Hi Randy - ♡

I hope you enjoy Furax. If you do, please tell the world. With love,*

Steve

THE FURAX CONNECTION

*from Claudia + me,

A Novel

by

Stephen L. Kanne

Fireside Publications
Lady Lake, Florida

This book is a work of fiction. Names, characters, businesses, organizations, places, events and incidents, with the exception of (a) government and military locations and procedures, (b) the Chicago, Ft. Wood and Plattsburgh areas and surroundings, (c) sporting events and facts, and (d) items noted by endnotes, are either the product of the author's imagination or are used fictitiously. Except as noted in the previous sentence, any resemblance to actual persons, living or dead, is entirely coincidental.

Published by:
Fireside Publications
1004 San Felipe Lane
Lady Lake, FL 32159

www.firesidepubs.com

Printed in the United States of America

First Edition: July 2009
ISBN: 978-0-9814672-6-9

Visit www.firesidepubs.com to order additional copies.

The Furax Connection

The last thing Louis Rosen expected of his son, Billy, was that he would volunteer for the draft after graduating from Harvard in 1949 with highest honors; and the last thing Billy expected of his father was that he would become a partner in a criminal enterprise known as "Furax Unlimited." Yet, when these two events unexpectedly collide and connect, Billy's life is changed forever.

The Furax Connection chronicles Billy's struggle for survival during his initial weeks in uniform when, unwittingly, he becomes entangled in a web of deceit and intrigue from which he must either extricate himself or suffer the shame and disgrace of a dishonorable discharge. That he survives at all is testimony not only to his resourcefulness and strength of purpose, but to his uncanny ability to forge relationships. And, as Billy struggles to survive, he discovers that, contrary to the civilian world of indifferent strangers he left behind, the military is a close-knit family of good and decent people who unselfishly care for their own.

This is a terrific novel. The authenticity and attention to detail are top notch, especially the depiction of military life. A good story with plenty of suspense. The sections on the M1 Garand Rifle are spot on, a rare treat. Highly recommended!

Robert Seijas, Chairman Emeritus
The Garand Collectors Association

I found Steve Kanne's novel, The Furax Connection, to be a great read. All the military information is on the mark and totally believable. An interesting note: When I served during the Vietnam War materiel theft and corruption were rampant both in and out of the war zone, so this supports Steve's subplot perfectly. This is one book that definitely makes the reader turn the pages and forces him to constantly assess where the storyline is headed.

A.J. Broomall
Former Naval Aviator
Naval Academy Class of 1966

The Furax Connection has it all: mystery, action, suspense, and intrigue. Author Steve Kanne blends his first-hand knowledge of Army basic training in the 1950's with well-defined, colorful character descriptions and a storyline that makes for a real page-turner. An exciting novel that you'll find hard to put down.

Warren Kerzon
Former Wild Weasel Pilot, Lt Col, USAF (Ret)

Acknowledgments

When I began *Furax* more than eight years ago I never realized what an all-consuming undertaking it would turn out to be; nor did I anticipate all the help I would need in getting it published. Without the assistance and kindness of so many people it never would have happened. Although never intended, *Furax* became a journey for me as well as for my characters. It brought me in contact with people I hadn't seen or talked to in years (including friends from my days in the service) as well as new people. Then there were my editors who put me through numerous rewrites. And, finally, there were my "beta-testers," those who read various versions of the manuscript and gave me their feedback. There are too many of you to name. Nevertheless, I thank you all.

Having said the foregoing, I do want to mention just a few who were key to getting *Furax* published:

Lois Bennett of Fireside Publications.

Claudia, my wife, who helped me edit the manuscript.

Patty Isensee who helped me edit and restructure the manuscript.

Stephanie Ball who assisted in the cover design.

Karen Linick, my unbelievably talented proofreader.

Bob Seijas, Chairman Emeritus, The Garand Collectors Association, Inc., who generously helped me with the complex details of M1 training and firing.

Rochelle Linick whose incisive comments transformed a vapid story into a novel.

Steve Bowes who, at the outset, jolted me into writing a much better book.

Al and Harriet Efron who went to unbelievable ends to help me.

Irwin Lazarus, my coach who kept cheering me on.

Beth Wiles, Executive Director, Pulaski County Tourism Bureau.

Ann Newmark of American Safety Razor Company.

Larry Wolf, Norma Barger, Col. Michael Linick, Joan Green, Jim Harvey, Yolanda and Len Farr, Arthur Schleifer, Tom Markus, Bob and Cindy Miller, Jerry and Barbara Mehlman, Reeve Chudd, Ken and Linda Halaby, Nancy Lewis, Bev deGraw, Gary Fields, Col. Peter Gleichenhaus, Carroll Peterson and Lorna Appel who all helped me in a variety of other ways.

Finally, the magnificent photograph of the Pentagon on the cover was taken by Master Sergeant Ken Hammond, USAF.

Steve Kanne

To Claudia

My love, my very best friend

Glossary of Terms/Abbreviations

Foreign Language

Boytchik—An affectionate term for "boy" (Yiddish)
Cacasenno—smart-ass (literally, "one who shits wisdom") (Italian)
Latkes—Potato pancakes (Yiddish)
Mishpochah—family (Yiddish)
Vos makhtsu?—"How are you?" (Yiddish)

Military

4F—A U.S. Selective Service classification designating a person physically, psychologically, or morally unfit for military duty
AG—Adjutant General
AWOL—Absent Without Leave
BAR—Browning Automatic Rifle
CB—Construction Battalion
CID—Criminal Investigation Command [Note: The U.S. Army's Criminal Investigation Command was originally known as the "Criminal Investigation Division." Its name was later changed to the "Criminal Investigation Command." However, it is still referred to widely as the "CID."]
CO—Commanding Officer
CQ—Charge of Quarters
DAC—Department of the Army Civilian
IG—Inspector General
KIA—Killed in Action
KMAG—Korean Military Advisory Group
KP—Kitchen police duty or kitchen patrol duty
NCOIC—Noncommissioned Officer In Charge
NCO—Noncommissioned Officer
NKPA—North Korean People's Army
OCS—Officer Candidate School
OD—Officer of the Day
OJT—On the Job Training

OR—Orderly Room
PFC—Private First Class
PIO—Public Information Office
ROK—Republic of Korea
SFC—Sergeant First Class
TDY—Temporary Duty
TRB—Training Regiment (Basic)
USAREUR—United States Army Europe

Other

REA—Railway Express Agency
VMI—Virginia Military Institute

Prologue

First Platoon Barracks, Company B, Fourth Battalion, Second Training Regiment (Basic), Fort Leonard Wood, Missouri, Sunday, 4 June 1950, 2300 Hours.

An hour after lights out Billy Rosen lay on his bunk in the darkened barracks unable to sleep. His head was feverishly spinning. Those nagging questions again. They were coming at him like a series of loud incessant sonar pings. *"Ping! Ping!"* Why had Sergeant Sack singled him out that first day for such unprecedented harassment? *"Ping! Ping!"* Why had Sack been rummaging through his medical records? *"Ping! Ping!"* Why had Sack and his wife offered him sanctuary in their home? *"Ping! Ping!"* How had General Haslett known his last name that night? And why had his daughter, Chris, sent him that puzzling note of warning? *"Ping! Ping!"* Was his father involved in Furax' nefarious schemes?

Billy knew he desperately needed sleep. Reveille would sound in a few hours and he'd be useless the next day without it. But to fall asleep he needed a focal point, something specific to carry over into his dreams.

His thoughts sidestepped the questions and drifted back to Chris Haslett as they had so often these past weeks. He visualized her lips moving. Now he could hear her voice as she spoke to him: "You're way too full of questions, Sport. You'll have your answers in time. Just be patient." She smiled. "Come over here, Billy. Now!"

He saw himself approaching her, extending his hands toward hers…

It was at this moment that the lights suddenly came on. No yelling. No screaming. No fanfare. Just the goddamn lights.

"What's goin' on?" Billy heard someone shout.

"Turn off the damn lights, for Christ's sake," someone else cried out. "We gotta be up early tomorrow. Hey!"

"Gentlemen," a voice said. "I am sorry to disturb you. But I'm afraid I must."

Billy and a few of the others looked down the aisle toward the doorway where they thought the voice was coming from. It was the CO, Captain Schtung. He was standing there in his Class A uniform. Behind him stood First Sergeant Sack in fatigues.

"Please," Captain Schtung said in a quiet but forceful voice, "may I have your attention."

The men looked up, but didn't get out of their bunks.

"This will only take ten or fifteen minutes of your much needed sleep," Captain Schtung continued, now appearing somewhat sad.

Still no yelling, no screaming, no profanity. What the hell was going on?

Then Sergeant Sack yelled, "Outta your bunks! Now! Atten…hut!"

The men were fully awake. They scrambled out of bed and stood at attention at the ends of their bunks. They were only wearing skivvies.

"At ease, gentlemen," Captain Schtung said, still speaking in a muted voice. "Again, I apologize for waking you. But there is a serious matter which must be dealt with immediately, so please listen carefully." Captain Schtung reached into the back pocket of his trousers, withdrew a handkerchief, and wiped his brow. Then he replaced it.

"In my army career, gentlemen, this has never happened before, and I am deeply saddened to have it happen tonight." He took a moment to clear his throat.

The men were puzzled. So, it appeared, was Sergeant Sack. Sergeant Gomez, the Platoon Sergeant, had managed to slip into his fatigues. He was standing at the end of the aisle near the door to his small private room. He too looked confused.

"I am not very good at this," Captain Schtung continued, "and, like you, I don't want to be here at this late hour. Neither does your First Sergeant." He motioned to Sergeant Sack. "But something has been brought to my attention which cannot wait. It involves only one of you, but I need the cooperation of everyone because what I am about to relate to you I find…" he hesitated, "shameful, even un-American. It goes to the very heart of why we are all in the Army. Let me tell you.

"You see, gentlemen, the reason I am in the Army is that I believe in our great country, what it stands for, and how its citizens are treated. As a boy, I came here from Nazi Germany where the rights of individuals were trampled upon by the state. I know what it is like to live in fear, to live under totalitarianism. I am in the Army to ensure that this will never happen to us. I believe the things our constitution guarantees, things like freedom and liberty, are worth fighting for, even dying for. That's why I've chosen the Army as a career. Many of you, probably most of you, will leave the Army in two years. But if a war breaks out you may be called to duty, just as Sergeant Sack and I were called in during the last war. We fought side by side, your First Sergeant and I, to defend our great nation. We love this country, and we believe you do too. We understand that being in the Army, particularly going through basic training, is not fun. KP and guard duty are not fun. These things aren't meant to be fun. What we are trying to do is train you to become soldiers in case your country calls. That's really what this is about. And I must say that all of you are doing splendidly. You will, if called upon, serve your country with honor and distinction—that is, all but one of you.

"There is one among you who is a total disgrace. At the time of induction he attempted to lie his way out of the Army. He would have succeeded except for the officer who interviewed him." Now Captain Schtung's voice was becoming louder. He began to scream. "No, not a disgrace, a fucking disgrace. I hate him. I hate what he stands for. He's a liar and a goddamn coward. I want him out of my sight, out of the Army. If I could, I would strip him of his citizenship—which he doesn't fucking deserve." Captain Schtung was now shaking with rage, his face had turned red, and he was sweating profusely. Again, he reached for his handkerchief and wiped the sweat from his forehead.

The men were beginning to react. Without being ordered to do so, each was now standing motionless, at rigid attention. No one made a sound.

"This man, gentlemen, is shit. I order you to shun him. You must avoid him. You must not speak to him. I hope he voluntarily leaves the Army, and I will do everything I can to see that he does." Now Captain Schtung lowered his voice once again.

"So what did this man do? I will tell you. At the time of induction he falsely claimed he had an injured foot which would prevent him from serving. He claimed he was so severely disabled that he should be classified 4F. But, gentlemen, he lied. We in the Army knew he was a cross-country runner and that his claimed disability was a fraud."

When Billy heard the term "cross-country runner" his heart sank. "Christ," he thought, "Schtung is talking about me. But that's impossible. I wanted in, not out. No!"

"You!" Captain Schtung screamed, pointing at Billy. "You, goddammit. You are not fit to live with these men, to eat with them, to march with them, to soldier with them. And, because of that, you shall not be allowed to have any contact with them. I will not permit you to despoil them. Do you understand, Rosen? Do you know what 'despoil' means?" Captain Schtung continued to stare at Billy. "Answer me, Rosen!" he screamed.

Billy was stunned. Never in his life had he been so assaulted. He could hardly speak.

"Rosen!" Captain Schtung continued to scream. "Answer, goddammit!"

"I understand, sir. But what you say…it's not true."

"You're a goddamn liar!" Captain Schtung replied.

Then he turned to Sergeant Sack. Speaking just loudly enough so he could be overheard by Billy and the others, he said, "First Sergeant, beginning now, Rosen is to sleep by himself in the furnace room. Please see to it that his things are moved there at once. I personally will speak to Cookie in the morning. He's to eat alone in the mess hall at a table in the corner facing the wall. And during the day he is not to take part in any training. He is to remain in the furnace room except during meals or when he needs to shower or use the latrine. Please confiscate all of his reading and writing materials. He is to have no phone privileges. I will speak to him only if and when he wishes to apply for a dishonorable discharge from the Army. And I hope that will be soon."

"Very good, sir," Sergeant Sack replied, expressionless, trying hard not to look at Billy.

"And now, First Sergeant," Captain Schtung continued, "I'm going home. Please make sure Rosen's things are moved to the furnace room tonight and that my orders are carried out."

As Captain Schtung turned and headed toward the doorway, Billy's shoulders began to sag. A sickening feeling of isolation took hold of him and he bowed his head, looking down at the floor. He had never felt more alone, more isolated, more demeaned. His knees began to wobble and he was about to fall when Sergeant Gomez grabbed hold of him from behind. Propping him up, he walked him outside, around to the back of the barracks, and into the darkened furnace room. Within minutes, some of the men carried in his bunk and footlocker.

***

Once inside, Billy looked up at the one bare light bulb which was to illuminate his new home for the remainder of basic training. He saw particles of coal dust, ash, and soot floating in the air. As he breathed these in, he began to cough uncontrollably. This caused his recently healed throat and nasal passages to throb in pain. But most of all, Billy ached from the injustice of it all. Placing one hand against the cold furnace, he leaned forward and silently began to weep

And as he wept, Billy now felt himself consumed by a new question which dominated all the others: "How in God's name had it come to this?"

Part I

An Inauspicious Beginning

Chapter 1

Padraig's of Lauderdale Stone Crab Restaurant,
Fort Lauderdale, Florida,
Tuesday, 16 December 1947, 1930 Hours.

Tradition had it that Louis Rosen, his wife, Doreen, and their son, Billy, always spent their Christmas holidays at the Roney Plaza Hotel in Miami Beach. This held true for the current year, 1947, when Billy was a junior at Harvard. But contrary to tradition, on this particular trip Louis Rosen had left his wife and son to fend for themselves for an evening so that he could dine with two longtime friends. At the moment he was seated at a corner table in Padraig's of Lauderdale Stone Crab Restaurant, an hour and fifteen minutes by chauffeur-driven car from the Roney, nursing an Edenbrau beer while he awaited their arrival.

Louis Rosen was an extraordinarily handsome man, almost celebrity-like in appearance. At forty-six he was lean and muscular with a full head of black hair. His complexion was slightly dark but his eyes were a piercing pale blue. His facial features were classic in appearance and bore a striking resemblance to Tyrone Power. And he always dressed impeccably, on this occasion in a dark blue suit custom made by his Chicago tailor, along with a white polished cotton shirt with his initials monogrammed in black on the cuff of the left sleeve, a deep red silk tie, and black plain-toe soft leather shoes which had been made for him by a shop on London's Bond Street the previous summer. Beneath his exterior of good looks and expensive clothing lay Louis Rosen's most extraordinary quality: his IQ. By all acceptable standards he was a genius. He not only possessed a photographic memory and an ability to do lengthy mathematical calculations in his head, but his creative instincts were unsurpassed. He was also unusual in one other respect. He was completely ambidextrous, probably an indication that each side of his brain functioned as well as the other.

Louis Rosen relaxed as he sat. And as he did, he took in Paddy's success as evidenced not only by the long line of people just inside the main entrance waiting to be seated, but also by the extreme noise of the place: a cacophony of waiters and patrons talking, even shouting; the clatter of dishes and flatware; and the incessant popping and clacking as diners opened cracked claws in search of morsels of stone crab.

Suddenly, almost as if someone had thrown a switch cutting off the power to a sound amplifier, all was silent. Everyone in the large dining room had stopped talking and eating. All heads were turned in the direction of the restaurant's doorway where two men, one much shorter than the other, had entered and immediately walked to the head of the line. The shorter man, barely five feet in height, had beady eyes, a recessed chin, a large straight nose which was bent to one side, and a lower lip which protruded slightly beyond his upper lip. He was attired in a poorly fitting off-the-rack dark brown suit, a white shirt, a dark green tie, scuffed black shoes, and a fedora with an overly large brim. He stood slightly in front of his companion and seemed to be in charge. He also commanded the undivided attention of Guido, the maître d'.

"Mr. Rosen arrived a short while ago, sir," Guido said. "He's been waiting for you and your brother. May I escort you to your table?"

The shorter man had been surveying the room. "Not necessary," he replied in a surprisingly high voice that carried a noticeable lisp. "C'mon, Sammy." With that, the two started walking in Louis Rosen's direction. And, while the other diners continued to stare, the shorter man began to smile broadly.

***

"Hey *boytchik*," the shorter man said to Louis Rosen, reaching up and warmly clasping his shoulder, "*vos makhtsu*?"

"Hi ya, Louie," the larger man said in a guttural voice. "Good to see you." He proffered a flabby hand which Louis Rosen grasped. In sharp contrast to his smaller brother, he was almost six feet tall and weighed over two hundred pounds. His huge head was beginning to bald and his puffy face was covered with acne scars. His dress was suggestive of a common laborer. He had on a pair of wrinkled denim pants, a light blue shirt, and a yellow sleeveless sweater which bore a number of stains and food splatterings. His footwear consisted of leather work boots.

"Sit, boys," Louis Rosen said. "I've already ordered for us." Within seconds a waiter arrived carrying a tray. He placed two plates in front of each man. On one, an unusually large entrée plate, there were half a dozen cracked stone crab claws, home fries, creamed spinach, and Paddy's special mustard-horseradish sauce; and on the other, a salad plate, there was a cone of coleslaw with peanuts garnished with a dollop of mayonnaise and pickle relish.

"What're you drinking, Moe?" Louis Rosen asked.

"Edenbrau, same as you," the shorter man said. "Might as well keep it in your family." He smiled. "So Leibel," he continued, addressing Louis Rosen by his Yiddish first name even though he had been called "Luigi" by his Italian mother and "Louie" by just about everyone else, "how's the *mishpochah*?"

"Doreen's fine and Billy's setting the world on fire in his own arena. He's right at the top of his class with a few others, and I'd be surprised if he didn't graduate with honors a year from June."

"Nice," Sammy said as he unceremoniously removed a piece of crab shell from between two teeth.

"Harvard, right?" Moe continued.

Louis Rosen nodded.

"Pre-med?"

"That was last year. This year it's chemical engineering."

"You know my kid's a research chemist?" Moe said.

"I do. I guess your son isn't interested in coming in with us?" Louis Rosen asked.

"Not even slightly. What about Billy?"

"Billy? Hardly," Louis Rosen said. "He's straight out of a North Shore cookie-cutter. Either got his nose in a book or he's out running."

"Think he's had his ashes hauled?" Sammy asked grinning salaciously. His lips bore a repugnant greenish hue colored by an overflowing mouthful of creamed spinach.

"Probably not, but who knows?" Louis Rosen replied. "He's as tight-lipped as they come."

"Kids today," Moe said. "I wish to God I knew what they were thinking." Then he motioned to his brother.

"Louie," Sammy said, "me and Moe wanna congratulate you on being so brilliant. That food scheme you dreamed up is making us a fortune. We got it goin' on both coasts and in the Midwest."

"Sammy's right," Moe interjected. "The deal's like the Bureau of Printing and Engraving, a goddamn cash cow. Probably the best thing we got goin'."

Louis Rosen smiled. "I had no idea you guys were pursuing it. Aren't your bookie operations keeping you busy enough?"

Sammy laughed. He withdrew a blank sheet of stationery from his pants pocket, unfolded it, and handed it to Louis Rosen. "Here, Louie, take a look."

Louis Rosen examined it. He had a puzzled expression on his face. "I don't get it…the moniker."

"Hah! So he doesn't know everything," Sammy said.

The first line of the stationery's letterhead contained a business name in large bold lettering:

Furax Unlimited

Immediately below it in slightly smaller type there was a post office box address and a phone number, both in New York City.

"Louie," Sammy continued, as he passed the stationery to his brother for safekeeping, "we've made you a one-third partner in our little venture. We'll settle up with you next time we're in Chicago. And here's something we owe you." Sammy handed him an envelope.

Louis Rosen folded back the flap of the envelope and glanced inside. "Thanks," he said.

***

After dessert of Key lime pie followed by coffee, Moe motioned to Guido who immediately came over to their table. "How 'bout the check, pal?"

"No way," Louis Rosen said. "This is on me."

"I'm afraid I'll have to disappoint you both, gentlemen," Guido said. "Paddy insists on picking up the tab."

Surprised, Louis Rosen looked over at Moe. "I guess we owe Paddy."

"You tell Paddy thanks for all of us, Guido," Moe said. "We don't forget things like this."

"I certainly will, Mr. Schwartz," Guido replied. "And Paddy wants you to know he considers you one of his best customers. He said to tell you you're always welcome here."

***

After bidding the Schwartz brothers goodbye, Louis Rosen stood alone outside the restaurant next to the curb. As he awaited his chauffeur-driven car, two large FBI types with crewcuts and wearing charcoal gray suits approached. He remembered seeing them in the restaurant. One grabbed him under the arm. "Hey, asshole, you been doing a little business back there with Mutt and Jeff?"

"Wha…?" Louis Rosen replied, obviously taken by surprise. "And take your filthy hands off me!"

"Really?" the man replied. Then turning to his companion he said, "He thinks I got filthy hands, Jinks." With that, he spat into the palm of his free hand and wiped it across the lapel of Louis Rosen's suit coat.

Louis Rosen's reaction was instantaneous. In one smooth quick motion he brought his right knee up hard into the man's groin. As the man collapsed crying out in pain, Louis Rosen turned and walked off down the street.

"Not so fast," Jinks cried out. He withdrew his thirty-eight from its shoulder holster, took aim, and yelled "FBI! Freeze!" But Louis Rosen kept on walking. Moments later there was the sound of a gunshot. Louis Rosen felt a searing pain on the left side of his chest as he fell to the sidewalk.

"Okay, let's have it," Jinks barked as he stood over Louis Rosen.

"Have what?" Louis Rosen was having trouble breathing.

"The fuckin' envelope Tweedledum and Tweedledee passed to you."

Louis Rosen heard a siren blare in the distance. He was beginning to lose consciousness. As his eyes were closing he felt a hand reach inside his coat pocket and remove the envelope.

***

"You're not gonna believe this," Jinks said as he handed his partner the single sheet of paper he'd taken from the envelope. "'*Latkes.*' It's a fuckin' recipe!"

***

Back at the Roney that same evening Louis Rosen learned to his relief that the bullet had only grazed his side.

And three days later, after he'd fully recovered from his misadventure with the two federal agents, Louis Rosen's thoughts turned to the new partnership, "Furax Unlimited." Why hadn't he known what "furax" meant? Embarrassed by his own ineptitude, he called Billy into his hotel room. "How 'bout going over to the library and finding out for me," he said.

Later on that day in the Miami Beach Library, Billy began his search. He knew that "furax" wasn't in the English dictionary, but he looked anyway. He was right. It wasn't there. Then where? He thought for a minute or two before it finally it came to him: a Latin term! He went into the stacks and found an old dusty Latin to English dictionary. And just as he'd suspected, there it was: ***"furax"—"thievish" or "inclined to steal."***

Chapter 2

Office of the U.S. Army Chief of Staff, The Pentagon, 3E650, Washington, D.C., Monday, 22 December 1947, 1505 Hours.

Two middle-aged men, both wearing khaki pants and Egyptian cotton khaki shirts, their collars unbuttoned and their ties pulled down, were seated opposite one another at a small conference table located near the far end of a large wood-paneled Pentagon office. One, slightly older and balding, had a jutting chin and a flat pugnacious face. The other had a full head of silver gray hair and movie-star good looks. A cardboard file storage box rested on the floor between them. On one side of the box the words "WATER WALKER" were printed in large bold capital letters. The younger man, General Thaddeus Watson, Vice Chief of Staff, U.S. Army, was in the process of withdrawing the contents of the file box, fifteen file folders labeled "W-W #1" through "W-W #15," and placing them on the tabletop. His companion, General Glen Conroy, the Army's Chief of Staff, looked on.

"We should be meeting more often on this, Thad," General Conroy observed. "Or at least I should be getting regular updates."

"Agreed on both counts, Glen. It's just that you and I are so damn busy. And besides me, who else is there to give you updates?"

"I take your point," General Conroy said. He hesitated. "So where are we on our fifteen Water Walkers?"

"Not where I'd like to be, that's for damn sure."

"Meaning?"

"Meaning as of right now we've only got five."

"Five! For Christ's sake, how can that be?"

"I was afraid you were gonna ask that. We've had eight washouts and one death."

"One death?"

General Watson handed the W-W #7 file to General Conroy. "The details are all in here."

"C'mon, Thad. I don't have time for this. Just tell me."

"He hung himself."

General Conroy appeared stunned. "Jesus!" he said. Then he thought for a moment. "That's only fourteen. What about the fifteenth?"

"Water Walker #15 hasn't been selected."

"Hasn't been selected? How come?"

"Our man's been on this thing less than six months, Glen."

"Huh," General Conroy said in surprise. "Who's our guy, Thad?"

"Name's Harkavy. First name Kenneth. Bird colonel. Highly decorated. We both know him."

General Conroy smiled slightly. "I remember him well. Bright and tough; plus he's got ice water in his veins. I guess we let him take all the time he needs."

"I guess we sure as hell do."

General Conroy thought for a moment. "Thad, from now on nothing takes precedence over Water Walker. I don't care how busy we think we are. Let's meet quarterly on it. Last Thursday of the month work for you?"

"That's fine," General Watson said. He got up and walked over to the brown leather couch on which he had neatly placed his uniform coat more than an hour before. Picking it up by the collar, he withdrew an appointment book and a Parker 51 pen from an inside pocket. He flipped the book open to the page headed "Thursday, March 25, 1948," their next meeting date, and made a notation on it.

"1400 hours okay, Glen?"

General Conroy nodded and General Watson made a second notation on the same page of the appointment book.

Background Check: The North Shore

Chicago's North Shore consists of a string of affluent suburbs beginning at the city's northerly boundary, Howard Street, and proceeding northward along Sheridan Road roughly following the contour of the nearby westerly shore of Lake Michigan: first, Evanston (home of Northwestern University); then Wilmette, Kenilworth, Winnetka, Glencoe, Highland Park, and Lake Forest; and, finally, Lake Bluff (Highwood, not nearly as upscale and somewhat out of place, is located between Highland Park and Lake Forest, as is Fort Sheridan, a large U.S. Army installation).

Two distinct characteristics set the North Shore apart from most other areas: first, its tiny suburbs are excessively wealthy; and second, it is populated by an inordinately large number of high achievers.

As an example, in 1950 the Village of Glencoe had a predominately white Protestant Republican population of roughly 7,000 (only sixteen percent were Catholic, ten percent were Jewish, and less than six percent were black); the average annual family income was $14,700 (the amount which a mid-level executive of a major corporation would expect to earn at that time); and 87% of its graduating high school seniors—who had either attended private preparatory ("prep") schools or the local public high school, New Trier—went on to college (many to Ivy League schools), with a startling 90% of those graduating.

Thus, it was no surprise that the North Shore spawned far more than its fair share of renowned persona: writers, poets, artists, musicians, actors, and entertainers (including those of the Hollywood variety); professional athletes; lawyers and physicians; educators; CEOs; political leaders; and heads of various branches of government service. One of its greatest luminaries, Archibald MacLeish, born in Glencoe in 1892, served as a Captain in the U.S. Army in World War I; was an editor of Fortune Magazine; taught at Harvard Law School, Harvard College, and Amherst College; was a Librarian of Congress, a speech writer for FDR, and an Assistant Secretary of State; and was the recipient of an eclectic group of awards including three Pulitzer Prizes, the Presidential Medal of Freedom, a Tony, and an Oscar.[1]

In 1945, during his senior year at New Trier in Mr. Mortenson's Advanced English Literature class, Billy Rosen became fascinated with many of the works of MacLeish. Some he read over and over again. Perhaps this is why he adopted as his life's credo the simple concept that "life is living." He would always wonder whether it was purely coincidental that MacLeish would write twenty-three years later that:

> It is not in the world of ideas that life is lived. Life is lived for better or worse in life, and to a man in life, his life can be no more absurd than it can be the opposite of absurd, whatever that opposite may be.

Mulling those words over many years later, Billy would reflect upon his life's experiences as periodically alternating between the absurd and its opposite. Then he would smile—although sometimes when he was alone, more often than he wished, he would lapse into moments of unbearable sadness consumed by memories of friends and companions whose lives had ended so abruptly and unexpectedly.

Chapter 3

553 Sheridan Road, Glencoe, Illinois,
Friday, 28 April 1950, 0600 Hours.

Billy Rosen, Harvard Class of 1949, *summa cum laude* (in chemistry and physics), awoke with a start at 6:00 AM to the ringing of the gold-plated Swiss travel alarm clock his Great Uncle Hatch had given him for graduation nearly a year ago. Almost immediately he felt a painful throbbing alongside his right temple, obviously the result of his excessive drinking the night before. That irked him. Why hadn't he used better judgment?

Slowly, excruciatingly, he wrenched himself from his bed and made his way to the bathroom. There he swallowed a tall glass of water and two aspirin before peeling off his pajamas and stepping into the shower.

Beneath the spray of cold water Billy thought about his going away party the night before. Despite the stag movies, the poker game, the cigars, and the camaraderie, in his eyes it had been a disaster. And it had seriously upset and unsettled him.

Prior to the party Billy had been completely at ease with his decision to volunteer for the draft and go into the Army as an enlisted man for two years. But afterwards, after his friends had badgered him with question after question about his motives or, rather, his sanity, well…he wasn't sure. Moreover, it was the barrage of questions that had propelled him to the bar where he remembered ordering a sixth gin and tonic, this time heavy on the gin. And now, the morning after, he was hung over and filled with doubt—so much so, in fact, that he felt compelled to go over his reasoning one last time.

Before leaving Harvard Billy had been accepted by MIT into its chemical engineering graduate program. Although he hadn't entered the program last fall, he'd called the MIT admissions office and explained to them that he wanted to work for a year before starting graduate school. They had gone along with this and had assured him that he could begin a year later. So this was still an option, although now he was no longer interested. His job as a research assistant at Merritt Pharmaceuticals in North

Chicago over the past nine months had convinced him he'd be bored stiff working as a chemical engineer.

Nor did he have any interest in becoming a doctor. That was something he'd never seriously considered even though a few years ago he'd told his father he was thinking about medical school.

And law? Billy hated "lawyer think." Two plus two? Well, arguably four, but when you considered this factor and that one, well, also arguably, it wasn't four. Billy's scientific mind could no more cope with this than his personality could with the thought of a mind-numbing engineering career.

Business school: a place where they worked you to the bone and you learned next to nothing. Why in the world would he want that? And truth be known, Billy had never really been interested in business. He couldn't even remember the last time he'd picked up a copy of *The Wall Street Journal*.

In thinking about it now—as he had so often in the past—Billy again came to the same conclusion: he really didn't know what he wanted to do with his life. But even if he didn't know, at least by volunteering for the draft and spending two years in the Army he'd be getting his military obligation out of the way. And after that? Well hopefully by then he'd know.

So, despite the seeds of doubt sown at last night's party, his earlier decision still stood. He would leave for the Induction Center within the hour. With renewed resolution, he stepped out of the shower, dried himself off, and walked over to the sink where he completed his morning's ablutions.

Back in his room Billy slipped into his clothes (jockey shorts, a white t-shirt, khaki pants, a button-down long sleeve plaid shirt, white sweat socks, and dirty white bucks) before making his way downstairs to the kitchen. The family retainer, Odessa, an elderly black woman who'd been with the Rosens as far back as Billy could remember, had a sumptuous breakfast awaiting him which he devoured as quickly as he could.

"Your momma ain't stopped cryin' for almost a week," Odessa said. "And Mr. Rosen..." she rolled her eyes.

Trying to appear unmoved, Billy put his arms around Odessa and gave her a hug. "Your cooking's gonna be what I'll miss the most," he said.

Now came the moment he'd been dreading. He went upstairs to the master bedroom to face his parents who were in bed.

"Well, I'm off," he said.

With this, his mother began crying. And predictably his father locked, loaded, and fired off his standard sarcastic salvo, the one he used when he thought Billy was assuming the role of a know-it-all: "Glad we had a chance to discuss this one, *Mr. Cacasenno*." On hearing this, Billy reddened slightly. But then, regaining his composure, he kissed his mother on the forehead, squeezed his father's shoulder, and waved goodbye. For all intents and purposes, his two years of military service had begun.

"Kid doesn't know it," Louis Rosen said conspiratorially to his wife after Billy left the room, "but I'm gonna make sure we see an awful lot of him in the next two years. Maybe have him stationed in the Chicago area. I've already made some calls."

***

Glencoe's Chicago & Northwestern Railroad Station, better known simply as "the Station," was, some said, an imposing edifice, at least when compared with Glencoe's other early twentieth century architectural standouts such as the Methodist Church, the Library, the Adams Drug Store Building, Central School, and the Glencoe Theater. Mary Tate, one of the more articulate members of Billy's high school class, had once remarked that "it was classic Romanesque." "Right," Billy had thought when overhearing this learned pronouncement, "and if bullshit were music then Mary'd be Beethoven." In fact, the Station was an ugly, broken down structure replete with its repulsive odors of disinfectant, tobacco, and perspiration; its railroad dust and grime; and its officious uniformed employees. Billy considered it the cornerstone of a way of life which caused stomach acid to rise in the back of his throat: *the commute.*

Mornings and evenings of each weekday of each year orderly legions of businessmen either marched or were driven to and from the Station along Glencoe's avenues, streets, roads, and walkways. Once on a spring morning for a project in Miss Collins' eighth grade English class Billy and Richie Linden, his good friend, had met at the Station at 6:00 AM and, until around 8:30 AM, had jotted down their observations in spiral notebooks: about half the commuters had arrived by car, driven by hastily-dressed unbathed women wearing no makeup and probably with rancid breath (Richie referred to them as "unmade beds" and told Billy to cover his watch lest one of them break it with her ugliness); something like 97% of the commuters wore suits, ties, and wing-tipped shoes; and about three out of four carried briefcases, many of which, Billy knew, contained nothing remotely relating to work but instead were filled with sandwiches, candies and other snacks, beverages, cards, books, newspapers, and magazines. Zeke Wigman, a friend of his father, not only carried his lunch and recreational reading material in his briefcase, but also packed it with a small thermos of pre-mixed martinis which, winkingly, he referred to as his "see-throughs for the train." After that morning Billy and Richie had argued over which was more lethal, the commuting process itself or being married to one of those women, Billy taking the position that a life of commuting would put you in the ground faster than living with one of those clock-stoppers.

But on this particular Friday morning as he walked to the Station, Billy paid little attention to the ant-like migration of walking and riding commuters. His thoughts were elsewhere, specifically, on the new and altogether different life he was about to begin, a life which would require that he depart the familiar and venture into the unknown. And how would he cope with the notion that, for two long years, he would be leaving that pre-defined path he had followed since as far back as he could remember, a path designed to bring him financial success and its trappings, namely, a beautiful wife and well-behaved children, a house with a white picket fence, new cars every other year, a country club membership, luxury vacations, and, of course, happiness? He just didn't know. He would have to wait and see.

When he entered the Station, he found, to his surprise, an unusually short line at its only ticket window; probably, Billy supposed, because most commuters bought their passes around the middle of the month. Within five minutes, and at a cost of $1.08, he purchased a one-way ticket to Chicago's downtown Northwestern Station. He looked at his watch. 7:20 AM. He had seven minutes before the train's scheduled arrival. Billy's eyes wandered to the two stacks of newspapers on a ledge next to the door leading out to the tracks, one containing the Sun-Times and the other the Tribune. "Not this morning," he thought. He wanted his train ride and his ten to fifteen minute walk from the Downtown Station to the Van Buren Street Induction Center to be completely unhampered by news items, the sports page, obituaries, and editorials. He wanted a last chance to think.

At 7:25 Billy's train arrived and the people split into four groups, each making its way toward an entry door of one of the four commuter cars. Billy joined the group bound for the last car. A conductor dressed in a black C&NW uniform with a frayed lapel and shiny pants motioned to Billy and the others to enter. Billy ascended the steps into the musty car and noticed that only a few of its two-place cushioned seats were occupied. He chose an unoccupied one in the middle of the car, sat next to the window, rested his right elbow on the sill, cupped his chin in his hand, and was about to close his eyes when the conductor reappeared and asked him for his ticket. He handed it over. Within a minute or two the train began to lurch forward. This time he took a deep breath just as he had when he was about to begin a difficult final exam or compete for Harvard in a cross-country race. Then he exhaled and allowed his mind to wander to the train's pleasant rocking motion. Soon he fell into a deep sleep, so deep in fact that by the time the train pulled into the Winnetka Station, about five minutes later, he had developed an erection.

Chapter 4

On Board C&NW Railroad's Commuter Train, Friday, 28 April 1950, 0727 Hours.

Despite wet dreams, masturbation, and occasional sexual encounters, like almost all of his male contemporaries Billy lived in a sea of sometimes overpowering testosterone. And so, as he slept, vast numbers of tiny molecules of this libidinous substance began to overwhelm him, unconsciously forcing him to relive his first sexual encounter just as he had done so often in the Dunster House Library at Harvard when his sex drive overcame his will to study:

Billy's mind was afloat. He was seventeen years old. He and two friends, Jed King and Lon Berg, were about to receive their initiation into manhood in a small hotel on Chicago's Near North Side.

It all began when a pimp Jed knew by the name of Sky Bosley met them in front of a hotel in the Loop. Sky told them to wait in the lobby while he checked upstairs to see if the girls were available. And so they waited...and waited...and waited. For almost forty-five minutes. Then Sky returned. He was sorry, but the girls weren't available. But if they wanted to they could go elsewhere, to another hotel on the Near North Side, the Louella. They wanted to. Then the three drove to the Louella. In fact, they cruised past it and parked six blocks down the street attempting to preserve their anonymity. It was at this point that Billy's heart began to race.

"You sure we got enough cash?" Lon asked nervously. Neither Jed nor Billy responded. They had been over this before. Instead, Billy got out of the car. "C'mon," he said, "let's go. Just make sure the car's locked." Previously the three had put their valuables in the glove compartment, and they each now carried only twenty dollars in cash. After Lon checked to make sure the doors were locked, they walked back to the Louella and entered the lobby. They told the clerk at the front desk that Sky had sent them. Replying with a bored nod, he told them the girls were on the fourth floor.

"That'll be three dollars each," the clerk said extending his hand. "And there'll be a one dollar charge for each of you to the elevator operator."

As they made their way to the elevator, the clerk picked up the phone and dialed a number. He waited a moment, and then said, "Three cherries on the way."

Dutifully, the three entered the rickety elevator operated by a short man wearing a stained sport jacket as his uniform coat. After collecting his money, the elevator door closed, its interior gate clanged shut, and the man rotated the operating handle downward. The elevator rose, clonking its way up to the fourth floor.

When Billy and his two friends stepped out into the dingy gray-green hallway, they saw that there was an unusually small hotel room on their immediate left which was missing a door and which had been converted into something resembling a parlor or waiting room. Each of its four walls had a worn green naugahyde bench attached to it, some with tears patched by tape. With Lon in the lead, they entered the room and took seats on the bench at the far wall.

As if on cue, almost immediately five women filed into the room and sat squeezed together on the bench opposite them. Billy looked up and swallowed. Close to five seconds of uncomfortable silence ensued. Finally, in a somewhat ambiguous gesture which might have been considered pointing, Billy raised his right hand in the direction of the redheaded woman seated opposite him who appeared to be in her late twenties. She had a soft rather pretty face and long dyed red hair which was beginning to blacken at the roots. She smiled slightly, probably because she was the first to be chosen, got up, motioned to Billy to follow her, and proceeded down the hallway and into one of the rooms.

As he entered behind her, she stood there facing him, assessing him with one eyebrow raised. She wore a synthetic silk red and black floral-patterned dress which came down to her knees. It was low cut and emphasized her cleavage and well proportioned breasts. With a quick motion, she reached behind her neck and undid a clasp. Then with both hands she tugged at the dress and it slipped off her shoulders and fell to the floor around her ankles. To Billy's surprise, she wore nothing under it.

She was completely naked except for her red high heel shoes. Billy looked down at the dress. The inside portion that had covered her breasts had a cloth and wire support attached to it which resembled a built-in brassiere. Billy had heard of this kind of dress, something someone once told him they called a "trick suit."

"Hi, honey," she said, stepping away from her dress. "I'm Lorraine. So what do they call you anyhow?"

"Scott," Billy replied, not wanting to give his real name. "Or sometimes Scotty." As he spoke he found he couldn't stop staring at Lorraine.

"Yeah…well Scott, honey, so what's your pleasure? Straight party? Or maybe something a little more exciting, like a French? Or what? But just so you know, I'm not into any kinky stuff, like from behind."

The back of Billy's throat had begun to tighten, and he cleared it with a cough. "How much…I mean for a straight party?" he asked, his nervousness apparent. "And what's a French?"

While Billy spoke, Lorraine was still studying him closely: tall, almost six feet; a healthful complexion; dark brown hair, almost black; piercing pale blue eyes; a classically handsome face: long and angular with high cheekbones, a thin straight nose, a friendly mouth, and a strong chin; and, although covered by his clothing, what appeared to be a lean hard body, unusually muscular for someone his age. She found herself strongly attracted to him and also to his innocence and naiveté.

"Why, you're as ripe as can be, aren't you, baby? Well, you all just let little ol' Lorraine take care of everything. Oh, baby, just wait 'til you slip inside Lorraine's happiness. So slippery comfy smooth…"

As he listened to her, Billy began to understand what she was doing: delivering a well-rehearsed speech, one which she'd probably given many times in the past. And as she spoke, Billy also realized that Lorraine had just this moment taken on the role of a demure southern belle. And yet he found there was something erotically sensual in her voice, and in the way she looked directly at him. And suddenly he began to feel himself being swallowed up in the moment, in her nakedness, and in the strangeness of the whole experience. Now he no longer heard her words, only her voice.

"I'll make it special for you, honey. French and straight party, eleven dollars. And don't you worry your little head over what's going to happen. You let my little head do that." She smiled at her double-entendre.

As she continued to speak, Billy began to feel dizzy, as if he'd been caught up in an eddy. His head started spinning and his equilibrium began to slip away. He felt himself begin to sway from side to side, and, when his breathing became more difficult, he reached out for the edge of the bed in an attempt to steady himself.

"Eleven dollars," she repeated.

This time he appeared to hear her words. He reached into his pocket and withdrew a wad of bills. Lorraine was still watching him closely and saw that he was holding what appeared to be more than eleven dollars. She also saw that underneath his pants he had an erection.

"Tell you what. I'm gonna give you an extra special treat. Something you'll remember for the rest of your life."

She reached over and took all the money out of his hand. "Just you take off those pants, honey." She turned, took hold of a robe hanging from a hook behind the closet door, and disappeared out into the hallway leaving Billy alone, slightly confused.

Billy unbuckled his pants, slipped them off, and put them on the floor next to the bed. Then he looked around the room. It was dingy, even slightly depressing in its drabness. The only furniture was a double bed covered by an old wrinkled bedspread with a bed stand next to it. There was a sink in the corner. Near the sink there was a towel bar attached to the wall, and immediately below it a wastebasket half full of trash. The walls of the room were covered with greenish flocked wallpaper, but there were no pictures; and the beige carpet on the floor was stained and pockmarked with cigarette burns. The room's one window which faced the street looked like it was permanently sealed from the many coats of white paint that had been applied to its frame and sill, and below it there was a radiator painted silver from which hissing steam emanated.

Billy shivered. He felt cold. He walked over to the radiator and touched it. It was hot and he quickly withdrew his hand to avoid burning it. He looked out the window onto the street below where, six blocks away, he knew the car was parked. He closed his eyes and breathed in deeply, trying to slow his heart rate and relax. His erection was beginning to subside, and he wondered whether he shouldn't just get dressed and leave when, as abruptly as she had disappeared, Lorraine reappeared. He noticed that she was holding several hand towels.

"Well, my goodness," she said, removing her robe and letting it fall to the floor, "where's that little pokey you all had for me?" Then she smiled at Billy as she placed the towels on a small shelf above the sink.

"Why sweetheart," she said, "you got to make a little stiffy for Lorraine. How else am I gonna pleasure you?" She smiled, again seeming pleased with the way she was delivering her lines.

"Anyway, sweet thing, I just gotta check you out. Rules of the house." As she spoke she grasped the elastic top of Billy's jockey shorts with both hands and pulled them down to his knees.

"My oh my, honey," she said. "You are special. I've never seen one that large!"

Billy knew of course this was utter bullshit. He knew from locker rooms he had changed in over the years that he was not unusually large. But for some reason he didn't care.

"Lorraine," he said, playing her game, "you really are beautiful. I'm..." he hesitated, trying to find the right words to flatter her. "I'm...God, I'm so lucky to be with you."

Few of her customers had ever said this to her, and Lorraine appeared flustered. Suddenly she had been caught so completely off guard that she had forgotten her lines. And he was sorta cute. Well...sweet, anyway. He was so young. And he did have a nice hard body.

"But honey, we been doing way too much talking. We got to get started."

She took his hand and gently pulled him to the sink. She turned on the water, testing it to make sure it was warm, not hot, and then she began to wash him while at the same time looking carefully for signs of infection: puss, scabs, and redness. When she finished she took one of the hand towels and dried him.

"You're just fine, sweetness. I knew you would be. And...oh, you smell so so good."

"And how nice," she thought, "that he didn't come while I was washing him like so many of the first timers." Now she could have him, something she'd wanted ever since first laying eyes on him in the parlor.

Taking his hand again, she led him to the bed. She removed the bedspread and gently pushed him down on his back.

"You just lie like that, honey, and let's you and me get started."

Then she leaned over and slowly took his erection into her mouth, her head beginning to bob up and down.

"God, this is it!" Billy thought as he closed his eyes and decided to try to enjoy the moment. But he really didn't seem to be able to. Sadly, after waiting all these years for this first encounter, he was disappointed by Lorraine's efforts to transport him to somewhere he'd never been.

"How we doing, honey?" Lorraine asked. "That was nice, wasn't it?" Without waiting for a reply, she went on, "That's a French, honey.

"Now we start in with the real fun." Saying this, she mounted him, sliding him into her as deeply as she could.

Billy's eyes were still closed. Now he felt her thighs on either side of him as she began to move her body over him causing the bed to squeak. As her full weight came down upon him and then was raised up again, and as this was repeated over and over again, each time at a faster pace and with greater force, Billy slowly felt himself being pushed up a steep precipice toward its edge. Then he was falling over the edge into space. And as he fell he experienced a cathartic surge accompanied by a glowing sensation of warmth and release. Suddenly he felt tired and completely relaxed.

"Lover," she said, "you are the greatest. I could do this with you all day and night."

Another rehearsed speech, Billy knew. Now it was his turn.

"God, Lorraine, that was so wonderful. You're so very special."

"Am I, honey? Am I really? Oh, God, honey, please visit me again. Oh Scott." She paused for perhaps two or three seconds. "Oh dear," she said.

Billy wasn't sure what she was trying to say. But then she leaned over and kissed him gently, it seemed with genuine affection, on the neck…as if to thank him.

"Please, sweet boy, come back again."

"Dear Lord," she silently said to herself, "what am I doing?" Even she didn't know. "Jesus Christ!" she whispered. She shook her head as if to clear it, and then sadly looked away.

Slowly she got up and slipped into her dress while, at the same time, staring back at Billy trying, it seemed, to make sure she would remember the moment. But, Billy knew, she wouldn't. Then she left the room. She was gone. It was over.

But was it over for Billy? Not really. His initiation into manhood so skillfully and caringly orchestrated by Lorraine would always be a part of his memory bank. So in a way it wasn't over at all.

***

Billy was putting on his clothes, getting ready to leave, when he felt a strange good feeling come over him. There was something about Lorraine he actually liked. But what was it? He searched for words to describe her, but couldn't find them. Well, then, how would his father have described her? Suddenly he knew. His father would have bestowed upon Lorraine the ultimate compliment. To him she would have been a "standup guy." "Yes," Billy thought, not at all bothered by the term's masculine gender, "that's exactly what she is." Reaching for a shoe, he looked toward the door knowing of course that she wasn't there and couldn't hear him. "Hey, Lorraine," he said, "you're the best."

Chapter 5

Northwestern Station, Chicago, Illinois, Friday, 28 April 1950, 0756 Hours.

Billy awoke with a start as the train came to an abrupt stop. "End of the line. Chee...Caw...Go Main Station," he heard the conductor call out.

Billy had been in a deep sleep since shortly after the train pulled out of the Glencoe Station. Now he felt surprisingly rested and completely relaxed.

He was due at the Induction Center at 9:00 AM. He looked at his watch. 7:58 AM. Plenty of time. He rubbed his eyes, stretched his legs, and was about to stand up when he looked down at his pants and saw with horror *a large wet stain* at his crotch.

"Jesus!" he screamed. And then again, "Jesus!" He held his head in his hands and began rocking it from side to side; and then he started banging his fists on the back of the vacant seat in front of him.

"How could I possibly have friggin' done this?" he said to himself. "A goddamn wet dream!"

"Shit, shit, shit!" he screamed, still banging the seatback.

One of the passengers in the front of the car who was in the process of removing a package from the overhead rack heard him and began staring in his direction.

"Sorry," Billy said, calling out to the man. "I just realized I forgot something important."

The man nodded understandingly, removed his package, turned, and began walking toward the exit.

Billy didn't know what to do. He hadn't brought a coat with him which he could drape over his arm to hide the stain while he walked. And he'd have trouble trying to buy another pair of pants at this time of morning even though he had enough money. "Dammit!" he said.

Billy looked down and saw a section of the Sun-Times on the floor half under the seat in front of him. Grabbing it in his right hand, he draped it over his left arm so that it would cover the stain.

He thought maybe he could get out of the car and make it to the men's room in the station unnoticed. He'd give it a try.

By this time there were only a few other people left in the car so he was able to step down out of it without being noticed and then walk along the platform to the station proper. Keeping his head up, he looked straight ahead trying to appear relaxed and invisible.

Three minutes later he was alone in the men's room of the station. He looked at his watch again. 8:07 AM. Shit!

He entered one of the stalls, closed the door, and pulled off his pants, carefully examining the stain. It was still there. Shit, again! And his jockey shorts were soaked. He took them off, balled them up, and threw them with disgust to the floor. Then he put his stained pants back on and listened carefully. Still alone, thank God! He exited the stall and put his soiled shorts in the waste receptacle. He felt better without the stickiness between his legs. Grabbing the section of the Sun-Times he had used when he'd gotten off the train, he went out into the station again trying to appear as inconspicuous as possible.

Once he was outside on the sidewalk where he saw fewer people he looked down. He could see that the stain was beginning to dry and fade, although there was still a dark outline which probably wouldn't disappear without washing. Could he go as he was to the Induction Center unnoticed? He doubted it. And then, as he looked up, he saw it: "Salvation Army Second Hand Store." "Maybe," he thought. "Just maybe." Still trying to hide the stain with the newspaper, he walked toward the store.

***

Safely inside, he spotted a large table littered with old clothes in disorderly piles. He began sifting through several stacks of pants, but found nothing.

A man appeared from somewhere in the back of the store carrying a large cardboard box. He had a tag pinned to his shirt with his name written on it in longhand. The word "Volunteer" appeared in print below his name.

"You looking for some pants?" the man asked as he approached.

Billy nodded, making an effort not to look down at the stain.

"These just came in. I usually go through 'em first to make sure there's nothin' in the pockets." He pulled a pair of faded blue jeans from the box which appeared to be too big, but otherwise were in fairly good shape. "Here," he said. "Try these."

"Thanks. Do you have a changing room?"

The man looked at Billy incredulously. Where did this college kid think he was? In some upscale men's store, for God's sake? Next thing you know, he'd be asking for alterations!

"Over there," the man said, pointing to a corner of the room partially sectioned off by an old sheet which hung from a sagging wire.

Billy stepped behind the sheet and put the jeans on. Christ, they really were too large: by about four inches in the waist and they were dragging on the floor. Billy pulled his belt out of the khakis and slipped it through the loops of the jeans. Then he hauled them up, chest high, so they no longer touched the floor. He tightened the belt as best he could, leaving several large folds in his now elevated waist. When he finished he transferred his wallet, keys, change, comb, and some papers to the pockets of the jeans. He folded the khakis, placed them under his arm, and walked back out to the cash register.

"Here," he said, handing the man a dollar bill. "Will that cover it?"

"I suppose," the man replied. "But we can always use a little more."

Billy quickly withdrew a second dollar bill from his wallet and handed it to the man. Then he took a deep breath and walked out onto the sidewalk, but not before noticing that the man was staring at him. He had a strange indescribable look on his face. Had he seen the stain? Billy wondered.

Billy thought for a moment about the khakis. Should he keep them or throw them out? He walked over to a trash bin, looked to make sure no one was watching, and dropped them into it.

Then, compulsively, he reached into the pockets of his jeans searching for the form letter he had received from the Induction Center several weeks before. When he found it he reread it for the hundredth time. There it was: 9:00 AM on today's date. The letter had been signed by the Center's CO, Colonel Kenneth Harkavy.

Chapter 6

U.S. Army Induction Center, Chicago, Illinois, Friday, 28 April 1950, 0850 Hours.

At ten minutes to nine Billy finally reached the Induction Center. It was located in a three-story building on Van Buren Street at the southerly perimeter of the Loop. Its ugly stone exterior was a dirty brown, and beneath its arched entryway were double doors with brass handles which had recently been polished. On the building wall next to the entryway there was a metal plaque on which *U.S. Army Induction Center, Chicago* was written in raised brass letters, also recently polished.

When Billy entered the building lobby he saw that there was a line of six men, all younger than he was. He joined it. He noticed that a few of the men were carrying small hand duffel bags.

The second in line, a large fat man, almost boyish in appearance, turned and looked at Billy. "Hey, would you get a load of that!" he said. "Where the fuck you get them pants, man? A fuckin' local yokel. Jesus!" He turned and laughed, trying, at the same time, to see if the others would join in. They didn't.

"Shut up, Jerry, you stinkin' asshole," the young man just in front of Billy said. "Anyway, he looks a lot better 'n you do, you tub o' lard." Then speaking even louder so he could be overheard by everyone, he said, "We better all goddamn learn to stick together from the beginnin'. And if you don't like it, Jerry, let's settle this now. 'Cuz I'll knock you on your fat ass." He stared directly at Jerry who quickly looked away.

"Sorry, man," he said to Billy. "I been listenin' to his bullshit since I came in ten minutes ago. See, I don't judge people by what they wear. Name's Craig Billington. From Decatur. I'm enlisting. I'm thinkin' about an army career." He extended his hand to Billy.

Shaking Craig's hand, Billy said, "Nice to meet you. Name's Billy. I'm from just north of here."

Another young man with long hair cut strangely so that it stuck out in a disheveled ring around his head, but not on the top of it, turned to Craig. "You got that right," he said. "I live on the South Side and that's the way we make it...by hanging together."

He pointed proudly to the symbol of a snorting dragon sewn on the front of his black silk jacket. "Vin," he said making a fist which he extended toward Craig and which Craig touched with a fist of his own. Vin then turned to Billy. "Hey, man, I don't give a flying fuck about your pants."

"Thanks," Billy replied.

Just then a door was pushed open and a tall black sergeant entered. His appearance was immaculate. His uniform was neatly pressed, the brass on it shown, and his shoes gleamed. On the right side of the chest of his olive drab Eisenhower jacket was a name tag with "Marks" on it, and on the left side were five rows of ribbons. One, in the top row, Billy recognized: the Silver Star. On each sleeve were chevrons denoting the rank of a master sergeant, and sewn below those on his left sleeve was a column of gold "overseas bars"—too many for Billy to count—followed by eight "hash marks," each representing three years of service.

"At ease," he said speaking in a surprisingly low yet commanding deep voice which Billy found difficult to hear without listening carefully. "Men, I'm Sergeant Marks. We're gonna begin, so listen up.

"You're gonna go into that room over there, Room One," he motioned with his head toward a doorway to his right, "where you're gonna fill out some forms and take our Achievement Test. Then you're gonna move on to Room Two. Strip, except for your socks, and put all your clothes in a locker. If you don't have a duffel bag, there are paper bags in there. Either put your valuables in your duffel bag or in one of the paper bags. But carry your valuables with you until you get dressed again. Got it?" He waited, looking at the group, and then continued. "Okay, after you've stripped you're gonna go into Room Three for a physical exam; and when that's over you go back to Room Two and put your clothes back on. Someone'll meet you there in about two hours. Any questions?" There were none.

"One more thing: the Achievement Test. We do not cheat, I repeat, we do not cheat in this man's army. There will be three proctors in Room One watching over you at all times. If any of you is caught cheating, that man will automatically get a grade of zero on the test. What that means is that after basic training, he will be assigned to a duty company. And that means the shittiest duty we've got for you for the rest of your time in the service. And just so you know it, *I fucking hate cheaters!"* It was the first time Sergeant Marks had raised his voice or used profanity, and it had the intended effect. He had gotten their attention. "Do you read me?" he asked. They nodded. "No, goddammit, I wanna fucking hear it!"

"Yes, Sergeant!" they yelled back in unison.

"You know," he said, speaking normally again, "there just might be a soldier or two in this group." He smiled. "So what're you waitin' for? Move out!"

Billy and the others got up and went into Room One. There was a blackboard on one wall and two dozen classroom-style desk chairs lined up facing it. To the side of the room there was a long table with stacks of papers on it. Three corporals were waiting for them in the room, each also immaculate in his appearance down to spit-shined shoes.

"Morning," one of them said. "I'm Corporal Ward. Take a seat." Then the other two corporals passed out various forms for the men to complete which asked questions about background, medical conditions, and education. "Fill these out as best you can; and don't worry if you can't come up with some of the answers," Corporal Ward said.

***

After they had completed the forms and passed them in, Corporal Ward stood up. "We've just finished the easy part. Now comes the Achievement Test. You've all been warned about cheating, right?" They all nodded. "Fine. Now listen up. We'll be passing out the test in a few minutes. It consists of a hundred multiple-choice questions. You use a Number Two pencil, and you're to fill in the answers on this test card." He held one up for them to see. "It's graded by a machine, and we'll have your grades ten minutes or so after you've finished. If you want to change an answer you can, but be sure to erase your first answer completely or the machine will think you answered the question incorrectly. We don't normally tell you the results, but you can't fail. Your results just tell us something more about you which we'll use in assigning you after basic. Now the last thing—and this is important—you'll have exactly one hour to complete the test. We come 'round after the hour's up and collect the cards even if you haven't finished. And if the hour's almost up and you've got a bunch of unanswered questions left, I recommend that you don't guess because this, on average, only lowers your score. In other words, you're penalized more for an incorrect answer than for no answer. Oh yeah, one more thing: no talking while you're taking the test.

"Anyone have a question?" No one did. "Okay," he said, "we'll pass out the test."

Billy skimmed the test after it had been handed to him. He'd taken so many tests that this one looked like all the rest, except that there seemed to be a lot more questions than usual involving simple logic and common sense. He began; and twenty minutes later he put down his Number Two pencil. He got up and handed in his card and the test to one of the corporals.

"What's the fuckin' matter, highpockets?" the corporal asked in a whisper, staring at Billy's ridiculous pants. "Didja drop your pencil in them jeans and forget to take the test?" Then he turned to the other two corporals and the three started laughing.

"I finished the test," Billy replied, flush with embarrassment.

"That a fact? Well, then, move on out to the changing room. When you're bare-ass go on into Room Three for your physical. But if I were you I'd carry them jeans with me 'cuz somebody's liable to steal 'em." Again, he and the other two corporals laughed.

All of this commotion seemed to be disturbing the others. This was the last thing Billy wanted, so he quickly exited the room.

After Billy's departure, Corporal Ward left the room with Billy's test card.

***

"Just stand back a ways from the wall," the doctor said. "Lean over and spread your cheeks as wide as you can so I can see in between. I got good eyes and I can see enough from here. I don't need to be within sniffing distance." Billy did as he was told.

"Fine. Now come on over here and let me listen to your heart and chest, and poke around a bit." The doctor listened and poked.

"Okay, now grab your pecker and skin it back for me so's I can get a good look." Billy was confused. "Skin it, son. You gotta have had some practice doin' that," the doctor said with a slight grin. Billy reached for his penis and slid the skin back as far as he could. "Feels kinda good, doesn't it? Wanna do it again?" The doctor laughed at his own joke.

"Now walk all the way over to the side of the room and back for me." Billy did as he was told while the doctor watched intently. "Any pain? Discomfort?" Billy shook his head.

"Ever had any sprains or broken bones?"

Billy thought for a moment. "Yes, sir," he answered.

"Tell me about that, son. And who was your doctor?"

"When I was around twelve I was told I had a smashed left heel cap. I hardly felt it and it's never really bothered me, but my orthopedist, Dr. Phillip Ehrlich, put my foot in a cast for six weeks."

"Red Ehrlich treated you?"

"Yes, sir," Billy replied, somewhat surprised. "You know Dr. Ehrlich, sir?"

"Sure do. We golf together every Saturday. Fact is, we're on for tomorrow." The doctor smiled.

"Any other orthopedic problems?"

"No, sir," Billy said.

"Okay, you're done. Get dressed."

***

While Billy was putting his shoes back on in the changing room, Vin, Jerry, and the others filed in and began removing their clothes. But Craig wasn't with them.

"What happened to Craig?" Billy asked Vin.

"I dunno. He was just sitting there in the test room when we left."

"Oh-oh," Billy thought as he got up and headed for the doorway.

***

A short time later Billy was back in the changing room seated on a bench awaiting the return of the others from their physicals. He had been there for some time when he heard someone enter. It was Sergeant Marks. "C'mon, Rosen," he said. "Let's move out. I want the Colonel to see you."

"Huh?" Billy replied, not quite believing what he'd heard.

"I said I want the Colonel to see you, so let's move out, goddammit!"

"I'm coming, Sergeant," Billy said.

"Shit," he thought. "It's the blue jeans."

***

Billy followed Sergeant Marks down a long corridor. At its end there was a large door. Sergeant Marks opened it, entered, and motioned to Billy to follow.

They were in a reception room. At the far wall a middle-aged secretary sat at a desk busily typing.

Sergeant Marks looked at Billy and then pointed to one of the couches. "Sit down," he said as he walked over to the secretary. "Hi Mildred. Is Colonel Harkavy in?"

"He just went out to run some errands. After that he's got a one o'clock dentist appointment."

"It's kinda important."

"I'll see if I can track him down," she replied as she picked up the phone.

Sergeant Marks looked at his watch. It was 11:05 AM. Three hours and ten minutes later they were still waiting. Billy had begun to doze off and Sergeant Marks was engrossed in a magazine article when the door opened and Colonel Harkavy rushed in. He was carrying a manila envelope. Before Mildred could speak, he motioned to Sergeant Marks to follow him into his office.

***

"Have a seat, Wally. And what's so important?"

"Well, Colonel, as you know I always look over the new kids when they come in. Sometimes I pick up some interesting stuff. That's more or less what happened this morning.

"There's a kid sitting in your reception room who came in a couple of hours ago wearing blue jeans about six sizes too big that just about came up to his chin. Looked like some kinda hayseed in baggy pants. And you know we get a lot of weirdoes, so I didn't think much of it, that is, until Ward showed me this." Sergeant Marks handed Billy's graded test card to Colonel Harkavy who examined it and then raised his eyebrows.

"You and I've been here for close to three years, Colonel. Ever seen anything like that before?"

"No, Sergeant, I haven't."

"Then Ward tells me Baggy Pants finished the test in twenty minutes. Another first? Right, sir?"

The Colonel nodded.

"Well, now I'm becoming interested so I get hold of the forms Baggy Pants turned in. He's from Glencoe, sir. That's high end. Went to New Trier High School and then on to college, form doesn't say where, but he wrote on it that he graduated with a degree in chemistry and physics." He paused.

"A few more interesting things, sir. I spoke to Ward. He told me that one of the other kids didn't finish the test and was just sitting there in Room One in sort of a daze. Ward was about to tell him to move out into Room Two when Baggy Pants came in. Ward overheard their conversation. He said the other kid told Baggy Pants that he was thinking of an army career, but that he'd blown all hopes of that when he didn't finish the test. Ward said that Baggy Pants told him not to worry because that wasn't what soldiering was about, that performance on the rifle range was a lot more important than test scores, and that he was gonna make a great soldier, someone Baggy Pants and the others would be proud to serve with. Seems the other kid was pretty moved by what Baggy Pants said. Guess I would be too, Colonel. You and I both know that a word or two of encouragement at the right time and place can make a world of difference. So I'm thinking that maybe Baggy Pants isn't the weirdo he appears to be. And I'm also beginning to like him."

Sergeant Marks stopped for a moment before continuing. "Then Doc comes in and lays something on me which I never expected. He tells me he has a call in to Baggy Pants' former doctor, guy by the name of Phil Ehrlich who happens to be one of Doc's golfing buddies. Doc says he thinks that Baggy Pants probably should be 4F, but he wants you, Colonel, to make the call. 'Why?' I ask. 'Because,' Doc says, 'he's pretty sure there's something seriously wrong with his left foot and he thinks it'll hurt like hell on any kind of a march or field problem.' But he's waiting to speak to Ehrlich to confirm this."

"You talking about Rosen?" Colonel Harkavy asked.

Sergeant Marks nodded in surprise.

"I just came from Doc's office. He's already talked to Ehrlich. Here, Wally. Take a look at this." Colonel Harkavy handed Sergeant Marks the manila envelope he'd been carrying. Inside there was a memorandum typed on an Induction Center multi-page interleaved carbon form. Sergeant Marks took a moment to read it:

Interoffice Memorandum
U.S. Army Induction Center
Chicago, Illinois

To: Col. Kenneth Harkavy

From: Col. George Gunderson, MD

Date: 28 April 1950

Subject: William Rosen

Ken—

There's a youngster I saw earlier this morning by the name of William Rosen (I also discussed him briefly with Sergeant Marks). When I questioned him about sprains or breaks, he told me that when he was a teenager he had a smashed heel cap, and that his left foot was put in a cast. He also gave the name of the physician who originally treated him (who, by the way, happens to be a friend of mine). I called him and he told me that, on top of the smashed heel cap, Rosen had a condition known as "Sever's Disease." Normally kids recover from all this, but he said that in Rosen's case the problem was severe and he wasn't sure whether there had been a complete recovery. He didn't have an opinion on how Rosen would fare in the service.

When Rosen told me about his left foot he said it never really bothered him.

Frankly, I'm dubious. For this reason I think he probably should be classified 4F, but I want you to interview him; when you do ask him about that foot. Then you decide. But the bottom line is that if he's going to be inducted he'd better be told that his left foot could hurt like hell on long marches and field problems, etc.

For my file, please return a copy of this Memo to me countersigned by you advising me of the action taken.

Thanks.

Doc

*Reply*____

When Sergeant Marks finished reading the memo, Colonel Harkavy asked, "So what do you think?"

"I honestly don't know, sir. I'm not a doctor. I guess you'd better discuss the foot with Rosen."

"Right," Colonel Harkavy said. "Send him in."

"I will, sir. But before I do I think I'd better tell you a couple more things about him:

"First, Rosen wasn't drafted. He's here voluntarily for two years.

"Second, on the form he filled out he lists his father as 'Louis Rosen.' Ring a bell, Colonel?"

Colonel Harkavy shook his head.

"Well it did with me, so I made a quick call to a friend over at the Sun-Times." Sergeant Marks stopped for a moment, taking time to look directly at Colonel Harkavy. "Sir, this kid's father is gonna be a royal pain in the ass. He's wealthy and powerful, knows everyone. He's also supposed to be able to do large numbers calculations in his head. Something like a genius. Sir, all's I can say is that I wouldn't want to be making any problems for his kid. Never can tell how the father would react."

"Christ, Wally, what else, for God's sake?"

"Nothing, sir. But remember, you always told me to be on the lookout for…" He hesitated. "Well, you know, sir."

"Thanks, Wally. I read you loud and clear. Why don't you just let me and Baggy Pants have a little one-on-one. At this point I think I'm about as curious as you are."

"Thought you'd be, sir." Sergeant Marks got out of his chair and opened the door to the reception room.

"Rosen," he said, "come on in."

Because his father knew just about everyone, and because he seemed to get a buzz out of introducing Billy around, Billy had, long before arriving at the doorway of Colonel Harkavy's office, met a number of so-called "notables" in his short lifetime. They included CEOs and politicians; the President of Harvard (when he was told he was graduating *summa*); celebrities like Groucho Marx, Danny Kaye, and Eddie Cantor; high-ranking military people including a couple of generals and admirals; sports figures; and even a few of the "guys" like little Moe Schwartz. And Billy recalled that his father had once said to him, "Hey, kid, they're just like you and me: they put on their pants every morning one leg at a time." Billy knew of course that his father was right. So even though he didn't know why he was being called into Colonel Harkavy's office, he wasn't even slightly impressed or, for that matter, intimidated.

With his hands in his pockets, he stepped into Colonel Harkavy's office and stood, not knowing exactly what to do.

"Rosen," Sergeant Marks groaned, "for Christ's sake, get your hands out of your pockets and stand at attention!"

Billy stood rigidly before Colonel Harkavy trying desperately to comply with Sergeant Marks' order even though he felt sure he could never properly stand at attention in his oversize jeans.

"Sir," Sergeant Marks continued, "this is brand new recruit William Rosen. And, sir, I emphasize the 'brand new.'"

"Thank you, Sergeant Marks. I believe I can take it from here," Colonel Harkavy said, trying as best he could to keep from laughing at the sight before him. "Oh, and by the way, would you find this young man a pair of khakis."

"Be glad to, Colonel," Sergeant Marks said as he left the room.

Colonel Harkavy raised his hand to his mouth, coughed, and then cleared his throat. Billy couldn't help noticing his MIT ring.

"Well, Rosen," he began, "it seems we've got a lot to talk about, and neither you nor I have all that much time. So why don't you take a seat and let's begin." He waited while Billy sat down in one of the chairs.

"First, I'm a bit puzzled by your ill-fitting pants. Would you please explain to me what the hell's going on?"

"Certainly, sir," Billy replied. "I ruined my khakis on the way to the Induction Center this morning, so I bought these at the only store that was open, a second hand store, and threw my khakis away."

Colonel Harkavy nodded.

"Second, Rosen, what do they call you?"

"'Billy,' sir. But of course 'Rosen' is fine; or even 'Private Rosen.'"

"I think I'll try 'Billy,' but just for this meeting, not afterwards. Okay?"

"Sure, sir."

"Anyway, even if I wanted to I couldn't call you 'Private Rosen' since you're not officially in the Army and won't be until you're sworn in later today—if that happens."

Billy looked up. "What do you mean, sir, 'if that happens'?"

"Well, I'm not sure you're going to be able to go into the Army. See, Doc Gunderson, the physician who gave you your physical, has advised me and Sergeant Marks that he thinks you probably should be 4F with that bad left foot of yours. So why don't you tell me what that's all about."

Billy looked puzzled. "'Bad left foot,' sir? If you mean my heel, it's fine."

"Look, Billy, if Doc tells me you've got a problem, then, trust me, *you've got a problem.* Doc's one of the best. Ranked first in his class at Johns Hopkins more years ago than he'd like to remember. So what I want you to do is tell me what you recall happening to that left foot of yours."

Just then Mildred opened the door. "Colonel, I know you're on a diet and never eat lunch. But that boy in there does. Why, he must be hungry as all get-out."

Colonel Harkavy looked at his watch. It was 2:35 PM. "Christ," he said, "the day's almost gone." Then turning to Billy he asked, "Would you care for something to eat? Mildred's buying."

"That's correct, Colonel, I am buying." She turned to Billy. "So, young man, what would you like?"

"Any kind of a sandwich, ma'am, and maybe a soft drink."

"Would a tuna sandwich on toast and a Pepsi do?"

"Perfect," Billy said.

Colonel Harkavy got up from his desk chair and walked over to the doorway where Mildred was standing. "Here," he said handing her two dollars. "It's on me."

"If you insist," she replied taking the money and then closing the door.

Colonel Harkavy returned to his chair. "Well, Billy, where were we?" He thought for a moment. "That left foot of yours."

"Well, sir, as I told the doctor today, I smashed my left heel cap when I was about twelve. It didn't bother me much, but when I did see an orthopedist about it he put me in a cast for six weeks.

And after he took off the cast my foot's never bothered me. Actually, it didn't bother me much before."

"Yeah, well...Doc seems to feel there's still a problem there. You ever have any trouble on hikes or long walks?"

"Well, sir, sometimes I used to tire a little faster than my friends did. That seemed to go away, though, after I started running cross-country in college. But I don't recall any kind of a problem with my left foot."

"Okay, Billy. Here's what we've got. Doc says it's my call whether you're 4F. But he also says that on field problems—and I'm assuming he's thinking in terms of long marches, particularly with a full field pack—your left foot might start hurting like hell. So I think I'm probably gonna classify you 4F. How do you feel about that?"

"Colonel, if my mother or father heard what you just said I think they'd break out the champagne. But me...well, frankly, I'm pretty disappointed. It may sound unbelievable, but I was sorta looking forward to two years in the Army. I thought they just might turn out to be fairly interesting. It'd give me a chance to get in better shape and to be around people I've never mixed it up with before. Yeah, I have to say I don't think I feel like celebrating at the moment."

"So would you like me to forget about it then?"

Surprised, Billy said, "Sure, sir, I really would."

"Well, understand, Billy, if we do forget about your foot and let you in the Army you might really suffer on those marches. You sure you still want in?"

"Sir, please pardon my language, but, yes, I want in, and to hell with an occasional sore foot."

"Okay, Billy, you got it."

"I appreciate it, sir. And may I request that this be between you, me, and Dr. Gunderson; because if my folks ever found out they'd probably go nuts. See, they're not exactly thrilled about me being in the Army, particularly coming in the way I am."

"Not a problem, Billy," Colonel Harkavy said. "It'll be strictly between you, me, and Doc, with one minor exception: there'll be some notation about it in your 201 File. But that will be it."

"Thanks, sir. So I guess that's what you wanted to see me about?"

"We're not quite finished. Mind if I ask a few questions?"

"Not at all, sir."

"Okay, for starters, where'd you go to college?"

"Right down the street from your alma mater, sir. Harvard."

"And how would you know where I went to school?" Colonel Harkavy asked, mildly surprised.

"The beaver."

"The what?"

"On your 'Brass Rat,' Colonel. Your MIT ring."

"Right," Colonel Harkavy said glancing down at his left hand.

"Honors, Billy?"

"Is it really all that important, sir?"

"I think it is, Billy. *And, remember, I'm doing the questioning, not you*," Colonel Harkavy replied with a forcefulness which caught Billy off guard.

"Well," Billy thought, "I think I just got a glimpse of the real Colonel Harkavy."

"I graduated *summa*, sir."

"Kinda what I figured," Colonel Harkavy said, half talking to himself.

"So, Billy, let me lay the sixty-four dollar question on you. What in hell are you doing here? Why, for Christ's sake, aren't you in grad school?"

"Well, Colonel, I was accepted by MIT in their chem engineering grad program. But I felt I'd be bored working as an engineer. So I decided to go into the military."

"Yeah, but why as an enlisted man? Don't you think you could make a more important contribution as an officer?"

"I guess I never thought of it in terms of a contribution, sir. Just getting my military obligation out of the way."

"Okay, let's switch gears for a second, Billy. Have you got any idea how you did on the Achievement Test?"

"Okay, I guess. It was fairly standard."

"Yeah, well, just so you know, you finished in record time and got every question right; and that's the best I've seen in the nearly three years I've been around here. I consider that impressive."

"Really, sir? I wouldn't. I don't think doing well on a short answer test is what soldiering's all about."

"In a way it is, Billy. When you think about it, the Army's like any other large organization. We need technical people who are expert at firing an M1, tossing a grenade, driving a tank, that sort of thing. But most of all we need people with brainpower who can think their way through problems. That's what any large organization needs. And, frankly, both Sergeant Marks and I feel that that's what you've got to offer the Army: your ability to think."

Colonel Harkavy watched Billy closely to see how he reacted to this.

"So that's why you're in the Army, sir: because of your brainpower?"

"No, not exactly. But I can't get into that. Today I'm gonna have to limit our discussion to you." He looked directly at Billy.

"So here's the bottom line. You said you want in. You got it. But both Sergeant Marks and I think it would be a damn waste of talent if you came in as an enlisted man. We want you to come in as an officer. Much better opportunity to use that brain of yours. So here's what I propose: Instead of being sworn in today, you go on home, but with the understanding that I'll be in touch with you in about six weeks. At that time I will have worked out your admittance to OCS. When you've finished there you'll be a second lieutenant. Only difference is you'll have to serve for three years instead of two. But those three years will be interesting for you and, as I said, you'll be making a far more important contribution to the Army than you'd be making as an enlisted man. How does that sound?"

"I hear you, Colonel, but, with respect, for several reasons I'm just not comfortable accepting your offer." Billy stopped for a moment and tried to pull his thoughts together. He didn't want to offend Colonel Harkavy but, at the same time, he wanted to be completely forthright. He knew he was walking a fine line.

"First, sir, like I said, I'm really here only to satisfy my military obligation. I'd be misleading you if I told you otherwise. And if that's my goal, as I believe it is, why increase that obligation by another year? What I want to do is serve honorably in the military for two years and then move on. When I get out of the service I'll try to make whatever contribution I can, but it'll be in a different arena, not in the service. At the same time, I can't go for a 4F classification even though I may come by it legitimately. It just rubs against my grain." Billy took a deep breath. Had he totally pissed off Colonel Harkavy? He hoped not.

"Secondly, sir, I don't want to be around the same kind of people I've spent my entire life with: college graduates who are in the Army as officers. I can't imagine being in an officers club with them most every night. What I want is to be around the kind of guys I met on my way in here this morning." He saw that Colonel Harkavy was listening intently.

"Finally, Colonel, as I mentioned, I really wanna go through basic. May sound crazy, but I'm looking forward to the physical training, living in a barracks, and even pulling KP and guard duty. OCS would be just another college course with some PE tossed in."

Colonel Harkavy didn't respond immediately. Instead, he sat there silently, Billy guessed for at least five seconds. Then he said, "Well, Billy, I suppose I have no choice. I'll go along with your decision. You'll come in as an enlisted man."

"Thank you, sir," Billy said.

At that moment Mildred entered. In her right hand she was carrying a small open cardboard box containing two sandwiches, a twelve-ounce bottle of Pepsi, two apples, and some napkins; and in her left she held a pair of khakis. She placed the khakis on the desktop and then handed the box to Billy, but not before removing one of the apples from it. "Enjoy your lunch, young man. And you enjoy yours too, Colonel," she said, handing him the apple. "By the way, I found these pants on my chair."

Taking a bite of his apple, Colonel Harkavy pointed to the khakis. "Try putting those on. Use my washroom over there." He motioned to his right.

"Thank you, sir," Billy said. He went into Colonel Harkavy's private washroom and slid out of his jeans and into the khakis which were only about an inch too large in the waist, but the correct length. After he'd transferred his belt and valuables to his new pants, he walked back into the office carrying the jeans. "I have money, sir. May I pay for the khakis? Or would you like them returned in a few weeks?"

"Forget it, Billy," Colonel Harkavy replied. "And don't worry about the jeans. We'll dispose of them. Let's just say that you owe me one and we'll leave it at that."

Chapter 7

U.S. Army Induction Center, Chicago, Illinois, Friday, 28 April 1950, 1530 Hours.

Earlier, while Billy had been in with Colonel Harkavy, twenty-one other recruits had arrived at the Chicago Induction Center by bus from Waukegan. This brought the total to twenty-eight, all of whom, including Billy, were now seated in a room which resembled a small auditorium. At the front of the room there was an elevated platform on which a podium rested. Several recessed ceiling lights shown down upon it, and an American flag stood at the far corner of the platform behind and to its left. Sergeant Marks was sitting in the first row of chairs. He stood up. "Atten…hut!" he shouted, and all the recruits rose to rigid attention as Colonel Harkavy entered the room.

"At ease, gentlemen," he said, as he made his way to the podium.

Colonel Harkavy had on his uniform coat and Billy noticed that there was only one item pinned to its front, a name tag. Nothing else. Billy was puzzled. For someone like Colonel Harkavy who'd obviously been in the Army a number of years there should have been more—particularly ribbons—unless, of course, he'd spent his entire career behind a desk. That, Billy felt, was highly unlikely.

Colonel Harkavy began to speak. "Good afternoon. I'm Colonel Harkavy, Commanding Officer of the U.S. Army Induction Center, Chicago. I want to welcome you. By now you've had a physical exam and taken our Achievement Test. If you're still here it means you've passed the physical. And, as Sergeant Marks told you, no one flunks the test. We just use the results in assessing your skills for assignment purposes.

"Technically, at this juncture, not one of you is in the Army. And you won't be until you've taken the Oath which I'll be administering to you in a few minutes. Once you've taken it, and then taken one step forward as I will order you to do, each of you will officially have been inducted into the United States Army with the rank of Private and with a distinct serial number which you should commit to memory." He took a moment to clear his throat.

"The Oath which you are about to take is historic. All members of the military, past and present, have taken it." Colonel Harkavy stepped from behind the podium and nodded in the direction of two corporals who were standing next to the doorway at the far wall. Almost immediately they began passing out copies of the Oath to the men.

Billy glanced around the room. He noticed that Craig had a concerned look on his face and a slightly furrowed brow; that Fat Jerry was making a commotion—talking loudly while gesticulating at the same time—trying to attract as much attention as possible; and that Vin's demeanor was completely out of sync with what Billy would have expected. Wearing an expression of intense pride, he stood motionless looking directly ahead, his feet spread apart, his back arched, and his hands clasped firmly behind him.

When each man had received a copy of the Oath, Colonel Harkavy stepped to the podium once again. "Please follow along with me," he said. Then, from memory, he began: "*I,* and then you state your name, *do solemnly swear that I will support and defend the Constitution of the United States against all enemies, foreign and domestic; that I will bear true faith and allegiance to the same; and that I will obey the orders of the President of the United States and the orders of the officers appointed over me, according to regulations and the Uniform Code of Military Justice. So help me God!*"

As he almost always did, Colonel Harkavy took a moment to look over this group of youngsters who would shortly be inducted. He knew how drastically their lives were about to change.

"Any questions?" he asked. There were none. The room was silent. Colonel Harkavy waited a moment before beginning.

***

At 3:57 PM on Friday, April 28, 1950, Billy became Private (E-1) William Rosen, Serial Number ER16548889.

Chapter 8

U.S. Army Induction Center, Chicago, Illinois, Friday, 28 April 1950, 1630 Hours.

It was late in the afternoon when Colonel Harkavy returned to his office. Mildred had just cleared her desk and was reaching for her coat. "Mildred," he said, "would you do me one small favor and get Sergeant Marks in here. Then you can take off."

"Sure, that's easy," she replied. She dropped her coat over the back of the desk chair and went down the hall looking for Sergeant Marks.

A few minutes later Sergeant Marks was seated in Colonel Harkavy's office. The speakerphone was on, and the phone was ringing. They heard someone pick it up.

"Good afternoon, General Haslett's office, Captain Martin speaking, sir."

"Hi, Captain. This is Colonel Harkavy, Chicago Induction Center. General Haslett available?"

"Hold one, sir." A moment later he was back.

"Sir, he's in his office with Colonel Paulson. He'll be on momentarily."

Less than a minute later the General's voice boomed over the speaker. "Ken, how are you?"

"Doin' fine, sir. And you?"

"I'm okay, I guess. Normal pressures of running a basic training regiment. But with guys like Jon Paulson, I'll make it."

Brigadier General Stanton M. Haslett, II commanded the Second Training Regiment (Basic), Fort Leonard Wood, Missouri, and was responsible for putting more than twelve thousand recruits through basic training every year. Lieutenant Colonel Jonathan Q. Paulson was CO of the Regiment's Fourth Battalion. Both were longtime acquaintances of Colonel Harkavy and Sergeant Marks.

"Sir, I've got Sergeant Wally Marks in here with me. That okay?"

"Wally," the General said with obvious pleasure, "glad you're there. How's it goin'?"

"Great, General," Sergeant Marks replied. "But to be honest, sir, I'd just as soon be back on post. Chicago's getting old."

"Don't blame you, Wally. Never could stand big cities myself. So, Ken, what's so important that you're calling me when you should be heading home? And is it anything Colonel Paulson should be privy to 'cause he's right here with me?"

"General, I really think we ought to restrict this conversation to you, me, and Wally."

"No problem. Just a sec'." General Haslett could be heard mumbling something. Then he got back on the phone. "Okay, Ken, Jon's not in the office. So what gives?"

"Well, sir, you know Wally and I've been in this assignment for almost three years now sitting on our hands—and it's really driven us both nuts—that is, until today *when I think we finally found the guy I want.*"

He waited for General Haslett to respond, but there was silence. Finally General Haslett replied, "You know what you're saying, don't you, Ken?"

"Yes, sir, I do."

"What about you, Wally? You concur?"

"Hundred percent, General."

"Fact is, Wally found him and brought him to my attention," Colonel Harkavy interjected.

"Hmm. Well, dammit, fill me in. I want to know everything. I mean *everything*."

"Well, sir, early this morning this kid walks in wearing these baggy blue jeans. Looks like a real hayseed. He's part of the 9:00 AM lineup. Well…"

General Haslett listened intently to Colonel Harkavy for close to ten minutes without saying a word. When he finished, General Haslett said, "I look forward to getting him here. What's his name?"

"William Rosen, sir. Goes by 'Billy.'"

"Son of a bitch!" General Haslett screamed into the speakerphone. "This is the fourth call I've received today about Private William Rosen. Shit!"

Colonel Harkavy and Sergeant Marks were stunned. "What do you mean, General?" Colonel Harkavy said. "I'm not understanding, sir."

"Yeah, well, listen up then. At eight-thirty this morning I get a call from Jimmy Steeger, Fifth Army CO. 'Hey, Stan,' he says, 'I got this good friend in Chicago, Louie Rosen. His kid, Billy, is fresh outta Harvard and being inducted today. My friend's really upset. Thinks his kid should be in grad school, or at least coming in as an officer. So anything you could do to keep the boy in the Chicago area after basic sure'd be appreciated.' And, goddammit, that's only the first call. 'Bout an hour later Congressman Ian Morgan calls me. Same damn drivel. A good friend of Louis Rosen's, etcetera, etcetera. So you'd think that'd be the end of the phone calls, right? Well, wrong! Now it's about noon and Dan Forrester, CO at Fort Sheridan, calls me. Seems his first cousin is one of Louie Rosen's closest friends; and Dan also knows him. Seems Rosen and his wife are very upset 'cause their kid's comin' in today as an EM instead of a Second John and couldn't I at least make sure he gets some interesting assignment near home. And now, of all things, I hear from you that after about three years of searching you've finally found someone you want; and, coincidentally, he just happens to be Private William Rosen! All I can say is it's a good thing my office is on the first floor, because I'm just about ready to go out of the friggin' window."

"Jesus!" Colonel Harkavy said. "Wally told me his father had influence, but I never expected this, particularly so early in the game. But sir, with respect, it doesn't change things. Wally and I feel this youngster's exceptional, and we just can't lose him to pushy parents."

"But Ken, be realistic for Christ's sake. How am I gonna be able to put this kid to the test? Think about the pressure I'm under today plus the pressure his family'll bring to bear if he complains about the way he's being treated during basic or if he isn't assigned close to home afterwards. I wouldn't be at all surprised if I started getting calls from the President himself." Colonel Harkavy and Sergeant Marks could sense General Haslett's frustration.

"Sir, Wally and I have been on the lookout now for close to three years. I say we ignore the pressure. I say we go for it."

"Wally?" General Haslett asked.

"I agree with Colonel Harkavy, General."

"Okay, then I guess I'll have to consider him a keeper. After all, Ken, it's your call, not mine. But let's have the following understanding: I'm gonna have the absolute maximum amount of shit thrown at him during basic. And if, as I suspect, he turns out to be a whiner or a pussy, well then, Ken, we call this whole thing off; and after basic I'll see to it that he gets some stupid-ass plush assignment near his home. And if he comes through with flying colors, as you geniuses predict he will, then I guess I'll just have to figure out some way to duck the heat. That sound fair?"

"Yes, sir," both Colonel Harkavy and Sergeant Marks replied.

"And just so you know it, I'm gonna have Rosen assigned to Jon Paulson's battalion. I'll fill Jon in. In a way, I feel sorry for Private Rosen. He's gonna catch an awful lot of crap in the next eight weeks. Poor bastard." General Haslett hung up.

Chapter 9

Franconia Ballroom, Franconia Hotel,
St. Louis, Missouri,
Friday, 28 April 1950, 2000 Hours.

Harley Lutz was a large man who took pride in his build. As a boy he'd been impressed by the ads about the muscular guy who lorded it over the skinny weakling making him look like a fool in front of his girl. Early on he'd decided that he was going to be the one who made the puny guy with the girl look like a twerp, not the other way around. And so he'd started working out. It had paid off because now, in his early thirties, he had a bodybuilder's physique. The way he came across—as a big beefy guy—had helped him get work, including his present employment. He gave the impression that he was someone who could handle the diciest of situations, even if it involved slapping a few people around. To a certain extent the impression wasn't entirely accurate because Harley suffered from extraordinarily poor eyesight as evidenced by the quarter-inch thick eye glasses he always wore. Without them, he was blind as a bat and incapable of handling any situation, dicey or otherwise, or slapping anyone around. In fact, without his glasses Harley couldn't punch his way out of a paper bag.

On a certain level, Harley was a man of conscience. He clearly knew right from wrong. As a result, he had come to despise his current job although he liked the money. Correction: he *loved* the money. And he desperately needed it not only to support his wife and three young children but to feed his ravenous gambling habit. Despite this, no one had to tell him that he'd sacrificed principle for the holy dollar when he'd signed on with Furax Unlimited ten months ago. In his own eyes he was nothing but a whore.

When Harley had joined Furax his wife, Marie, had quizzed him about his new position. He had given her the same bullshit that had been fed to him: "It's a chance to do good, dear," he had said. "Food is donated to us which we dispense to the needy."

Unbeknown to Marie and most others, Harley's work required him to wear two hats. He headed up a fictitious charity known as the "Brothers of the Hungry" and he also managed "Furax Distributors," a food wholesaler. The Brothers' ostensible mission was to solicit donations of food which was on the verge of spoiling or being thrown out. This food was then supposed to go to food banks from which it could be withdrawn by those in need. In fact, the whole setup was a ruse. The donations which the Brothers received were the direct result of hefty bribes Harley paid to people having access to food in bulk. And the items of food—which were always fresh, not anywhere near spoiling or being thrown out—never reached a single food bank; instead, they were almost immediately resold by Furax Distributors, sometimes to the very same people who had donated them. A nifty scheme with negligible costs.

As it turned out, the "chance to do good" had netted Harley more money per month than he'd ever imagined. And he was so proficient in doing the good work of the Brothers and in reselling the food via Furax that he'd been promoted to District Manager, Midwest Division. His boss, someone known to him only as "Mr. Samuels," never showed up, although Harley did find in the envelopes containing the Midwest Division's bank statements some canceled checks showing that a "Samuel Samuels" was receiving a sizeable monthly paycheck…larger than his by at least a factor of three.

As part of his duties as District Manager, Harley was required to throw a series of dinner parties for various groups of food donors. This evening he was hosting the first of these bashes. That was why he'd booked a table for seven at the Franconia Ballroom. He'd had Marie help him with the table arrangements: a place card for each guest, and at each place setting two bottles of wine, one red and one white, and two Cuban cigars. Owing to the nature of the after-dinner entertainment he'd arranged, wives and girlfriends were excluded. Harley was not particularly looking forward to the evening. No matter how viewed, he considered it strictly business.

As his guests began to arrive, Harley was overcome by a feeling of loathing. He loathed his guests; but most of all he loathed himself. Furthermore, he felt like a fool bedecked in the black and red Salvation Army-like uniform of a Colonel in the Brothers of the Hungry.

Ian Baldwin was seated on Harley's immediate right. He was the most productive member of this particular group of suppliers; but, at the same time, he was also the most boisterous and obnoxious. He tended to drink to excess. And when he did, he was like a broken record. He would continually talk about women and pussy. At the first mention of some woman, Baldwin would always comment, "She takes it in the head."

Seated next to Baldwin on his right was stolid overweight Quentin Ratsil. He was more interested in the evening's menu than in money or entertainment. He too liked to drink, and the more he imbibed the quieter he became. A good source of donations; almost as good as Baldwin.

The other four guests were rather new to the Brothers, brought in by one of Harley's salesmen. One had begun making donations just three weeks before, and the other three had been on board for only two months. Harley didn't know much about them, and part of his evening's work was to learn as much as he could about each of these newcomers.

For the appetizer, Harley had ordered shrimp cocktail. That was followed by a Caesar salad. Then came the main course: roast beef with Yorkshire pudding, peas, and mashed potatoes. For dessert Harley had chosen a chocolate parfait; then coffee followed by an after dinner drink (the guests had their choice of brandy, crème de menthe, or coffee liqueur); and, finally, a cigar or two.

Despite Ian Baldwin's crassness, the dinner had gone swimmingly. Now, while the men were puffing on their cigars, Harley got up. "Friends," he said, "I want to thank each one of you for your efforts on behalf of the Brothers. You have allowed us to help feed the hungry, so you should feel a true sense of satisfaction. We at the Brothers truly appreciate your efforts. And, as a token of our appreciation, well…here." Harley handed each man an envelope containing a one hundred dollar bill.

"Christ," Harley thought to himself, "do they really buy off on this? What kind of a charity pays bribes to get donations, hosts a fancy dinner party, and then hands each guest a C-note?"

But the men were happy and tipsy.

Now came the *coup de grâce*, the women. Harley had engaged the services of six hookers who showed up just after he handed out the envelopes. One for each guest. They whispered in the men's ears, loosened the men's ties, ran their hands inside the men's shirts, kissed them with open mouths, and, finally, began rubbing the men's crotches, at the same time gently pulling them away from the table and out of the ballroom to one of six rooms upstairs in the hotel which Harley had reserved.

When a dyed blonde in her late thirties with sagging breasts finally hoisted Ian Baldwin from his chair, he began to sway back and forth and then suddenly he vomited, fortunately missing her dress and the table. "Sorry, Colonel" he said, slurring his words.

"Not to worry," Harley replied. "Stomach flu hits us all from time to time."

Baldwin looked over at the blonde. Gesturing to her with the hand he had just used to wipe his mouth, he said, "Whaddya think, Colonel? She take it in the head?"

"I wouldn't be at all surprised," Harley replied, repulsed at the thought of even being in the same room with her.

Hearing this exchange, the blonde came over to Harley and whispered in his ear, "Not on your life, pal. This guy smells like a bucket of puke."

Harley winked at her and handed her a ten dollar bill.

"Well, okay," the blonde said, continuing to whisper to Harley. "But you gotta admit I'm gonna earn my keep tonight!"

Harley nodded, as the woman again began pulling Baldwin toward the ballroom's main doorway.

"God," Harley thought, "what we do for a dollar!" But he knew that he'd cemented his relationship with each of these suppliers. At the same time he cringed at the thought of hosting even one more of these damn wing dings.

Chapter 10

Main Gate, Fort Leonard Wood, Missouri, Saturday, 29 April 1950, 1330 Hours.

In the early afternoon on the day following Billy's induction, a World War II-vintage army bus in which he and the others were riding ground to a halt at the main gate of Fort Leonard Wood, Missouri, one of the largest basic training centers in the United States. The driver, a chain-smoking PFC in his late thirties whose hands shook from the DTs, reached under his seat for a clipboard, thumbed through some papers, muttered something to the MP on duty whom he appeared to know, and then put the bus in gear. It lumbered forward down a winding roadway. About ten minutes later it came to a stop in front of a large building which, like every other building Billy had seen since entering Fort Wood, was painted white and had a green roof.

"Let's move it," the PFC yelled in a hoarse voice. Billy and the others filed out. The last to exit the bus was Corporal Ward who had shepherded the group on its journey from the Induction Center in Chicago to St. Louis by overnight train and then on to Wood by bus.

Corporal Ward stepped to the front of the group. "Remain at ease," he said. "I'm gonna arrange to have someone meet you." He went inside the building, reappearing a few minutes later. "All set," he said. "They'll be here in about fifteen minutes. So try to enjoy the next eight weeks, mother fuckers! And if things get really tough just think of your ol' buddy Ward slipping the sausage to some beautiful Chicago broad." He grinned. Then, waving goodbye, he reboarded the bus which turned around and headed back in the direction of the main gate.

Craig groaned. "What a gaping asshole." Someone nearby—Billy wasn't exactly sure who—chimed in, "On the fuckin' money!" And then people began talking. Some started to smoke. One began playing the harmonica, while Fat Jerry, on Billy's immediate right, nervously picked his nose. Vin pulled out a comb and began teasing his hair so that it stood out in the same circle around his head, but even straighter than before.

Billy felt awful. He couldn't remember when he'd been so

tired. He'd tossed and turned all night in the lower berth on the train. And he also felt sticky and grimy because he hadn't bathed since leaving home. He ran his tongue over his teeth. They felt rough and unbrushed, and his mouth was dry and bitter tasting. What he'd give for a hot shower and a decent night's sleep. He breathed in deeply and winced at the unmistakable stench of unbathed men.

And so they all waited—for close to half an hour—until they saw a Jeep approaching. It contained two NCOs, both sergeants. The taller of the two was driving.

"Attention!" the large Sergeant cried as he got out of the vehicle. "Welcome to Fort Leonard Wood, your home for the next eight weeks. I'm Master Sergeant Sack; you know, like the 'Sad Sack' in the Army cartoons from WW2. Yeah, well, I ain't him. I'm in the 'fuckup-free' army! And after eight weeks that's where you'd better goddamn be." He looked to his right. Pointing to the other Sergeant, he said, "Okay, Whitney, take the roll."

The second Sergeant, a short slight man who wore three stripes, walked to the front of the group. He withdrew a long form from a manila envelope. Holding it in his tiny hands, he began to call out names. When someone answered he made a pencil mark on the form.

"Armstrong."

"Here."

"Billington."

"Yo!" Craig replied.

"Demmings."

"Here, Sergeant."

"Foggerty."

"Here," Vin said.

"Krazinski."

"Present," Fat Jerry answered.

And so it went until he finally called out, "Rosen."

"Here, Sergeant," Billy said.

"Stop, Whitney," Sergeant Sack ordered. "I didn't hear that."

Looking at Billy, he said, "Hey, pussy, I didn't fuckin' hear you. So let's fuckin' try again. Call his name again, Whitney. Right now!"

"Rosen," Whitney called out.

"Here, Sergeant," Billy replied in a voice as loud as the others who had already answered.

"You *are* a fuckin' pussy!" Sergeant Sack screamed. "Goddammit, answer like a soldier!"

The others in Billy's group began staring in Billy's direction as he replied in an even louder voice, "Here, Sergeant."

Sergeant Sack turned to Sergeant Whitney, speaking loudly enough so he could be overheard. "Take down that asshole's name. He just joined my shit list."

Craig glanced at Billy who appeared perplexed.

The roll call continued. But no one else was singled out.

When the roll call ended Sergeant Sack walked over and grabbed Billy by his shirtfront. In one swift movement he spun him sideways and then kicked his feet out from under him. Billy slammed to the ground, and Sergeant Sack planted a boot foot on his chest. Staring down at him, he began screaming, "Now listen to me, you no good cocksucker. You start to shape up or I'm gonna have you on KP cleaning the fuckin' grease trap for the next eight weeks. Matter of fact, you're on KP tomorrow. I'd put you on today but you got other things to do. And, by the way, get cleaned up. You fuckin' stink!"

"Yes, Sergeant," Billy replied, yelling as loudly as he could.

"Hey, whaddya know," Sergeant Sack said, grinning as he lifted his foot from Billy's chest, "I think I finally heard something come outta this little turd's mouth."

Sergeant Sack straightened up, brushed away some dust from his pants, and walked over to the Jeep. Reaching into his pocket for the keys, he got in and drove off.

***

"All right," Sergeant Whitney cried out, trying to be as authoritative as his weak voice would permit, "form a column of twos at the doorway." He pointed to the main entrance of the building.

"This is haircut and shot time, so go on in—in groups of four. First room on the right; then follow the arrows on the floor. When you're done, come on back out. Let's go!"

The men did as they were ordered. The first four went into the building. Ten minutes later they returned with shaved heads.

One was rubbing his upper arm.

Billy noticed that Vin who had been near the front of the line was now at its very end. Billy walked over to him.

"Hey, Vin, you okay?"

"No, man, I ain't. Shots don't faze me, but losing my hair's like...well, losin' every fuckin' thing I got. I thought I could do this, but I just can't."

"Aw c'mon, Vin," Billy said. "You know they're jes' tryin' to make us the same in basic. That's all it is. Can't have you being better than the rest of us. Whole point is to level the playing field. That's why they're chopping off our hair...so we'll all look alike." He looked at Vin, who still appeared apprehensive.

"Hey, Vin, know what? After basic you'll be able to grow your hair back. Probably not as long, but long enough so you'll be in a class by yourself."

Vin looked up at Billy. "You think so?"

"Honest. After basic we'll both grow our hair back. Anyway, I hear hair grows a lot faster after it's been cut." Billy saw he was making headway. "Vin, just forget about your hair for the next eight weeks and concentrate on getting through basic."

"I'll try," Vin said. "I'll really try. But, man..."

"You think it'll be tough on you without your hair? How'd you like to be me, on Sack's shit list?"

"Yeah, I heard all that. What in hell didja do?"

"I dunno," Billy replied. "But I do know we need each other. So let's make a pact, you and me. Let's agree to get through basic no matter what. And if things get tough for either of us, we'll just remember our agreement." Billy paused. "Deal?"

Vin thought for a moment before extending his hand which Billy grasped.

Vin smiled, amazed that someone like Billy, or anyone for that matter, needed his help. He felt surprisingly good. "Fuck the haircut," he thought. "Me, Billy, Craig, and the rest: hey, we're soldiering!"

As Billy and Vin waited at the end of the line for their haircuts and shots, Billy saw that Vin was grinning. But he knew this was only temporary and that soon Vin would sorely be missing his hair.

***

After the men had been given their GI haircuts and received their shots, they were taken into a part of the building which turned out to be a clothing supply center. In many ways it resembled a cafeteria. Each man was issued a large army duffel bag and then, as he walked past a series of long tables, soldiers standing on the other side stuffed various items into it, including boots, clothing, outerwear, towels, washcloths, linens, and toiletries. At the end of the line there were several dozen ink pads, and also stamps which could be adjusted to print combinations of numbers and letters.

"Okay, listen up," a corporal shouted. "Take a stamp. Adjust it so it prints the first letter of your last name followed by the last four numbers of your serial number. You, over there, what's your last name?" He pointed to Fat Jerry.

"'Krazinski,' Corporal."

"Okay. So that's 'K.' And what're the last four numbers of your serial number?"

"I dunno," Jerry replied.

"Well, asshole, what's your fuckin' serial number?"

"I guess I forgot."

"Okay," the corporal said, "for those of you who can't remember your serial number, Sergeant Whitney over there has a list of 'em. But, goddammit, learn your serial number 'cuz that's who you are from now on. Anyhow, in the next few days you'll be issued dog tags. You'll have to wear 'em all the time, and they'll have your serial number on them. So if you forget it, look at your fuckin' dog tags." He looked around. They were all listening.

"So if you need to find out your serial number now, get it from Sergeant Whitney. And, again, fix a stamp so it prints the first letter of your last name followed by the last four numbers of your serial number. Test it out on a piece of paper. Make goddamn sure it's right. And when it is, then stamp your duffel bag and every goddamn thing in it with that stamp at least once. Everything! It's the way we ID stuff 'round here. And if you need help, raise your hand." No one did, so he pointed to the ink pads and stamps. "Okay, let's do it," he said.

***

It was shortly after 7:00 PM and things had finally begun to settle down. Earlier, the men had been trucked from the clothing supply center to the company area where they had been assigned to First Platoon Barracks, their new home. There they had showered, shaved, and changed into fatigues. Next, they had gone to the mess hall for chow. Then they had returned to the barracks to make up their bunks and stow their gear. They were all now officially members of First Platoon, Company B, Fourth Battalion, Second Training Regiment (Basic). They had been told that the following day they would meet their Company Commander, Captain Emil Schtung, his Executive Officer, First Lieutenant Barry Fuller, and their Platoon Sergeant, SFC Manuel Gomez. They had already met the Company's First Sergeant, Master Sergeant Sherman Sack. So tomorrow would be an important learning day for all of them—for everyone, that is, except Billy who would be on KP.

Billy was seated on his carefully made up bunk. At its end his foot locker rested on the floor with all the items from his duffel bag neatly placed inside it. There was really nothing more for him to do except prepare mentally for tomorrow's ordeal.

Billy felt exhausted and slightly feverish. No sleep last night on the train. And now his arms ached from those damn shots. But most of all he was totally drained from his unexpected run-in with Sergeant Sack. What was that all about? Billy tried to think. What had he done? The best he could come up with was nothing, not a damn thing. Anyway, not much he could do about it right now. Better to get a good night's sleep, especially since he'd be facing KP in the morning.

Even though it was more than two and a half hours before lights out, Billy pulled down the covers and crawled into his bunk. He was sound asleep in less than two minutes.

Chapter 11

First Platoon Barracks, Company B, Fourth Battalion, Second Training Regiment (Basic), Fort Leonard Wood, Missouri, Saturday, 29 April 1950, 2047 Hours.

Billy felt as if he were in a small skiff on a very rough sea. The waves were high, perhaps in the one hundred-foot range, and his skiff was rocking, tossing, turning—completely out of control. He was holding on for dear life, about to get tossed overboard.

"Get the fuck outta that bunk, asshole. Who the fuck said you could sleep?" There was no response.

"Answer me, asshole! Goddammit!"

Billy, who had been in a deep sleep, awoke. He realized his bunk was swaying back and forth. Then he felt it go over on its side as he fell to the floor. Now the mattress was on top of him, and the bunk had overturned.

"If you don't fuckin' answer me, I'm sending you to the stockade, asshole. Who said you could sleep? Tell me, goddammit!"

Adrenaline coursed through Billy's veins and he balled his fists preparing to strike out at his assailant. Suddenly he remembered. He was in the Army. He was being assaulted by Sergeant Sack and the old rules no longer applied.

Then he heard it, the clatter as the contents of his footlocker were dumped on the floor.

"Get up, asshole. Now!"

He slid out from under the mattress and saw Sergeant Sack looking down at him, as if relishing the whole scene.

His fists still balled, Billy slowly got to his feet and drew himself up to attention.

"Okay, asshole. Apparently you don't understand that in this man's army we have lights out at 10:00 PM, and that you're mine until then. Maybe for the rest of the night, you miserable turd.

"So clean up this fuckin' mess—make your bed and stow your gear—and be out front in fatigues in three minutes. Think you can do that, pussy?"

"Yes, Sergeant," Billy replied as loudly as he could, glaring at Sergeant Sack.

"Well, we'll see. 'Cuz you and I are gonna work through a little field problem out there in the boonies. Just the two of us, and over 60,000 acres to play in." Sergeant Sack stomped out of the barracks.

***

Craig, Vin, and a few of the others Billy hadn't met rushed over. "Hey, man," Craig said. "Jes' forget the bunk and your gear. Get dressed. Go on out there. We'll take care of your stuff." Vin nodded.

"No way," Billy said. "You don't wanna be involved. I'll deal with this mess when I come back." He pulled on his fatigue pants and shirt and slipped into his combat boots. Leaving them unlaced, he raced out the door. While standing in front of the barracks he managed to lace up his boots before Sergeant Sack returned wearing running attire.

"Well, now, Rosen, seems you got your ass in gear for once. That's a start at least. Just wait here." Sergeant Sack turned and went back into the barracks.

Billy's heart sank. He knew his things were strewn everywhere.

"Sonofabitch!" Sergeant Sack swore as he came out again. "Anybody else have anything to do with that?" He gestured back toward the barracks.

Billy remained silent.

"Hey," Sergeant Sack said, "didja' hear me? Anybody else help you out in there? How 'bout an answer, fuckhead."

Billy continued to remain silent.

"So that's the way it is, is it? Okay, you little shit, I'll deal with your fuckin' insubordination tomorrow. Right now I got some other things in mind…like our little field problem." He waited a moment staring hard at Billy.

"All right, let's go. We'll just see if that left foot of yours holds up." He smiled. Then he stopped, horrified, realizing the enormity of his blunder. "Christ!" he thought, "if this kid figures out what I just said, Schtung and the Colonel will have my ass for breakfast."

Sergeant Sack's concerns were, in fact, justified. The moment he'd mentioned Billy's foot, Billy realized that Sack must have been rummaging through his medical records and that something strange was going on, far more than trainee harassment.

***

The field problem Sergeant Sack had in mind on this evening of Billy's second day in the Army was, in fact, a grueling twelve-mile run: six miles up a sloping dirt road to the top of a low hill and then back down a second curving road to their starting point. Sergeant Sack was an avid runner, and, except when the company was on bivouac, he did this particular run at least five times a week. It was the only thing he found that helped relieve the pressures of managing a basic training company.

"Hey, pussy, see that fucking hill?"

"Yes, Sergeant," Billy replied as loudly as he could.

"Well, that's where we're going; coming back down the other road over there." He pointed. "Think you can handle it?"

Billy intentionally hesitated. "I'll try, Sergeant."

"Let's go." With that, Sergeant Sack began to jog up the road. Billy followed.

About ten minutes later Sergeant Sack looked behind him. Billy was right there.

Before he had been so rudely awakened, Billy had gotten just enough sleep to recharge his body. He actually felt good. And the place Sergeant Sack had chosen for their run was ideal: the beautiful natural landscape of Fort Leonard Wood—low hills punctuated by clusters of trees, for the most part oaks, elms, and an occasional silver maple. Moreover, it was invigoratingly cool, in the low 40s; cool enough so that there were no annoying bugs. Billy listened to the sounds of the night: the nasal buzzing call of a woodcock competing with the hoots of a barred owl, both against a background of chirping crickets. He was beginning to unwind, to enjoy the run.

"So how we doing?" Sergeant Sack said.

"Okay, Sergeant," Billy shouted.

"Think we can ratchet up the pace a bit?" Sergeant Sack asked, as he increased his speed.

Feigning difficulty breathing, Billy replied, "Yes, Sergeant."

"Yeah, well, you fuckin' stick with me." Sergeant Sack increased the pace again.

Ten minutes later Sergeant Sack looked over his shoulder. Billy was still there. Hardly sweating. Again Sergeant Sack speeded up just as the road's grade increased.

By the time the two had run three miles Sergeant Sack was at his maximum speed, and Billy was right behind him. It was at this moment that Sergeant Sack began to wonder whether Billy was a runner. Anyone else would be falling on his face—or at least breathing heavily. Then he heard Billy say something.

"Hey, Sergeant. Any possibility we could go a little faster? These boots are kinda propelling me forward."

"'Propelling me forward,' my ass." Sergeant Sack thought. "I've been had. This kid can run. Lucky if I can keep up with him."

"Sure, asshole. We'll push it a little. I wouldn't wanna overdo it your first day of basic." And with that he increased the pace. But he was beginning to tire. And Billy kept on coming.

"Tell you what, Sergeant. I'll just go on up to the top, and then head back. I'll wait for you below." Before Sergeant Sack could answer, Billy passed him and ran up the road leaving him far behind.

***

It was about thirty-five minutes later when Sergeant Sack finally arrived back at the starting point. He found Billy lying on his back, his hands behind his head gazing up at the stars. Winded, Sergeant Sack sat down nearby. Billy knew he was waiting for an explanation.

"Hey, Sergeant," Billy finally said. "I gotta fess up. I'm a running nut like you."

"Yeah, I'd say so, *kid*," Sergeant Sack replied.

"*Kid*?" Had Billy heard Sergeant Sack correctly? "*Kid*?" Not "asshole," "turd," "fucker," "fuckhead," or "pussy"?

***

They were walking back to Billy's barracks when Sergeant Sack said, "Hey, Rosen, Captain Schtung wants you present for tomorrow's orientation. So we'll postpone KP for a while. But it's only a postponement."

"Okay, Sergeant," Billy yelled.

"For Christ's sake, Rosen, not so fuckin' loud. You'll wake up the troops. There's your barracks over there." Sergeant Sack pointed to a building whose lights were out. It was 11:30 PM. "Night, *kid*," he said.

Background Check: The "Schtungmen"

When he first heard the name "Emil Schtung" it should have registered with Billy. It didn't. But if someone had mentioned the name to Billy's Step-Uncle, Matt Irwin, he would have known it immediately.

Matt was a mechanical engineering graduate from the University of Wisconsin, Class of 1920. He was in the printing business, but that was really a sideline because he spent about ninety percent of his time on University of Wisconsin alumni business as president of its National Alumni Association. As a result, he knew almost everything there was to know about the University, both academic and athletic. He was famous for attending every football game, at home and away, and he was extremely active in recruiting Wisconsin football players. So if he had heard that someone by the name of Emil Schtung was Billy's CO, he undoubtedly would have been both surprised and delighted because a Wisconsin football player by that name whose family had fled Nazi Germany and settled in Madison had not only been a first-string All-American guard, but had captained the U's team to two Big Ten championships. Emil Schtung was one of the best known football players in the University's history; for certain, despite his bizarre muscular physique (he was 5'7" tall and almost as wide), he was the quickest guard ever to play for the Badgers. Unfortunately, just before he had begun his senior year in 1942, he had been drafted into the Army and, so far as Matt knew, he had disappeared forever. But had Matt gone looking for him, he would have discovered that Emil Schtung had had a distinguished military career while in the South Pacific, receiving a battlefield commission and more medals than his wide chest could accommodate; that he had fallen in love with army life and had opted for a military career as a regular officer; and that he now commanded a basic training company at Fort Leonard Wood, Missouri, by sheer coincidence the basic training company to which Billy had been assigned.

In fact, Emil Schtung loved being a company commander. And he particularly loved commanding a basic training company, for in this he was given the opportunity to mold the character of young men, as many as seven hundred in any given year.

In addition, Schtung saw in the organization of his company a certain order to things, an assignment of tasks and a necessity for teamwork, all of which caused it to function. This pleased him. From time to time he would stare up at the bulletin board in the Orderly Room displaying the company's "TO&E" (its Table of Organization and Equipment) and luxuriate in the thought that he was in charge of a well-oiled carefully crafted military unit made up of experienced, dedicated professionals. With the exception of his newly arrived executive officer, First Lieutenant Barry Fuller, about whom he knew almost nothing, he was indeed proud of them all: Master Sergeant Sherman Sack, his first sergeant and longtime friend; SFC Manual Gomez and the other three platoon sergeants; SFC Tom Blackman, his roly-poly upbeat supply sergeant; Mess Sergeant Ian "Cookie" Baldwin and his five PFC helpers who had a deserved reputation for preparing the best meals in the battalion; Corporal Arvin Svendsen, the dowdy armorer who cared for the company's weapons as no other could; Buck Sergeant Don Whitney, the company clerk whose pristine morning reports were unsurpassed; and likable dull-witted Buck Private Dewey La Droop, whose job it was to serve as a sort of errand boy for the company regulars and perform other odd jobs. These men Captain Schtung relied upon to make it all happen, to transform the other members of his company, the trainees, into soldiers during the eight short weeks of their basic training cycle.

To Schtung, all members of his company, both the permanent cadre and the trainees, were his "Schtungmen." They were his team. As in his football days, he was their team captain. And, like the championship Wisconsin football teams he had played on and captained, his company always won—in every way and on every type of playing field the Army served up. He demanded perfection, that his company be the best. And, thanks to its permanent cadre who, to a man, worshiped Schtung, it always was. Schtung had forever deleted the phrase "second best" from his vocabulary. He demanded the same of his Schtungmen.

Chapter 12

Drill Field, Company B, Fourth Battalion, Second Training Regiment (Basic), Fort Leonard Wood, Missouri, Sunday, 30 April 1950, 0755 Hours.

It was five minutes to eight on Sunday morning and the members of each of the company's four training platoons, with its platoon sergeant out in front, were standing at rigid attention on the drill field in front of the Orderly Room building. They had been at it for approximately twenty-five minutes waiting for Captain Emil Schtung, the CO, to show up. The remaining members of the company were lolling about in the vicinity of the Orderly Room also awaiting the Captain's arrival. They, along with the platoon sergeants, made up the company's Headquarters Platoon.

As inconspicuously as he could, Billy glanced in the direction of the Orderly Room doorway. There he saw an NCO and a short officer talking. Billy noticed that each was wearing a bright red armband on his right arm a few inches above the elbow. There were no markings on it. Then Billy saw that the other members of Headquarters Platoon congregating near the side of the OR building were also wearing the same armband. And looking straight ahead he spotted the armband on Sergeant Gomez, his platoon sergeant.

A moment later an enlisted man, his back to Billy, appeared in the doorway. He was dragging a large red loudspeaker out through it. When it had cleared the doorway, he picked it up and carried it to a spot in front of the building. He went back inside and came out with a long insulated cord and a microphone stand with a microphone inserted in its end. He plugged one end of the cord into the microphone and the other end into the speaker. Then he uncoiled a second cord from the back of the speaker. Carrying its end with him, he disappeared back into the OR. A minute or two later a shrill screech could be heard emanating from the loudspeaker. It stopped, and, as if this were a signal, Sergeant Sack, the short officer and the NCO with whom he had been speaking, and the other remaining members of Headquarters

Platoon lined up at attention in front of the OR. Next, Sergeant Sack half-turned so he could be seen by the troops behind him. He raised his index finger to his lips obviously calling for silence in what appeared to Billy to be a completely unmilitary gesture.

Ten minutes later, with everyone still standing silently at attention, the suspense began to mount. Then Billy saw it out of the corner of his eye, a cloud of dust approximately half a mile down the road, and an old dilapidated dark green VW Bug careening toward the company area. A minute later it came to a skidding halt in front of the OR building. The door opened, and a short stocky muscular man emerged. He was in uniform and was carrying the billed hat of an officer. He stood for a moment looking up at the sky and breathing deeply. He stretched, placed the hat on his head, looked in the direction of Sergeant Sack whom he casually saluted, and marched in a waddled gait to the microphone which he thumped with his thumb and forefinger. A clicking noise could be heard coming from the loudspeaker, and he nodded in satisfaction. Then he cleared his throat, coughed, and reached into his pants pocket withdrawing a crumpled handkerchief. He blew his nose and replaced the handkerchief

"Please, gentlemen, stand at ease." He waited for a moment while the men relaxed.

"I am Emil Schtung, CO of Company B. I want to welcome you to your new home for the next eight weeks. You will see. We do well here. And we will be happy, you and I, as long as you do three things: first, follow orders; second, do not make mistakes; and, third, win."

Billy thought he detected a very slight German inflection as the Captain spoke: not only in occasional mispronunciations, but also in his choice of words. He also wondered what the hell Captain Schtung was talking about. Win? Win what?

"Sergeant Sack and I do not tolerate losers. We have rifle and drill competitions with the other basic training companies of the battalion. The company winning those gets the Best in Battalion Award. And we have won that every time for the past two years. And this streak will continue unbroken. You will see."

Then, pointing a stubby finger at the company, he said menacingly in a much louder voice, "We lose and you pay dearly!

Yah!" Balling his right hand into a fist, he forcefully smacked it into the palm of his left hand.

Billy could feel every member of the company tense at Captain Schtung's words.

"And now, my Schtungmen, I tell you my rules. Only two. First, teamwork and good attitude. And second, teamwork and good attitude. When we win the Best in Battalion Award you will wear our red armband. And for the next eight weeks, gentlemen, you will get in shape, learn to be soldiers, and have a good time. You will look back on this as one of your most interesting experiences. And we will come to respect one another. And now, First Sergeant Sack, please take over."

***

"All right, listen up," Sergeant Sack said. He addressed the company without using the microphone. "You just met the CO. I've been in the Army fourteen years, and he's the best. And just so you know it, you're now members of a very elite group, Captain Schtung's company. We are all Schtungmen. And damn proud of it." He watched their reaction for a moment.

"See this armband? Well, it's red, same as the University of Wisconsin's colors. Captain Schtung was captain of two Big Ten championship football teams there. Also All-American. Before he finished his last year he was drafted into the Army as an EM and sent to the South Pacific where he received a battlefield commission and was awarded more medals than I can count. But just for openers, I'll tell you that he has three Silver Stars. That's right, three. The men in his unit—and I was one of them—we lived alongside him for months and we learned to respect him. So did his Wisconsin teammates when they elected him captain. He's a leader and he's been a great friend to me and my family. Fact is, he once saved my life. So the least I can do, the least we all can do, is our very best for him. He served his country with distinction, so he deserves a little payback. So what does this mean? Absolutely no screw-ups, no disciplinary problems, and teamwork. We pull together. And together we'll win that Best in Battalion Award for the Captain. We expect nothing of you we haven't done. I pulled KP when I joined up; so did the Captain when he was drafted; and so will you. Same applies to everything else you'll be ordered to do during basic." Sergeant Sack waited a moment before continuing.

"Okay, we begin." He turned toward the Orderly Room. "Private La Droop," he called out, "the envelopes!"

The enlisted man who had set up the microphone came running out of the OR and handed Sergeant Sack four large envelopes. Sergeant Sack beckoned to the four platoon sergeants who hurried over to him. Each took an envelope, opened it, withdrew the contents, and distributed a single sheet of paper to each member of his platoon. This took approximately ten minutes.

"All right," Sergeant Sack said. "Before you head back to your barracks, take a moment now to read the words of our company song. And listen to its music." Then he nodded in the direction of La Droop. Billy smiled as he heard the University of Wisconsin Fight Song blaring from the loudspeaker.[2]

Sergeant Sack let a minute or so pass. Then he nodded toward La Droop. The music ceased, and he began again. "And when you march on out of here I want you to be singing. And I wanna fuckin' hear it." Turning in Billy's direction, he yelled, "Hey, Rosen, know what I mean?"

"Yes, Sergeant," Billy shouted at the top of his voice.

"Okay," Sergeant Sack went on, "here's the skinny. When I dismiss you, you're to march on back to your barracks singing. When you get there you're to clean yourselves up and straighten your gear. The Captain and I will be along in about an hour to inspect. No one fails. For today, it's a learning experience. And you'll see we inspect everyone and everything in your barracks, including your platoon sergeant's room and his gear. And afterwards we'll have calisthenics. We all do 'em. Even the Captain and Lieutenant Fuller. Then comes close order drill. By the end of the day your gear'll be in shape, you'll ache, and you'll be marching to the company song. And you'd better be hoarse! Tomorrow we introduce you to your new best friend, your M1. And, as I said—and don't ever fuckin' forget this—your performance, and it better be a goddamn winning one, is Captain Schtung's payback. We do not tolerate losers 'round here." He waited for a moment. "All right, you're dismissed. Move on out.

On the double! And lemme hear it!" Again Sergeant Sack nodded in La Droop's direction, and the music resumed.

And, as if they had done it many times in the past, the men of Company B's four platoons marched off to their barracks shoulders high, in perfect cadence. And as they marched, they sang in voices loud and clear to the music of the University of Wisconsin Fight Song:

We are Schtungmen, we are Schtungmen,
we are trained to fight
to protect our nation's honor
through each day and night!

Because…
We are Schtungmen, we are Schtungmen,
we love liberty;
and we pledge
to keep our country free!

As they were singing, Captain Schtung came out of the Orderly Room and stood next to Sergeant Sack. Reaching up, he placed his hand on the latter's shoulder. "Well, old friend," he said, "our magic is beginning to take hold. Our *kinder* start out on their journey."

"Yes, sir, never fails," Sergeant Sack replied. Then he looked down at the ground and remained silent for a moment. The two had been together so long that Captain Schtung knew immediately there was something of importance on Sergeant Sack's mind.

"What is it, First Sergeant?"

"You and I gotta speak about this kid, Rosen, sir. I got a real problem with him."

"Bad apple, eh?"

"No, sir. Just the opposite. Something's wrong with those orders we got."

"Well, we have about an hour before inspection begins so we'd better talk this over right now, First Sergeant. You know Colonel Paulson's orders."

"Yes, sir."

They both turned and went into the Orderly Room, heading for Captain Schtung's office. They entered, closing the door behind them. Their meeting, for which they allocated about an hour, wound up lasting roughly ninety minutes and involved six phone calls, four between Captain Schtung and the Battalion CO, Colonel Paulson, and, unbeknown to Captain Schtung and Sergeant Sack, two between Colonel Paulson and General Haslett. At discussion's end, Captain Schtung and Sergeant Sack had their marching orders: Under no circumstances were they to let up on Billy. To quote Colonel Paulson, they were to "put the fuckin' blocks to Rosen, and that's a direct order!"

Chapter 13

Base Library, Fort Leonard Wood, Missouri, Sunday, 7 May 1950, 1530 Hours.

While the other members of First Platoon were enjoying their initial break from basic either indulging in the pleasures of the flesh dispensed by prostitutes working out of nearby trailer parks or drinking beer to excess at the EM Club, Billy, wearing his Class A uniform, was seated at a reading table in Fort Wood's library staring out into space. He was thinking, trying as best he could to piece together the events of his first week of basic training, attempting to make some sense out of them. But he wasn't getting very far. And he was beginning to wonder whether he had made a mistake. Perhaps he should have accepted Colonel Harkavy's offer to go into the Army as an officer. Too late for that now.

As he slipped deeper into thought, he began to daydream, to relive the past six days:

They had not only been exhausting and demanding, but emotionally draining as well, mostly because he now seemed to be at the top of Sack's shit list—this despite the fact that during their first evening run he thought he'd gotten a few signals to the contrary. But he'd obviously been wrong because "kid" had once again been replaced by "asshole," "fuckhead," and "pussy." True, there were some interesting moments, particularly when he had been introduced to the M1 rifle and had learned to field strip it, then detail strip it, and, finally, reassemble it blindfolded. And there were other things like the manual of arms, close order drill, and calisthenics—all typical basic training activities he'd heard about before entering the Army—which he also found somewhat interesting, perhaps even enjoyable. But what little enjoyment came his way was always more than offset by Sack's maddening antics. He was forever on his case and had a way of turning every single positive experience into a colossal negative.

Every night there'd been a field problem which Sack had dreamed up for him. Each was more onerous than the prior one—except for last night's when Sack had told him to do whatever he wanted to do, and Billy had gone for a badly needed run.

Then there were Sack's sadistic daytime projects. It hadn't taken Billy long to conclude that his first sergeant was some kind of a goddamn ghoul. Whenever other members of First Platoon were enjoying some off time, Billy would consistently be detailed to perform a miscellany of unpleasant and, in his view, often stupid tasks. These included being on KP and cleaning Mess Sergeant "Cookie" Baldwin's grease trap and washing out his rancid garbage cans; uselessly cutting, raking, and bagging weeds and brush from the hill immediately behind the company area; cleaning out the interior of several antiquated coal furnaces which were no longer in use; and, worst of all, cleaning the floor and polishing the urinal and six commodes of his barracks' latrine.

Sergeant Sack had introduced him to this last enterprise the previous afternoon by the following enlightening orientation delivered while he had been resting on his bunk: "Hey, fuckhead. Get up and follow me!" Then Sergeant Sack led him down the barracks' center aisle to a doorway at the far end of the sleeping quarters. He walked through it into a room which contained a partially enclosed shower area on the right, and washbasins with mirrors above them on the wall to the left. Straight ahead was a second doorway to the latrine which he proceeded on into with Billy right behind. It contained one large eight foot stainless steel urinal at the far wall and, out in the open, six commodes lined up in two rows of three facing each other, all apparently designed to eliminate privacy, as much a part of the basic training humbling process as those ugly shaved haircuts he and the others had received a few days before.

"Okay, asshole. See these commodes and that urinal?"

"Yes, Sergeant."

"Well don't fucking stand there. Start cleaning. I wanna see them shine, inside and out. No sign of piss or crap on any of them. And mop the goddamn floor while you're at it. Do I make myself clear?"

"Yes, Sergeant."

"Okay. I'll be back in two hours, and you'd better be finished by then."

Billy began. Periodically he had to stop because of the sickening odor. But the real problem came about twenty minutes later when one of the men had to move his bowels, and three others had to urinate. Soon Billy discovered that his assignment was in fact a series of moving targets. No sooner had he finished cleaning the urinal then it had to be cleaned again. The same held true for several of the commodes. All the while the smell continued to overpower him.

Approximately fifteen minutes before Sergeant Sack's scheduled return, Billy shut and bolted the door to the latrine and, for the last time, went over the six commodes, the urinal, and the floor, finishing just before Sergeant Sack reappeared.

"Not bad, asshole. And now that you're experienced, we got similar work for you in the other barracks." He laughed loudly, and then continued, "See you tonight at 8:30 out front for our nightly field problem. No need to show up with a full field pack; just your fatigues."

"Goddamn him," Billy thought after Sergeant Sack left. "How I'd enjoy shoving his miserable head into one of those stinkin' toilet bowls."

At 8:30 PM Billy was standing in front of his barracks as ordered, dressed only in his fatigues. Twenty minutes later Sergeant Sack showed up dressed as he had been earlier in the day. Billy noticed that he appeared to wobble slightly as he walked, and that he was carrying a package under his arm.

Standing within a foot of Billy, Sergeant Sack began to speak in a raspy voice. "Here, Rosen." He flung the package to the ground. "I'm through with you until Monday morning." Turning his head to one side, he coughed and spat. "Have a good run, or just go on back to your barracks. I don't give a shit what you do." And then, almost inaudibly, he continued in a whisper drawing even closer to Billy, "I wanna tell you one thing, goddamn you. You've fuckin' ruined my life. Just thought you'd be happy to know that." Sergeant Sack spat again before hurriedly turning around and making off into the darkness, swaying slightly as he walked away.

Billy thought he smelled alcohol on Sergeant Sack's breath when he was speaking. And, for the life of him, Billy couldn't understand what Sergeant Sack was saying. How could he possibly have ruined his life? Clearly, it was the other way around.

Billy bent down, picked up the package, and opened it. It contained a pair of gym shoes, his size, and some running shorts. Billy shook his head in confusion before going back to the barracks to change into the shoes and shorts. Then he took off on an exhilarating six-mile run which did wonders in ridding his body and soul of latrine stench, anger, and frustration. But he was still confused. What had he done to bring ruin to Sergeant Sack's life?

***

Billy's daydreaming at the library table ended abruptly when he heard a rather loud rustling noise close by. To his immediate left a rather elegant elderly woman was beginning to lose her grip on several books she was carrying.

"Here, ma'am, let me help you," Billy said, jumping up. He walked over quickly and caught the books just as they were about to fall. "May I carry them for you?"

The woman stopped for a moment and looked at Billy. Then she smiled. "Thank you, young man. Can you imagine how long ago it's been since someone first offered to carry my books? That was when I was in high school. And do you know what that led to? Many wonderful years of marriage. That's how my late husband and I met." She smiled again. "I will accept your kind offer if you don't mind a short walk. I try to walk every day."

"Ma'am," Billy said. "Could you wait here a moment? I was going to check out a book, and…well, I guess I never did get to that."

***

A few minutes later Billy returned with a large volume he had checked out along with a paper bag he'd gotten at the front desk. He placed the woman's books along with his own in the bag. "Shall we?" he asked.

"Only if I can take hold of your arm. My arthritis is bad and it will make walking easier."

"My pleasure," Billy said, extending the crook of his left arm to her into which she placed her hand. Together they walked through the library's main doorway to the outside.

"Where are we going?"

"Over there," the woman replied, nodding with her head slightly inclined to the right. "I'll just lead the way. And so we won't be strangers on our little walk, I'm Emma Durban. But please call me 'Em.' And what do they call you?"

"William Rosen, ma'am. My friends call me Billy."

"Billy." She smiled again. "All right then, Billy."

It was a beautiful spring day, and, as he gazed down the street, Billy saw large expanses of green lawn on either side. Far away in the distance he also saw green-roofed white army buildings; but here, near the library, it was strangely quiet, almost suburban. Basic seemed a long way off. For a moment Billy thought he might even be back in Glencoe. He glanced at Em. He was sure he heard her humming as they walked. Truly, she was striking. Almost as tall as he was, and slender, with perfect upright posture. Her features were classic: sparkling brown eyes bordered by crow's feet obviously the result of frequent laughing, a fine nose, and a delicate mouth and chin. Her hair, cut short, was a burnished brown streaked with gray. But what caught Billy's attention was Em's unusual complexion. Her skin was a smooth creamy youthful hue, like that of the more attractive Radcliffe and Wellesley women he'd met back at Harvard. Billy knew he'd have difficulty guessing her age—somewhere between 55 and 75—but where, he wasn't sure.

"So, Billy, tell me about that book you just checked out. What kind of reading do you do?"

"All kinds, I guess; but, unfortunately, not much over the past few days," he replied. "I've sorta been busy. But the book, well, to tell you the truth, I've been missing my family, so I got an 'old friend.'"

"Really? And who would that be?" Em asked.

"I don't know if you know him, ma'am, but the author is John Dos Passos, and the 'old friend' is the first book of his USA trilogy, *The 42nd Parallel*."

"So by 'old friend' do you mean you've read your book before?"

"Yes ma'am, several times. I like the way Dos Passos writes, and I like what he writes about. He was born in Chicago and his books contain some fascinating descriptions of early Chicago—which is where both my parents grew up. But I also like his characters, maybe most of all his World War I people: like J. Ward Moorehouse who winds up as a public relations man but, as Dos Passos says, is really a phony, a big bag of wind, a human megaphone. This book, and the others in his trilogy, give me a good feeling. And sometimes I just need to be with certain books for comfort, for companionship. It's important to me."

Em took a moment to respond. Billy's comments were unusual, and she found them moving.

"Billy," she said, "you're what my father would have called a 'damnable bibliophile.' Know what that means?"

"Yes ma'am. A lover of books."

"Right. And we bibliophiles have to stick together. I guess I also suffer from the same infirmity. Without my books, well...there'd be a major void in my life. Books have meant so much to me. One, I think, even saved my marriage."

"How so?" Billy asked.

"I'm sure you've read *Main Street*."

"If it's by Sinclair Lewis, I have."

"That's the one, and it held my marriage together. It all began in high school in Chicago where I met my future husband, Mark."

"When he offered to carry your books?" Billy asked.

"That's right," Em said, smiling. "And in those early years we saw a lot of one another and grew to be close friends. Shortly after our high school graduation Mark and his family moved to Durango, Colorado. Unfortunately, there was no college there so he went to work clerking for a local attorney. Meanwhile, I enrolled at Northwestern. In my third year Mark came back to Chicago to complete his law studies. When we got together that special attraction between us was still there, stronger than ever. So we married. That was in 1900. A year later our daughter was born and Mark was working as an attorney in a prestigious Chicago law firm. We spent the next nineteen years in Chicago and loved it. And so did our daughter. It was a stimulating place with theater, opera, concerts, lectures, the Art Institute, and all of our friends, people we had known since childhood. But then, when our daughter was a freshman in college back East, Mark's father died. The family business in Durango was a successful sporting goods store in desperate need of management and Mark felt we had no choice: we had to move to Durango so he could take over the store." She paused. "Am I boring you?"

"No, ma'am, not at all."

"Well, I can see that I am. So I'll shorten all this. You see, I had a terrible time adjusting to a tiny town like Durango, especially after living in an exciting place like Chicago. Several months after we moved there I told Mark I couldn't take it, that I needed the environment of a large city. It was 1920 and *Main Street* had just been published. It was quite the literary rage. Mark gave me a copy and told me to read it. I did. I was able to identify with Carol Kennicott who was grappling with similar problems living in Gopher Prairie. I read and reread the parts of *Main Street* in which Lewis describes how Carol overcame those problems. It truly helped me make a greater effort to get along in Durango, and soon I was beginning to enjoy my life there. Poor Mark passed away ten years ago. Yet I still live in Durango. I love it for its intimacy, its friendliness; but most of all I love my friends there. That book, Billy, was a godsend to me. So, like you, I think books can be very important."

As they walked, they came to a corner. Em gently tugged on Billy's arm. "This way," she said as she turned to the right. "Over there." Billy saw a large white three-story wood frame house. It was set back some thirty feet from the sidewalk by a neatly manicured lawn bisected by a flagstone pathway bordered by spring flowers; a gravel driveway ran alongside the lawn providing access to a garage. The house had a covered front porch in which an upholstered love seat hung by chains from the ceiling above. An attractive woman, perhaps twenty-five years younger than Em, sat in it knitting while gently rocking. An ancient Golden Retriever was curled up next to her sound asleep. The woman looked up and waved to Em.

"Mother, where have you been? I was getting a little concerned."

"Not to worry, dear," Em replied. "I've been out and about, and I've picked up this nice young man. We've had quite an afternoon's assignation."

"Mother, for God's sake!"

"Please, dear. You know I've always liked the company of men. I saw something I wanted, and I grabbed him." With this,

Em squeezed Billy's arm tightly pulling him toward her. "Isn't he precious?"

"Mother, you're embarrassing all of us, particularly your guest. He must think you're some kind of a camp follower."

"I should hope so," Em replied. "It's so dull around here. That's precisely what we need in this household, a good old-fashioned camp follower. Then I'd have some wonderful stories to tell about my customers. If my grandchild turns out to be as stodgy as you and that husband of yours, we'll never have another marriage in this family." Then Em started to laugh, and Billy could see her eyes begin to sparkle. "She's just plain fun," he thought.

Em turned to Billy. "That lady, there," she pointed, "happens to be my overly correct daughter, Beth Haslett." Turning back toward her daughter, she went on, "And this young man is William Rosen. His friends call him 'Billy,' and so do I. And I want him given something to eat and to drink; but please never forget, he's mine." She laughed again and squeezed Billy even closer to her.

Chapter 14

124 Sibert Lane, Fort Leonard Wood, Missouri, Sunday, 7 May 1950, 1715 Hours.

After Beth Haslett retreated into the house, Em gently tugged Billy up the front steps onto the porch and then through the front door. He was now standing alone in the hallway where she'd left him before proceeding on into the kitchen. Billy could hear Em speaking, and he could hear another voice, but he couldn't make out what was being said.

A few paces down the hall to his right Billy saw a polished wooden staircase. On the wall angling upward in line with the stairs were a number of framed black and white family photographs, some turning brown with age. The nearest one caught Billy's eye. It was of a tall young man dressed in what looked like a military school uniform. He had piercing eyes and a full head of black hair. Each of the sleeves of his tunic was adorned with seven large chevrons and there were several medals on his chest. One looked like a circular rifle target hanging by tiny chains from a small horizontal bar. The man's shoes were polished to a gleam, and he had a serious look on his face. In the background were several buildings built of stone, and on the ground there were patches of melting snow. "A cadet in his last year at some military academy, maybe West Point or VMI," Billy thought. Then he heard footsteps and felt movement from the stairs, as someone began to descend. Billy looked up and saw a large man in civilian clothes about his father's age approaching: the man in the photograph, but many years later.

The man saw Billy and then looked to his right, down the first floor hallway. Beth Haslett, who apparently had also heard him coming down the stairs, was walking toward them. "What have we got here?" he asked.

"Oh, a young man Mother met, dear."

"One of her strays," the man said. Then he turned to Billy. "No offense, son. But Mother Durban is continually surprising us. What're you doing 'round here?"

"I was in the Base Library, sir. Em—I mean Mrs. Durban—had a lot of books so I offered to carry them for her."

"That was decent of you, son. So I guess you'll be heading out now?"

"Yes, sir," Billy replied as he turned to leave.

"No he won't, Stan. You mind your own business. He's my guest, and he needs something to eat." Em had just come out of the kitchen and was approaching them. Then turning to Billy, she said, "This is my son-in-law, Stanton…" But before she could finish she was interrupted.

"Now wait a minute, Mother Durban. This young man is obviously in basic training and there's a mess hall over at his company area. Plenty of food there."

"No, you wait. You're not ordering me around. I just spoke to Benny and he's joining us for dinner." She smiled and came over to Billy's side reaching for his arm.

"It's okay, Em. I really have to go."

"Not an option, Billy," Em replied pulling him along. "We're going into the living room where we can relax for a few minutes before dinner." They both disappeared through a doorway down the hall on the left. Neither had noticed the large man's eyebrows rise slightly when he'd heard the name "Billy."

"Leave Mother alone, Stan," Beth said to her husband. "She's very fond of that young man. He's been nice to her and she needs someone to talk to besides us."

"Okay. But as you just heard, I think he feels a bit uncomfortable."

"Don't you worry about him. Mother will make him feel welcome." With that, she walked to the foot of the stairs. "Chris," she called, "dinner will be starting in ten minutes." She got no reply.

***

In the dining room the polished antique mahogany table was set for five. Beth sat at one end, her husband at the other, and Billy sat next to Em on the left side. The chair on the right side in front of a single place setting was conspicuously unoccupied. And although no one seemed to notice, Em was smiling contentedly. A moment before she had glanced over at Billy and, just as she'd suspected, he seemed perfectly at ease in the Haslett family's formal dining room, so entirely different from his company's mess hall. It confirmed to her something she had known all along: that her taste in men was impeccable.

The swinging door from the kitchen opened and a cart overflowing with hot rolls, butter, a large tureen of beef barley soup, a ladle, and five soup bowls on serving plates was expertly guided through the doorway by Benny, a middle-aged Filipino steward wearing a spotless white coat. He positioned the cart a few feet from Beth on her left before reaching for the ladle.

"Chris," Beth called out. "Soup's on." Again there was no response.

"Stan, would you please call your daughter," Beth asked.

"You're damn right I will," he replied. "Hey, Chris, get on down here. We're all having dinner and there isn't gonna be a special sitting for you. Now!"

Still, there was no response.

As Benny was ladling soup into bowls, Billy noticed a tall slender exceptionally attractive young woman leaning against the side of the dining room doorway. She was staring at him intently. She appeared to be squinting through horn-rimmed glasses. Her gaze was direct and unflinching—and distinctly unfriendly.

In fact, Chris Haslett was very annoyed at what she saw: another of her parents repeated attempts at matchmaking which she had warned them against. "Damn them!" she thought. "They just never give up!"

"'Bout time, miss," Beth said. "Is this the way it works at school? You can show up for meals whenever you want?" Chris Haslett didn't respond. She continued to stare at Billy. Then she pointed to him.

"What's he doing here?"

"This is Billy, a friend of Gram's," her mother replied. "She met him at the library and invited him to join us for dinner. Billy is our guest this evening."

"Lord!" Chris thought. "Gram's in on this too! Why can't they just leave me alone!"

Now Chris was incensed. "They want a show?" she thought. "I'll give them one. I'll send their 'guest' packing." Feigning a smile, she began.

"Don't you feel weird here?" she asked, making direct eye contact with Billy, trying to goad him into reacting. "All this army stuff—saluting and the rest of the silliness—and you're just a private?"

Billy was puzzled. What was she talking about?

"Chris," her mother said, "please sit down!" But Chris didn't move. She continued to stare at Billy.

"I'm waiting for an answer, Sport. Don't you feel weird here? And what are you really doing here?"

Now Billy could feel himself growing angry. At the same time he sensed that he'd better answer, because Chris Haslett wasn't going to let up until he did.

"All right," he said, "I'll answer. First, I'm here because your grandmother invited me.

"Second, I don't feel uncomfortable or, to use your term, 'weird.' Your folks offered me the hospitality of their home and I've accepted. I may be a lowly private, and your father is probably an officer, but what difference does that make? Extending a hand, offering hospitality, just treating another person with common decency—because that's what your folks have done so far as I'm concerned—well, that doesn't make me feel weird; truth be known, it makes me feel good. And maybe it makes them and your grandmother feel good. Anyway, I don't understand why, but I guess it makes you feel weird." He stopped and noticed that Chris' jaw had dropped slightly. He continued.

"And where I grew up, there's something that goes along with being a guest. Guests are special. In my home, and obviously in this home, they're welcome." Now Chris' eyebrows rose, and her face began to redden slightly.

"Finally, I take offense at your characterization of military tradition as 'silliness' because it isn't silly. I may not be making a career of the military, and, even though I'm just a private going through basic, it's the armed forces of our country that help preserve the things you and I cherish…you know, those little things we take for granted like freedom, liberty, the rule of law, and…" he looked directly at her, "the right to talk back to your parents." Chris turned an even darker shade of red.

"And I'll tell you where we'd be without the armed forces: probably under Nazi or Japanese domination. So I don't think there's anything silly about the military or its traditions. And saluting is just the way things work in the military, their way of acknowledging a chain of command." Then Billy turned to Em.

"Sorry, Em," he said, getting up from his chair. "I really didn't mean to climb on a soapbox or embarrass your family. I guess I sometimes can't hold my tongue. And I didn't mean to insult you or your daughter and her husband." He nodded toward them. "So I think I'd better go. I really had no intention of putting a damper on your Sunday dinner."

"Sit down, son," Chris' father said. "Never enjoyed a Sunday meal as much as this one."

Chris watched as Billy returned to his seat. "Dammit," she thought, "this has nothing to do with matchmaking. I think I just made a complete fool of myself!" Embarrassed, she sat down.

***

After Benny had finished serving the entrées, Beth turned to Billy. "So, Billy, tell us a little about you. Where are you from?"

"Chicago area, ma'am."

"Where, exactly?"

"Glencoe, a little village on the North Shore."

"Really," Beth said. "We know the area well, don't we, dear?"

"We get to Fort Sheridan fairly often," her husband replied.

Billy noticed they were all looking at him.

"What about college?" Beth asked.

"I finished. I'm in the Army for two years because I really don't know where I'm headed career-wise."

"That's nice. But if you're a college graduate you certainly could have gone to OCS."

"Mother, for God's sake, leave him alone." This was the first time Chris had spoken since sitting down. "I for one don't care even slightly whether he's an officer or a 'lowly private.'"

Just then Benny walked over to Chris' father. "Telephone for you, General Haslett."

"General Haslett," Billy thought to himself. "I wonder who he is?"

"Excuse me," the General said. "I have to take this call." He got up and walked out of the room.

After her father had left, Chris looked over at Billy sheepishly. "I'm so sorry…and ashamed, Sport. I mistook this whole thing for something it wasn't: I thought my family was trying to play matchmaker again. Will you please accept my apology?"

Now Billy understood. He too hated it when his relatives or their friends tried to fix him up.

"I will," Billy replied, "but on one condition."

"Which is?"

"That your grandmother and I can continue to date." Billy winked at Em.

"Could I maybe tag along?"

"No you cannot, dear," Em replied, trying as best she could to keep from laughing. "He belongs to me."

Billy smiled. He could only imagine the potential of someone like Chris Haslett, the product of a warm military family possessed of her father's intelligence, her mother's decency, and her grandmother's graciousness and humor. "Sad," he thought, "that I'll never really get to know her."

***

Dinner over, they were all getting up from the table when General Haslett returned. He walked up to Billy. "I enjoyed meeting you, son. Good luck." He shook Billy's hand. Then turning to Em he said, "Mother Durban, why don't you show Private Rosen out."

***

It had turned dark and Billy had been walking in the direction of his company area for approximately five minutes when he suddenly realized that General Haslett had referred to him as "Private Rosen." Billy was puzzled. How had he known his last name? To the best of his recollection no one had ever mentioned it in the General's presence. Billy remembered Em introducing him to Beth Haslett as "William Rosen." Maybe Beth had told her husband—probably while Billy and Em were in the living room those few minutes before dinner. But that seemed highly unlikely. Just before going into the living room with Em, Billy recalled that Beth appeared preoccupied and had rushed off into the kitchen.

And, except for that brief moment, Billy was certain he'd been with the General and his wife whenever the two had been together. And he'd never once heard his last name mentioned. Then how had General Haslett known?

Chapter 15

First Platoon Barracks, Company B, Fourth Battalion, Second Training Regiment (Basic), Fort Leonard Wood, Missouri, Sunday, 7 May 1950, 2107 Hours.

Billy was stretched out on his bunk reading the first book of Dos Passos' USA trilogy, *The 42nd Parallel,* when the commotion began. Four bunks down to his right a group of trainees, including Craig and Vin, had surrounded Fat Jerry's bunk.

"Stay away from me, you mother fuckers!" Fat Jerry screamed. "Stay away, goddammit!"

"Sorry, Jerry," Vin said. "We warned you plenty, and you haven't done shit. You stink, and we can't stand it. So c'mon, let's do it."

"I ain't doing nothing. Leave me alone!" Jerry screamed again, this time in a higher pitch.

Billy put his book down, got up, and walked over to see what was going on. He noticed that several of the men were holding large bars of tan soap, and each was holding a scrub brush.

"What's up?" he asked Craig.

"Hasn't taken a shower in over a week. He reeks, and we can't stand him. So we're gonna have a little GI party, get him cleaned up."

"Leave me alone, you assholes. None of your goddamn business!" Jerry cried. Then seeing Billy, he cried even louder, "Help me, Billy! Please!"

"Where'd you get the bars of soap and the brushes?" Billy asked Craig.

"Platoon sergeant gave 'em to us. He wants Jerry cleaned up as bad as we do. Man, he smells like something died. Take a whiff."

"No thanks," Billy replied. "But lemme see what I can do. Gimme a few minutes."

"No way. He's ours now."

"I said lemme see what I can do!"

Craig and the others, surprised by Billy's sudden forcefulness, stepped back and let him through.

***

"Listen, Jerry," Billy said. "You want me to help, right?"

Jerry nodded.

"Then grab a towel, a bar of soap, and follow me."

Jerry looked at the men around his bunk suspiciously. Then he got up, pushed his way through them, bent down and got a towel and soap out of his footlocker, and followed Billy down the aisle to the shower room. When they entered, he turned to Billy.

"Okay, man, you guard the door while I take a shower. I'll be finished in a few minutes."

"No you won't, Jerry. Twenty minutes minimum." Billy waited in front of the doorway. He heard the water running.

Approximately twenty minutes later Jerry emerged with the towel wrapped around his waist. He was carrying his boots and clothing.

"Okay," Billy said. "Put on clean underwear tonight, and for God's sake have those clothes washed. And you'll have to take a shower at least every other day." He smiled. "I know. I'll guard the door like tonight."

Jerry stared at Billy. "Hey, man, how'd you know?"

"Know what?" Billy said.

"That I needed to be alone in there."

"I just had a hunch. But why do you, Jerry?"

"Never mind, man. But thanks," Jerry replied.

"Jerry," Billy said, "I wanna know so I can help you."

Jerry shook his head. Then he turned and walked back to his bunk. As he did, Craig, Vin, and the others looked at him. They could see he had showered. Craig walked over and whispered to Billy. "What the hell did you do? We've been trying to get him in the shower for days."

"Nothing, really," Billy responded quietly. "I just let him do it in private. I figure he's embarrassed about his weight or something."

Craig nodded. "Probably should'a thought of that myself," he said.

***

In the mess hall the following morning Billy had just sat down when Jerry came over to him.

"Gotta talk to you, man. Let's go now while the others are eating. Please!" He beckoned to Billy to follow him and then turned and walked out the door.

Billy immediately got up, leaving his tray full of food on the table. He went out and found Jerry behind the mess hall sitting on the ground. Jerry looked up at him. "Will you promise to keep what I tell you between us?"

"Sure," Billy replied.

"Okay," Jerry said. Then he looked around making sure they would not be overheard. "Man," he said, "I got this problem. I'm kinda freakish."

"'Freakish'? Meaning what?"

Jerry looked around again. Billy could see this was difficult for him.

"Well, it's like this." He hesitated. Then he looked around for a third time. "See, I only got one ball." He stopped. It was as if he couldn't say any more.

"So?" Billy said, trying not to show any reaction to what Jerry had said, but beginning to understand.

"Well, in my freshman year of high school I was in the shower and these guys saw the way I was. Told everyone, including all the girls. I felt like shit, and never went back to PE again. Couldn't take any girls out either 'cuz they all knew I was a freak. So I just ate and got fat."

"Okay, Jerry, I get it. Now listen, I wanna discuss this with the first sergeant. Between the two of us I think we can help you. Will you give me permission to talk to him?"

Jerry hesitated. "Why should I? What can he do besides just tell everybody?"

"I'm not sure what he can do. Certainly more than I can do. And I don't think he'll be telling anyone," Billy said.

"You really think he'll keep it quiet?" Jerry asked.

"I'll ask him to agree to it before I tell him."

"Okay, go ahead," Jerry said.

***

One hour later Billy was in the Orderly Room. Sergeant Whitney was at his desk filling out forms, and Private La Droop was seated at a second desk with his feet up on top of it, his chair tilted back. He was reading a comic book.

"Hey, La Droop, I gotta speak to the first sergeant."

"He's got no time for assholes, so buzz off," La Droop replied, not bothering to look up. Sergeant Whitney continued on with his paperwork ignoring Billy and La Droop.

"Listen, La Droop, I told you I have to speak to him now!"

"Okay, but it's your funeral, not mine, asshole." With that, La Droop reluctantly got up, turned around, and walked over to a closed door on which the words "First Sergeant" were painted in black letters. He knocked.

"Who is it?" Sergeant Sack called out from inside where he was seated at his desk working through a pile of papers of his own.

"Me, First Sergeant. Rosen insists on seeing you."

"No shit. Well tell the little turd I don't wanna hear any of his belly aching; he and I have a field problem for tonight, and I don't wanna see his ugly face until then."

La Droop turned to Billy. "You heard that, didn't you?"

Billy nodded. Then he walked over to the door and, raising his voice, said, "First Sergeant, it's not about me. Please, it's important."

The door opened and Sergeant Sack reached out and grabbed Billy by the front of his fatigue shirt, yanking him into the office. Then he slammed the door.

"What the fuck you doing here, Rosen?" he said releasing Billy. "And how come you're not with your platoon?"

"Sergeant Gomez gave me permission, First Sergeant."

"And you say this doesn't concern you?"

"It's about someone else. But I can't tell you unless I have your word you won't discuss this with anyone without my okay. The person involved asked me to have you promise that."

"You're fuckin' crazy, Rosen, walkin' in on me like this. But okay, you got my word. So go ahead."

"You know Private Jerry Krazinski?"

"The fat kid in your platoon?"

"Yes."

"I know who he is. So what?"

"Well, First Sergeant, I'm not a doctor, but I think he needs to see one. He has a condition where one of his testicles is probably up in his abdomen, and I think that could cause him real problems."

"Yeah? How do you know that?"

"He told me. But he swore me to secrecy. Except he said I could tell you. He hasn't been taking any showers 'cuz he's afraid someone in the barracks will find out and then they'll all start riding him about it. He said that's what happened to him in high school."

"Well, this isn't high school, Rosen."

"I know, First Sergeant. That's why I wanted to bring this to your attention."

Sergeant Sack was silent for a moment. Rosen had a point. "Krazinski's probably self-conscious as all hell about that; guess I would be too," he thought.

He turned to Billy. "You wait outside while I call my wife. She's an RN. I do have permission to discuss this with her, don't I?"

"Sure," Billy said, as he walked out of the office and sat down in a chair in the Orderly Room outer area. He looked over at La Droop who was still engrossed in his comic book, while Sergeant Whitney pressed on with his work.

***

"Hi. It's me," Sergeant Sack said speaking into the phone in the deferential tone he reserved for his wife of nine years.

"Sherman," his wife said. "Haven't I asked you to respect my mornings? This is my private time."

"I know, Velma, but I got a problem with your name on it. One of my men has a medical condition, and I thought maybe you could help me figure out what to do."

"You mean you're calling to help someone, Sherman? How unlike you. But go ahead…tell me."

"Well, I got this kid. Been hidin' the fact that he's only got one testicle. He won't shower 'cuz he's afraid the others in his platoon will find out and make fun of him. Ever heard of his condition, Vel?"

"'Course I have, Sherman, and it's no big thing. Called an 'undescended testicle.' Not all that uncommon."

"So is it dangerous?" Sergeant Sack asked.

"Probably not. It's usually surgically repaired when the child's an infant so it won't cause emotional problems like it has with your recruit. Wonder why they let him in the Army in the first place?"

Ignoring her question, Sergeant Sack continued. "So what should I do, Vel?"

Velma hesitated before answering. "Send your boy to the hospital tomorrow. I'll see if I can get Dr. Stone to take a look at him. He's about the best surgeon over there."

"Okay. Assuming he's operated on, do you think I'll have to pull him out of his basic training cycle?"

"My guess is he'll do just fine and probably won't have to spend more than one or two nights in the hospital. He might not be able to march for a few days after surgery. But that'd be about it." She thought for a moment.

"Poor boy. Probably embarrassed as all get-out." For several seconds she remained silent. "Sherman, was this your idea?"

"Yes," he lied.

"Tell you what. Why don't we have a special little dinner tonight? You know, just the two of us and some candlelight. You come on home early. Say about five-thirty. You being so nice and all has kinda warmed me up. And come to think of it, you're due for a complete workup anyway."

He heard her laughing as she hung up.

Sergeant Sack wiped the grin off his face, opened the door to his office, and motioned to Billy to come in.

"Listen, fuckhead. Forget about our field problem for tonight. And tell that fat friend of yours to get his ass over here on the double."

"Thanks, First Sergeant," Billy said.

As Billy was departing, Sergeant Sack said in what he hoped was his gruffest voice, "Yeah, well…just keep out of my sight, asshole."

Left alone, Sergeant Sack couldn't stop thinking about Billy: "Why in God's name would that kid take on someone else's problems—particularly when he had so many of his own?"

Chapter 16

First Platoon Barracks, Company B, Fourth Battalion, Second Training Regiment (Basic), Fort Leonard Wood, Missouri, Tuesday, 9 May 1950, 0330 Hours.

Understandably, Vin Foggerty would never forget his first day on KP.

It had all begun at the ungodly hour of 3:30 AM when he felt himself being shaken out of a deep sleep. Sergeant Whitney, the CQ, was making his rounds looking for bunks with towels tied around their ends which signified that their occupants had pulled KP. "You're due in the mess hall in thirty minutes," Whitney had whispered to Vin, trying not to wake the others. Reluctantly, Vin pulled himself out from under the covers, stepped onto the barracks' cold wood plank floor, and headed for the latrine.

***

On arriving in the mess hall's dining area twenty minutes later, Vin saw that one of Cookie Baldwin's five PFC helpers, Ben Cross, was holding a clipboard with a sign-up sheet clipped to it. When he approached, Cross handed the clipboard to him and he signed in.

"Sit over there, Foggerty," Cross said, reading Vin's last name from the sign-up sheet. "Ever been on KP?" Vin shook his head. He joined four others at one of the dining area tables. "Where's Rosen?" Cross asked, looking at his watch. It was 3:58 AM. Just then the front door was pulled open and Billy entered. Cross nodded to him before proceeding.

"I'm gonna assume none of you've been on KP before 'cept Rosen, so listen up. Cookie don't like no military bullshit. He just wants the job done. And that's where you come in. You'll be helping him do it."

"You two," he pointed to two of the men. "You're the inside men. You set the tables for the NCOs and officers, take their orders, serve them, and clear their dishes. After each meal you clean up the entire dining area. That means wiping down all the tables and chairs, sweeping the floor, and mopping up. And after that you'll work the vegetables: cut beans, prepare potatoes for the peeling machines, shuck corn, whatever else we got goin'. Okay?"

The two men nodded. From what they had heard, they knew they had been selected for the easiest job.

"Good. In just a few minutes I'll show you how we set the tables."

Then he pointed to two others. "You two wash and dry…the dishes and trays, not the pots and pans. I'll demonstrate later."

Finally, he came to Vin. "You're outside man. Meaning you empty the garbage cans into the dumpster; then you clean 'em; and you keep the loading dock hosed down. You and Rosen will be going to the food warehouse with me later on this afternoon to pick up a bunch of stuff. Cookie's gotta give us a list." Then he turned to Billy who was standing next to the table.

"And Rosen, somethin' a little different for today: pots and pans. First Sergeant sends greetings; he had us save 'em for you from last night. Plus you still got the grease trap. It stinks—needs cleaning from yesterday and the day before. And after that do another cleanup on it just before you leave tonight."

Billy got up, a tired expression on his face, and headed into the kitchen.

"The rest of you wait, and, like I said, I'll show you the ropes," Cross continued. "Cookie and the other helpers should be along in about an hour."

Vin looked at his watch. 4:10 AM. He cringed at the thought of at least sixteen, maybe seventeen, more hours of this shit. And he hadn't even begun.

***

By the time lunch was over and the men had completed their chores, Cross approached Vin and Billy who were taking a break outside on the loading dock. Vin was smoking. "I got a truck out front. Let's go. We're heading to the warehouse. Before we leave I want you," he pointed to Billy, "to get me that list from Cookie. I'll also need a requisition. Meet us at the truck."

***

Billy had never been in Cookie's office before, although he knew where it was. He approached the white door marked "Mess Sergeant" and knocked. He heard someone inside call out, "Come."

When he stepped into the office he saw that Mess Sergeant Ian "Cookie" Baldwin was seated at his desk reading a girlie magazine, and that plastered all over the walls were pictures of nude men and women engaged in various sexual acts. One large poster on the wall immediately behind Cookie's head showed a photo of two women and a man. The man had his head between one of the women's legs, his tongue licking her vagina, while, at the same time, the other woman was performing oral sex on him. The whole scene made Billy uncomfortable, and he began to feel his throat constrict. He knew that on a certain level the photo was beginning to titillate him.

"Sergeant Baldwin," he said. "Cross sent me to pick up a list and requisition."

Without looking up from the magazine, Cookie pointed to an envelope on his desk. Billy grasped it, and turned to leave…but not before staring once again at the poster of the *ménage a trois*.

***

In the warehouse Cross pointed to some large flatbed pushcarts. "Each of you get one of these and follow me." He walked over to an area containing canned goods. None of the cans was less than a gallon in size.

"Let's see," Cross said, as he read from the list. "Get me four cans each of peaches, pears, corn syrup, tomato paste, chipped beef, shortening, and chocolate syrup. Put 'em on your cart, Rosen."

Billy and Vin did as they were told.

"Okay. Now follow me over here." Cross led them to an area where items bagged in burlap sacks were resting on shelves. "Four bags of rice, sugar, and flour."

To the right of the bagged items, were large boxes of fresh vegetables. "Six boxes of potatoes and three boxes each of spinach, string beans, and corn," Cross called out.

Next, Cross went to an area containing huge refrigerators. "Get me four boxes of eggs, twenty gallons of milk, and two cases of butter."

Finally, Cross approached an area marked "Freezer." He pulled open a heavy door. He motioned to Vin, whose cart was still empty. "Bring your cart in. You come in too, Rosen."

As they entered, Billy noticed an area to his left where circular gallon containers of vanilla ice cream were stacked three high. He also saw large sides of beef hanging by hooks attached to an overhead track. Motioning to the ice cream, Cross said "A dozen of those." He waited while Billy and Vin put the ice cream containers on the cart. Then Cross pointed to the nearest side of beef and said, "Grab that one and lay it sideways on the cart." Billy and Vin hoisted the slab of meat up and off the hook and laid it on the cart next to the ice cream. "That'll do it for this trip," Cross said. "Let's get everything into the truck."

***

Back at the mess hall Billy and Vin unloaded the truck. Cross ordered that everything which didn't go in the refrigeration room or the freezer be piled up outside on the loading dock. Vin and Billy didn't have time to discuss how strange they thought this was because almost immediately Billy was back dealing with the dirty pots and pans that had accumulated in his absence.

***

It had been a long day, much longer than Vin had anticipated, and he was beat. It was now 8:25 PM and by his count he had been up almost seventeen hours and had been working steadily with only three thirty-minute breaks. As he looked up from where he was standing on the loading dock, he saw Billy and Cross approach.

"I'm goin' home," Cross said. "Before you two leave I want this place shipshape. And I want you out of here by nine o'clock. Cookie will be looking things over in the morning, so no fuck-ups. Otherwise your ass is grass!" Cross stared directly at Billy. Then he turned and disappeared into the kitchen.

"You on KP again tomorrow?" Vin asked incredulously.

"Not tomorrow; but the next two days."

"That Sack is one first-class fucker," Vin said. "I still can't figure out why he has it in for you."

"Forget about it," Billy replied. "I better get back in there and finish up."

***

Some time later Vin looked at his watch. It was after nine. He was about to go inside and grab Billy when he heard what he thought was the sound of a car or truck in the distance. The sound grew louder and less than a minute later he saw it: a large eighteen-wheeler approaching. It glided past the mess hall, stopped, and then slowly began backing up to the loading dock, coming to a halt when it was less than an inch away. The engine shut down and the door to the driver's side of the truck's cab was opened; then it was slammed shut. He saw a large muscular man in orange coveralls wearing thick glasses climb up onto the loading dock and open the back of the truck.

"Hey kid," the man said, "I'm here for my pickup. Gimme a hand. There's a fast buck in it for you."

"What?" Vin replied.

"I'm from Brothers of the Hungry. Food on the dock's ours; plus some stuff inside."

"'Brothers of the Hungry'…what's that?"

"A charity. We pick up food that's about to go stale; take it to food banks where poor people can get it."

"I think there's a mistake, sir. This food's fresh. Me and a couple of other guys brought it in from the warehouse this afternoon. You sure you got the right mess hall?"

"'Course I'm sure. I come here every Tuesday night. Now let's get moving. I got other stops tonight." In fact, the man's next stop was in an hour, at the Fort Wood Commissary where he was going to resell the food for $500.00 cash—*cash which his employer would never know anything about and which he desperately needed by tomorrow afternoon at the latest to pay off an East St. Louis loan shark who had been hounding him for the money.*

"You have some kind of paperwork on this?" Vin asked. "Like a requisition or something."

"Listen, soldier, I told you. I come here every single week. Now if you're not gonna help, move out of the way so's I can load up the truck."

"I'm sorry, sir," Vin said. "This is government property. I need something in writing."

"Well I've never needed anything before. I just get a call from Sergeant Baldwin to pick the stuff up. I work for Furax, the Brothers' administrator. Name's Harley Lutz. Here's my card if that'll help. I'm District Manager." The man pulled out one of his cards and handed it to Vin.

Vin studied the card before slipping it in his pocket.

"Why don't you go ask Baldwin?" Harley continued.

"He's gone home, sir. You'd better come by in the morning because I'm not letting this stuff off the dock without proper army paperwork. That's final, sir." Vin wasn't sure he was doing the right thing, but he smelled a rip-off.

"That so?" the man said as he reached into a back pocket of his pants, withdrew a heavy object and, in a surprisingly swift move, hit Vin on the side of his head knocking him face down on the dock. With his foot the man shoved him aside and began loading his truck. Vin groaned loudly. As he did, Billy came out onto the dock. He was holding a bucket of grease trap slop.

"Vin!" he cried. But Vin was only semi-conscious and unable to reply. Billy turned to the man.

"What the hell's going on?"

"Kid's been interfering with my pickup. That's our food on the dock. Plus we got some in the freezer and the refrigerator. Little prick wouldn't let me at it without some kind of paperwork."

"Little prick?" Billy said, in surprise. "Little prick! He's right. This is army stuff and no one's touching it without proper authorization. So leave."

"Whoa!" the man said. "Look, kid, take it easy. Sorry I hit your buddy. I don't want no trouble. I got a call from Sergeant Baldwin. He told me to come by for the stuff."

By this time Vin was beginning to recover from the unexpected blow. He turned to Billy. "He's full of shit," Vin cried out. "Says he's supposed to be picking up food that's about to spoil, not fresh stuff." Now Vin was beginning to pull himself to his feet. He was heading for the man.

"Stand back, Vin," Billy yelled. "Lemme handle this." He looked directly at the man.

"Get outta here or I'm calling the MPs! You understand?"

"Goddammit," Harley thought. "Fuckin' kids!" His hand moved to his back pocket.

"Watch out, Billy!" Vin cried. But Billy was ready. Holding the handle of the bucket in his right hand, he grabbed its bottom with his left hand and pitched its contents into Harley's face. As Harley staggered back, Billy placed his left leg behind Harley and shoved him with all his might. Harley's heavy body came crashing down onto the dock.

"Can't see!" Harley cried out as he reached for his glasses now covered with thick grease trap slop. It was at this moment that Billy's boot came down on Harley's neck just beneath his chin choking him and pinning him to the dock.

"Here," Vin said, handing Billy the business card. "Says he's involved with some charity. Should I call the MPs?"

Billy glanced at the card. "Furax Distributors." Instantly he remembered his father asking him about "furax" several years before. Was there some connection? "Shit!" he thought as he pocketed the card.

"Let's not make too big a thing outta this, Vin," he said. Reaching down, he removed Harley's glasses and handed them to Vin. "Go inside and wash these. Then bring 'em back."

"Now listen, mister," Billy said with a forcefulness which Harley found disquieting. "I want you out of here! And don't come sneaking on back tonight 'cuz we'll be guarding this place. Come back tomorrow—or later on—and sort all this out with Baldwin. You understand?"

Although he could hardly see, Harley looked up at Billy. There was something about this kid—he wasn't exactly sure what—which told him he'd damn well better do as he was told. The money guy in East St. Louis would just have to wait a day or two longer. "Okay," he said. "Just gimme back my glasses."

***

After Harley had left, Vin turned to Billy. "I heard what you said. We really gonna have to stick around here all night?"

"'Course not," Billy replied. "I just said that so our four-eyed friend would stay away until Cookie showed up in the morning. I don't want any stuff going out of here on our watch."

As he lit another cigarette, Vin smiled. Billy was right. If that food were heisted during the night they both might be hauled up on the carpet. And for damn sure neither of them wanted that.

***

The two had just left the mess hall and were on their way back to the barracks when Billy stopped abruptly. "You go on ahead, Vin," he said. "I've gotta make a call." With that, he turned and started walking in the direction of the EM Club.

***

With a handful of change which he'd gotten from the EM Club's bartender, Billy entered a nearby phone booth and took Harley Lutz' business card out of his pocket. There were two phone numbers on it, one in St. Louis and a second in New York City. He dialed the operator and asked her to place a call to the St. Louis phone number. When no one answered and the operator came back on the line Billy asked her to connect him to the New York City phone number. Shortly after that a female voice answered. "Furax. How may I assist you?"

"I'd like to speak to Mr. Louis Rosen, ma'am," Billy said, his heart racing.

"Mr. Rosen is not at this number. However, if you'll leave your name and phone number I may be able to have someone contact you."

The response confused Billy. "I don't understand. Was Mr. Rosen ever at this number, and can I leave a message for him?"

As if reading from a script, the operator repeated herself. "Mr. Rosen is not at this number. However, if you'll leave your name and phone number I may be able to have someone contact you."

Still confused, Billy hung up.

Chapter 17

11276 Hodiamont Avenue, St. Louis, Missouri, Wednesday, 10 May 1950, 0220 Hours.

Harley Lutz had never been more frightened in his life. To put it mildly, he was scared shitless. He knew what guys like his East St. Louis money lender did when they weren't paid on time, and he figured that his chances of getting Baldwin to meet him back at the mess hall this morning were about as good as those of a snowball in hell—although he'd give it a shot. But since he'd more or less concluded that Baldwin would be crapping out on him, he'd decided to return to his home in St. Louis where he could fall back on Plan B, his contingency plan.

Harley stared at the empty master bedroom. Marie and the kids were gone. She had taken them to visit her mother in Des Moines. Well, in a way that might turn out to be a blessing in disguise.

Harley reached for the phone. He lifted the receiver and the operator came on the line. "Number please."

"Long distance. Rolla, Missouri. RO4-2187."

"One moment, sir."

Harley listened as the phone rang. On the fifth ring he heard a rustling noise and then someone say "Yeah."

"Sergeant Baldwin, this is Colonel Lutz of the Brothers. We got a problem."

Harley heard coughing. "Yeah, Colonel. What's up?"

"I couldn't make my pickup tonight. A couple of your men interfered with it. Said they'd be around 'til morning guarding the mess hall."

"Fuck!" Harley heard Baldwin say.

"Look. I *have to* make that pickup before noon. Meet me at the mess hall in about four hours." Harley emphasized the words "have to."

"Oh yeah? Over my fuckin' dead body," Baldwin replied. "Forget it. I'll get back to you in about a week. I may stop this whole thing. But I'm not laying thirteen years of armying on the line for a fuckin' pickup in broad daylight."

"Look, Baldwin, you've made a lot of money with me. It's absolutely critical that I make that pickup. Can you meet me at the mess hall, say around six?"

"Fuck you, Colonel! I said forget it! I gotta get to the bottom of this. And you ain't doin' nothing 'til I do. Nothing!" Harley could hear him cough again.

"And I wanna know who those soldiers were."

"The first guy was named 'Vin.' He called the other one 'Billy.' That's all I know."

"Yeah, well you'll hear from me in about a week. Meantime, stay the fuck away! Plus I want the dough you owe me from the last couple'a pickups." Harley heard him slam down the phone.

As he replaced the receiver in its cradle he noticed that his shirt was sopping wet. Obviously from perspiration. But he hadn't been surprised by Baldwin's refusal. Still, it depressed him. He turned and walked to the laundry room at the back of the house. A five gallon container rested on the floor. He grabbed it by the handle and made his way to the front door via a long hallway, pouring gasoline as he went. Just before exiting he struck a match and tossed it as far back as he could into the hallway. He heard a "whooshing" sound accompanied by a burst of flames.

A few minutes later he drove off in the truck. In the rear view mirror he saw something which could only be described as a raging inferno. He wondered how much insurance money his handiwork would generate.

***

Harley backed the truck up into its space in the lot next to the Furax building. Then he went inside and called a cab. He had decided to take the first train to Cairo, Illinois, where his spinster sister lived. He hadn't seen her in a month of Sundays. "Cairo," he mused. "Might not be a half-bad place to raise a family."

Background Check: "The Boys"

Buck Sergeants Johnny Ludrakis and Frank Kaye could best be described as "wheeler-dealers." In army parlance, they were "expediters." Whatever the job, no matter how difficult, they always figured out a way to get it done.

"The Boys," as they were called by most, had almost always worked together. In fact, when it came to togetherness, they pushed the envelope: they had been together as best friends in high school in Newark; they had joined the Army together the day after graduation; they had gone through basic together; and they had worked side by side (together) throughout their army careers, now in the fifth year. Together they even shared an apartment in Rolla. When they spoke, they sounded alike. They laughed at the same things, and their values were virtually identical. They were something like conjoined twins, with one surprising exception: religion.

Frank was a Conservative Jew (Conservative rather than Orthodox because he refused to keep kosher, wear Orthodox regalia in synagogue other than the traditional yarmulke or skull cap, or attend services where men and women sat separately and where he felt women were relegated to a role of lesser importance). Johnny, on the other hand, was a staunch Greek Orthodox. Having been an altar boy in his early years with thoughts of becoming a priest, he loved the pageantry of the church service. The feelings it gave him were dazzling.

So on weekends The Boys separated, with Frank in temple beginning Friday evening and continuing on into Saturday, and with Johnny in church early Sunday morning.

Because there was only a smattering of Jews at Fort Wood and in Rolla, Frank would get in his shiny dark blue '40 Packard coupe and drive into St. Louis every Friday. With the permission of the Assignments Section CO, Captain Pete Reston, he normally left around 2:00 PM so that he'd arrive at his destination, a large home owned by his Aunt Bell and Uncle Gene at 766 Center Polo Drive in Clayton, about 5:00 PM, give or take half an hour depending on traffic. This would give him ample time to shower, shave, change clothes, and make it to the synagogue in University City by 6:30 PM where he normally sat in the third row next to

Missy Landsbauer, a voluptuous divorcee in her mid-thirties who was also a regular at services. The routine was always the same. He would take his seat, close his eyes and inhale deeply for a long moment, trying to fill his lungs with as much of Missy's distinct musk as he possibly could. He loved her sensuous odor, a titillating combination of perspiration and perfume. Then he would tap her lightly on her upper arm and nod. She would nod in return. After this ritual was completed, he would remove a prayer book from the seatback in front of him and immerse himself in the services knowing that when they were over he would be having dinner with Missy followed by the glorious pleasures of her bed and warm body which she so generously and energetically shared with him. The next day, Saturday, he would be back in temple.

Frank's absence from the Rolla apartment he shared with Johnny was all part of The Boys' planned weekend separation. While Frank was in St. Louis, Johnny was able to use it to indulge in one of his great passions, womanizing.

Where and how Johnny found his women was a puzzle to those who knew him; but find them he did: from among the DACs working at Fort Wood; from its scant WAC population; from offices and small businesses in Rolla and neighboring communities; from his church; from the many school teachers in and around Rolla and Fort Wood; from movie theaters; from grocery store checkout lines; from bars and clubs; and from a variety of other places and sources. And occasionally he would even take up with a lonely housewife. In this endeavor his resourcefulness seemed boundless, and he was almost always successful in finding companionship each weekend.

Johnny's *modus operandi* with his women was somewhat complex, for it was not only his aim to sleep with each for a night (though this was of prime importance), but also to become a new friend of sorts, subject to a strict caveat made abundantly clear at the onset that any kind of a repeat evening, or extended, permanent, or romantic relationship was absolutely out of the question. Most of the women he met bought off on his terms, allowing almost always for a pleasurable evening of fine dining followed by a night of unrestrained sex. But once the sun began to rise on Sunday morning the date came to an end. The woman would be shown out of The Boys' apartment, handed one of

Johnny's cards, and told to call if he could ever be of help. Then Johnny would head for church. The fact that it was over did not seem to bother the women, and later on Johnny would occasionally receive calls from a few of them for help or assistance which he graciously rendered if the request was within reason. His goal was never to cause hurt or pain, but, instead, to cultivate goodwill…and also to add to his ever-growing list of contacts. And sometimes, but not often, he would call upon a few of his women to help him…which they almost always did. The entire arrangement worked well for him and seemed to generate a warm feeling of contentment propelling him into his upcoming week with a certain enthusiastic gusto.

The Boys would always reunite at 3:00 PM Sunday afternoon at Corwyn's Restaurant in Rolla for their traditional Sunday supper: a house salad with Roquefort dressing; a T-bone steak, medium rare; a baked potato with "everything"; and, for dessert, a slice of chocolate fudge cake à la mode. At this meal The Boys never discussed their weekend adventures. Instead, they focused on their clients' business for the week ahead, things like making last-minute travel or hotel arrangements; getting theater or opera tickets on short notice; taking care of a parking or speeding ticket; lowering a real estate tax bill, local politics permitting; or, for people headed overseas, swapping dollars for foreign currencies at optimal exchange rates. They operated in all parts of the US and abroad. And their forte was performing seemingly impossible tasks. Anything was fair game for The Boys. Anything! Though it wasn't true, some said The Boys had every judge in the country in their pocket. The Boys weren't alone in their endeavors. There were others like them at various military installations throughout the country and overseas who did more or less the same things. They, along with The Boys, formed a loose network of "wheeler-dealers" who occasionally worked together.

In addition to performing the impossible, another specialty of The Boys was their uncanny ability to gather information which they discreetly but effectively put to good use when the occasion arose. As an example, there was very little they didn't know of the goings on at Fort Wood.

Whatever services The Boys provided were far from free. Their fees were stiff, and they expected prompt payment. Bills would be issued from their firm, "The Boys, Inc.," headquartered at their apartment in Rolla and administered by their hard-nosed secretary, Rose Applebaum. All of this was in addition to performance of their army duties which took them almost no time at all and which consisted of finding appropriate assignments for basic training graduates.

Above and beyond their varied and widespread business activities and their military duties, The Boys cherished their friendships. Their select group of friends came from all walks: officers, enlisted, and civilian. They considered friendship a sacred lifetime commitment. If you were fortunate enough to be one of their friends, you knew you could always count on them for help, given freely and unconditionally.

It was clear that The Boys not only loved their weekends, but that they also relished their work and their relationships. As anyone who knew them could easily surmise, life for them was good, about as good as it could ever get.

Chapter 18

Outer Office, Assignments Section (EM),
Second Training Regiment (Basic),
Room 482, Headquarters Building,
270 Constitution Avenue, Fort Leonard Wood, Missouri,
Thursday, 11 May 1950, 0925 Hours.

Chris Haslett's relationship with The Boys went back a long way. In fact, it spanned roughly the five years they'd been in the service.

It all began in the summer of 1945 when The Boys were first assigned out after basic to the USAREUR Assignment Team at Fort Dix, New Jersey. At the time the Dix Post Commander just happened to be then Bird Colonel Stanton M. Haslett, II who had recently taken up his new duties after returning from Nazi Germany following its unconditional surrender. His office was two floors above the Assignment Team's offices.

Shortly after Colonel Haslett moved in, his bored sixteen-year-old daughter, Chris, had wandered into the Team's offices and wheedled out of its CO, Captain Tim Kline, the job of temporary office boy for the remaining six weeks of her summer vacation. It hadn't been particularly easy for Captain Kline to hire her given two factors: first, his non-military employees were supposed to be civil service-qualified, which Chris certainly was not; and second, he had absolutely no money to pay Chris. But he conveniently forgot about the civil service requirement, and, somehow, he dredged up enough money to pay her a salary plus a generous bonus when she departed.

It was while working at the Team's offices that Chris and The Boys got to know one other. The attraction was instantaneous. The Boys found this slender wisp of a high schooler bright, fun, and exceptionally resourceful; and, for her part, Chris found The Boys intriguing. Their ability to accomplish the impossible was something she wanted to master, and she discovered that The Boys were outstanding teachers of their particular art form.

When Chris' six-week stint with the Team ended, The Boys discovered how sorely they missed her, not only for all the help she provided, but for the wonderfully upbeat way their office functioned while she was on board. Thus, unbeknown to her (and perhaps even to them, for there was no formal ceremony), The Boys inducted Chris into their fraternity of friends. It was obvious that they adored her; and, if asked, they would confess that they would do just about anything they could to help her.

And so, on this particular Thursday morning four days after she first met Billy Rosen at her parents' home, when a smiling Chris Haslett stood in front of the desks of Sergeants Frank Kaye and Johnny Ludrakis, it was not surprising that something resembling a festive reunion erupted.

"Hey Frank. Take a look!" Johnny cried out.

Frank, who had been reading through a stack of papers on the credenza behind his desk, swiveled his chair around. "Whoopee!" he cried. He grinned broadly and yelled, "Hey, Princess!" Then he jumped up, ran around the side of his desk, and embraced Chris in a bear hug.

"Gosh, it's wonderful to see you, beautiful," he said. But before he could continue, he felt himself being pried away.

"My turn," Johnny said, giving Chris a hug. "We were starting to wonder whether you'd be a no show."

"Hi Boys," Chris said smiling. "Sorry, but with family and all I just couldn't make it over here until now. How've you been?"

"Great," Johnny replied. "Still doing our thing. How's everything at Smith?"

"I absolutely love it."

"Rumor has it you're going into politics."

"Law. I'm gonna be a lawyer."

"Yeah, well, please make it quick, because you never can tell when we'll need a lawyer. Our deals are getting more and more complicated," Johnny said. "Right, Frank?"

"Personally," Frank said, "I avoid lawyers like the plague. They kill every deal you try to make. All we wanna do is 'do business,' and then they come along and draw up fancy contracts with big words no one understands. Me, I'm happy with a handshake from a guy I trust."

"Now, Boys," Chris said. "Let's not start poking holes in my chosen profession. If you keep it up I may just change my mind and become an expediter. Go into competition with you. Probably put you out of business."

"No question about that," Johnny said. "Particularly with your looks." He smiled.

"So what brings you here, Chris?" Frank asked. "And how can we help?"

"First off, I need plane reservations back to school next Tuesday. I'm only here for a few days during what Smith calls the 'Reading Period.' My finals begin in a little over three weeks. And second…well, I just want to run something by you. It's…" she hesitated, "personal in a way."

"First things first," Johnny said. "What time would you like to leave?"

"I really don't care. But some time so I won't get in too late. Smith's an hour later than we are here, and it takes me about ninety minutes by bus to get there from the Hartford-Springfield Airport."

Johnny nodded.

"And the second item of business?" Frank said.

"Well, it's been on my mind for a few days and…" Again she hesitated.

"C'mon, Chris. It's us, The Boys. You know you can speak freely to us, and whatever's said we'll keep confidential."

Chris nodded. "Is there somewhere we can talk in private?"

"Sure," Johnny said. "We can use Captain Reston's office for a few minutes. He won't mind, particularly since it's you." The three went into the Captain's office shutting the door behind them.

"Okay, Chris, what gives?" Frank asked.

Chris looked at each of them for a moment. Then she began. "Well, you two know me. I don't mince words or play games. I see something I want and I go after it. I think I learned that from you two some years ago."

Both of The Boys nodded.

"So that's really what this is all about," she continued. "A few days ago I met a recruit. Actually, my grandmother met him first. Brought him home and insisted he have dinner with us. When I got to the table I thought he was a pawn in a match-making ploy orchestrated by my family so I decided to try to goad him into leaving. And in the process I think I made a total fool of myself. I asked him why he was having dinner with us and whether he didn't feel weird sitting there. And his response wasn't particularly friendly. He really put me in my place. Told me my parents had offered him hospitality and that he was simply accepting it. He said that even though he was a lowly private in basic he didn't feel weird. Said he thought I was the weird one." She paused.

"But while I was listening—and realizing how wrong I'd been about him—I was also looking him over. There was something about him I found attractive. I can't explain it. So at this point I just want to know more about him. That's all." She looked up, but neither of The Boys said anything. After a moment she continued. "Well, women aren't all that different from men, are they?"

"Hey," Frank said. "No big deal. You just liked what you saw. Happens to us all the time." He turned to Johnny. "Right?"

"Not to me," Johnny replied, laughing. Then he winked at Frank. "Hey, pal, get your wallet out 'cuz I think you're gonna owe me big."

Chris had a confused look on her face. What was Johnny talking about?

Holding a cupped hand to his mouth, Johnny coughed, clearing his throat, as if preparing to say something important.

"So, Princess, what specific information would you be wanting about Private William Rosen?" He waited a moment. Then he saw a surprised look on her face. He continued, smiling broadly, "Because I pulled his 201 File and I've been holding it for you for the past few days. And I made a little wager with my friend Frank here that you'd be by asking some questions about him. Well?" He glanced sideways at Frank.

"Jesus," Chris said, "you two know everything, don't you! Even what goes on in my head!"

Johnny slapped the palm of his hand against his desktop. He was now convulsing in laughter. So was Frank.

"Aw, c'mon, Princess. We're not exactly mind readers," Johnny said. "But you gotta remember that Fort Wood's a tiny community, and we generally know what's going on 'round here. Hey, that's our business. In this case, if you'll keep it confidential, we'll even tell you how we know."

"Promise," Chris said.

"Okay. It was from Benny."

"Our steward?" Chris asked.

"The very same," Frank replied. "We met him Monday night at a bar in town. He gave us all the details. Said he'd never seen you so blown away by a guy."

Chris felt embarrassed. "Looks like I wear my emotions on my sleeve."

"I'd say that's a fair assessment," Johnny said.

Then he turned to Frank. "Hey, Frank, why don't you go out and get that 201 File. It's on my desk."

"I'll be right back," Frank said. He got up, opened the door to Captain Reston's office, and left.

Moments later he returned carrying a file. "Here, Princess, take a look." He handed Chris Billy's file. "Just stay as long as you want. If Captain Reston returns before you're done, we'll let him know you're in here going over a file."

"Thanks," Chris said. Even before they were out the door she'd begun to read.

***

Forty-five minutes later Chris came out of Captain Reston's office and handed the file back to Johnny. "I don't feel quite as loony as I did before seeing this," she said. "It's obvious he's pretty bright."

The Boys nodded. Then Frank asked, "Notice anything strange in the file?"

"No, why?"

"See, right here," Frank said, pointing to the routing slip attached to the inside of the file jacket. "Take a look at the travels this file has had: first, it was in Chicago where he was inducted; then it went to 'Captain J. Martin,' your father's aide; next, it went to 'Master Sergeant S. Sack,' his basic training company's first sergeant who kept it for a few hours; and finally, it went back to 'Captain J. Martin' before being sent to us." He waited for a moment watching Chris.

"I mean this whole thing is highly unusual because normally the file simply leaves the Induction Center, Chicago, or wherever, and winds up directly in our office."

"Interesting," Chris said. "Anything else?"

"Yeah. You read the typed interview report?" Frank asked.

"I did. But who interviewed him?"

"We don't know. We think it may have been the Induction Center CO, a Colonel Harkavy, but we're not sure."

Chris smiled. "Really?" she said. "I know the Colonel well. A good guy."

"Did you notice the little notations in the margin: 'HUSCL' and '4F'?"

Chris nodded.

"They mean anything to you?"

"Not really. Obviously he's not 4F if he's in the Army so I don't understand why the '4F' is there. And I don't have the foggiest idea what that other notation means. Do you?"

"Nope," Johnny replied. "Except for what's in the interview report—the fact that Private William Rosen comes from a comfortable North Shore home, aced the Army Achievement Test in record time, and, as a kid, hurt his left foot—we know almost nothing about him. But when you couple that with his problems in basic, we're like 99.99 percent sure something's not kosher."

"'His problems in basic'...what are you talking about?" Chris asked.

"Well, we know a private who works in his company's OR, Dewey La Droop," Johnny said. "He may not be the smartest, but he's reliable. He tells us that Sergeant Sack, the first sergeant, has been on Rosen's case like you wouldn't believe from day one; that he won't let up; that Rosen has a field problem every single night; and that during the day while the others are free Sack keeps dumping misery on him. La Droop says he's never seen anything like it." He looked at Chris and thought he saw her wince slightly.

"So when you add everything up, something's terribly wrong. Maybe he's a rotten apple; or maybe something else is going on. We're completely in the dark. And we probably should know because if he finishes basic we're gonna have to assign him out."

"What do you mean, 'if he finishes basic'?" Chris asked, now slightly alarmed.

"I mean that there's been so much crap dished out to him that he might not make it for any number of reasons," Frank replied. "The first that comes to mind is that he could break and put his fist through someone's face...like Sack's. Or maybe he's got an attitude problem and doesn't make it because of that."

"That's not likely," Chris said. "I met him. There's no attitude problem there, at least not when it comes to the military—which he went out of his way to defend at our dinner table."

"Well then, why the harassment?" Johnny asked.

"I don't know," Chris replied.

"Neither do we," Johnny said. "But we'd sure as hell like to know what's going on."

"That makes three of us," Chris responded.

Then Johnny said, "Chris, make sure we have your phone number at school."

"'Course," she replied, writing it on a piece of paper which she handed to Johnny. "And thanks, Boys." Smiling, she walked behind their two adjacent side-by-side desks, leaned over, kissed one on the cheek, and then the other.

As she was about to leave, Chris said, "You know, with so many people after him, I'd say Private Billy Rosen needs a few good friends. Wouldn't you?"

Johnny and Frank looked up at her, hesitated for a brief moment, and then nodded.

Chapter 19

Building CR-C, Second Training Regiment (Basic), Fort Leonard Wood, Missouri, Tuesday, 16 May 1950, 1120 Hours.

There were dark clouds on the horizon threatening rain as the rays of the overhead Missouri sun bore down mercilessly on the dull black curved metal roof of Building CR-C, a World War II-era Quonset hut that was being used as a classroom. The extreme heat of the day, along with unusually high humidity, had converted its interior into something akin to a steam bath. Inside, its occupants, the forty-odd members of Company B's First Platoon, sweltered.

Billy sat next to the hut's one small window. Even though it was wide open, he felt no air movement, and his fatigues were blotched with sweat. And he, like the others, thirsted for water. But there was none to be had. The five-gallon bottle atop the single water cooler next to the far wall was empty as was his canteen and the canteens of most of the others, emptied earlier that morning during their quick time march from the company area to Building CR-C, some six miles distant.

Despite their discomfort, the men sat uncomplaining in folding chairs which had been neatly arranged in five rows inside the hut. A few of them had nodded off, while some of the others were talking quietly among themselves. Jerry Krazinski, however, was the one noisy exception. Ever since his manhood had been surgically restored, he had become increasingly boisterous and obnoxious—causing some members of First Platoon to conclude that he was far more tolerable before when he stank.

Billy looked around. At the front of the room he saw a raised platform with a lectern on it. Attached to the wall immediately behind the lectern was a large blackboard with "*Smith John NMI PVT RA 16123456 M5-11-7/2377842 (4/44)*" printed on it.

His platoon sergeant, SFC Manual Gomez, appeared to be unaffected by the heat. He was standing at the right side of the room gesticulating animatedly as he spoke to a tall NCO with a large protruding beer belly. The latter looked at his watch, said something to Sergeant Gomez, and then stepped up onto the platform and walked over to the lectern. He leaned forward on it, took a moment to study the group of recruits before him, cleared his throat, and began.

"Good morning, gentlemen," he said. He waited but there was no response, so he said it again, "Good morning, gentlemen." Still there was no response. "Dammit," he said in a louder voice, "when someone says 'good morning' to you, what's the normal fuckin' response?"

There was silence. After a while a muscular curly-haired man in the back of the room spoke up. "Good morning, Sergeant?"

"Finally!" he said. "So let's hear it from everyone. Now!"

All the men replied in unison, "Good morning, Sergeant."

"That's more like it!" He nodded in apparent satisfaction. Then he coughed, cleared his throat again, and continued. "I'm Staff Sergeant Burlingame. And I'm here to give you instruction in the use of your gas mask which we're gonna issue to you today. So pay attention, because this little device might just save your ass." He waited a moment letting what he said sink in.

"Okay. See that pallet behind you over there?" He waited, allowing time for the men to turn and look. "Well, there's a large packing crate on it, and inside are a bunch of boxes 'bout the size of shoe boxes. Each box contains a brand new M5-11-7 Assault Gas Mask. This is the one we used in the Normandy invasion." He looked around and saw he had their attention.

"So here's what I want you to do. Without talking and in some semblance of order, I repeat, no talking and in some semblance of goddamn order, go on over to the pallet and take one of them boxes from the crate. Open it up, take out the package that's inside, and remove the wrapping paper. Throw the box and wrapping paper in one of them cans over there." He pointed to a group of large trash cans lined up at the left side of the room. "Then go on back to your seat and hold your gas mask in your lap. Do not, I repeat, do not, remove your gas mask from the canvas bag it's in." He looked at his notes. Satisfied that he'd covered everything, he said, "Okay, let's do it!"

The men got up slowly, turned, and walked over to the pallet. Ten minutes later they were back in their seats with their bagged gas masks in their laps.

"Okay," Sergeant Burlingame said. "I'm going to be handing out forms like this here which'll be passed on down each row."

He held up a sheet of paper with printing on it. "There'll be a line for each of you on the form. Fill it out like I've done for Private John Smith up there on the blackboard: with your last name, first name, middle initial, rank, and serial number; and, for the gas mask, the type, which is M5-11-7, and the manufacturer's identifying number and the date of manufacture. Since this information is on the gas mask itself, not the bag, you'll have to take the mask out of the bag." He waited for a moment. "One more thing. If you got no middle initial, like John Smith up there," he motioned toward the blackboard, "then write in the letters 'NMI.'"

"Questions?" There were none. Then he passed out a ballpoint pen and a clipboard with the form clipped to it to the first man in each of the five rows.

Fifteen minutes later Sergeant Burlingame had retrieved his pens and clipboards. He was ready to proceed.

"Okay, now I want you to put your mask back in the bag, and put the bag's adjustable strap around your neck tightening it or loosening it so the top edge of the bag is lined up with your titties." He looked around and smiled, obviously hoping some of the men would laugh. But none of them did. He continued. "This is the normal position for carrying your gas mask into combat." He hung his gas mask bag around his neck demonstrating.

"When you've got the carrying position correctly set, I want you to leave the bag around your neck and take the mask out again." He waited a few moments.

"Now this here is one of the best gas masks around. When the straps are properly adjusted, it fits anyone. And it's lighter than some of the older models. Plus the canister, which holds the filter, doesn't hang by a tube which could break, say if you were crawling on your belly while you had it on. Okay, here's how it goes on." He held up his mask.

"See these six straps? Well, they can be loosened or tightened. Now make sure they're loose enough so's you can slip the mask on." He waited a moment.

"So here's how you put it on. First, place your chin in the cup just below this here round flutter valve, like this." He slid his chin into the mask.

"Next, pull the mask and straps up and over your head, and then down, making sure your ears aren't under any straps. And then tighten the six straps." He demonstrated. Then he loosened the straps and removed the mask.

"You can pretty well tell if the mask is on right 'cuz when you breathe, air will flow in and out through the little round flutter valve." He pointed.

"Okay, give it a try. Put your gas masks on."

Billy and the others did. And when Billy breathed, air entered and exited through the small circular valve at the front.

"Raise your hand if you're having problems and either Sergeant Gomez or I will come 'round."

A few of the men had difficulty with their masks but eventually got them on.

"Okay, put 'em back in the bags and listen up," Sergeant Burlingame said. "Now at this point you don't know shit about your gas mask. For all you know it's somethin' designed for a Halloween party, not a gas attack. So we're gonna have you use it and prove to you it works." He looked up. Now the men were listening intently.

"Outside, across the path, there's a small shack with one room. We've sealed it off and pumped tear gas into it. And we're gonna put each one of you in that room for four minutes. Without that mask, your eyes, nose and throat will burn like hell. What we do is get you in that room without your masks on. Then you gotta put 'em on and stay in there the full four minutes. We bar the door so you can't get out. Sergeant Gomez and I are on the outside, and we don't pay attention to hollerin'. So forget about yelling for help. Just get in there and put your masks on. And don't worry 'cuz everyone does just fine." He looked out over the men. Some appeared uneasy.

"You go in the shack a squad at a time, with no more than twelve men in a group. Got it?"

He waited, but there were no questions. "Okay, move on out. When you get outside line up by squads."

Billy and the others got up. Billy took out his gas mask again and slipped it over his head, cinching down the six straps. It not only felt comfortable, but when he breathed in and out, it worked perfectly. He put it back in the bag.

When the men were outside and lined up, Billy heard Sergeant Gomez shout, "First Squad, get ready. Go! Go! Go!" Billy, who was in the Second Squad, watched as the eleven men of First Platoon's First Squad walked through the doorway into the shack's smoke-filled interior. Four minutes later they were back outside. They quickly removed their gas masks and walked over to the side. One looked over toward Vin, who was in Billy's squad, and gave him a "thumb's up."

"All right, Second Squad. Ready. Go! Go! Go!" Sergeant Gomez shouted as Billy and the others in Second Squad entered the shack. As soon as they were inside the door slammed shut. Billy could hear its latch fall into place.

Billy made an effort not to panic. He reached into the bag on his chest, withdrew his gas mask and put it on, making sure he first put it under his chin, and then pulled the mask and straps back up over his head. Then he cinched down its straps. Satisfied that the mask was on correctly, he took his first breath. But instead of an inflow of air entering through the flutter valve, he felt warm gas coming in next to his left nostril. He reached up and felt it: *a large tear in the face of the mask.*

Billy's instinctive reaction was to try somehow to seal off the leak. He pressed the palms of both hands over the tear, but this did no good. He was breathing in tear gas, and his nose and throat were beginning to burn. And inside his mask the gas was seeping up into his eyes. Probably a little over three minutes remaining. Then he heard it: a few of the others were making gasping noises.

Billy tried to cry out, but his voice wasn't working. He was also beginning to weaken from lack of oxygen.

He looked around. There! On the wall in a flush glass case: a fire extinguisher and a *fire ax*. He rushed over, grabbed the handle of the door to the case and pulled with all his might. It wouldn't budge.

He grabbed for the canteen hanging from his webbed belt. He unsnapped its canvas pouch and yanked it out. Then he began hitting the glass with the canteen's bottom, all the while growing weaker. But instead of the glass breaking, the aluminum canteen simply gave way and dents appeared in its bottom.

Suddenly Craig was at his side. He began pounding the glass with his fist. It shattered as his right arm went through it. Billy saw blood spurt out as Craig withdrew his arm. There, embedded in his forearm just below his elbow, Billy saw an ugly six-inch shard of glass. But the case was broken. Billy reached in, opened the door from the inside, and grabbed the ax. As he was making his way toward the shack's door he collapsed into unconsciousness.

***

When Billy came to he was outside on the ground. Sergeants Burlingame and Gomez were staring down at him. Then he felt it: a terrible burning in his throat and nose. And his eyes hurt like hell; he had to squint to see. He coughed and began spitting up heavy yellowish phlegm.

He looked to his right. Craig and another member of Second Squad Billy barely knew, diminutive Jason "Jack" Russell, were lying nearby. There was a tourniquet tied around Craig's right forearm just above the elbow.

And then he saw that Sergeant Burlingame was holding several gas masks. Billy heard him say to Sergeant Gomez, "Goddammit, Manny, fuckin' leakers! I'm calling a halt to this."

"Jesus Christ," Sergeant Gomez groaned, "what we gonna do, Burly?" He hesitated, then asked, "Should I get an ambulance and have 'em taken to the hospital?"

"No goddamn hospital!" Billy heard Craig cry out. "I ain't goin' to some damn hospital and have to start basic all over. Just take us back to the barracks!"

Sergeant Gomez thought for a moment. Then he turned to Sergeant Burlingame. "You got a vehicle handy, Burly?"

"Yeah. My pickup over there," he said, pointing to a truck parked over to the side. "Here, take the keys." He held them out to Sergeant Gomez. "And, Manny, don't worry none about the others. I'll get 'em back to your company area. That's the fuckin' least I can do."

Background Check: Waynesville

The tiny town of Waynesville, Missouri (population 2,196), lies less than one mile to the north of Fort Leonard Wood, just across US 44. In addition to its homes, rental housing, and trailer parks, it boasts a three-man police department; a volunteer fire brigade whose membership varies from three to twelve depending upon whether it's hunting season, fishing season, or some other time of the year; a six-member Town Council; a two-man Public Works Department; a doctor; a pharmacy; a Rotary Club; a grocery store; an eatery referred to by locals simply as "Dale's"; a beauty salon; The Old Whitehorse Inn, a traveler's rest stop built in 1837 located in the downtown square next to Roubidoux Creek; a barber shop with one barber and three chairs; a grammar school named, not surprisingly, after Mark Twain; an Octane-Plus gas station; a realtor; an Abstract Title & Trust Company office; a town hall; and the Pulaski County Administration Building containing a County Recorder and County Clerk's office, a Sheriff's Department, a two-man jail, the County Board's chambers, and a courtroom for Pulaski County's only judge, the Honorable Lon A. Gordon.

If you choose to live in Waynesville and you need something you can't find there, you'll have to go elsewhere, either to Rolla, twenty-five miles to the northeast on US 44, or on up to St. Louis, another one hundred five miles.

Despite its small size and limitations, Sherman and Velma Sack never for a moment considered living anywhere but in Waynesville when, just over two years before, Sergeant Sack received orders assigning him to Fort Leonard Wood as first sergeant of a basic training company to be commanded by his wartime companion, Captain Emil Schtung. Velma also liked the idea of living there because it was close to Fort Wood's Base Hospital where, as an experienced civilian RN, she felt certain she could find work.

With the help of Dave Rice, Waynesville's only real estate broker, the Sacks found what they were looking for in less than two hours: a small white two-story rental home on a quiet street on the north side of town. When they first went through it, Velma was a bit skeptical. Although she liked the warm beige color of its freshly painted interior, she had hoped for three bedrooms; instead, it only had one bedroom and a convertible den, both upstairs. In addition, she was a bit uncomfortable with the new wall-to-wall carpeting sculpted in a pattern so popular at the time. She would have preferred something plainer. But then she saw the kitchen, and that was the closer. "My Lord, Sherman," she said. "Look! A portable dishwasher and one of those new garbage disposals!" These were things she thought you only found at home furnishing shows. "We'll take it!" she exclaimed excitedly.

The next day the Sacks moved in. Their household goods were in transit from Germany, but this didn't put Velma off in the slightest. As an army wife she was used to moving, and she knew how to make do. She went to the PX and the Commissary at Fort Wood and got the things she needed to tide them over until the movers arrived.

And today, two years later, when she thought of how a dishwasher and a garbage disposal had seduced her, she smiled. "Doesn't take much to get into my pants," she thought. But she knew the house had been a good choice, and that for sometime now she and Sherman had considered Waynesville home. Moving to the next post wouldn't be nearly as easy.

Chapter 20

336 Pippen Road, Waynesville, Missouri, Tuesday, 16 May 1950, 1330 Hours.

"Sherman," Velma called from downstairs. "Pick up the phone. It's for you. Whatever are you doing up there?"

But whatever Sherman was doing in their upstairs den was absolutely fine with her, and she was happy to answer the phone because today was Sherman's 32nd birthday. She had insisted that he take the day off. She had done the same because, as she had said, "Not so many birthdays left after this one, honey, before you reach the big '4-0!'"

Velma had done her best to make last night and today special. She had sent away for a lavender-colored negligee which she'd worn to bed. Sherman had undressed her, first with his eyes and then with his hands, and afterwards they had made love. Then Sherman had told her how beautiful she looked, and that alone was worth all the trouble she had gone to. "Damn him," she thought. "He sure knows how to treat a woman!"

This morning they had slept in. Around 11:00 AM she had prepared his favorite breakfast for him: fresh orange juice, honeydew melon, scrambled eggs, Canadian bacon, homemade biscuits, and a new brand of Columbian coffee she'd ordered by phone from a specialty store in Chicago. After that she'd given him his birthday present, a large box containing a model sailboat which the man at Grant's Models in Rolla had assured her could be put together in only an hour or two. She had seen it assembled and resting on the stand that came with it, and she had loved it. She thought Sherman would too. Shortly after she handed the box to him he had disappeared upstairs into the den.

But now his birthday was being interrupted by a damn phone call.

"Who is it?" he called down to his wife.

"Sergeant Gomez, I think he said."

"Aw hell," Sergeant Sack mumbled to himself.

"Vel," he continued, "Ask him if it can wait; tell him to leave a number and I'll call him tonight. Tell him…" he thought for a moment, "that I'm pretty busy most of today with personal stuff." He waited.

A few minutes later he heard her call up to him: "Sorry, dear. Says it's important. Can't wait."

"Damn!" he swore, as he picked up the phone.

"Hi, Manny. What gives?" he asked, trying to feign pleasantness.

"Sorry to bother you at home, Top, but we got a serious problem. Real bad, and I need you to tell me what to do."

"Shoot, Manny."

"Three guys in my platoon were taking gas mask training, and turns out their masks were leakers. They got exposed to large amounts of tear gas. All three seem to be suffering from burns in the nose and throat. Eyes don't look too good neither."

"Son of a bitch!" Sergeant Sack cursed under his breath.

"Where are they, Manny?"

"In the barracks on their bunks, Top. I thought about taking them to the hospital, but one didn't wanna go. Said he didn't wanna start basic over again."

Sergeant Sack was silent for several seconds. Finally he asked, "When did all this happen?"

"Between one and two hours ago, Top."

"How'd the three get to the company area?"

"Burlingame loaned me his pickup."

"Burly was NCOIC?"

"Yeah."

"And the rest of your platoon?"

"In the barracks too. Burly marched 'em on over."

"Last question, Manny. What're their names, the three guys?"

"Billington, Russell, and Rosen, Sarg," he replied.

Had Sergeant Gomez been with Sergeant Sack, he would have seen the latter stiffen slightly at the mention of Billy's name.

"Okay, Manny, here's what I want you to do. First, go on over to the OR. If the Captain's there, tell him what's going on, and that I'm handling it. Then get back to the barracks; make sure they're cleaned up 'cuz I don't know who'll be comin' by. Get the men outside, close order drill or something. Let the three stay in their bunks. Make sure they have water. I'll be around in about thirty minutes."

"Okay, Top. But I think someone should stay in the barracks just in case Billington's arm starts bleeding. It was cut pretty bad. I bandaged it and put sulfa powder on it. Still and all, I think someone should be there."

"Good thought, Manny. You stay with them after you get back from the OR. And when you go to the OR get Lieutenant Fuller to give the others close order drill."

"Top, Lieutenant Fuller's playing mumbly peg[3] behind the OR with La Droop, so I can't bother him. You know the way he is."

"Yeah. Well, get someone else. Anyone, I don't care. Just get the men out of there and make sure they're doing something. See you shortly at the barracks." Sergeant Sack hung up.

***

"Velma," Sergeant Sack called, "I need your help."

Sergeant Sack heard his wife coming up the stairs. "Okay, birthday boy, what is it?" she asked pleasantly.

"Honey, looks like the birthday celebration just ended. We got an emergency. Three of my men were pretty badly injured by tear gas." He went on to explain what he had just found out from Sergeant Gomez. "They're in the barracks, and I'm not sure what to do. I said I'd be over there pretty soon."

Velma thought for a moment.

"Okay, Sherman, here's what I want. You get into your Class A's. I'll need to make a call before we leave. Probably should put on my nurse's uniform in case we have to go to the hospital." Velma left the room. A few minutes later she was on the phone.

***

"Fort Wood Hospital," the operator answered. "How may I direct your call?"

"Hi, Muriel. It's Velma Sack."

"Oh, hi, Velma. How're you?"

"I'm okay, but I need to speak to Dr. Stone as soon as possible. He around?"

"I think so. I saw him earlier today. Hold on." The operator put Velma on hold, and a minute or so later a man's voice came on the line.

"Colonel Stone."

"Hi, Dr. Stone. It's Velma Sack."

"Oh yes, Velma. What's up?"

"Sir, I need your help. Three men in my husband's company have been injured by tear gas. They're in their barracks. First Platoon, Company B, Fourth Battalion of the Second TRB. If it's not too much trouble, could you meet us over there in about half an hour and have a look at them?"

"Why aren't they in the hospital, Velma?" Dr. Stone asked.

"I'm not really sure, sir. But before we move them, if we have to, could you possibly see them in their barracks?"

"I guess so," Dr. Stone replied reluctantly. "Where are you now?"

"At my home, sir. In Waynesville."

"You got a pharmacy in town?"

"Yes, sir."

"All right, then, here's what I need." Dr. Stone gave Velma instructions which she wrote down. "See you in around half an hour," he said.

As Velma Sack was hanging up the phone, her husband came downstairs dressed in his OD uniform.

Chapter 21

First Platoon Barracks, Company B, Fourth Battalion, Second Training Regiment (Basic), Fort Leonard Wood, Missouri, Tuesday, 16 May 1950, 1607 Hours.

The weather had finally turned, and it was pouring rain when Velma's 1941 powder blue Ford convertible pulled up to the entrance of First Platoon's barracks and parked next to a 1939 silver gray LaSalle sedan which Velma recognized as Dr. Stone's car. Sergeant Sack, who had been driving, turned off the engine. Then, facing his wife who was sitting next to him in the front seat, he said, "Vel, before we go on in, I need to say something."

Velma looked over at her husband. "Sherman, Dr. Stone's waiting for us."

"I'll make it quick. I don't want one of the three men, Private William Rosen, goin' into the hospital. It'd probably mean he'd be recycled, and I don't want that. He's been through enough. So please, Vel, use your charm, whatever. Just keep him outta the hospital."

"Sherman, you're always talking in damn riddles, you know that? You're just lucky today's your birthday or you and I'd be getting into it. But, okay, I'll see what I can do. Just remember, though, I'm not that boy's doctor."

"Thanks, Vel," Sergeant Sack said.

Velma reached into the car's back seat and withdrew a paper bag containing the items Dr. Stone had told her to get at the pharmacy. Then she got out of the car and walked up four wooden steps into the barracks, her husband right behind her.

***

Contrary to Sergeant Sack's instructions, all members of First Platoon were in the barracks. Sergeant Gomez ran over.

"Sorry, Top," he said. "Too wet for close order drill."

"Manny," Sergeant Sack said, "would you please make sure the men are decent. There's a woman in the barracks." He turned, intending to introduce his wife to Sergeant Gomez, but she had disappeared. Then he saw her down at the end of the row of bunks bending over a sleeping figure. A bird colonel was standing next to her.

"Jesus," Sergeant Sack mumbled, as he walked quickly over to his wife.

"Honey," Velma said, "this is Dr. Stone."

"Hi there, Sergeant," Dr. Stone said extending his hand.

"Sir!" Sergeant Sack replied coming to rigid attention.

"None of that please, Sergeant. I'm just a disguised faith healer in colonel's garb."

"Yes, sir. And thank you, sir, for coming out here to see these men."

"My pleasure." He looked at Velma and Sergeant Sack. "There a place where we can talk in private for a few minutes?"

"I think so, sir," Sergeant Sack replied. Then he called out, "Manny, can we use your room for a few minutes?"

"'Course, Top," he said, leading them into his small bedroom in the far corner of the barracks. When they were inside, he stepped back out into the barracks proper closing the door behind him.

***

"Okay, here's the deal," Dr. Stone said. "The little guy, Russell, that you and I just saw, Velma...he'll be fine. I want him to shower several times before going to bed tonight. Give him one of those eye cups. Before he turns in he's to rinse his eyes every hour with the eye solution you got at the pharmacy."

Velma nodded. "I'll tell the Platoon Sergeant."

Dr. Stone continued. "I'm not sure what his schedule is tomorrow, but I want him here in the morning. I'll be by at 9:00 AM to see him." He paused.

"Now I want the same treatment for Billington. But I also want him on penicillin for that gash in his arm. Before you arrived I put eight stitches in it which I'll take out in a few days. He should also take two aspirin every four hours for pain. He's to remain in the barracks for the next two days. And if you want me to, I can admit him to the hospital. But when I talked to him he was adamant about not going. Something about not wanting to start basic training all over again."

"If it's okay with you, sir, I'd like to keep him here," Sergeant Sack said.

"I've got no objections at the moment," Dr. Stone said. "But if he takes a turn for the worse, I'll have to put him in the hospital."

"Fair enough, sir," Sergeant Sack replied.

Dr. Stone reached into his bag. "Here's the penicillin, Velma. I assume you've got aspirin?"

"Yes, sir," she replied.

"Okay, now we come to the tough one, Rosen. I really don't like what I see. He's been badly burned in the throat and nose. But it's his eyes that have me worried. They're red as hell and should be irrigated. And I need to have him seen by an ophthalmologist. So I want him out of here right now and on his way to the hospital. We can't chance an eye burn or an infection."

Velma glanced at her husband. He was looking at her, as if pleading for help.

"Does he really have to go to the hospital?" Velma asked. "I know Sherman here, I mean Sergeant Sack, doesn't want to risk the possibility that any of his men will be taken out of their basic training cycle." She looked over at her husband. "Right, dear?"

Sergeant Sack nodded.

"I understand all that," Dr. Stone said. "But I don't see how I have a choice. Either you take him in your car or I'll take him in mine. I'll schedule an ophthalmologic consult for him first thing in the morning. And until then we can keep him under observation at the hospital."

"How about this?" Velma said. "We'll take him to our house where I can look after him. That way he'll have his own private nurse and you can have the eye doctor drop by in the morning. If he says that Rosen has to go into the hospital, I'll take him there myself. Then he'll probably be recycled. But if he doesn't need hospitalization, we can keep him 'til he's ready to go back to his company."

Sergeant Sack, who had been listening intently to his wife, appeared relieved. But he felt he had to add something.

"Dear," he said, "his stay at our house will have to be confidential; you know, strictly between the three of us and, of course, the eye doctor?"

"Christ!" Dr. Stone said. "What's going on here?"

"Sir," Velma said. "Even though my husband isn't supposed to treat his recruits differently, just between us he considers Rosen special. And he'd very much like him to stay with his basic training group." She looked up at her husband. "Wouldn't you, dear?" He nodded.

"This is all highly irregular," Dr. Stone said. "But what else is new? Anyway, since it's you, Velma, I guess I'll go along with your program. But, frankly, I still don't know what the hell is going on."

Dr. Stone reached for his small black physician's bag, closed it, and then said, "Jay Pearlberg, my ophthalmologist buddy, should be by your house around nine tomorrow morning. I'll call him tonight. And I'll tell him that Rosen's stay there is a state secret." He thought for a moment.

"I guess I'll need your address."

"336 Pippen Road, Waynesville," Velma replied as she scribbled it on a small piece of paper which she handed to Dr. Stone.

Just before leaving, Dr. Stone turned to Velma. "You know, Nurse Sack, you owe me big for this one. I hope you realize that."

"Indeed I do, sir," Velma replied, batting her eyelashes. "And I look forward to repaying you in full, Doctor—preferably in kind." Then she giggled.

Neither Velma nor her husband could see that Dr. Stone had turned a deep shade of red as he made his way out of the barracks.

Chapter 22

336 Pippen Road, Waynesville, Missouri, Wednesday, 17 May 1950, 0830 Hours.

"Morning," Velma Sack called as she entered the den. "Time to rise and shine! Doctor should be here in about thirty minutes!"

Billy had been in a deep sleep on the den's sofa bed dreaming he was in Miami Beach where he'd gotten sunburned over most of his body, so badly, in fact, that he ached everywhere. And so, when he heard a strange female voice calling out to him—he couldn't pinpoint exactly from where—trying to awaken him, his instinctive reaction had been to stay in his dream, to remain in sunny Miami Beach.

"Private Rosen! You hear me? I said wake up! The doctor's coming in half an hour!"

Doctor? What doctor? Billy's mind was a muddled blend of thoughts, pain, and confusion.

"Private Rosen! Get up, now!"

This time Billy awoke. He looked up. There, staring down at him, was a pleasant-appearing woman dressed in white. But he was having trouble seeing. His eyes felt sticky as he struggled to open them.

He shook his head trying to clear it. The he realized it was the nice lady who had ministered to him through the night making sure his eyes were irrigated. But he couldn't remember her name or where he was. "I'm sorry," he said, "I'm not sure who you are or where I am."

"I'm a nurse, Private Rosen. I'm Velma Sack. You're in my home. Get up! Doctor will be here shortly."

"But…"

"No 'buts.' Just get up now! Bathroom's over there." She pointed. "There's a robe in there. C'mon! Up! You can brush your teeth, comb your hair. When the doctor's finished, you can shower, shave, and put on fresh pajamas. Then I'll get you some breakfast. You must be hungry 'cuz you didn't eat a thing last night."

"Yes, ma'am," he said, as he managed to pull himself out of bed and make his way to the bathroom.

***

"All right, son," Dr. Pearlberg said as he removed an ophthalmoscope from his bag. "Just lie back on the pillow while I take a look-see. I understand you were exposed to tear gas?"

"Yes, sir," Billy replied.

"Any idea for how long?"

"Well, we were supposed to be locked up in that shack for four minutes, so it wasn't longer than that. But one of the guys got us out a little sooner. I'm not sure when, because I passed out."

"How'd you get exposed, son?"

"My gas mask had a leak in it. It trapped the tear gas up around my eyes."

Dr. Pearlberg shook his head. Then he said, "What you've got is what we call a 'chemical burn.' Dr. Stone did the right thing by having you start irrigating it yesterday. And that's what I want you to continue to do today: keep your eyes irrigated. This means holding an eye cup over each eye for at least five minutes every hour." He looked down at Billy. "Think you can do that, son?"

"Yes, sir," Billy replied.

"Good."

Then, turning to Velma, he said, "Forget about that eye wash he's been using. Make sure the cup is filled with distilled water." Velma nodded. "And call me at the hospital tomorrow and the next day. But I think by Friday he should be able to go back to his barracks."

***

"Well, soldier, how was breakfast?" Velma asked.

"Great," Billy replied. "I can't tell you how much I appreciate all this, Mrs. Sack. You are Sergeant Sack's wife, aren't you?"

"That's me. But forget the 'Mrs.' I'm Velma." She smiled. "And you're Private Rosen."

"'Billy,' ma'am."

Velma nodded. "I'm off to work, but I'll be home this evening. There's a radio over there." She pointed. "You just relax today. Try to get as much rest as possible. There's food in the fridge and there's a package for you which someone dropped off at the company. I've put it on the kitchen table. And whatever you do, don't forget to keep irrigating those eyes. I put two bottles of distilled water in the bathroom." Smiling warmly, she looked down at him. "Hey, soldier," she said, "you're gonna be fine."

***

A few minutes later Billy heard the front door close, an engine start up, and a car drive off. Suddenly, for the first time since his induction into the Army more than two weeks ago, he was alone in civilian surroundings. Those two weeks seemed like an eternity. And how strange he felt being in the Sacks' home. Stranger yet, he missed the turmoil of basic training and maybe even the incessant harassment by Sergeant Sack, his arch nemesis, now apparently his host. And why were the Sacks offering him sanctuary? He was utterly confused and still very tired.

***

When Billy awoke again it was three o'clock in the afternoon. He felt weak, slightly dizzy, and hungry. Again he went into the bathroom to irrigate his eyes. They were not as sticky as they had been earlier in the day, and he was able to open them almost immediately. After using the eye cup, he took a wash rag, ran cold water on it, and wiped his face. That felt refreshing. He reached for the robe and went downstairs to the kitchen.

***

Billy was seated at the kitchen table eating a sandwich Velma had left in the icebox. A half-full glass of milk rested on the table. Next to it lay the package. By its contour he was almost certain it was a book. He tore away the brown paper wrapping: *Manhattan Transfer* by John Dos Passos. An old friend he'd read several times. Now he knew who had left it: obviously Emma Durban. Inside the cover there was an envelope with his name printed on it. He opened it and withdrew a smaller sealed envelope and a handwritten note.

Tuesday AM

Dear Billy:

I'm off to Durango tomorrow. I thought you might enjoy another Dos Passos book. I hope you haven't read it, but, knowing you, you probably have.

Thanks so much again for rescuing me in the library and for livening up our Sunday evening.

Please stay in touch. And let's continue to be friends.

My address and phone number in Durango—

Emma Durban

627 East Third Avenue,

Durango, Colorado

DU9-2164

Fondly,

Em

P.S. Please read over the note in the small envelope. It's very important!

E. D.

Billy opened the smaller envelope. It contained a second handwritten note, but in an altogether different handwriting.

Christine Durban Haslett
124 Sibert Lane
Fort Leonard Wood, Missouri

Monday, May 15th

Hi Sport,

By the time you get this note, I'll be back at school. I fly out tomorrow morning.

I've concluded that you'll definitely be needing some good friends in the weeks ahead. You'll know when. Rest assured, you've got them.

And when the time comes, here's what you <u>must</u> do: Call me first at Smith. If you can't get hold of me, try either Sgt. Johnny Ludrakis or Sgt. Frank Kaye.

For me: Call my dorm in Northampton, Massachusetts, NO5-3097. (Call collect. I'll accept the charges if I'm in.)

For Johnny or Frank: Call Fort Wood Extension 1351. If you can't reach one of them at their Extension, try their business number in Rolla, RO4-7755. Leave a message with their secretary, Rose, if they're not in. Their company is The Boys, Inc.

I know this all sounds mysterious, and you obviously have questions. I'll explain when I see you. Meantime, it's vitally important that you commit these names and phone numbers to memory. Then tear up this note.

You've got to trust us, Sport.

With affection,

Chris

Alarm bells were going off in Billy's head when he finished reading Chris Haslett's note. He read it over and over again. If it had been written by anyone else, he might have dismissed it as gibberish, some form of silly cloak and dagger craziness.

But he seriously doubted that Chris Haslett was crazy. Certainly Emma Durban was not. And in her postscript Em had told him to read Chris' note. "*It's very important*," she had said.

So this couldn't be craziness! He'd better memorize those names and phone numbers immediately. He had a sinking feeling he'd be needing them.

***

Later that day Billy read Chris' note one last time. It had been written with her characteristic directness. He tried to conjure up an image of her, but he was having difficulty. After all, they had been together for such a short time and he'd been nervous and distracted by the others. Now he closed his eyes and tried hard to remember: tall, slender, dark hair, casually dressed, those horn-rimmed glasses, her warmth after she'd apologized to him. But that was all, and he desperately wanted more.

Alone in the Sacks' kitchen there could be no answers, only Billy's intuition which told him that Chris Haslett was going to become much more than a casual acquaintance.

Chapter 23

444 High Street, Cairo, Illinois, Thursday, 18 May 1950, 1310 Hours.

After camping out at his sister's home for over a week, Harley knew he was getting on her nerves. He had to make a move. So far he'd been able to keep his wife in the dark, mainly because she was at her mother's in Des Moines. On the day he'd left St. Louis he'd called her from the railroad station and told her he had to go to New York on business; and that's where she thought he was. He hadn't mentioned anything about the fire. Now it was time to call her again. He got up and went out, heading for a phone booth at the end of the block.

***

"Honey, I'm back from New York. I've been transferred to Cairo, Illinois, and I'm staying with Sis. I want you and the kids to come on down here immediately. And Marie, you tell no one about this. Otherwise I'll lose my job."

"But Harley, I've got to go home first."

"No! Grab the first train you can. Come here directly." Harley hung up. Now was not the time for a long-drawn-out conversation.

Leaving the phone booth, Harley began walking back to his sister's home. When Marie and the kids arrived they would all have to stay with Sis. He could only imagine how that would play out. Even though he was running dangerously low on cash, he knew he'd better do something to assuage her irritation. Maybe take her out to dinner and a movie. Anyway, in a few days they'd all be gone. He'd use the insurance proceeds to buy a car, and then he'd drive off with Marie and the children to a place unknown where he'd change his name, get a new job, and start over. He was confident that by burning down the house there'd be no trail for the East St. Louis money guy to follow. His only remaining tie to St. Louis was through his insurance agent who'd told him to expect a sizeable check in a matter of days.

***

As Harley approached the front door to his sister's home he noticed a panel truck parked directly across the street. He saw a short overweight elderly black man wearing a mail carrier's uniform get out of the truck and limp toward him. A mail pouch was slung over his right shoulder, and he held a letter in his left hand.

"You Mr. Harley Lutz? 'Cuz if you is I gots a Special Delivery for you."

"That's me," Harley replied. The insurance check! It was arriving even earlier than expected.

"Well you gots to sign for it." He handed Harley a pen and a sheet of paper.

Harley looked down at the paper. There was nothing on it. He was puzzled. "I don't get it," he said. Then he felt something cold pressed against his temple.

"You will, old friend. You will."

Harley heard a loud explosion and suddenly everything went blank.

Chapter 24

Orderly Room, Company B, Fourth Battalion, Second Training Regiment (Basic), Fort Leonard Wood, Missouri, Friday, 19 May 1950, 1440 Hours.

Billy felt unsteady and dizzy as he stood outside the door to Sergeant Sack's office. He still hadn't completely recovered from his accident. When Velma had dropped him off at the OR La Droop had come running over and told him that Sergeant Sack wanted to see him first thing. So, at the moment, he was simply following orders.

While he'd been at Sacks' home he'd seen a great deal of Velma but hardly anything of Sergeant Sack. In fact, he'd seen him only once. And that was for just a brief moment. At the time they hadn't spoken.

As he stood there, Billy tested his eyes, opening and closing them several times. They still felt slightly sticky and irritated. Taking a deep breath, he reached up and knocked.

"Come," a voice called out from within.

When Billy entered he saw that Sergeant Sack was on the phone. He stood there waiting. A moment later Sergeant Sack looked up and pointed to one of the two pull-up chairs. Billy took a seat. Several minutes after that Sergeant Sack hung up and turned to him.

"I just wanna let you know that Dr. Pearlberg ordered your return to the company as of today. Tell Sergeant Gomez you're on light duty until Tuesday."

"And during my off duty time, First Sergeant?"

"Far as that goes, you're on your own. But the doctor wants you to take it easy."

Then looking directly at Billy, Sergeant Sack continued, "One more thing, Rosen. And I want you to listen carefully. If anyone asks—I mean anyone—you were in the hospital the last few days. You understand?"

Billy nodded.

"Okay, you can go."

As Billy walked out of Sergeant Sack's office he smiled. With all his gruffness, what Sergeant Sack had just told him was that if anyone found out about his rather unusual stay at the Sacks' home, Sergeant Sack would be in deep grease. And now Sergeant Sack knew—probably to his great relief—that Billy would never let that happen, no matter what.

Chapter 25

***Orderly Room, Company B, Fourth Battalion,
Second Training Regiment (Basic),
Fort Leonard Wood, Missouri,
Tuesday, 23 May 1950, 0945 Hours.***

In the OR outer area First Lieutenant Barry Fuller, the company executive officer, and the supply sergeant, SFC Tom Blackman, were having a heated discussion about the St. Louis Cardinals' disappointing second place finish in the National League pennant race the prior year, and whether their manager, Elmer Posley,[4] was to blame.

"Posley's just not with it, Lieutenant," Sergeant Blackman said with conviction. "Muffed it last year and he'll do it again this year. Some guys just can't run a team. Takes a certain mystique. You know that."

"I dunno, Tom," Lieutenant Fuller replied. "I think he did a helluva job. Did you know the Cardinals led the league in hitting? Batted .277. Beat out Brooklyn by three percentage points."

"Don't sucker me, Lieutenant. Percentages don't mean jack shit. Yeah, percentage-wise the Cards were on top. But let's talk about runs. How 'bout that, huh?"

Sergeant Blackman smiled triumphantly and then continued. "Cards season total was 766 runs. Know what the Dodgers' total was?"

Lieutenant Fuller shook his head.

"Yeah, well, it was 879. There's your difference, Lieutenant. Posley don't know how to bring in runs. Dodgers averaged 5.63 per game to the Cards 4.88. See, Lieutenant, where I come from it's runs that count, not batting averages. *But then again I only graduated from high school.*"

Sergeant Blackman's last remark might, under some circumstances, have been considered insubordinate. But he and Lieutenant Fuller had come to a tacit understanding that when they were discussing baseball he was permitted an unusual amount of latitude in what he said to the Lieutenant in order to emphasize a particular point or to enliven the conversation. In addition, on a certain level he and the Lieutenant were friends.

"You're being way too tough on Elmer Posley, Tom," Lieutenant Fuller said. "After all, the Cards wound up 96 and 58 versus the Dodgers 97 and 57. That's pretty close. They were only one game out at the end of the season. I'd say that's pretty good management. Wouldn't you?"

"Hey, Lieutenant, who won? Huh? Tell me that, will ya."

"You're a hard man, Tom," Lieutenant Fuller said, smiling. "We'll just see how Posley does this year. Far as I'm concerned, the Cards and Dodgers finished in a dead heat last year."

"Right, Lieutenant. So did Truman and Dewey in '48. But who's our President, huh?" Sergeant Blackman smiled again. He always felt good when he debated with Lieutenant Fuller. He knew he could more than hold his own, and he had never even gone to college like the Lieutenant. Sometimes after one of these exchanges he even felt like he should have become a lawyer, or at least gone into politics.

"Well, Tom, I guess you got me there," Lieutenant Fuller said. "I'm the last one to quarrel with success. But still and all, Posley did a pretty good job last year, I'd say. Anyhow, what are your thoughts about this year?"

"Well, same problem this year as last. Cards got a great team. Look, they got Musial and Slaughter. Those two guys batted .338 and .336 last year. Only Jackie Robinson did better. And they got the best pitching. Their overall ERA of 3.44 last year was the lowest in the league. So they should win the pennant. But again it's back to that lamebrain, Posley. He just can't manage. So I say that this year it'll be the Dodgers all over again."

Lieutenant Fuller remained silent for a moment. He knew that Sergeant Blackman was probably right, that it was time for Posley to go. He was just about to respond when he was interrupted.

"Ah…excuse me, gentlemen," Sergeant Sack said as he walked over. "Don't mean to disturb such an earthshaking debate, but, if I might, sir," he said, turning to Lieutenant Fuller, "I'd like to have a word with you."

"With me?" Lieutenant Fuller said, surprised. He and the First Sergeant rarely spoke; and, in fact, in the seven months since he'd been with the company, Lieutenant Fuller had never had a discussion about anything of significance with Sergeant Sack.

Their only verbal exchanges had been limited to meaningless niceties like "good morning," "good evening," or "have a nice day." On one rare occasion Sergeant Sack had commented about the weather, how beautiful it was. But that was it.

"You sure you got the right person, First Sergeant?"

"Absolutely, sir. I really need your assistance." Sergeant Sack cringed as he said this. He knew full well that while Lieutenant Fuller had been with the company all he had done was piss away his time. Now Sergeant Sack had decided to see if he could figure out something useful for the little shit to do.

"Wow-wee!" Lieutenant Fuller said with enthusiasm. "So what gives?"

"Jesus!" Sergeant Sack thought to himself. "Not only looks like a gaping asshole, acts like one too."

Sergeant Sack truly couldn't stand the sight of Lieutenant Fuller. He was not only unsoldierly in appearance (he was only 5'4", his posture was poor, and he was overweight), but he was a royal slob as well. For openers, he wore a shirt that badly needed laundering and pressing which had been buttoned so that every button was in the wrong buttonhole; second, all his brass needed polishing; third, he was in dire need of a haircut; fourth, his nails were dirty and needed clipping; fifth, his boots had never been shined and were badly scuffed; and lastly, his badly wrinkled pants, which should have been tucked into his boots, dragged on the floor. "Lord," Sergeant Sack thought, "what a revolting specimen!"

"Sir," Sergeant Sack said, "could you come on into my office so we can discuss this?"

"My pleasure, First Sergeant," Lieutenant Fuller said.

The way Lieutenant Fuller had responded seemed to have alerted Sergeant Sack to something, but he wasn't exactly sure what. Was it just the slightest change in the Lieutenant's demeanor? Sergeant Sack wondered.

***

"Sit down, sir," Sergeant Sack said, as Lieutenant Fuller slid into one of the two pull-up chairs in front of the desk in the first sergeant's office.

"Sir, we've had a problem which I now feel compelled to bring to your attention. I hadn't mentioned it to you before because I didn't want to take up the Lieutenant's valuable time." Sergeant Sack knew he was laying it on pretty thick, but this was the way he would have broached the subject with any other officer, so he thought he'd speak to Lieutenant Fuller in the same fashion.

"Please continue," Lieutenant Fuller said, his voice deepening as he leaned forward and began to squint. Sergeant Sack saw with disgust that the Lieutenant's demeanor was changing. The little prick was assuming an air of self-importance. "Christ," Sergeant Sack thought, "what a jerk!"

"Well, sir, last week three of our men in the First Platoon were injured during gas mask training. Seems they were exposed to tear gas for several minutes when their gas masks failed. They received burns to the eyes and throat. One man also suffered a gash in his forearm which required stitches." Sergeant Sack cleared his throat and was about to continue when Lieutenant Fuller interjected a question.

"And how are the three men now, First Sergeant?"

"They're all fine, sir. Took a few days, but I'm happy to report they're one hundred percent."

"Good man, First Sergeant. That's what I like to hear. You're to be commended!"

"Son of a bitch," Sergeant Sack said to himself. "This turd suddenly thinks he's a big shot, that he has the right to hand out compliments."

"Thank you, sir," Sergeant Sack said.

"Now, First Sergeant, I believe I have several things on my plate that I'd like to have us address."

"Fucking asshole," Sergeant Sack thought. "This little shit has decided to take over. Jesus!"

"Yes, sir?"

"Well, for openers, tell me about the gas masks, First Sergeant."

"Sir, I spoke with the NCOIC of the training, Sergeant Burlingame. He told me they were the D-Day masks."

"Figures, First Sergeant. That damnable M5-11-7 Assault Gas Mask. The Army shit-canned it in '47. It was made of neoprene rubber and suffered from a condition called 'cold set' which means if it was subjected to low temperatures it would crack."

"Christ, how would you know that, sir?" Sergeant Sack said.

"I dunno, First Sergeant. But what I do know is that the Army replaced them with the E48 which became standard issue in 1947. Why in hell we still have some of the old M5-11-7s around is a puzzler."

By this time, Sergeant Sack was in a state of shock. How in God's name could this little fucker know something about army equipment he didn't know?

"So tell me, First Sergeant: exactly what happened to our three men? I must know."

"Well, sir, it's like this." Sergeant Sack explained in detail how Craig Billington, Jason "Jack" Russell, and Billy had been injured.

"So if it weren't for the fast action of that Rosen kid and uh, what's his name...Billington, we could be looking at three dead recruits? Am I hearing you right, First Sergeant?"

"Yes, sir."

"Interesting; so here's what I want you to do," Lieutenant Fuller said as he nervously began picking his nose. "First off, I want you to prepare two letters of commendation for my signature, one for Rosen and the other for Billington. Have them ready for me to sign by tomorrow morning."

Sergeant Sack began taking notes.

"Second, please set up a meeting in the OR outer area for 0630 tomorrow. I'll be there and I want you and all of the platoon sergeants to attend. For that meeting, please send Private La Droop over to Building CR-C and have him pick up an M5-11-7 gas mask. I happen to have an E48 in my billet which I'll bring to the meeting. I want to be able to display the two masks and explain the differences between the two. Naturally, I'll conduct the meeting."

"Naturally, sir," Sergeant Sack said, trying hard to refrain from sounding sarcastic. "But, sir, why so early in the AM?"

"0630 is an excellent time, First Sergeant. Before the platoon sergeants begin their daily training. And, besides, we all know that knowledge is best digested on an empty stomach."

"Of course, sir," Sergeant Sack replied. He had no idea where Lieutenant Fuller had ever heard anything like that.

"Third," Lieutenant Fuller continued, "please make an appointment for me to see Lieutenant Colonel Paulson just as soon as possible. Let his office know this is critical. I personally want to explain the problem to him face to face so that no other recruits in the battalion are injured. Let me know when he can see me." He cleared his throat.

"And finally, First Sergeant, please make sure Captain Schtung is fully briefed on all of this."

"Yes, sir," Sergeant Sack said.

"Good man," Lieutenant Fuller said, smiling with satisfaction. "Well," he continued, "I think that about does it. And I think, First Sergeant, you've handled this whole thing rather nicely."

Then Lieutenant Fuller extended his grubby little hand to Sergeant Sack which the latter reluctantly clasped.

As Lieutenant Fuller was leaving the First Sergeant's office, Sergeant Sack knew in his heart of hearts that when Lieutenant Fuller had said "you've handled this whole thing rather nicely," his comment hadn't been directed to Sergeant Sack at all. Instead, the little fucker had been congratulating himself.

Chapter 26

***Orderly Room Outer Area, Company B,
Fourth Battalion, Second Training Regiment (Basic),
Fort Leonard Wood, Missouri,
Wednesday, 24 May 1950, 0630 Hours.***

In the OR outer area Sergeant Sack and the four platoon sergeants, including SFC Manuel Gomez of the First Platoon, were seated in chairs which, one-half hour earlier, Lieutenant Fuller had arranged in a single row placed directly in front of a large work table. In the table's center, but next to its back edge, three phone books were stacked one on top of the other forming a makeshift lectern. A manila file containing Lieutenant Fuller's working papers rested atop the uppermost phone book, and on the table nearby lay two gas masks.

When he took his seat, Sergeant Sack immediately noticed that from the waist up Lieutenant Fuller looked different. His hair, still badly in need of a haircut, had been combed and slicked down with some kind of greasy tonic or oil. And his fatigue shirt was freshly laundered and pressed, although, to Sergeant Sack, it didn't seem to fit. The polished brass crossed rifle infantry insignias pinned to it gleamed uncharacteristically. But below his waist nothing had changed: same unshined brass belt buckle, same wrinkled pants which hadn't been tucked into his boots, and same unshined scuffed boots. Then Sergeant Sack saw that Lieutenant Fuller was holding something in his hand. He looked closely. A goddamn gavel. "What is this?" he wondered. "A Rotary Club luncheon or something?"

At exactly 0631 hours Lieutenant Fuller, who had taken his place immediately behind the table, rapped the gavel against its surface.

"Good morning, gentlemen. It is indeed with great pleasure that I call our meeting to order this fine morning. Although I do not intend to adhere strictly to Roberts Rules of Order, I find it incumbent upon me to speak first. Following my presentation, which I estimate should last no longer than forty-five minutes, there will be a question and answer session if that proves necessary." He looked up. "Any questions or comments so far?"

Sergeant Sack glanced to his left. Sergeant Gomez was rolling his eyes. On his right he saw that Sergeant John Lupe of the Third Platoon had raised his hand.

Nodding in the direction of Sergeant Lupe, Lieutenant Fuller said pleasantly, "Please, Sergeant."

"Well, sir," Sergeant Lupe said, "generally 'round 6:45 or 7:00 I have to take a crap."

"Interesting point, Sergeant Lupe," Lieutenant Fuller replied unflustered. "I am indeed indebted to you for bringing it up at this juncture because I strongly suspect you are not alone. But I believe your concerns can be assuaged if we take a ten-minute break at, say, precisely 7:00 AM. Would that do it for you?"

"Not exactly, sir," Sergeant Lupe said. "While I shit I usually have a cup of coffee and skim the *St. Louis Post-Dispatch*. Normally takes about twenty minutes."

"Hmm," Lieutenant Fuller mused. "Hadn't thought of that. Well, I regret that you'll have to forego the coffee and paper until after this briefing has been concluded, Sergeant Lupe. Sorry, old chap, but that's the way the cookie crumbles."

He smiled. He was extremely pleased with his last well chosen phrase, particularly the "old chap" part. He knew it was perfect under the circumstances because he'd first heard it used in an old World War II movie in which some RAF flyers were being briefed on a particularly hazardous mission.

"Any other questions or comments?" he asked. When no one spoke up he decided to press on.

"As you see, gentlemen, we have here on the table two distinctly different types of gas masks." He picked one up. "This one is gray. It is known as the M5-11-7 Assault Gas Mask, or the Combat Service Gas Mask. It was carried by our troops when they landed at Normandy. But it is inherently and irremediably flawed."

He waited, trying to see if the import of what he had just said had hit home. But before he could determine this, Sergeant Lupe farted. Normally, this would have unnerved the average speaker, but not Lieutenant Fuller who occasionally bestowed the same indignity upon others. In fact, he hardly noticed it and instead soldiered on as if nothing out of the ordinary had occurred.

"When this mask is subjected to cold temperatures it develops a condition called 'cold set' which will cause its neoprene rubber masking to crack. Three of the men in Sergeant Gomez' First Platoon were injured while undergoing gas mask training. They were using this mask, and I believe their masks failed because of the 'cold set' problem. So the bottom line is: never ever use this mask in gas mask training other than to demonstrate how a gas mask should be put on and taken off." He looked around. The men were listening. He had their attention!

"The M5-11-7 was taken out of service by the United States Army in 1947. There should be none around here, but apparently there are. They were replaced by this mask." He held up the other mask so the men could see it.

"Notice, it's black. It's the E48. This is the only one your men should be using for insertion into the tear gas shack." He was about to continue, when Captain Schtung entered.

"Ah! Good morning, gentlemen. A pleasure to see you hard at work, particularly you, Lieutenant Fuller. I see the masks. A little training. That is good." Having said this, he retired to his office and closed the door.

Lieutenant Fuller had a pleased look on his face. As just confirmed by Captain Schtung, he had been right to initiate this training session. He had almost finished. He was thumbing through his working papers when Sergeant Lupe raised his hand.

"Yes, Sergeant," Lieutenant Fuller said.

"Sir, I gotta go."

"Of course, Sergeant. We shall break now." With that, Sergeant Lupe bolted out the door.

"Sir," Sergeant Sack said.

"Yes, First Sergeant?" Lieutenant Fuller answered.

"The platoon sergeants have to get back."

"Yes, of course, First Sergeant. And I believe we've covered most of what I wanted to cover."

Overhearing this, the three remaining platoon sergeants exited the room.

***

Alone with Lieutenant Fuller, Sergeant Sack said, "Sir, I think you did a credible job, all things considered."

"Do you indeed, First Sergeant?"

"Yes, sir. And I have the two letters of commendation you requested. You might want to sign them now so I can give them to Sergeant Gomez later today. He'll hand them out to Billington and Rosen."

"Great, First Sergeant. I had almost forgotten about the letters."

"By the way, sir, your fatigue shirt?"

"What about it?" Lieutenant Fuller said.

"It appears to belong to someone else, sir. The name tag on it says 'Harvey.'"

"Well it sort of belongs to me because my neighbor in the BOQ told me I could borrow it. So in a way it's mine."

"If it were me, sir, I wouldn't be wearing that shirt because Captain Schtung is a stickler about someone not wearing things with someone else's name on them."

"That's where he and I part company, First Sergeant. Unlike gas masks, names are unimportant. But since he's my superior, I shall accede to his foibles."

"Makes sense, sir," Sergeant Sack replied. "One more thing, sir."

"Yes, First Sergeant?"

"Those airborne wings on the shirt: you never went through airborne training, did you?"

"Not precisely, First Sergeant."

"Well, sir, I'd suggest that you not wear that shirt not only because it has someone else's name on it, but also because you didn't precisely go through airborne training."

"I'm not so sure that's the thing to do, First Sergeant," Lieutenant Fuller said. "I did seriously think about going into the airborne at one time."

"That certainly sheds some new light on whether you're authorized to wear that shirt, sir. But I think I'll leave the matter in your hands."

"Good thinking, First Sergeant," Lieutenant Fuller said in perhaps the most pompous voice he had used all day. "And now, if you'll excuse me, Private La Droop and I have scheduled a performance evaluation behind the OR."

"Of what, sir, if I may ask?"

"Oh, we're evaluating the Swiss Army Pocket Knife. If it proves to be as effective as we believe it is, I intend to propose that it become standard issue for our troops."

"Right, sir," Sergeant Sack said shaking his head in disbelief. "I'm certain the Quartermaster General will appreciate that."

"Exactly what we think, First Sergeant," Lieutenant Fuller replied.

Chapter 27

Apartment 4D, 97 Central Park West, New York City, New York, Thursday, 25 May 1950, 2015 Hours.

Moe Schwartz was a night person. Without question, he did his best thinking at night. His wife and servants knew better than to disturb him after the dinner hour. But on this particular evening Moe had made an exception. He had scheduled a meeting with two business partners, his brother, Sammy, and Louis Rosen. At his request, the latter had flown in from Chicago. Sammy had picked him up at LaGuardia a short while ago and at the moment the two were on their way back to Moe's apartment.

Moe was seated in a red leather winged armchair in his study reading a particularly challenging work on the life of James Madison, the fourth president. He had been thinking about Madison: a great writer, thinker, and legislator, but a total flop as president. In his view, Madison was about as practical as tits on a goose when it came to running the country. His obsession with the embargo as a cure-all was absurd; and, besides, he'd gotten us into that stupid-ass War of 1812.

Moe heard a knocking at the door to his study. "Yes," he called out.

Sterns, a tall elderly Englishman who served as Moe Schwartz' major-domo, opened the door several inches. "Sir," he said. "Your brother and Mr. Rosen are here."

"Show them in," Moe replied, laying down his book. "And while you're at it, bring us some tea."

The door opened. Sammy and Louis Rosen entered, and Moe Schwartz rose to his feet.

"Leibel," he said warmly, "thanks so much for coming. I really felt we had to meet on this. We gotta make a decision. And I wanted to bring you up to date."

The two shook hands as Sammy stood by.

"Not a problem, Moe. I always have things to do in your city." He smiled and then sat down. "So tell me what this is about, because all I know is that it involves our cash cow."

"It does. And it also involves your son who, in a way, recently made his bones."

Hearing that, Sammy started laughing.

"Billy killed someone?" Louis Rosen said in disbelief.

"Well not exactly. But he sure showed us he's a chip off the old block. And he may even have saved our asses."

"Billy's in basic training at Fort Leonard Wood, Missouri. There's gotta be a mistake…"

"We know exactly where he is," Sammy interrupted. "And there's no mistake. Louie, you're gonna love this: Your kid just cut our income by a third."

"Christ, boys, stop talking in riddles, will you!" Just then Sterns entered carrying a tray.

***

"See," Sammy began, "a couple days ago a guy by the name of Baldwin calls and leaves a message with our answering service that he needs to speak to someone at Furax. I call him back. He's one of the Fort Wood company mess sergeants our guy down there, Harley Lutz, has been doing business with. I'm supposed to know all about each of them, but I never heard the name 'Baldwin' before…which tells me that maybe Lutz is stealing from us. Anyhow, Baldwin is pissed. Says he hasn't been able to get hold of Lutz, that Furax owes him $275, and that he wants his money. I tell him 'thanks,' 'sorry about the money,' and that I'll send it to him ASAP. But then I also tell him I'm concerned about Lutz because he hasn't checked in with me in over two weeks. This is like opening a floodgate, because now I'm able to get Baldwin to tell me everything he's found out. And here's where your kid comes in, Louie." Sammy reached for a glass of tea, spooned some strawberry jam into it, and took a sip.

"Seems Baldwin is the mess sergeant in Billy's company. This doesn't particularly surprise me 'cuz we got deals at just about every mess hall down there. Anyhow, Baldwin tells me that about two weeks ago Billy and one of his buddies, a kid named Foggerty, are on KP. They're finishing up at the end of the day when Harley shows up for a pickup. Billy's inside and Foggerty's out back. Apparently Foggerty smells a rip-off because he tells Harley he's not letting any stuff out the door without proper authorization. Harley tries to talk him out of it, but Foggerty won't budge. So Harley coldcocks him. That's when your son shows up. When he sees what's happened to his buddy, he knocks Harley down and forces him to leave.

"Now what impressed me is that I know this guy Lutz. He's a big palooka, bodybuilder. And he can be a mean son of a bitch. I wouldn't wanna tangle with him. Anyhow, Billy did. I guess he didn't wanna let his buddy down." Sammy and Moe looked over at Louis Rosen. They saw he was smiling.

"But that ain't the whole story. Seems when Billy had Harley pinned down he talked to Foggerty about calling the MPs. But then he decided not to. Instead, he just told Harley to take off, come back in the morning and clear the pickup with Baldwin. This may have saved our entire operation at Wood, Louie. If it'd been me, I probably would'a called the MPs…or reported this thing. But Billy didn't do nothin' like that."

Moe looked over at Louis Rosen. "Leibel, your son know anything about Furax?"

Louis Rosen shook his head. "I never discuss business with him. No, wait a minute…I did ask him to look up the meaning of 'furax' at the library a few days after you first showed me our stationery. But that was more than two years ago."

"So if Billy heard the name 'Furax' mentioned in that scuffle it might have alerted him to a possible connection with you, right?" Moe looked over at Louis Rosen. The latter was silent.

"Maybe, Leibel, that's what happened. Maybe that's why he didn't call the MPs and told Harley to take off instead."

"I don't know," Louis Rosen said. "I guess we'll never know the answer to that."

"Tell me this, Leibel. If Billy knew you were connected with Furax would he have tried to protect you?"

Louis Rosen thought for a long while. He felt himself beginning to choke up. Then he nodded. "There's this strong bond…"

"That's okay, Leibel," Moe said. "It's special, isn't it? The way we feel about our kids. And the way they feel about us."

Louis Rosen bowed his head.

"Jesus! Let's not have you guys start goin' soft on me," Sammy said. "'Cuz we gotta decide what to do about Harley. The more I think about it, I'm positive the guy's been pickin' our pockets. And we've been good to him."

"What's to decide?" Louis Rosen replied. "I say whack him."

"I agree, Leibel," Moe said. "And we won't replace him 'til your son and this Foggerty have left Fort Wood."

***

Several days later when Louis Rosen was back in Chicago he received a phone call from Sammy Schwartz.

"On that Harley Lutz thing, Louie. He's in the morgue in Cairo, Illinois."

"Nice work, Sammy."

"Yeah, but not ours. Somebody else beat us to the punch."

Chapter 28

Reception Area, Office of the Commanding General, Second Training Regiment (Basic), Room 400, Headquarters Building, 270 Constitution Avenue, Fort Leonard Wood, Missouri, Thursday, 1 June 1950, 1325 Hours.

General Haslett's aide, Captain Jess Martin, was seated at his desk in the Reception Area of the Office of the Commanding General, Second Training Regiment (Basic), reading the current edition of the *St. Louis Post-Dispatch* which, along with the *New York Times*, the *Washington Post*, the *Boston Globe*, the *Chicago Tribune*, and the *Los Angeles Times*, made up the background material he used in preparing the General's daily news briefing. This day he found the world events particularly disturbing on three counts:

First, in Yugoslavia, Marshall Josip Broz Tito, who had been thrown out of the *Cominform* two years earlier by Stalin, had been irritating the Russian dictator. Captain Martin felt certain it was only a matter of time before this resulted in an invasion by the armies of the Soviet puppet state Bulgaria.

Second, Stalin and his armies seemed to be lusting for a communist takeover of Turkey and Iran. War there appeared inevitable.

And third, Russia had concentrated an unnecessarily large number of troops in East Germany, far more than was needed for occupation and administrative purposes. Captain Martin also felt certain that this boded ill.

He took a sheet of typing paper from a drawer in his desk, inserted it in his typewriter, and began to type. He had just completed the first paragraph when General Haslett returned from lunch.

"You eaten yet, Jess?" General Haslett asked.

"I'm gonna pass, sir. I've decided to resign from the 'tight pants club.' I figure if I cut back by just a hundred calories a day, that's three thousand per month, which means I'll lose a pound a month. That way I'll be outta the club in about a year and a half."

"We'll see how that plays out," General Haslett said, chuckling.

He was just about to enter his private office when Captain Martin said, "Oh, sir, Colonel Harkavy called. Wants to speak to you. You have his number?"

"Got it, Jess. I'll call him right now. Thanks." With that, the General pulled the door to his office closed.

Seated at his desk, General Haslett thought for a moment. Obviously, Harkavy was calling about that recruit, Rosen. He'd be wanting to know how his special training was going. General Haslett picked up the phone and dialed Fourth Battalion headquarters. Approximately two seconds later a voice came on the line.

"Fourth Battalion HQ, Colonel Paulson speaking, sir."

"Jon, since when do you answer the battalion phone?"

"Oh, General," Lieutenant Colonel Paulson replied. "Sorry, sir. Everyone here is out except me. Sergeant Williamson should be back in five to ten minutes. What's up, sir?"

"Jon, Ken Harkavy called. Wants me to call him. Before I speak to him I probably should have an update on Rosen."

"Glad you called, sir. I'd been meaning to speak to you because there is some news which you probably should be aware of. Shortly after Rosen was injured during his gas mask training, which you know all about, he and another recruit, Private Craig Billington, each received a Letter of Commendation from Schtung's exec, Lieutenant Fuller, for taking the initiative and bulling their way out of that tear gas shack with a fire ax. Fuller of course doesn't know anything about what's going on with Rosen, General."

"Interesting," General Haslett said. "Anything else I should know, Jon?"

"Well, sir, let me see. Only other thing I can think of is that Rosen has been tolerating the harassment fairly well." He paused. "I think that's about it, sir."

"Thanks, Jon," General Haslett said as he hung up.

Then General Haslett leaned back in his large desk chair, closed his eyes, and tried for a moment to picture the young soldier who had dined at his home more than three weeks ago. But all he could remember was a mildly amusing spat the boy had gotten into with Chris, how he had put her in her place, and how, also, he had defended the military. And, in addition, General Haslett distinctly remembered coming away from that dinner liking the young recruit.

General Haslett reached for the telephone.

***

"Colonel Harkavy's office," a female voice answered on the third ring.

"Hi there, Mildred," General Haslett said.

"Good afternoon, sir," Mildred replied, immediately recognizing the General's voice. "Colonel Harkavy has been waiting for your call. Just a moment and I'll fetch him."

General Haslett could hear the phone being put down on a hard surface. A moment later Colonel Harkavy came on the line. "Afternoon, sir," he said.

"Hi, Ken. I'm returning your call."

"Thanks, General. I appreciate it. I'm calling about Rosen, sir. How's he holding up?"

"I anticipated your question, Ken. In fact, I just got off the horn with Jon Paulson. Seems Rosen and two other soldiers were injured during gas mask training when their masks leaked. But Rosen's okay. He and one of the other two used a fire ax to force their way out of the tear gas shack. Jon tells me that Schtung's exec, a Lieutenant Fuller, gave them each a Letter of Commendation for their quick thinking. Second, according to Jon, the harassment hasn't bothered Rosen all that much. He's taking it fairly well. That's about it, Ken, except maybe there's one other thing you should know."

"What's that, General?"

"Well, through no fault of mine or his, I spent several hours with Rosen."

"How could that be, General?"

"If you'd ever met my seventy-two-year-old mother-in-law you'd understand, Ken. She was in the Base Library having difficulty carrying some books. Rosen was also there and offered to help. She had him walk her home and next thing I knew he was having Sunday dinner with us."

"Did he know who you were, General, and did he know that you knew all about him?"

"My answer to both your questions, Ken, is 'No.' I think he knew I was an officer—maybe a general—but that's about it."

"So what did you think of him, sir, if I may ask?"

"You know, Ken, I found him surprisingly likable. Maybe even charming. At dinner he had a chance for a few minutes to tell us what he thought of the armed forces, and I was impressed by what he had to say. He's very savvy and knows our country would be in trouble without a strong military. Yes, I definitely liked him."

"Did he say anything about his harassment, General?"

"Not a word, Ken. That also impressed me."

"Anything else, sir?"

"Not really, Ken. I guess we all liked him. That was about it."

"Well, General, you're probably not gonna go along with what I'm about to say, but I've been doing a lot of thinking about Rosen, sir, and I honestly feel I haven't been hard enough on him. So this is what I propose—and I recognize it's pretty drastic. But given the circumstances, I think it's warranted."

Colonel Harkavy then told General Haslett what he had in mind for Private Rosen. General Haslett listened without saying a word. After Colonel Harkavy had finished, there was an uncomfortable silence. Then General Haslett spoke up.

"Dammit, Ken, what you're proposing is God-awful. This is a decent young man, for Christ's sake. He's just another draftee. What you wanna do is clearly out of bounds. Leave him alone, Ken!"

"No can do, sir," Colonel Harkavy replied. "With all respect, General, he's not just 'another draftee.' Far from it, he's extraordinarily exceptional, and I've gotta make sure he's much more than just a nice guy; or, to use your term, 'likable.' I've got to make sure he's one tough son of a bitch capable of withstanding the most vicious of onslaughts."

"Well, Ken, you said it. I didn't. What you're proposing is precisely that, 'the most vicious of onslaughts.' This whole thing stinks. If I could, I'd order you to put an immediate end to it. But I can't. So what I want is out. Now. I want out of the loop, Ken.

Whatever you do, you do without my participation or blessing. And I don't want Jon Paulson involved either. I guess I understand where you're coming from but, frankly, I think you're completely out of line. To put it in simpler terms, Ken, I think you're being a first class prick."

"You're probably right, General, but in my arena nice guys finish last."

"So tell me, Ken, how do you propose to work this thing now that Jon and I are no longer involved?"

"Well, sir, I'll just have to spend a little time with Rosen's CO, Captain Schtung. Perhaps invite him up to Chicago for a little talk."

"Well two things, Ken. First, don't have Schtung contacting Jon or me in connection with your nefarious plans. And second, Schtung's not exactly a pushover. I'm not so sure he'll cooperate."

"We'll see, sir. And believe me there's nothing personal in any of this. I've got a job to do, and I'm just doing it the best I can."

"Sorry to say this, Ken, but I think you've really gone overboard."

***

After he'd hung up, General Haslett felt overcome by a certain profound sadness. No person, least of all Billy Rosen, deserved this kind of devastating shit in his life. But General Haslett knew that his hands were tied, that there wasn't a damn thing he could do about it.

Chapter 29

***The Grill Room, Williston House Hotel,
Chicago, Illinois,
Sunday, 4 June 1950, 1210 Hours.***

Seated at a corner table in The Grill Room, an upscale restaurant in one of Chicago's finest hotels, the Williston House, Captain Emil Schtung, CO, Company B, Fourth Battalion, Second Training Regiment (Basic), couldn't remember when he'd felt more ill at ease. Not only did the thought of having a protracted Sunday lunch with some bird colonel he had never met make him uncomfortable, but he now realized how inappropriately dressed he was for the occasion: his dark blue woolen suit, which he hadn't worn in two years (when he'd been eighteen pounds lighter), barely covered his massive frame, and he was unable to fasten even one button of its suit coat; the starched collar of his white shirt, although buttoned, was badly creased and one point was bent at an ungainly upward angle; and his floral-patterned necktie, which he had acquired in the mid-40's, measured more than four and one-half inches across at its widest point and was obviously very much out of style when compared with the narrower foulard patterns currently in vogue.

By contrast, Colonel Kenneth Harkavy, Captain Schtung's host, appeared completely relaxed as he sat across the table from Captain Schtung. He was flawlessly attired in his freshly pressed officer's pinks and greens. On the left breast of his tunic were four rows of ribbons. They included, among many others, the Distinguished Service Cross, the Silver Star, the Bronze Star with two Oak Leaf Clusters, the Purple Heart, and the French *Croix de Guerre*. By itself, centered, and immediately above the first row of ribbons there was another ribbon, this one blue in color with tiny white stars in it. Captain Schtung had never seen it before except pictured in books and magazines. It was the nation's highest military decoration, the Medal of Honor. It warranted a salute from persons of all ranks and bestowed upon Colonel Harkavy the right to apply for and receive a special lifetime pension of $200 per month.

"Find something on the menu?" Colonel Harkavy asked, looking up at Captain Schtung.

"Not yet, sir," Captain Schtung replied.

"Say, Captain, I've got a request. You were kind enough to accept my invitation to come up to Chicago for this luncheon, and what we're going to be discussing isn't strictly army business. What it amounts to more than anything else is that I need a little help from you. So, under the circumstances, I'd like you to call me 'Ken,' and, with your permission, I'll call you 'Emil.'"

"Of course, Ken," Captain Schtung replied, feeling a bit better already. He liked the idea of being on a first name basis with someone like Colonel Harkavy.

The waiter approached. He was holding a small notepad in one hand and a pencil in the other. "Have you gentlemen decided?" he asked.

"I'll have a shrimp cocktail, followed by your minute steak, rare, french fries, and an Edenbrau beer," Colonel Harkavy said.

"Very good, sir," the waiter replied. Then, turning to Captain Schtung, he said, "And you, sir?"

Captain Schtung was in fact ravenously hungry. He had gotten up at 4:00 AM so that he could catch the 5:45 AM "milk run," a military C-47 flight from Forney Army Air Field at Fort Leonard Wood, to Chicago's Midway Airport with an intermediate stop at Lambert Field in St. Louis. From Midway he'd taken a bus to the Loop, Chicago's downtown area, and from there he'd taken a cab to the Williston House located on the Near North Side. On the plane he'd had two cups of black coffee, but nothing else. And Fritzi, his wife, had been sound asleep when he'd left home so he hadn't had breakfast.

"I'll have your Dover sole," he said. "And instead of beer I'll have a glass of white wine. Do you have anything along the lines of a Liebfraumilch?"

"Certainly, sir," the waiter replied. "We don't carry a large stock of Liebfraumilch, but I believe we have some excellent vintages."

"How about one from the Rheinhessen region?" Colonel Harkavy asked, turning to Captain Schtung.

"I believe we have that," the waiter replied.

"That's a damn good Liebfraumilch, Emil," Colonel Harkavy said.

"Fine, Ken. I'll certainly go along with your recommendation since I'm far from being a wine connoisseur." Captain Schtung was pleasantly surprised, perhaps even flattered, that Colonel Harkavy was extending himself in this manner. He had seldom experienced such attention, not even from Fritzi.

"Then let's have that one, waiter," Colonel Harkavy said.

The waiter nodded, and was about to leave when a gentleman in a tuxedo who seemed to know Colonel Harkavy came over to the table. It was Roberto Calderas, the maître d'.

"Ah, Colonel Harkavy," Roberto said, "as always, so good to see you. How have you been?"

"Just fine, Roberto, and you?"

"No complaints, Colonel. And have you ordered?"

"We just did, and your colleague here," Colonel Harkavy motioned toward the waiter, "is doing an excellent job."

"Good," Roberto said. "And is there any way I may be of service, Colonel?"

"Everything's fine at the moment, Roberto. But please meet my good friend, Captain Emil Schtung. He runs a basic training company down at Fort Leonard Wood. He's one of the Army's best."

"'Schtung,'" Roberto said, cupping his chin in his right hand. "I've heard that name before. Why yes, of course." Turning to Captain Schtung, he said, "You captained the Wisconsin football team some years back, didn't you, sir?"

Captain Schtung nodded.

"Well I had the distinct pleasure of watching you play. I happen to love football, and you're a great talent."

Captain Schtung was smiling.

"If you'll allow me, Colonel, The Grill Room would like to host your beverage selection today for two reasons. First, The Grill Room is honored to have someone like Captain Schtung, a former All-American, with us. And, second, The Grill Room wishes to congratulate you, *General*." Roberto turned to Captain Schtung and winked.

"Is that right, Ken?" Captain Schtung asked, somewhat surprised.

"'Fraid so, Emil. The senate confirmation hearing on my first star is scheduled in a couple of weeks. They say it's pretty much a formality. So Roberto is probably correct."

"Congratulations, *sir*," Captain Schtung said, suddenly unable to continue calling Colonel Harkavy "Ken."

"Thanks," Colonel Harkavy said.

"With your permission, Captain, I would be pleased to offer you a bottle of our finest champagne, Williston's Private Reserve. With our compliments, naturally."

Since he wasn't quite sure how to respond, Captain Schtung looked over at Colonel Harkavy.

"Bring the bottle on over, Roberto," Colonel Harkavy said. "Emil and I will figure out a way to dispose of its contents."

"My pleasure," Roberto said, smiling.

***

"Well, here's to you, Emil," Colonel Harkavy said, raising his champagne glass.

"And to you too, sir," Captain Schtung replied as he swallowed the contents of his glass in one gulp. Colonel Harkavy reached over, took the glass, and refilled it.

"Again, Emil, I can't tell you how much I appreciate your making this trip to Chicago. I know it's a damned imposition, particularly on a Sunday."

"That's okay, sir," Captain Schtung replied, finishing his second glass of champagne.

"So Emil," Colonel Harkavy said as he poured Captain Schtung a third glass of champagne, "in the strictest confidence lemme tell you what I need. I'm hoping maybe you can help me."

"I'll try, sir," Captain Schtung said.

"There's a youngster in your company by the name of Rosen. Know him, Emil?"

"Yes, sir, I do. I was ordered by the Battalion CO to ride him pretty damn hard, and I'm having my first sergeant do that. I personally don't know him all that well, though."

"That's okay, Emil. Here's what we've got." As he spoke, Colonel Harkavy noticed that Captain Schtung's glass was empty, so he filled it again.

Captain Schtung picked up his glass. And as he sipped the champagne, a pleasant easy feeling came over him. He couldn't help wondering whether this was how a woman felt when a man had designs on her.

"Rosen comes from a wealthy family," Colonel Harkavy continued. "They, and people they know, have been putting a lot of pressure on the powers that be in the Army for special privileges and special treatment for Rosen. He's getting to be…" Colonel Harkavy paused, "well, sort of a pain in the ass. I think the Army would be better off without him. But we have no reason to discharge him. And that's where you come in. I'd like you to create a reason."

"Such as?" Captain Schtung said, somewhat puzzled.

"Well, here," Colonel Harkavy said, reaching down for a file which had been resting on the floor against his chair leg.

"This is Rosen's 201 File. I had my secretary call down to Wood and request it from the Second TRB's Assignments Section a few days ago." He opened Billy's file.

"If you take a look at this," he said, pointing to the page containing Billy's interview report, "you'll see the notation '4F'."

Captain Schtung looked and nodded.

"Well the story I get is that on the day he came into the Army, Rosen claimed that he had a bad left foot, the result of an injury in his teens. This was true. You'll see that in the medical report in the file. He tried to get out of the Army using this as an excuse. But his interviewer didn't buy off on that primarily because Rosen was an excellent cross-country runner in college. That's what that notation '4F' is all about. The interviewer apparently determined that this was a bogus excuse, and Rosen was inducted."

"So what you're telling me, sir, is that Rosen tried to bullshit his way out of the Army?"

"That's what appears to have happened, Emil. And, ironically, that's what I think will be our reason for getting him the hell out of the Army. Think you can figure out a way to use this to put maximum pressure on him so that he'll fold, go AWOL, or maybe even have some kind of breakdown? 'Cuz then we can discharge him."

"I know precisely how to handle dishonesty, sir," Captain Schtung replied. "As you may know, I was raised in Germany.

We had a very effective way of dealing with liars in school, and I think what you've told me amounts to lying. I also happen to know Rosen is one helluva runner based on what my first sergeant has told me—which confirms that his excuse was a goddamn lie."

"That's the way I figure it, Emil," Colonel Harkavy said as he poured Captain Schtung a fifth glass of champagne. "So tell me how you propose to handle this."

Captain Schtung explained to Colonel Harkavy how harshly liars were dealt with in his youth and how he proposed to handle Private William Rosen—*only even more harshly*.

"Pretty much what I had in mind, Emil," Colonel Harkavy said after hearing Captain Schtung out. "I doubt that Rosen will be able to stand up to that, particularly coming from his cushy background and all, but we'll see. And, oh yes, one more request, Emil. Can we move on this immediately? Could you take care of this when you get back tonight?"

"I guess so, sir, so long as I can have the first sergeant in there with me."

"Why would you need him there?" Colonel Harkavy asked.

"Sort of a show of solidarity, sir."

"Good point, Emil," Colonel Harkavy said. "So please get on with it as soon as you can."

"Will do, sir," Captain Schtung said, swallowing his fifth glass of champagne.

***

Captain Schtung and Colonel Harkavy were standing outside, next to the curb, immediately in front of The Grill Room's main entrance. Colonel Harkavy was holding the 201 File in his left hand as he and Captain Schtung shook hands.

"Emil, it was a real pleasure. Have a good trip back. And keep me posted on this Rosen thing, will you?"

"Certainly, sir," Captain Schtung said, his voice sounding just slightly slurred.

"One more thing, Emil. Take Rosen's file back with you, will you? No hurry, but when you get back to Fort Leonard Wood have it delivered to the Assignments Section."

"Glad to, sir," Captain Stung said, taking hold of the file. Colonel Harkavy noticed that Captain Schtung's hand shook slightly as he grasped it.

"Oh, by the way, Emil, I've arranged for your transportation back to Midway." Colonel Harkavy turned and motioned to the doorman. He nodded and made a gesture with his right hand. Almost immediately a long black Cadillac limousine drove up, and its chauffeur got out.

"Paul, meet Captain Emil Schtung."

"How do you do, sir," the chauffeur said to Captain Schtung. "Colonel Harkavy tells me your plane is at 4:00 PM out of Midway, so I think we'd better be on our way."

Captain Schtung had never ridden in a limousine. He couldn't wait to tell Fritzi.

"Thank you, sir," he said to Colonel Harkavy. Captain Schtung climbed into the limousine holding the file. Paul closed the door behind him. Then Paul got into the driver's seat.

As the limousine drove off, Colonel Harkavy turned and walked back into the restaurant. Roberto was waiting just inside the doorway.

"Roberto, my friend," Colonel Harkavy said, "you missed your calling. You're a born actor. Lemme pay and get the hell outta here."

"Thank you, Colonel," Roberto said. "Always a pleasure."

"Say Colonel, are those medals for real?"

"'Fraid so," Colonel Harkavy said.

"Jesus! Then how come you never wear them."

"Rob, I'm not much into medals. What I'm really into is that star I'm getting in a few weeks. Worked all my life for it. You can't imagine what it means to be a general officer in my line of work."

"Well then," Roberto said, "congratulations really are in order."

"I suppose so," Colonel Harkavy replied.

"In that case, Colonel, your lunch is on the house."

"Hey thanks," Colonel Harkavy said. "And even though you deserve an Oscar for your brilliant performance today, how 'bout this?" Colonel Harkavy handed Roberto a ten dollar bill.

A few minutes later Colonel Harkavy exited The Grill Room. From his inscrutable expression it would have been difficult to know just how pleased he really was. His luncheon with Captain Schtung had been a complete success on all fronts. Soon he would know the strength of the fabric from which Private William Rosen was cut, *a fabric which Schtung had promised to stretch to its absolute limits before the day ended.*

Part II

From Banishment to Resurrection

Chapter 30

***Furnace Room, First Platoon Barracks,
Company B, Fourth Battalion,
Second Training Regiment (Basic),
Fort Leonard Wood, Missouri,
Sunday, 4 June 1950, 2350 Hours.***

Billy Rosen sat disconsolately on his bunk in the half-lit furnace room. His cheeks were streaked with dried tears of anger and frustration. When his world had come crashing down less than an hour ago he had been devastated. And now Schtung's ranting rang in his ears:

"You! You are not fit to live with these men, to eat with them, to march with them, to soldier with them. And, because of that, you shall not be allowed to have any contact with them. I will not permit you to despoil them."

Billy remembered trying to defend himself—and Schtung's ugly response branding him a "goddamn liar" and ordering his banishment.

Billy began coughing uncontrollably. "Probably the soot, ash, and dust in the air," he thought.

He felt exhausted and deflated. He knew his body and mind needed rest. But first he had to get away from the furnace room's foul air.

With every ounce of strength he could muster, he dragged his bunk outside into the cold night. Then, shivering and coughing, he stretched out on it, pulling the thin GI blanket up over him, eventually falling into a deep sad sleep.

Chapter 31

Outside the Furnace Room, First Platoon Barracks,
Company B, Fourth Battalion,
Second Training Regiment (Basic),
Fort Leonard Wood, Missouri,
Monday, 5 June 1950, 0330 Hours.

It was pitch black and the air was chilly when, at 3:30 AM, Sergeant Sack walked over to the furnace room to which Billy had been banished a few hours before. He was carrying a flashlight and he had come by to make sure Billy was okay. He felt certain he was just about the only person around, aside from Velma, who even slightly cared about Billy's well-being.

Earlier, when he'd gotten home, which had been shortly after midnight, he and Velma had discussed at length what had occurred and, in particular, what had caused Captain Schtung to go off the deep end. Velma pointed out to her husband that even if what Captain Schtung had said were true, his punishment of Billy was not only long after the fact, but outrageously excessive. After all, Velma had said, kids try to duck the draft all the time.

They both agreed that it must have been something extraordinary which had prompted Captain Schtung into going after Billy. They also concluded that the Captain had obviously not been playing with a full deck.

"Hey, kid," Sergeant Sack called out in a loud whisper, "it's me, Sack. You okay, Rosen?"

Sergeant Sack waited a few minutes, but there was no response. He quietly pushed open the furnace room door. There on the floor was Billy's footlocker, but no bunk.

"Christ," Sergeant Sack thought, "he's fuckin' gone AWOL. Shit!" Then he heard it: a heavy coughing sound coming from outside and behind the furnace room. He closed the door and walked over to where he thought the sound originated. Ten feet from the rear wall of the building he saw what appeared to be the outline of a bunk. He turned on his flashlight, pointing it in the direction of the bunk. He could just barely make out a sleeping figure lying under a blanket. Cupping his hand over the lighted end of the flashlight, he walked over to the bunk.

"Hey, Rosen, you okay? It's me, Sack."

The figure stirred, and Sergeant Sack heard a weak groan.

"Rosen, it's me, Sack. You okay? Just came by to check up on you." Sergeant Sack took his hand away from the end of the flashlight and shined the beam down onto the bunk. To his horror, he saw Billy lying on his stomach under a thin GI blanket. His eyes were closed, his head was turned to one side, and his mouth was open. *Next to it there was a large pool of dark congealed blood.*

"Aw shit!" Sergeant Sack wailed as he sank to his knees. "What happened, Billy? Dammit, please tell me. I gotta know so's I can help. Please, Billy, speak to me. Lord God!"

Although weakened by loss of blood and the chill of the night, Billy seemed to understand that there was someone nearby trying to help; but in his present state he wasn't able to think clearly. "Couldn't breathe in there. Bad air. Nose and throat injured." But that was all he could say.

"I understand, kid," Sergeant Sack said. "We're leaving. Fuck the Army and all the rest of this." He made a sweeping gesture with his hand. "Hey, Billy," he said, "you're gonna be okay. I promise. Swear to God!"

Cradling Billy in his arms, Sergeant Sack carried him over to his parked car, gently placed him in the back seat, and drove off.

Once on the road, Sergeant Sack began to think. He knew his army career was probably over, but he really didn't give a shit. He hadn't much liked himself for what he'd done to Private Rosen over the past weeks, even though he'd been acting under orders. Maybe extending help today would constitute some small recompense. He hoped so not only for Billy's sake but for his own as well.

Chapter 32

Room 3420, Base Hospital,
Fort Leonard Wood, Missouri,
Monday, 5 June 1950, 1135 Hours.

A nurse and a physician stood beside an occupied hospital bed located in Room 3420 at Fort Leonard Wood's Base Hospital, one of the four corner rooms with two windows (and therefore one of the most desirable) on the hospital's third floor. To the best of the nurse's recollection, Room 3420 had never been occupied by a member of the enlisted ranks, let alone a lowly basic training recruit. However, the nurse in this case just happened to be one Velma Sack, a senior nursing supervisor, and her patient was Private William Rosen, someone both Nurse Sack and her husband, Master Sergeant Sherman C. Sack, considered very special to say the least. "Sad," Velma reflected, looking down at the sleeping figure in the bed, "that this boy couldn't appreciate this room." Translated, what Nurse Sack was referring to was the fact that when Private Rosen had been admitted earlier that morning he had been only semi-conscious and so damn sick he wouldn't have known the difference between a posh corner hospital room and a foxhole.

"So how's the patient doing, Vel?" Colonel David M. Stone, MD, asked.

"Much better, Doctor," Velma replied. "But thank God he arrived when he did. We've already given him four units of blood."

"I think your thankfulness is slightly misdirected, Vel," Dr. Stone said. "If I were you, I'd be thanking your husband, not the good Lord. After all, he was the one who brought him in. Probably saved that boy's life."

Dr. Stone walked over next to Billy and placed the chest piece of his stethoscope on the center of his chest. Then he moved it to various locations. Finally, after several minutes, he said, "Everything sounds okay to me."

"So what do you think, sir?" Velma asked.

"Let's continue as we are now," Dr. Stone replied. "I expect he'll be up and about by tomorrow or the next day. But I'm not discharging him for at least a week to ten days, maybe longer. And I obviously don't want him around a furnace room or any other dust-filled environment for quite some time. His throat and nasal passages have got to be given a chance to heal. We were doing just fine until he was moved into that furnace room." Dr. Stone paused.

"And, by the way, Vel, whose brilliant idea was that?"

"Can't say, sir," Velma replied, trying to avoid answering.

"C'mon, Vel. I need an answer. I have to know who was responsible for that order. This boy could've died, you know."

Velma looked up at Dr. Stone helplessly.

"Well, okay, Velma. Who's his CO, because he'll sure as hell know?"

"He's in my husband's company, sir. Company B, Fourth Battalion."

"We both know that, Vel. *Who's the CO*?"

"Captain Emil Schtung, sir. But, please, you didn't hear that from me." She looked at him pleadingly.

"Well you know I didn't, Velma," Dr. Stone replied.

***

Dr. Stone was seated behind the large desk in his office. He pushed a button on the intercom.

"Carrie," he said to his secretary, "please, as soon as you can, get Captain Emil Schtung on the phone for me. He's CO of Company B, Fourth Battalion, Second TRB."

Within a minute the intercom buzzed. "He's on the line, sir."

Dr. Stone picked up the phone. "Captain, this is Colonel Stone from the Base Hospital. Thanks for taking my call. I'd like you to come on over here as soon as you can. One of your recruits was admitted earlier today. He was a damn sick puppy when he came in, and you and I need to talk. I hope you'll be able to drop by within the hour." There was a pause. Then Dr. Stone said, "His name? It's Private William Rosen. I have his Serial Number if you need it." There was a second pause. Dr. Stone said, "Excellent," and hung up.

***

Approximately forty-five minutes later Dr. Stone's intercom buzzed. "Sir, Captain Schtung is here."

"Please send him in, Carrie," Dr. Stone replied. He rose as the door opened and Emil Schtung entered. Colonel Stone had never seen anyone quite as large from side to side, and he wasn't at all sure the Captain would fit into one of his pull-up chairs.

"Please have a seat, Captain. This shouldn't take long, and I know you're busy. But I felt a face-to-face meeting was important, given my patient's condition."

Captain Schtung forced his way into one of the chairs. Colonel Stone heard it creak as its two arms were pushed outward to their limit. When he was finally seated, Captain Schtung looked up at Colonel Stone. "Colonel," he said, "before we begin, I've a favor to ask."

"Of course, Captain."

"I've had a splitting headache all day. Aspirin doesn't seem to help. Could I get something stronger?"

"Not a problem, Captain. Just a moment." Colonel Stone reached into the center drawer of his desk and withdrew a bottle. "Here, Captain. Try two of these. They've got some Codeine in them which I'm sure will help. They'll take effect in a matter of minutes." As he passed the bottle to Captain Schtung, Colonel Stone noticed that his eyes were bloodshot and his hands shook. "Christ!" he thought. "The man's suffering from a Class A hangover."

Captain Schtung opened the bottle, poured out two pills, and immediately swallowed them, not bothering to ask for water. Then he sat back, closed his eyes for a moment, and began to think about where this meeting with Colonel Stone was heading. So far the Colonel had been more than cordial, so he figured it was safe to assume that the meeting was not intended to be confrontational. He therefore decided to dispense with all preliminaries. "Sir," he said, "I suppose you know that Rosen is a serious disciplinary case?"

"Hadn't heard that, Captain. But currently he's my patient, and my job is to see that he recovers, not that he's disciplined."

"Certainly, Colonel," Captain Schtung replied.

"So, Captain, I suppose you know a bit about my patient's medical background?"

"Not particularly, sir, other than he has a bad left foot and also that he was subjected to an overdose of tear gas a short while ago."

"Yes," Colonel Stone said. "The tear gas: that's my concern. He was recovering nicely until he was ordered to move into that furnace room. The dirt and dust particles in the air raised havoc with his nasal passages and his airway from his throat on down. He had a series of bad coughing spells. This induced severe bleeding and he's lost a fair amount of blood. So far he's been transfused with four units."

"I gave that order, sir. But I had no idea it would cause him physical harm. I'll see to it that whatever discipline is imposed in the future doesn't place him in harm's way. Frankly, my goal is to usher him out of the Army as soon as I can, not injure him. So far as I'm concerned, he's no damn good."

"That's interesting, Captain. I do know him because I treated him a while back and my impression was just the opposite. But then again I'm only a doctor, not a company commander." Colonel Stone hesitated for a moment. "If you would, Captain, could you possibly share with me what's going on, because it sounds pretty serious?"

"It's absolutely no secret, Colonel. Rosen attempted to lie his way out of the Army at the time he was being inducted. Specifically, he claimed he had a bad left foot which is true. He said he was entitled to a 4F classification because of it. But it didn't work. I'm told his interviewer knew he was a cross-country runner in college, and, if you'll pardon my language, didn't go for his bullshit. So he was inducted. That's really about it."

"Mind telling me where all this took place, Captain?"

"Not at all, sir. Chicago."

"Not good," Colonel Stone said, shaking his head. "I suppose you can back all this up?"

"I have it on the highest authority, sir," Captain Schtung said.

"Well, nevertheless, when he gets back to your company, which should be in about ten days to two weeks, you'll see to it that he is not placed in any environment that could damage his throat, his windpipe, or his nasal passages?"

"Absolutely, sir," Captain Schtung replied.

"Thanks, Captain," Dr. Stone said. "Pleasure meeting you. And I am sorry to learn about Rosen. He certainly had me fooled."

"He had a lot of us fooled, sir," Captain Schtung said as he wiggled free of the chair and lumbered out of Colonel Stone's office.

Chapter 33

Cafeteria, Base Hospital,
Fort Leonard Wood, Missouri,
Tuesday, 6 June 1950, 1145 Hours.

Because it was before noon, there was virtually no lineup at the hospital's cafeteria counter and Velma Sack was able to indulge in one of her great pleasures: the leisurely and deliberate selection of her day's lunch fare. By the time she approached the entrées with her two trays, she had on one of them a bowl (not a cup) of minestrone soup, a green jello salad, a large sourdough roll, some macaroni salad, a slice of carrot cake, and a large glass of chocolate milk; and, on the other, a cup of clear bullion and a large black coffee. Sliding her trays along, Velma stopped directly in front of a male cafeteria worker dressed in a white uniform wearing a chef's hat. He was standing behind a large wooden carving board on which a cooked tom turkey weighing over twenty-five pounds rested on its back beneath an amber floodlight. The man held a carving knife in his right hand and a large two-pronged fork in his left.

"Care for some turkey, ma'am?" he asked.

"I'm thinking about it," Velma replied. She hesitated. "Sure, why not? Give me an order, but white meat only."

"Dressing, gravy, and mashed potatoes?"

Velma nodded.

The man placed a helping of dressing onto a plate, carved two large slices of turkey breast and placed them atop the dressing, and scooped a healthy serving of mashed potatoes onto the plate as well, before smothering everything with thick rich turkey giblet gravy. As a final touch, he added a small paper container of cranberry sauce. Then, reaching out under a glass partition, he placed the plate on the tray with the bullion and coffee.

"Uh-uh," Velma said.

"Excuse me, ma'am?"

"Wrong tray." Velma said. "It goes on the tray with the food." She pointed. "I'm not the one on a diet."

Somewhat surprised, the man corrected his error, and Velma slid the two trays down to the cashier where she paid for both.

Then, after taking silverware and napkins for two from a nearby stand, she spied a vacant table at the back of the room. It took her two trips to bring her trays to it. She sat down and had just taken her first bite when Dr. Stone also sat down at the table, in the chair opposite her.

"Thanks," he said, positioning the tray with the bullion and coffee in front of him. He reached for a soup spoon and was about to begin when Velma's overloaded tray caught his eye.

"Velma," Dr. Stone said, "you never cease to amaze me."

"Why's that, sir?" Velma said, as she continued working away at the food spread over almost every square inch of her tray.

"Christ, shapely as you are, you can sure pack it away. I hate people like you. They never put on an ounce. What's your secret?"

Velma looked up. "Heavy exercise, sir," she said, smiling. "Sherman's got me in an exercise program. We work out regularly together. Builds up my appetite."

"Really?" Dr. Stone replied. "I knew there was a catch."

"You should try it, sir," Velma said.

"So when did you start this program?" Dr. Stone asked.

"On our wedding night, sir," Velma said. She was giggling. She looked up at Dr. Stone. He was blushing. "Lord!" Velma thought, "and he a doctor and all!"

"Well, Vel, I guess I understand. Only problem is I should be about twenty years younger." He saw that Velma was still laughing.

"Hey, Vel," he said, "how 'bout if I made your day? I think I've got some really nice news for you."

"What's that, sir?" she asked. She saw a look of triumph on Dr. Stone's face.

"Well, you know I read a lot of detective stories. I guess I've always wanted to be a member of Scotland Yard's finest, so I decided to do a little snooping into the Rosen matter on my own."

Now Velma was very interested. She put her fork down and began listening intently.

"Here's what happened. Shortly after you and I talked yesterday, I called Captain Schtung into my office. I thought I might have a hard time getting him to tell me about his involvement with Rosen's injuries, but it was just the opposite. It was almost as if he were bragging. He told me that he'd given the order banishing Rosen to that furnace room. He said he hadn't meant to physically harm Rosen, but that he wanted him out of the Army because he was no damn good. He said that he had it on the highest authority that at the time Rosen was inducted he tried to lie his way out of the Army by claiming he had a bad left foot which entitled him to be classified 4F. So I asked Schtung where all this took place, and he said Chicago. And that's all I needed."

"What do you mean, sir, 'that's all you needed'?"

"Well, don't you see, Velma, Schtung literally told me how to check this out. All I had to do was call the examining doctor in Chicago. Remember, this took place only a few weeks ago, right?"

"Yes," Velma said. "So you made the call?"

"Exactly," Colonel Stone replied. "You know how small the Army Medical Corps is. I know just about everyone in it, and I sure as hell know Doc Gunderson, the doctor who examined Rosen at the time he was inducted. So there's your proof."

"Proof? What proof, sir? All you've done is talk to the doctor who examined Billy. Where's the proof?"

Dr. Stone had been so absorbed in assuming the role of a methodical plodding detective that his train of thought had been derailed and, as Velma realized, he wasn't making sense. *"What did Dr. Gunderson tell you, sir? That's what I need to know. Please!"*

"Oh," Dr. Stone said. "Guess I forgot the good part, didn't I?" He took a moment to collect his thoughts. "Doc Gunderson and I go back a long way. He was a teaching fellow at Hopkins when I took my surgical residency there. That's where we met. He's smart as hell and we got to be pretty good friends. And after that we both became army docs, so our paths have crossed a number of times over the years. What I'm saying is that we're pretty tight." Dr. Stone stopped to catch his breath.

"Christ," Velma thought. "If he doesn't cut to the chase I'm gonna brain him."

"Anyway," Dr. Stone continued, "when I spoke to Doc it was like old home week. Then we got down to business. I told him that Rosen was a patient of mine and that I needed to know everything he knew about him. Doc said he remembered Rosen well because just a few weeks ago he'd discussed a condition Rosen had involving his left foot with three people: first with Rosen's orthopedist who treated him when he was a teenager; second, with the Induction Center's Sergeant Major, a guy named Wally Marks; and, third, with the Induction Center's CO, a Colonel Harkavy. He also said he handed Harkavy a typewritten memo about Rosen's foot in which he said that based on his conversation with Rosen's orthopedist Rosen probably should be 4F, but that he wanted Harkavy to interview Rosen and then decide. He asked Harkavy to reply in writing to the memo."

"Interesting," Velma said. "Do you think Dr. Gunderson has a copy of the memo he gave Colonel Harkavy?"

"Strange you should ask," Dr. Stone said, beaming. "When Doc and I spoke I asked the very same question. He told me he not only had a copy, but that on the bottom of his copy Colonel Harkavy had written in longhand that he'd offered Rosen 4F status and that Rosen had turned it down. So what do you think of that, Nurse Sack?"

"Doctor, you're amazing! You've done it. Billy is home free."

"Well not exactly, Vel," Dr. Stone said. "I haven't done it until I have a copy of that memo with Colonel Harkavy's handwritten comments on it in my hot little hands. You know, 'there's many a slip twixt the tongue and the lip.'"

"But that's only a matter of time, isn't it?" Velma asked.

"I hope you're right, Vel," Dr. Stone said. "As we speak, I think Doc is having his secretary run around the Loop trying to find a place that has one of those new-fangled copiers so he can get me a copy. I expect to see it in about a week or so. Think Rosen can wait until then?"

"I suppose so, sir. But in the meantime I can tell him, can't I?"

"I dunno, Vel. Let's assume you say something to him and then the word gets out about that memo. It's conceivable that the copy with Harkavy's original notation on it could conveniently disappear before our copy is made. I think we'd better play it close to the vest until we get that copy. I see a lot of disappointment on the part of that boy if we tell him and then our concrete evidence fails to materialize." Dr. Stone paused. "Why don't you just hold off on discussing this with anyone, even your husband, until the copy arrives. It'll just be a few days. Okay?"

"Well, all right, sir. 'Course we could ask Colonel Harkavy, couldn't we?"

"I don't think so, Vel. Something in my gut tells me not to be discussing this with anyone I don't know to be completely trustworthy. As I said, I know Doc well. I don't know Harkavy from Adam. And, remember, someone's behind all this nonsense."

"Okay, sir. I'll go along with that. I think Billy can survive for a few days without knowing."

While Velma was speaking, Dr. Stone noticed that she hadn't eaten a thing.

"Vel," he said, "I got some things to do in the hospital. But if you want, I'll sit with you until you finish."

"I'm done," she said.

"Done? You've hardly touched your food."

"I'm too excited to eat," Velma replied. "I just know Billy Rosen is on his way out of the woods…thanks to your outstanding detective work. How *do* you do it, sir?"

"Elementary, my dear Mrs. Sack, elementary," Dr. Stone replied in his very best British accent.

Chapter 34

Orderly Room Outer Area, Company B,
Fourth Battalion, Second Training Regiment (Basic),
Fort Leonard Wood, Missouri,
Wednesday, 7 June 1950, 1315 Hours.

First Sergeant Sherman Sack particularly enjoyed Mess Sergeant Ian "Cookie" Baldwin's lunch on Wednesdays: chef's salad with turkey, roast beef, ham, Swiss cheese, hard boiled eggs, and bacon bits, crowned with his mouth-watering thousand island dressing. Today had been no exception. His salad had not only been delicious and filling, but, in Sergeant Sack's mind, dietetic as well—because, after all, most of it was lettuce. Problem was, his perceived diet had taken a nosedive with dessert: brownies à la mode. He'd gone back for thirds. "Fuck it," he thought as he made his way back to the OR building, "we don't get brownies all that often."

As he mounted the steps leading into the OR outer area, Sergeant Sack reflected on his upcoming afternoon. In forty-five minutes all four platoons would be trucked off to the rifle range for their first day of actual firing of the M1. This would be an extremely important training session. Within ten days the men would be firing for qualification, as a Marksman, a Sharpshooter, or an Expert. And from among the Experts, six would be chosen to represent Company B in the battalion's inter-company rifle competition.

Once inside the OR outer area, Sergeant Sack was about to head for his office in the far corner where a stack of paperwork awaited his attention when something—or rather someone—caught his eye: Lieutenant Fuller. The door to the Lieutenant's office was open and Sergeant Sack could see that he was seated at his desk staring out into space, as if in a trance. On his desk there was a brown-jacketed file. Sergeant Sack watched for perhaps fifteen seconds, but Lieutenant Fuller didn't move. Sergeant Sack walked over to the doorway of the Lieutenant's office and peered in. Still no movement.

"Sir, sir," Sergeant Sack said. "You okay?" Lieutenant Fuller didn't respond.

"Sir, sir, are you all right?" Sergeant Sack said in a louder voice.

"Huh? Oh, yes, I'm fine, thank you." Lieutenant Fuller hesitated. "And why wouldn't I be, First Sergeant?"

"And why wouldn't you be?" Sergeant Sack thought. "Because you're fucking nuts! That's why!"

"No reason, sir. I just happened to notice that you appeared to be in sort of a trance. What's going on?"

"Why, I was just involved in some numerology."

"Pardon, sir. But what is *that*?"

"It's the study of numbers, First Sergeant. Numbers, you know, tell all."

"Like what, for instance, sir?"

"Ah, First Sergeant, that is the question, now, is it not?" Lieutenant Fuller paused, and then took the file that was resting on his desk and handed it to Sergeant Sack. "Like this file, for example."

"It tells all about this file, sir?" Sergeant Sack replied somewhat puzzled.

"Indubitably, First Sergeant. As I said, numbers tell all about us." Lieutenant Fuller smiled broadly.

"What are you talking about, sir?"

"Oh, please, First Sergeant, look at the file!"

Sergeant Sack glanced down at the file he was holding. He immediately recognized that it was a 201 File. Then he looked at the file tab: "Rosen, William NMI, ER16548889." He laid the file back down on the desk and was about to open it, when Lieutenant Fuller said, "Stop, First Sergeant. Listen to me."

Sergeant Sack looked up. "Wha..." But Lieutenant Fuller interrupted him.

"Before I begin the numerological analysis at hand, why don't we bring our CO in?"

"I doubt that this warrants his presence, sir," Sergeant Sack said, beginning to think that, as usual, Lieutenant Fuller had lost it.

"I disagree, First Sergeant. Please go get him. This will take at most two minutes of his valuable time."

"Your call, sir," Sergeant Sack said, leaving Lieutenant Fuller's office.

***

"Gentlemen," Captain Schtung said as he stood in front of Lieutenant Fuller's desk resting both hands on its desktop, "is this really all that urgent? I am preparing for the afternoon's marksmanship training, and you, First Sergeant, know how important I consider that."

"I do, sir," Sergeant Sack replied, "and you being in here is not my idea. It's the Lieutenant's. He wanted you in here before he proceeded with his numerology presentation." Then turning to Lieutenant Fuller, Sergeant Sack said, "Did I say that correctly, sir?"

"Indeed you did, First Sergeant. And sir," he said, addressing Captain Schtung, "please allow me a few minutes of your time so that I may proceed with my numerological analysis."

"Numer...what?" Captain Schtung said.

"Before you entered my office, sir, I told our First Sergeant here that I was engaged in a round of numerology. Numerology, as you undoubtedly know, is the study of numbers as it relates to the human condition. Specifically, sir, I was applying it to that file." He pointed to the 201 File on his desk.

"Sir," Sergeant Sack said, "that's Rosen's 201 File."

"What's it doing here?" Captain Schtung said. "Two days ago I specifically told La Droop to take it back to the Assignments Section."

"And that is precisely what he was doing when I intercepted it," Lieutenant Fuller replied.

"Dammit, Fuller, what right do you have messing with that file?" Captain Schtung asked with irritation.

"Every right, sir. Rosen is one of my men, and, from what I have learned, serious accusations have been leveled against him."

"Listen, Fuller," Captain Schtung said, his annoyance increasing, "the contents of that file and Private William Rosen are of no concern to you, so leave well enough alone if you know what's good for you! And by the way, you look like something the cat dragged in!"

While Captain Schtung was speaking, Lieutenant Fuller had nonchalantly rotated the wooden triangularly shaped name sign on his desk so that the side with his name on it was facing downward.

Now another side appeared to Sergeant Sack and Captain Schtung: "Genius at Work."

"Captain Schtung," Lieutenant Fuller continued, "am I not the executive officer of this company?"

"Big fucking deal," Captain Schtung snapped. "So what? What right does that give you to be messing in the Rosen matter?"

"Why, every right, sir. Subject to your supervening authority, he is, as I said, one of my men. But my greater duty is to protect you."

"You couldn't protect a gnat, Fuller. And I think I can pretty well take care of myself!"

"Perhaps you can, indeed, sir. But please hear me out."

"Okay, Fuller," Captain Schtung said. "But let's forget all the bullshit. What are you trying to say?"

At this point, Sergeant Sack was beginning to enjoy himself. He knew he would take pleasure in seeing Captain Schtung ream out this little turd.

"Simply this, sir," Lieutenant Fuller replied. "The chance that Rosen tried to lie his way out of the Army at the time of his induction is, I would conservatively estimate, no greater than one in ten million."

"Yeah, and how would you know that, Fuller?" Captain Schtung said. "Did you ever meet Rosen?"

"I have not, sir; nor do I need to, because, as I said, it's the numbers. They tell everything. You see, applying standard numerological principles, what Rosen has been accused of could not possibly have happened. Simply stated, it's an impossibility."

"Goddammit, Fuller, what are you talking about? What fucking numbers?"

"Why, here, sir, on the tab of Rosen's 201 File. Plain as the nose on your face."

Just then Sergeant Tom Blackman appeared at the open doorway. "Sir," he said, addressing Lieutenant Fuller, "we gotta make tracks for St. Louis if we're gonna be there for tonight's opening pitch. Remember, I gotta make a couple of stops before we get to the ballpark. Please, sir!"

"Gotta go," Fuller said. "I am, as you gentlemen are probably aware, currently involved in a significant management performance evaluation. Specifically, Sergeant Blackman and I are trying to determine what it is about Elmer Posley which causes his management style to be substandard." He got up, walked over to a coat rack, took his hat, and disappeared out the doorway.

***

"What a wacko," Captain Schtung said. "Any idea what numbers he was talking about, First Sergeant?"

"Only numbers I see are a part of Rosen's Serial..." Sergeant Sack stopped in mid-sentence. "Son of a bitch," he cried. "Goddamn that little fucker! He's right!"

"Right? What do you mean 'Right,' First Sergeant?" There was alarm in Captain Schtung's voice.

"Sir, take a look at Rosen's Serial Number!"

"ER16548889. So what?"

"Don't you see, sir?"

"No I don't, First Sergeant. What is it?"

"The 'ER' sir. The normal draftee's Serial Number begins with 'US.' But if you volunteer for the draft, you get an 'ER' Serial Number. Rosen obviously volunteered for the draft. What Fuller was saying in his round about way was that it's highly unlikely that someone who volunteers for the draft would try to lie his way out of the Army when he was inducted. And, sir, I'd have to agree with him."

Sergeant Sack saw that Captain Schtung's complexion had turned a ghostly shade of white and that beads of sweat were forming on his forehead.

"Sir," Sergeant Sack said, "I think you'd better sit down." He gently led Captain Schtung around behind Lieutenant Fuller's desk and the Captain collapsed into the desk chair.

"Sir, I've closed the door. Now I want you to start from the beginning. Tell me *everything*. I'll keep it strictly between us, but I have to know what in hell prompted you to accuse Rosen of trying to lie his way out of the Army."

"Harkavy, fucking Harkavy!" Captain Schtung screamed at the top of his voice. "He seduced me with his medals, his fancy lunch, all that champagne, his promotion to general in a couple of weeks, and that fucking limousine ride. He's the one. I'm gonna kill that son of a bitch!"

"Who's Harkavy, sir?" Sergeant Sack asked.

Captain Schtung paused. He was obviously very upset. Then he began. Speaking slowly, in a low shaky voice, he said, "Well, last Sunday I was asked to fly up to Chicago…"

***

When Captain Schtung had finished, Sergeant Sack took a moment to reflect.

"Sir," he said. "I don't want you feeling bad or foolish 'bout what happened with Harkavy. Man's a con artist. Truth is, if I'd been in your shoes I would have done the same thing." He saw that Captain Schtung was dejectedly looking down at the floor.

"What I'd suggest, Captain, is that we both take a deep breath and try thinking our way through this thing. How 'bout we give it, say, a week, maybe a little longer? By that time I'm pretty confident we'll be able to come up with a plan. Meantime, I don't think we should be discussing this with anyone, not even our wives. Okay?"

"Good, good, First Sergeant," Captain Schtung said with relief, although still extremely upset. "It just so happens Fritzi's out of town visiting family in Baltimore for the next week and a half. I certainly won't discuss it with her until she gets back."

"Perfect," Sergeant Sack replied. "One other thing, sir. Don't worry about Rosen. Lemme handle that. He's in the hospital for the next week or so—which means there's not much to be done for the moment. Only real concern I have is keeping him in basic. You and I know that if he's recycled Colonel Harkavy will con someone else into doing him in. And neither of us wants that."

"Exactly, First Sergeant. And I agree: from here on Rosen's your responsibility."

"Right, sir," Sergeant Sack said, getting up and opening the door to Lieutenant Fuller's office.

"Hey, La Droop," he called. Private La Droop appeared immediately. "Here," Sergeant Sack said. "This is Rosen's 201 File. Return it to the Assignments Section today or tomorrow at the latest."

"Will do, Top," Private La Droop replied, grasping the file.

Chapter 35

Third Floor Corridor, Base Hospital, Fort Leonard Wood, Missouri, Wednesday, 7 June 1950, 1930 Hours.

For the first time since his admission to Fort Leonard Wood's Base Hospital two days earlier, Billy was able to get out of bed and take a few short walks in the hospital's corridors. He felt weak and dizzy on his feet, and it still pained him to inhale and exhale; and his throat was sore, so damn sore, in fact, that he felt as if he had chugged a cup of scalding hot coffee. But he knew better. His fits of coughing in the furnace room had irritated his previously injured nasal passages and airway; that, plus the hemorrhaging that followed, had contributed to his current condition. Thank goodness Dr. Stone had assured him that this would all heal and that he would be fine, even though, as he said, it could take weeks, possibly months.

As he walked up and down the hospital's corridors, Billy pondered his predicament. He wanted to fight back, to prove his innocence, but in the barracks last Sunday night he hadn't been allowed to say one word in his own defense. So far as Schtung was concerned, he was guilty, and there was nothing more to be said. He knew he desperately needed help. "Maybe," Billy thought, "it was time to make one of those phone calls."

***

In the corridor adjacent to his room Billy lifted the receiver of a pay phone from its hook and dialed "O" for the operator. A voice came on the line. "This is the Long Distance Operator. How may I help you?"

"Hi. This is William Rosen. I'd like to place a collect call to Miss Chris Haslett in Northampton, Massachusetts, NO5-3097."

"One moment, sir," the operator said. A minute or so later Billy heard the phone ring and a female voice answer. "Warnall House, Sarah Childs speaking."

"This is the Long Distance Operator, ma'am. I have a collect call for a Miss Chris Haslett from a Mr. Rosen. Will she accept the charges?"

"Can you wait a minute, please?" Sarah Childs said. There was a minute or two of silence, and then she returned to the phone. "Operator, we can't find her, but we think she'll be back in about an hour. Please have the caller call back then."

"Did you hear that, sir?" the operator asked.

"I did," Billy replied. "I'd like to try another collect call, this time to anyone who will accept the charges."

"The number, sir?"

"In Rolla, RO4-7755."

"One moment, sir." Billy heard the phone ring, and again a woman answered.

"Good evening. The Boys, Inc. Rose speaking."

"Ma'am, this is the Long Distance Operator. I have a collect call for anyone from a Mr. William Rosen. Will you accept the charges?"

"You betcha!"

"There you go, sir," the operator said. "Have a nice evening."

"Thanks," Billy replied. Then he said, "Rose, I'm really sorry to bother you. This is important and I couldn't get hold of Chris."

"No problem, kid," Rose said. "Glad you called here 'cuz I wanted to get a chance to chat with you anyway. The Boys told me all about you."

"They did?" Billy said, somewhat surprised. "You know, we've never met?"

"Not to worry, babe. You're a friend of the Princess, so that means you're one of us."

"The Princess?" Billy said, slightly confused.

"Yeah, yeah, kid. You know, Chris Haslett. We just adore her 'round here, and any friend of hers is...well, tops on our list." Billy could almost feel Rose's warmth and good nature come across the phone line.

"So what's up, Billy Rosen? How can we help?"

"Rose, I'm in serious trouble. Sunday night just after lights out Captain Schtung, my CO, barged into the barracks and accused me of trying to lie my way out of the Army. He said that at the time I was inducted I falsely claimed I should have been 4F. He told the others in my Platoon to shun me, and then he had me moved into the barracks' furnace room where I was ordered to stay for the rest of basic. The air in there was so bad I had a series of coughing spells and I lost a lot of blood."

"Whoa! Slow down, kid," Rose said. "Let's backup and take it one step at a time. Where you at now?"

"In the Base Hospital. My first sergeant found me outside by the furnace room early Monday morning and brought me here. I'll probably be here for another week, maybe longer."

"And you say a Captain Schtung did this to you?" Rose asked.

"He's out to get me. Honestly, I wouldn't be calling if there were some way I could defend myself, but there isn't. He's convinced I'm guilty and he swore he'd make my life so miserable that I'd be begging for a dishonorable discharge. Last words he said were that he hoped that would be soon."

"And do you know why he thinks you tried to lie your way out of the Army?"

"I haven't a clue, and when I tried to explain he called me a liar in front of everyone in the barracks. He said he didn't want me around the others, that I didn't deserve to be a citizen, and that he wanted me out of the Army."

"Jesus!" Rose said. "Now what's this about you losin' all that blood?"

"Well three weeks ago I was injured during gas mask training. My nasal passages and wind pipe were burned by tear gas. They hadn't healed when I went into that furnace room. I guess when I breathed in all that dust, dirt, and soot something must have ruptured because I started hemorrhaging. So far they've given me four units of blood."

"Aw, Billy, that's terrible. Christ, I'm sorry," Rose said. "What's the prognosis?"

"My doctor, Colonel Stone, says I'll be okay, but it could take a while."

"Hey, kid," Rose said, "you just give us a few days, and we'll get everything straightened out with your CO. But you gotta do me one favor."

"What's that?"

"You gotta stop worrying and start concentrating on getting well. What room you in?"

"Room 3420."

“No foolin’! That’s VIP country, kid.” She paused. “Hey, Billy, you just sit tight. Figure on, say, around a week before things simmer down. Meantime, hang in there, and for God’s sake start getting better! Ciao.” Rose hung up.

Chapter 36

995 Lariat Lane, Rolla, Missouri,
Friday, 9 June 1950, 1900 Hours.

It was highly unusual for Frank and Johnny to be working on a Friday evening. This was particularly true of Frank who almost always was in St. Louis in temple at this time, breathing in the pleasant aroma of Missy Landsbauer. But despite custom, The Boys had been in their three-bedroom apartment, headquarters of The Boys, Inc., since Thursday evening, with only a few hours of sleep, engrossed in a special project they had started earlier that same day when they'd been on duty at Fort Wood in the Assignments Section's office. The project required not only their expertise, but also that of their secretary, Rose Applebaum. Finally, by the time Friday evening rolled around, they concluded that they had done just about everything they could do in connection with the matter at hand, namely, uncovering what in hell was going on with a certain Private William Rosen, otherwise known to them and to a very close friend of theirs as "Billy."

"You ready to pick up the extension?" Johnny asked Frank, "because I'm about to make the call."

"Yeah, go ahead," Frank said. "Lemme know when the operator comes on."

Johnny could hear the clicks as he dialed zero for the operator. Then he heard a voice come on the line. "This is the Long Distance Operator."

Johnny motioned to Frank to pick up the extension.

"Evening, ma'am," Johnny said. "I'd like to call Northampton, Massachusetts, NO5-3097."

"One minute, sir," the operator replied. Again, Johnny heard dialing. Then a voice answered.

"Hi, this is Sarah Childs."

"You're all set, sir," the operator said before leaving the line.

"Sarah, I don't think we've talked before. I'm Johnny Ludrakis, a friend of Chris'. My buddy, Frank Kaye, is also on the line. We're calling from Missouri and we need to speak to Chris."

"Hold on a sec' and I'll get her."

In less than ten seconds Chris came on the line. "Hi Boys," she said. "What's up?"

"Well, Princess," Frank said, "we think we've got some news for you. Wouldn't you say so, Johnny?"

"Yeah. For sure. And interesting too."

"I'm listening," Chris said.

"Well, you do know what happened to Billy, don't you?" Frank asked.

"I haven't heard a thing. Is there some kind of problem?"

"Yeah, a major league one," Frank said. He went on to describe in detail Billy's run-in with Captain Schtung in his barracks Sunday night, his banishment to the furnace room, his injuries, the hemorrhaging, and his rescue and hospitalization early Monday morning.

"My God!" Chris said, stunned. "Do you think my father's involved?"

"We don't know for sure," Johnny answered. "But all indications are he isn't."

"Princess," Frank said, "maybe you ought to jot all this down because there's a whole series of events that tie this thing together."

"I'm ready," Chris replied. "Go ahead."

"All right, then, here goes," Frank said. "First off, do you know that Billy tried to call you Wednesday night?"

"No. But come to think of it, Sarah did mention that someone called me collect when I was out. She didn't know who."

"Well it was Billy," Frank said. "And when he couldn't get through to you and it was too late to reach us at the Assignments Section he called Rose. He told her all about Schtung going after him late Sunday night, sending him to that furnace room, and how his first sergeant found him outside in the cold a few hours later and brought him to the Base Hospital where he wound up in a VIP room.

"After getting his call Wednesday night, we jumped right on this thing yesterday morning and we've been working it ever since. But about all we had for starters was that VIP room. Nothing else." Frank stopped to catch his breath before continuing.

"So we began by calling a guy we know who works at the hospital. He confirmed to us that Billy was brought in early Monday morning by his first sergeant, Sherman Sack. He's the one who's been riding Billy's ass since day one. Oops, sorry about that, Princess."

"That's okay, Frank," Chris said. "Just continue."

"Well, anyway, we couldn't figure out why Sack suddenly decided to make 'nice-nice.' But, assuming he's changed his tune toward Billy, then we think we know why Billy got that fancy room. It's probably because Sack's wife is a senior nursing supervisor and has a lot of clout at the hospital." Pausing to catch his breath again, Frank turned to Johnny.

"How 'bout you filling Chris in on what happened next?"

"Sure," Johnny said. "See, we knew where Billy was and we knew he'd be okay so long as he stayed in the hospital. We thought that maybe while he was there we could find some way of disproving Schtung's accusation that at the time of his induction Billy tried to lie his way out of the Army. That's when I called Wally Marks at the Chicago Induction Center."

"Who's he?" Chris asked.

"Wally's the top NCO there, a master sergeant. We work with him occasionally.

"Now you remember that we had Billy's 201 File here and you went over it in Captain Reston's office, right?"

"Right," Chris said.

"Well," Johnny continued, "shortly after that someone at the Induction Center asked us to send the file to them. So as a pretext, when I got Wally Marks on the line I told him I wanted the file back because I needed to know about Billy's physical condition for assignment purposes. I told him I understood that he had a bad left foot…which, of course, we knew a little about from what was in the file. And, guess what! I hit the jack pot. Wally said the file was on its way back to us. But, more important, he said he knew all about Billy's foot. He said that around the time of Billy's induction the examining doctor, he called him 'Doc Gunderson,' had spoken to him about it, and had also written a memo about it to Colonel Harkavy, the Induction Center CO. He said that Doc Gunderson felt Billy should be 4F but he wanted Colonel Harkavy to decide after interviewing him.

"Now here's the important part. Doc Gunderson insisted that Harkavy send one of the copies of that memo back to him with a handwritten notation on it telling Doc what the final decision was. I guess Doc wanted something in writing so that his backside would be covered if Billy was gonna go in the Army despite that foot. By the way, I got the impression from Wally that Billy's foot is pretty bad. Anyway, Wally said that Harkavy did send back a copy of that memo and in his own handwriting wrote on it that he offered Billy 4F status, and that Billy turned it down and asked to go into the Army as an EM."

"Wow! That's great!" Chris said. "All we need is the copy of that memo with Harkavy's comments on it and we can disprove Schtung's accusations."

"Exactly," Johnny said. "Only one problem. The copy has disappeared. Wally looked all over for it, but couldn't find it. In fact, he had me waiting on the phone for a while. Then he hung up so he could continue his search. When he called me back about a half an hour later he said it was gone. He thought maybe it might have recently been put into Billy's 201 File which is in transit to us."

"So it looks like all we can do right now is wait for the file and see if it's there?" Chris said.

"That's what we figured," Johnny said. "Frank, why don't you continue, because, Princess, there's more."

"Sure," Frank said. "Johnny's conversation with Wally Marks was around 11:30 AM yesterday. We went to lunch, and when we got back guess who's sitting on our doorstep?"

"Who?" Chris asked.

"Remember our little friend from Billy's company, Dewey La Droop, the gopher?"

"Not really," Chris said.

"Not important," Frank said. "Anyhow, La Droop is waiting for us. Of all things, he's got Billy's 201 File with him which he's been told to return to us. First thing I did was grab the file. I handed it to Johnny who began thumbing through it."

"Princess," Johnny said, "I swear I went through that file with a fine tooth comb and, dammit, the copy of that memo wasn't there. I knew finding it was a long shot, but, still, we were disappointed."

"Yeah," Frank said. "So lemme continue, because, remember, La Droop is still there. And here's where it really starts to get interesting. See, La Droop, just in case you don't know it, is a first class blabber mouth. And it seems that Wednesday while La Droop was in the company's OR, Schtung, Sack, and, the company exec officer, a real weirdo by the name of Barry Fuller, were all huddled in Fuller's office. The door was open and Fuller was speaking in riddles which everyone overheard but which no one could figure out. Then Fuller took off. That's when something caused the 'you know what' to hit the fan because Schtung started screaming and cursing about Harkavy and how he'd been seduced by his medals, a fancy lunch, champagne, his upcoming promotion to general in a few weeks, and a limousine ride. He even said he was gonna kill the son of a bitch. La Droop said the screaming was so loud that even if the door to Fuller's office had been closed you could'a heard it halfway across the company area." Frank stopped momentarily, trying to let Chris digest everything he'd said so far.

"So now Johnny and I are beginning to think that maybe it's Harkavy who's behind all this. And if I recall correctly, Princess, you told us you knew him, didn't you?"

"I've known him just about all my life," she said. "In fact, I call him 'Uncle Ken.' And this thing with Billy is absolutely not his style. I can't imagine that your friend—what was his name?—heard Schtung screaming 'Harkavy.'"

"Our friend La Droop swears the name he heard was 'Harkavy,' Princess. Right, Johnny?"

"Right. And after La Droop leaves, Frank and I figure it's time to go back to our apartment because we wanna get Rose involved. So we go there and then the three of us put our heads together, trying to figure out what to do next. Then Rose comes up with this stroke of brilliance. I guess you could call it feminine intuition. She figures that since it was pretty late last Sunday night when Schtung went charging into Billy's barracks like a madman that he had to be acting under some kind of a weird compulsion; otherwise he would have stuck it to Billy on Monday during normal business hours. In other words, Schtung couldn't wait; for some reason he felt he had to act immediately." Johnny paused, trying to collect his thoughts.

"The three of us then began to think about what it could have been that caused Schtung to act so impulsively, and we all came up with the same conclusion. Whatever it was that set Schtung off had to have occurred that Sunday, or a day or two before. So I gave Rose the job of finding out whether Schtung was up to anything unusual last weekend. And I think she hit pay dirt. Wait a sec' while I get Rose on the extension, because I want you to hear it from her direct."

***

"Hi Princess," Rose said. "The Boys are making some kind of a super sleuth out of me. I gotta tell you, it's been exciting. Johnny tells me you want to hear the results of my investigation."

"I do," Chris said.

"Well, for openers, I thought about what Dewey La Droop—I call him 'Little Dewey'—told us. You know, Schtung yelling about what Harkavy did to him…all that other stuff. So then I thought, 'Well, where is Harkavy?' And of course the answer is Chicago. 'So maybe,' I thought, 'Captain Schtung might just have taken a little trip up to Chicago last weekend where he met with Harkavy.' So I called over to Forney Field and spoke to Jeff Blatty and…"

"Whoa!" Frank said. "Better tell Chris who he is."

"Sorry, Princess," Rose said. "Jeff Blatty is the passenger scheduler at Forney. He has a record of passengers going back to the beginning of time. And he tells me that Schtung flew out of Leonard Wood early Sunday morning on the Milk Run to Chicago and came back Sunday evening. Bingo!"

"You guys are absolutely amazing," Chris said.

Smiling, Rose continued. "So anyway, now I gotta figure out what Schtung did in Chicago last Sunday. And I know this isn't gonna be easy.

"So what would you do, Princess?" Rose asked.

"I guess because La Droop mentioned that Schtung was screaming about a fancy lunch, I'd assume he went to lunch with Colonel Harkavy?"

"That's exactly what I figured," Rose said. "But proving it is something else. So let me tell you what I did. Remember that

Little Dewey mentioned that he heard Schtung screaming about a 'limousine ride'?"

"Yes," Chris said.

"Well how many Colonels have limos?"

"None that I know of," Chris replied.

"Same here," Rose said. "So what I figured was that the limo belonged to a limo service. That's when I picked up a Chicago phone book—which we just happen to have here in the apartment—and began making calls. The third call I made was to 'AA-Diamond Limousine Service.' And I got lucky. Seems a Colonel Harkavy hired a limo from them for Sunday afternoon. 'Who was the driver?' I asked. 'Oh, we can't give out that information,' the lady I was talking to told me. But then I said I was calling on behalf of the U.S. Army at Fort Leonard Wood and that we were looking for a missing file that might have been left in the limo. 'Oh, that's different,' the lady said. She put me on hold, and when she came back on the line she said the driver would call me in an hour or so. You with me so far, Princess?"

"Sure am. Go ahead, Rose."

"So about an hour later I get this call from the limo driver, a guy named Paul Stewart. He said he often works for Harkavy, and that he'd been instructed by him to be waiting in front of The Grill Room last Sunday at 1:00 PM to take someone to Midway. He said that at about 1:45 PM this huge guy, as wide as he was tall, wearing civilian clothes that hardly fit him came out of the restaurant escorted by Harkavy. They were laughing and Paul said that this guy was three sheets to the wind; that Harkavy poured him into the back seat of the limo, handed him a file, and then Paul carted him off to Midway for a four o'clock flight. Paul said that almost immediately after getting in the limo his passenger passed out. I checked, by the way, and the Milk Run back to Forney left Midway at 4:00 PM last Sunday. So from all this, we know that Schtung and Harkavy lunched together at The Grill Room last Sunday. Not bad, Princess?"

"Rose, you're the greatest," Chris said. "Is there more?"

"You betcha," she said. "I called the restaurant and spoke to the maître d', a guy named Roberto Calderas. He said he knows Colonel Harkavy well because Harkavy comes to The Grill Room often; and that last Sunday was special for Roberto for three reasons: first, he said Harkavy was wearing all his medals, and that Roberto never knew he had so many; second, he said he found out that Harkavy was being promoted to general in the next couple of weeks; and, third, he met one of the greatest college football players of all time, someone by the name of 'Emil Schtung,' a former All-American from the University of Wisconsin. Seems Roberto is wild about football. I asked Roberto about a file. He said that Harkavy was carrying it when he walked out of the restaurant with Schtung but that he didn't have it with him when he came back into the restaurant a few minutes later. And he also mentioned that Schtung, by himself, downed almost an entire bottle of Williston's Private Reserve champagne." Rose stopped to catch her breath.

"So that's about the end of my sleuthing. I'd say we know that Colonel Harkavy probably gave Captain Schtung a pretty good working over at that luncheon, but what exactly was said we'll never know. What we do know is that when Schtung got back to Fort Leonard Wood on Sunday night he marched into Billy's barracks and made those horrible accusations in front of everyone and then banished him to the furnace room. And I think we can pretty well conclude that all this was instigated by Harkavy. At least that's the way I read it."

"I'd say it all makes sense," Chris said. "Only problem I keep having is that it's definitely not Ken Harkavy's style." She paused for a moment. "Anything else?"

"That's about it, Princess," Johnny said. "At this point we're pretty sure we know what set Schtung off. But we really don't know what we should be doing other than looking for the copy of that memo."

Chris thought for a moment. "Boys, how 'bout if you let me think about all this for a while. Say, for an hour or so. If it's okay I'd like to call back?"

"Fine with us," Johnny said.

***

Exactly one hour later the phone rang in The Boys' apartment. Rose picked it up. "The Boys, Inc., Rose speaking."

"Just me again," Chris said. Then she heard the Boys getting on the line.

"We're on," Frank said. "Come up with anything?"

"I think I did," Chris said. "First, I think there's only an outside chance that we'll get hold of the copy of that memo. It's very likely that someone either destroyed it or is holding on to it. And even if we did get hold of it and cleared Billy of those charges, this wouldn't ensure that all this nonsense would end. What we have to do is pull this thing out by the roots. Second, we all seem to agree that Colonel Harkavy is behind this. It may be that he's doing someone else's bidding, but it sure seems like he's in charge. So getting him to stop probably will do a great deal of good, although it might not put a total end to all this if there are others involved. But I think for now it's about our best shot."

"Only thing is," Frank said, "I can't imagine how we're gonna get Colonel Harkavy to back off."

"Well, that's what I've been mulling over for the past hour. I'm gonna have to go speak to him myself…face to face. And the sooner the better."

"And what are you gonna say?" Frank asked. "Remember, he's a bird colonel and you're just a college kid. He thinks of you as his little niece from what you've told us."

"Here's what I'm considering," Chris said. Then she went on to describe her plan of attack.

"Hot damn!" Johnny said. "You're one tough cookie, Princess. Glad you're on our side."

"Look," Chris said, "this is not exactly some DAR badminton contest. This is hardball. Billy Rosen almost died because of all this. And I've never heard of anyone's integrity being impugned the way his was. Billy's a good person, and right now he's got to feel devastated."

"We'll get you your air tickets to Chicago and back," Rose said. "When do you want to do this?"

"I'll have to work around my exams. Let's say next Friday. I'll leave from Hartford-Springfield as early as possible that morning. First thing next week I'll call Harkavy's office and make a lunch date for 11:30 AM. That should give me plenty of time to catch a plane back to the East Coast at around 4:00 PM the same day. Our little meeting shouldn't last more than an hour."

"I'll make the reservations," Rose said.

"Do us a favor and get to Harkavy's office at least fifteen minutes early," Johnny said. "Then call us…just in case we have something else for you."

"Should I call the Assignments Section or your apartment?"

"Call the apartment," Johnny replied. "Rose will be waiting for your call. If there's anything else we wanna tell you, we'll make sure she knows."

"Perfect," Chris said. "And Boys…and Rose, thanks for everything. If we can pull this off I'll be indebted to you forever. And I know Billy will be too."

Chapter 37

336 Pippen Road, Waynesville, Missouri, Saturday, 10 June 1950, 0915 Hours.

Both Velma and Sherman Sack had the weekend off, and they had planned to have a picnic somewhere out in the boonies, although they weren't exactly sure where. Velma had spent several hours the previous evening making sandwiches, chili, and a sponge cake. Sherman had bought a bottle of especially good Chardonnay, and Velma had prepared a thermos of hot coffee.

"Sherman," Velma called, "you can start loading the car. The basket's ready to go."

As Sherman walked into the kitchen, he said, "Vel, I need to talk to you about something else. It'll only take a moment, but I need some help. Let's go into the living room."

***

Velma was seated on the couch and her husband sat in one of the two chairs positioned on the opposite side of the coffee table.

"Here's my problem, Vel. We started marksmanship training last Wednesday. And we're gonna continue on with it every day next week. Then a week from Monday the men start firing for qualification and..." But before Sergeant Sack could finish his wife interrupted him.

"So where does that leave Private Billy Rosen?"

"You got it, Vel. If he doesn't fire his M1, how in hell do I keep him in his basic training cycle?"

Velma frowned. What a shame if Billy had to start basic all over again, particularly after all the nonsense he'd already gone through. She thought for a moment. Then she smiled. She knew exactly what had to be done.

"Sherman," she said, "How 'bout trying something like this on for size: Supposin' you just happen to take Private Rosen on a little vacation down to the Ozarks. Say, to a dude ranch. And supposin' while he's there you let him play cowboy for a few days: you know, learn to shoot. Bet you anything his doctor would approve seeing as he feels his patient needs as much good clean fresh air as he can get. I know for sure his nursing supervisor would. Whaddya think of that?"

Sergeant Sack was starting to get excited. But then he realized he had a problem. "Jesus, Velma. What you're proposing is that I help this kid go AWOL."

"Sherman! For Christ's sake! For once will you forget your damn regulations and start being just a little creative. Who's gonna say Billy's AWOL? Captain Schtung? He might if Billy were back at the company; but he isn't, honey. He's officially assigned to the hospital where his doctor and his nursing supervisor will know exactly where he's at and when he'll be back. His first sergeant? C'mon, Sherman! That's you, baby!"

Sergeant Sack began thinking about his conversation with Captain Schtung in Lieutenant Fuller's office three days earlier—a conversation which he intentionally hadn't discussed with Velma—when the Captain had told him that Billy was his responsibility and how neither of them wanted him recycled. Could he possibly justify taking Billy away for a few days to get him qualified on the M1? He was silent for a moment. Then he smiled. "Sweetheart," he said, "you're a damn genius, you know that?"

"Sure do," she replied. "And, Sherman, this whole thing tells me something awful nice about you: that you're sweet as sugar being so concerned about that boy. And know what else, Sherman Cullum Sack?"

"What, Vel?"

"I love you very much, that's what. C'mon," she said, beckoning to him. Velma got up from the couch and started up the stairs.

"I thought we were going on a picnic?"

"We are, baby. But we're starting with dessert."

Chapter 38

Lori's Diner,
1612 St. Louis Street, Springfield, Missouri,
Tuesday, 13 June 1950, 1930 Hours.

Seated opposite Sergeant Sack at a window booth in a Springfield, Missouri, diner, Billy was having difficulty figuring out what was going on. Only adding to his confusion was the fact that Sergeant Sack was dressed in civilian clothes.

Earlier that day (at 4:50 PM, to be exact), forty minutes before the scheduled arrival of his dinner tray, something akin to a kidnapping occurred when Sergeant Sack burst into Billy's room at Fort Leonard Wood's Base Hospital and, in his own inimitable way, gently coaxed him into leaving: "Hey, Rosen!" he shouted, "get your ass outta bed, take off those pajamas, and put on some clothes!"

"Huh?" Billy replied.

"You heard me. Now!"

Then Sergeant Sack threw Billy's new uniform onto a table next to his hospital bed. It consisted of Billy's army combat boots, a t-shirt, a pair of undershorts, a pair of his khaki pants, and several other items of clothing Billy had never seen before including heavy socks, a pair of long underwear, a dark red heavy woolen shirt, and a rather well worn leather belt. Finally, Sergeant Sack took a U.S. Navy surplus black knit watch cap out of his pocket and jammed it onto Billy's head.

"Now, goddammit! We're movin' out! Get these on!"

As Billy looked up he noticed that there were two persons standing in the doorway of his hospital room, Colonel David M. Stone, MD, and Senior Nursing Supervisor Velma Sack. Both were laughing.

"Billy," Velma said. "Not to worry. I've decided that you and Sherman need to take a little vacation."

Billy thought for sure he was hallucinating or, perhaps, dreaming. A vacation with his first sergeant during his basic training? And sanctioned by his doctor and his nurse? Impossible!

Billy shook his head in disbelief, as if trying to clear it, but things didn't clear up. This wasn't a dream because Sergeant Sack, Senior Nursing Supervisor Velma Sack, and Dr. Stone were still there. Billy raised his hand to his head. The cap was still there too. And so were those items of clothing Sergeant Sack had tossed onto that table. Reluctantly Billy got up and, carrying the clothes with him, went into the bathroom. Ten minutes later he emerged fully dressed.

That had been a little over two hours ago. Since the time they'd left Fort Leonard Wood and, until his arrival at the diner, he'd been asleep in the back seat of Sergeant Sack's 1946 four-door burgundy Plymouth Special Deluxe.

Now, as Billy watched the chef in the diner's kitchen preparing platter after platter of cheeseburgers with fries, hot turkey sandwiches, buttermilk fried chicken, short ribs with lima beans, and t-bone steaks with hash browns, he realized he was getting hungry—in fact, very hungry.

***

As Sergeant Sack pushed his empty coffee cup to the far edge of the booth's table in an attempt to catch the waitress' attention, he turned to Billy. "Ever been to Springfield, kid?"

Billy nodded. "I remember visiting Lincoln's home and the State Capitol."

"Jesus, not that Springfield! Here. Springfield, Missouri, for Christ's sake!" He was about to continue when a waitress approached carrying a pot of hot coffee.

"Evenin', boys" she said. "Coffee?"

Sergeant Sack nodded, pointing to his cup and to Billy's. The waitress filled both.

"Aren't you dressed a little on the warm side, that wool hat and all?" the waitress said to Billy.

"You're probably right, ma'am," Billy replied as he reached up and removed his cap.

"Know what you'd like?" the waitress asked.

"Let's see," Sergeant Sack said. "How 'bout two t-bone steaks with hash browns and corn on the cob." The waitress nodded.

"How you boys like your steaks?" she asked.

Sergeant Sack looked over at Billy. "Well, kid?"

"Medium rare, Sergeant," Billy said.

"Same for me," Sergeant Sack said.

"Sergeant?" she said. "You all in the military or something?"

Sergeant Sack nodded. "On our way down to Arkansas, ma'am, on TDY."

"Well, you're always welcome here," she said. "My boy's an army captain stationed in Kitzingen, Germany."

"Know it well, ma'am," Sergeant Sack said. "They got a crooked tower there that looks like it's gonna topple over. My wife and I spent some time in a little town nearby, Wurzburg."

"No foolin'?" the waitress said. "I used to go shopping in Wurzburg when I was over there visiting my son."

Sergeant Sack smiled. "What's your boy's name, ma'am?" he asked.

"Jamie Billingsley."

"He in the MPs?"

"You know him?"

"Matter of fact, I do, ma'am. One of his men gave my wife a speeding ticket when we first got there. When he found out I had a few years in he just tore it up. 'In the interests of justice,' he said. Pretty nice of him, particularly since it would'a cost us a bundle in increased insurance premiums if he hadn't."

The waitress smiled. "I'm 'Lori' of Lori's Diner," she said.

"Thought you might be," Sergeant Sack said, extending his hand. "Lori, I'm Sherman Sack. This here is my friend, Billy Rosen. We work together." Billy nodded.

Lori smiled again. "Sherman," she said, "be sure and stop by here on your way back, will you?"

"We'll try," Sergeant Sack said. "And you be sure to say hi to Captain Billingsley for me. My wife and I still appreciate what he did for us."

***

Back in the car after they had finished dinner, Billy thought about Lori and how, when Sergeant Sack had asked for the check, she had come over to their booth and said, "Well, looks like Jamie started something with that ticket, so I guess I'll just carry on the tradition; dinner's on me. After all, we army people are all family, now, aren't we?" Then she had handed Sergeant Sack a brown bag with some sandwiches in it for the road.

"Nice having an extended family like that," Billy reflected. In a way, he felt that over the past few weeks he too had begun to accumulate new family members: people like the Sacks, Craig, Em, and Chris Haslett; perhaps even others he hadn't met, like the two Sergeants who called themselves "The Boys" and Rose, their secretary.

***

Still not understanding what was going on with what Velma had described as the "little vacation" he was to take with her husband, Billy reclined as best he could in the back seat of the Plymouth and almost immediately fell asleep again. And while he slept Sergeant Sack proceeded south on US 65 and, fifty-three miles later, crossed over into Arkansas. Some time after that the car slowed, awakening Billy. "We're comin' into a town," Sergeant Sack said.

Billy glanced sleepily out of the car's window. He saw a sign at the side of the highway illuminated by the car's lights:

PASSING SCHOOL ZONE

Still looking out, he saw four more signs appear in succession as they drove on:

TAKE IT SLOW

LET OUR LITTLE

SHAVERS GROW

BURMA-SHAVE®[5]

They were entering the town of Jasper. Thirty minutes later, at 11:10 PM, they arrived at what appeared to Billy to be a resort of some kind. There was a plain wooden sign at its entrance with "Elk Hill Dude Ranch" painted on it in white lettering.

Billy was able to make out several cabins. Sergeant Sack drove up to one of them, stopped the car, and motioned to Billy to get out. Billy saw Sergeant Sack enter the cabin and, almost immediately, a light came on from inside.

Chapter 39

Cabin #12, Elk Hill Dude Ranch, Jasper, Arkansas, Wednesday, 14 June 1950, 0630 Hours.

As the sun's rays crept up over the ledge of the window located alongside the lower bunk in which Billy was sleeping, they began to illuminate his face. Without awakening, he instinctively threw his right arm up over his eyes. But as the sun rose, his arm became less and less effective in blocking out its light. At precisely 6:42 AM he stirred; shortly thereafter he awoke.

Billy looked to his side. There, in the center of the cabin, he saw Sergeant Sack, who had obviously showered and shaved and was now fully dressed, reclining in what appeared to be a comfortable upholstered chair whose dark blue cushions were frayed and bleached. His feet were raised, and he was resting them on a companion ottoman. On his lap lying face down was a copy of an old magazine which he'd been reading. Sergeant Sack gazed over at him and smiled. Then he began to whistle "reveille."

After a few minutes, Sergeant Sack said, "Hey, kid, you been sawin' an awful lot of wood. You ever been told you snore like a trooper?"

"Sorry, Sergeant. I hope I didn't keep you awake."

"Not a problem, kid. I'm used to it. Remember, I'm married." Sergeant Sack laughed.

"Hey," he continued, "I put a paper bag with some more of your clothes in it on the shelf in the closet over there." He pointed. "Get your ass in gear. I want you to meet some friends of mine."

***

Billy and Sergeant Sack were seated at a large table made of hewn logs in the dining room of the ranch's main lodge eating breakfast. Jim Touhy, a tall thin sinewy man who appeared to be in his mid-forties and whose shoulders were unusually broad, sat at one end of the table; his wife, Nancy, a short slender slightly younger blonde woman was seated at the other. Sergeant Sack sat next to Billy on one side of the table, and Nancy's parents, Don and Virginia Ellsworth, sat opposite them.

"What a day!" Jim Touhy exclaimed with enthusiasm. "Bright; probably not too hot; nice breeze and a clear sky. Perfect day for teaching a youngster how to zero on in, wouldn't you say so, Sacko?"

"Hey, Tou," Sergeant Sack replied, "any day's okay with me if you're in charge."

Then turning to Billy, Sergeant Sack said, "Jim's probably one of the best shots I've ever met. Before he retired and joined the Arkansas National Guard, he was captain of the U.S. Army Pistol Team. They won all sorts of trophies. Pretty damn good with a rifle too."

Smiling, Jim said to Billy, "So I understand you need a little instruction in firing the M1?"

Puzzled, Billy looked over at Sergeant Sack. "You got it Tou," Sergeant Sack said. "That's why we're here. We've only got two days, and I need to have him qualify."

"In that case, we'd better get a move on," Jim said

"Go work your miracles, Major," Nancy said, making a "shooing" motion with her hands.

Then, turning to Sergeant Sack, she said, "C'mon, ol' buddy, grab some dirty dishes. As of right now you're on KP."

***

The rifle range at Elk Hill Dude Ranch located roughly one mile from the main lodge via a narrow bumpy dirt road resembled in almost every respect the rifle range of any U.S. Army training facility, with one exception: its pit was only large enough for two targets rather than a dozen or more. But otherwise, in terms of length and layout, it met all army specifications. Jim and Billy had driven to the range from the main lodge in the Touhys' World War II surplus Jeep. Billy sat in the passenger seat next to Jim, and in the back he noticed there were two leather gun cases and an olive drab metal army surplus ammunition container. There was also a large cardboard tube over six feet in length. When they arrived at the range, Jim opened the gun cases and extracted a well-oiled M1 Garand rifle from each. Then he took several bandoliers containing clips of

.30 caliber ammunition from the metal ammo container and handed one to Billy. Finally, he removed several paper targets from the tube.

"So, Billy, I understand you're familiar with the Garand. You know how to field strip it, detail strip it, and reassemble it?"

"Yes, sir," Billy replied. "We were taught to do all that blindfolded."

"How about blackening the sights, getting a proper sight picture, sighting in your rifle, the various shooting positions with and without the help of a sling, trigger squeeze, and breathing?"

"That could be a problem. I only learned about blackening the sights and adjusting the sling before I went into the hospital."

"Not to worry. I just want to get a feel for where we should be starting. One other question: How's your strength, particularly in your arms and torso?"

"I'm not really sure," Billy replied.

"Okay, we'll see," Jim said. "You right-handed?"

Billy nodded.

"Grab hold of this rifle. Place your right hand around the stock just behind the trigger guard and receiver, and place your left hand around the front hand guard."

Billy did as he was told.

"Now," Jim said, "when I tell you to begin, I want you to hold the rifle straight out in front of you parallel to the ground for as long as you comfortably can. Remember, it weighs over nine pounds so you may not be able to do this for very long. But, again, it'll give me an idea of where we're at." Jim paused, looking down at his watch's sweep second hand. "Okay, begin," he said.

Billy pressed the rifle out directly in front of him as instructed, while Jim concentrated on his watch. A little over three minutes passed and, finally, Jim could see the rifle beginning to quiver. "This is gonna be a cakewalk," he said. "But just so you won't worry, a good shooter doesn't strain when he's in the correct position. His bone structure supports the rifle, not his muscles. So if you're straining to hold the rifle steady, your position isn't right and we'll have to change it." Jim looked at Billy and saw he was getting through to him.

"By tomorrow evening you and the M1 will have become one. So listen to me now, and I'll tell you what, for want of better nomenclature, are the 'military secrets' to becoming a dead shot with what I consider to be the best weapon ever placed in the hands of a foot soldier; better, even, than the Springfield '03."

***

Jim had been talking and working with Billy for almost four hours, and, as he had done at Harvard, Billy was taking notes, not on paper but in his head. In addition, and although Jim didn't know it, before Billy had been in high school he'd done a fair amount of target shooting with a bolt action .22 rifle during the four summers he spent at a camp in Wisconsin, so he was somewhat familiar with Jim's explanations of the proper sight picture and shooting from the four positions required for qualification: prone, sitting, kneeling, and standing. But Jim's comments about sighting in a rifle were new to him and he found them fascinating.

First, Billy never knew that when you aimed a rifle upward or downward, no adjustment in the rear sight's elevation was required. In fact, he was surprised to learn that, with one exception, the only time there was an elevation adjustment was when the distance changed. The exception dealt with extreme light conditions. In bright light the shooter tended to aim slightly away from the light source, and in low light he tended to do just the opposite. This meant that in extreme light conditions either an elevation or a windage correction of the rear sight might be required.

Jim then asked Billy how he would correct for a shot group that was high and to the right.

"I suppose I'd crank in left windage and lower elevation?"

"Exactly, Billy. But how many clicks of each?"

"I'm not sure."

"Well, the M1 was designed to keep it simple, so it's the same for both: for every hundred yards, a single click moves the shot group one inch."

Next, Jim showed Billy how to calculate wind velocity. "With your back to the wind you grab a handful of dry leaves or dry grass. Then you drop it alongside where you're standing making sure your body doesn't act as a shield against the wind. To get the velocity, you estimate the angle between your body and where the stuff falls, and you divide that angle by four." Jim and Billy tested this, and Billy concluded that Jim's method was fairly accurate.

Jim then explained that if you knew the wind velocity you could determine the windage correction to the rear sight. The maximum number of required "clicks" of correction on the windage knob was equal to one tenth of the range in yards multiplied by the wind velocity. And whether you used the maximum number of clicks or only a few depended on the direction of the wind. Wind blowing from either the shooter's three o'clock or nine o'clock position required the maximum number of clicks; and as the direction of the wind moved toward the shooter's twelve o'clock or six o'clock position, the required windage adjustment became less and less.

"Finally, Billy, when you shoot for competition you'll get a chance ahead of time to zero in your rifle's rear sight for two hundred yards. Then it's no big deal once you understand the basics that we've gone over today to readjust it for other distances. And in combat the sight's generally set for three hundred yards, which is a fairly decent average distance."

"Okay," Jim continued, "I'm gonna assume for the moment that your rifle is properly sighted and that you're comfortable shooting from the four positions we discussed using either a hasty sling or a loop sling. This'll bring us to the two most critical factors in marksmanship: trigger squeeze and breathing. I'll go over them with you briefly now, and then I'd like you to practice them in unison for at least an hour. After that, I think we'll call it a day. Tomorrow, first thing, we'll begin shooting. By 1600 hours you should be ready for your qualification run."

***

Just before leaving the range, Jim said, "After dinner I'd like you to take a look at this." He handed Billy two printed pages. "A perfect score, all bull's-eyes, is 210; and I want you to start thinking about what's required to fire at least Marksman which is

140. That'll get you qualified on the M1 which, as Sacko said, is gonna be our goal tomorrow."

Billy took the handout. Later he would study it carefully, but for the moment he skimmed it:

Targets

Target A

Used for 200 and 300 yards and is a rectangle six feet high and four feet wide. It has a black circular bull's-eye 10" in diameter (value of hit = 5); an inner ring of 26" in diameter (value of hit = 4); an outer ring of 46" in diameter (value of hit = 3); and a border (value of hit = 2).

Target B

Used for 500 yards and is square, six feet in height and width. It has a black circular bull's-eye 20" in diameter (value of hit = 5); an inner ring of 37" in diameter (value of hit = 4); an outer ring of 57" in diameter (value of hit = 3); and a border (value of hit = 2).

Target D

Used for Sustained Fire and is square, six feet in height and width. It has in its middle a black silhouette 26" wide and 19" high representing a soldier in the prone position. The value of hits: in the figure, 5; in the space immediately outside the figure, 4; in the space immediately outside the 4 space, 3; and in the remainder of the target, 2.

Slow Fire

Range (Yards)	Time Limit	Shots	Target	Position	Sling
200	None	4	A	Kneeling	Loop
200	None	4	A	Standing	Hasty
300	None	4	A	Prone	Loop
300	None	4	A	Sitting or Squatting	Loop
500	None	8	B	Prone	Loop

Sustained Fire

Range (Yards)	Time Limit	Shots[*]	Target	Position	Sling
200	51 Seconds	9	D	Kneeling or Sitting from Standing	Loop
300	51 Seconds	9	D	Prone from Standing	Loop

Expert Rifleman..180

Sharpshooter..165

Marksman...140

[*] The rifle is loaded with one round initially, and reloaded with a full clip (eight rounds).

***

Back in the cabin at 7:00 PM after a long and exhausting day, Billy stripped off his sweat-soaked clothes. He wrapped a towel around his waist and sat down in the large upholstered chair that Sergeant Sack had occupied earlier that morning. He wanted a chance to think. He realized that tomorrow he'd be firing the M1 for qualification. The thought of this made him nervous. He knew he was obligated to do well, not only because Jim Touhy had spent so much time working with him, but also because the Sacks and Colonel Stone had stuck their necks out arranging his highly unorthodox leave of absence. In addition, Billy's nervousness was intensified by a nagging feeling of anxiety. Where did he stand with Captain Schtung? Was Schtung aware of this little outing? If not, and if he found out, would he accuse Billy of being AWOL? Sergeant Sack hadn't mentioned a word about his run-in with Captain Schtung, and Billy wasn't sure he should bring it up.

Billy got up from his chair and was about to enter the shower when Sergeant Sack came in.

"So, kid, how'd you do?"

"You won't believe this," Billy replied. "I didn't even fire off a shot. All we did was learn about the proper sight picture, shooting positions, sighting the rifle with corrections for factors like wind and light conditions, trigger squeeze, and breathing. And I even got a handout to study tonight which describes my qualification shoot."

"That's about what I figured would happen," Sergeant Sack said. "So tomorrow you'll put all the pieces together, start shooting, and then later on in the day you'll fire for qualification, right?"

"That's what Jim said I'd be doing," Billy replied. "But I'm confused. How will I actually be able to qualify?"

"Good question, kid," Sergeant Sack replied. "Tou's gonna write you up. He's got the authority seeing as he's a certified rifle instructor and currently a Major in the National Guard. Whatever you shoot will go into your 201 File."

Billy nodded. He was beginning to realize that the Army sometimes worked in strange—even unusual—ways.

"Lemme tell you something, kid," Sergeant Sack said. "You're learning it all the right way. In basic the other recruits only get lectures and group instruction. You're getting it one-on-one from the best there is."

"If what Jim has shown me works," Billy said, "I think I'll do okay."

"Guaranteed it will," Sergeant Sack said. "So let's get ready for dinner. I want you to turn in early tonight, because tomorrow's a big day. By the way, you got some earplugs?"

Billy shook his head.

"Well, I don't want your ear drums permanently damaged and your ears ringin' forever," Sergeant Sack said. He produced a small plastic box containing a set of shooters earplugs and handed it to Billy. "Better use these tomorrow. That M1 is a great weapon, but it's noisier than a goddamn cannon."

Chapter 40

Reception Area, Office of the Commanding Officer, U.S. Army Induction Center, Chicago, Illinois, Friday, 16 June 1950, 1110 Hours.

Chris Haslett should have been exhausted as a result of her seven-hour trip earlier in the morning from her two-bedroom suite in Smith College's Warnall House to the reception area of Colonel Kenneth Harkavy's office in downtown Chicago, but instead she felt energized. Her roommate, Sarah Childs, had been wonderfully supportive. She had gotten up with Chris at 3:30 AM and had driven her to the Hartford-Springfield Airport, some 48 miles from their residence hall. Then Chris had boarded the United Airlines DC-6 for her three-hour seven-minute flight to Midway. Finally, from Midway she'd taken a cab to the Induction Center. On the plane she'd had a chance to read through her notes and rehearse over and over again what she planned to say, each time honing her presentation. Chris knew she was ready for her upcoming confrontation with Colonel Harkavy in which she felt the life and good name of a very decent man were at stake—no matter that he happened to be someone she personally considered very special.

"Good morning, Miss Haslett," a lady who was obviously Colonel Harkavy's secretary said. "I'm Mildred. The Colonel will be with you in fifteen minutes or so. Would you like some coffee?"

"No thanks," Chris replied. "But I would like to use your phone."

"Certainly," Mildred said. "Over there on the end table next to the couch." She pointed.

It took Chris no more than a minute to place a collect call to the office of The Boys, Inc. As soon as Rose told the operator she would accept the call, she said "God, Chris, am I glad it's you. You won't believe what happened." Chris could sense excitement in Rose's voice.

"We got a copy of that memo with Harkavy's notes on it!"

Chris was stunned. "I don't believe it!"

"Apparently Billy's doctor here at the hospital, Colonel Stone, contacted the examining doctor right where you are now, Doctor Gunderson."

"But why?" Chris asked.

"All we know is that Doctor Gunderson had several copies made and mailed them to Dr. Stone. Carrie, Dr. Stone's secretary, brought one over to the Assignments Section around nine this morning and said Dr. Stone wanted it put into Billy's 201 File. Johnny gave it to me."

"Great," Chris said. "Can you read the memo to me, including the notes. I want to write it all down *verbatim*."

A moment later Chris was writing furiously.

***

At precisely 11:27 AM Chris Haslett walked into Colonel Harkavy's office. He was seated at his desk. He looked up. "Princess!" he said. "It's absolutely wonderful to see you."

He was about to get up when Chris went up to the front of his desk, leaned forward and, stretching, gave him a kiss on the cheek.

"Ken," she said, "you look great."

"I guess you've outgrown 'Uncle Ken' by now, haven't you?"

"Never, ever. I'm sure you'll always be my 'Uncle Ken,' and I'll always respect you, even after we've finished our little talk this morning."

"Talk?" Colonel Harkavy said. "I thought we were having lunch. In fact, I've made reservations at The Gascony Room."

"Lunch sounds great, Ken. But some other time. What I'm really here for is your help. I need your counsel with a problem I'm having."

Colonel Harkavy sensed that this little meeting involved something serious. "Sit down, Princess, and tell me what's on your mind."

"Ken," Chris said as she stared at him in what Colonel Harkavy sensed was anything but kindliness, "I want to request that you hear me out. Let me have my say before we get into any discussion, okay?"

Warning bells were sounding, and Colonel Harkavy was beginning to feel uncomfortable. "Sure, Princess, if that's what you want. Go ahead."

Chris drew a deep breath, and began. "A week ago Sunday night Private William Rosen—you and I know him as Billy—was mistreated in a way which, in my view, has brought shame upon the people involved as well as the Army as a whole. Not only was his integrity impugned, but he was physically abused."

At the mention of Billy's name, Chris could see a look of alarm on Colonel Harkavy's face. She saw his back arch slightly and his head rise up. She continued. "Specifically, his company commander, Captain Emil Schtung, barged into his barracks sometime after ten o'clock at night and accused him of trying to lie his way out of the Army at the time he was inducted right here at your Induction Center. Then Schtung banished him to a furnace room for the remainder of his basic training. Finally, he instructed the other men in Billy's barracks to shun him." Chris noticed a look of shock on Colonel Harkavy's face.

"Before all this took place Billy's nasal passages and airway had been badly burned in a tear gas accident. So when Billy went into that furnace room and inhaled its foul air—full of dust, dirt, and ash—he eventually began to hemorrhage. He lost at least four units of blood and probably would have died if his first sergeant hadn't found him early the next morning and rushed him to the Base Hospital…which, by the way, is where he's at right now."

By this time Colonel Harkavy's color had blanched, and he was beginning to perspire.

"Now, Colonel," Chris continued, "we—and there are a number of us—began to wonder what it was that prompted Captain Schtung to act so rashly. It seems he felt compelled to do Billy in that particular Sunday night. In other words, he was unwilling to wait even until Monday. And, after doing some investigating, we now know."

By now, Colonel Harkavy's demeanor had changed entirely. He had placed the palms of both hands on the surface of his desk as if to balance himself so he wouldn't topple over.

"Colonel, I can assure you we have done our homework. We know all about Schtung's little trip to Chicago that same Sunday; his luncheon with you at The Grill Room including all the gory details, such as his consumption of almost an entire bottle of Williston's Private Reserve champagne; and even the trip back to Midway courtesy of Paul Stewart and AA-Diamond Limo Service.

We even have a copy of the memo Dr. Gunderson sent to you on the day Billy was inducted, on which you personally wrote that you offered him 4F status which he turned down. That document, by the way, completely disproves all of Schtung's accusations. But most important of all, when Schtung apparently found out that what he'd accused Billy of was untrue, we have witnesses who overheard him screaming in anger to his first sergeant that he'd been seduced by you and your medals, your fancy lunch, the champagne, and that limousine ride. And Colonel, he even went so far as to call you a son of a bitch and say he was going to kill you."

Chris paused.

"Now, Ken, I understand that you will deny telling Schtung to go after Billy. But I'm afraid the evidence will weigh against you, what with Schtung's testimony as well as what happened to Billy. But of course it needn't go that far. All I want from you is your word—which I still value—that once I walk out of this office all this nonsense with Billy will stop. And I want to define what I mean by 'nonsense.' I have no objection to Billy Rosen being put on KP or guard duty, or things of that nature which any recruit would have to endure as a normal part of basic training. But what I do object to, and what must stop immediately, is any type of harassment which causes him to be treated differently or unfairly, which causes him physical harm, or which assaults his character. When I leave here you and I must have an understanding that these types of things are completely off limits. I feel certain that further elaboration on my part is unnecessary and that you understand perfectly well what I mean." Chris looked over at Colonel Harkavy. He had been listening intently. Then she said, "Your turn, Ken."

Colonel Harkavy's expression seemed to change. Chris could see a look of confidence return.

"Princess," he said. "I commend you and your friends on the investigative work you've done. And most of your facts are correct. For example, I readily admit that Captain Schtung and I had lunch together at The Grill Room the Sunday before last. But you're wrong about some things. First, though, let me respond about Billy, okay?" Colonel Harkavy smiled.

Chris nodded.

"Billy Rosen is an unusual young man. He and I spoke just before he was inducted, and, frankly, I liked him. I'm not quite sure what your involvement is with him, but whatever it is, he's exceptional. And I'm very pained to learn about his physical condition and that he has suffered a personal attack of any kind, including one on his character. And I sincerely hope that he's improved since his admittance to the hospital. Can you fill me in on this?"

"He's recovering nicely and, so far as I know, he'll be fine," Chris said. "I just don't know how long he'll have to remain in the hospital."

"Well, one solution I can suggest," Colonel Harkavy said, "is that he be given a medical discharge—which I think he deserves considering the fact that his physical condition has been aggravated by tear gas injuries and hemorrhaging. Don't you agree, Princess?"

Now Chris was getting angry. Colonel Harkavy was trying to stall, and she wouldn't buy it. "Colonel," she said, "cut the crap! You and I both know that Billy Rosen would never agree to the Army cutting him loose because of a medical condition. I have the papers to prove that at the time he was inducted he wouldn't; and he certainly won't now. So let's get to the bottom line, because I have a plane to catch. Are you or are you not going to call a halt to this. A simple 'yes' or 'no.' Because if you're not, I'll be contacting Ruth Walker, and I'll be seeing you in a few weeks. And here," Chris said, as she withdrew a piece of letter size paper from a manila envelope she was carrying, and thrust it at Colonel Harkavy.

Colonel Harkavy took hold of the paper and read it. It contained a list of names:

```
Private William Rosen
Captain Emil Schtung
Master Sergeant Sherman Sack
Master Sergeant Walter Marks
Colonel George Gunderson, MD
Colonel David M. Stone, MD
Velma Sack, RN
Sergeant First Class Manuel Gomez
Private Dewey La Droop
```

```
Private Craig Billington
Private Vincent Foggerty
Private Jerome Krazinski
Sergeant John Ludrakis
Sergeant Frank Kaye
Rose Applebaum
Roberto Calderas
Paul Stewart
Jefferson Blatty
```

"Princess," he said, although he was becoming exceedingly uncomfortable calling her that, "I don't understand any of this."

"Ruth Walker, Colonel, is Recording Secretary of the Senate's Committee on Armed Services and the list contains the names of the persons I intend to have the Committee subpoena as witnesses at the hearing on your promotion to brigadier general." Chris saw a look of surprise cross Colonel Harkavy's face.

"And yes, Colonel, I know about that too.

"Ruth tells me that normally these hearings are *pro forma*, that everything is automatically approved, unless someone requests otherwise. Colonel, if I walk out of here without that commitment I want from you, I will personally see to it that such a request is made. Furthermore, I'm going to assume that once each of these persons is called to testify under oath, he or she will tell the truth. And by the way, Colonel, in case you don't know it, your promotion hearing is in Room 253 of the Senate Office Building at 2:00 PM exactly two weeks from today." Chris stopped. She saw that what she had said was having an effect.

"Finally, Colonel, I am willing to tell you what I think each one of these witnesses will testify to, although in most cases you probably already know."

"No, Princess, I don't think that's necessary. And…" he hesitated for just a moment, "you've got my word. It will stop." There was a long tense pause.

"Thanks, Ken," Chris said, her voice softening. "When I walked in here I said you'd always be my 'Uncle Ken.' I meant it then, and I mean it now. I've always liked you. I know deep down you're a good person and that you felt there was some very compelling reason for doing what you did. I personally don't want to know what that reason was. It's none of my business. I'm just happy all of this is going to end for Billy. And just so you know it, I don't propose to tell him or anyone else about our little chat today, although I am going to tell Billy and a few others that this thing is now finally over."

Colonel Harkavy nodded. "Chris," he said. "May I ask one question?"

"Sure."

"What's your involvement with Billy?"

Chris smiled. "Colonel, you know my mother. But did you ever meet my grandmother?"

"Of course I know your mother; but your grandmother...well, let me see. I don't think I've ever met her. But I seem to recall she's from out West somewhere."

"She lives in Durango, Colorado. And the reason I ask is because, if you think about it, you'd realize that the women in our family are, for want of a better term, 'proactive.' We control the events that control our lives, at least as best we can. I have decided that, for better or worse, Billy Rosen is my man. In a sense, he belongs to me. Do you understand that, at least just a little?"

"I guess so, Princess," Colonel Harkavy said. "But does Billy Rosen know about this?"

"Not entirely, Colonel. But rest assured he will in good time." Colonel Harkavy could see that Chris was still smiling.

"Oh, and by the way, Colonel, here's something that may come in handy." Chris reached into her purse and withdrew a small black velvet box and handed it to Colonel Harkavy. "Use them in good health, Colonel." Before leaving, she extended her hand to Colonel Harkavy which he grasped.

"Don't worry, Chris," he said. "My word is good."

"Never doubted it for a moment," Chris replied just before leaving. "See you soon, I hope," she said as she left.

***

"Mildred," Colonel Harkavy called. "Can you come in here for a minute, please."

When Mildred was seated in a chair in Colonel's Harkavy's office, she glanced over at him. She was surprised to see that much of the color had drained from his face.

"Would you mind canceling my reservation at The Grill Room?"

"You mean The Gascony Room, sir?"

"Right...The Gascony Room."

"You okay, sir?"

"I'm fine. Maybe just a little tired, I think." He paused. "Mildred, as soon as possible would you also get Captain Emil Schtung, CO, Company B, Fourth Battalion, Second Training Regiment, at Fort Leonard Wood, on the phone for me. And don't bother telling anyone who's calling him."

***

For a time after he had completed his somewhat brief phone call with Captain Schtung, Colonel Harkavy sat motionless at his desk. He thought about his meeting with General Haslett's daughter. "Interesting," he reflected, "how in such a short time Billy Rosen had enlisted so many good people to his cause." There was no doubt whatsoever in his mind. He and Wally Marks had made the right choice.

Then he looked down at his desktop. On it lay the small box Chris had given him. "Use them in good health, Colonel," she had said. He reached over and opened the box. Inside were two silver stars obviously designed for the uniform of someone receiving his first promotion to the lofty rank of a general officer.

Chapter 41

336 Pippen Road, Waynesville, Missouri, Friday, 16 June 1950, 1750 Hours.

Velma Sack was seated in her living room trying to get back into a book she'd started some weeks before, but she was having difficulty for two reasons: first, she was so elated by the document Dr. Stone had handed her earlier in the day she could hardly think of anything else—and she desperately wanted to show it to Sherman; and second, she just plain missed Sherman. And he had been gone only four days.

Velma got up and walked to the kitchen. From a cupboard she withdrew a cookbook. She opened it to a well worn page: the recipe for Sherman's favorite double chocolate cake. Thirty minutes later Velma poured the batter she had made into an oblong pan and placed it on the middle shelf of her heated oven. This comforted her. In a sense, a part of Sherman was now with her. And, inexplicably, it made her feel even more assured that he'd be home soon.

Velma returned to the couch in the living room where she'd been sitting and began to read, but she still couldn't concentrate. Within minutes her eyes closed and her book slipped quietly to the floor.

***

Velma was awakened by a buzzing noise: the oven timer. Then she felt a breeze. She looked up. There, standing in the half-open front doorway, she saw Sherman. He was holding a large cardboard tube over six feet in length, and he was smiling broadly.

"Seems like I got here just in time," he said. "Something sure smells good…and I think it's you!"

Surprised, Velma instinctively raised her right hand to her head trying to determine whether her hair needed combing.

"Sherman," she said, "least you could have done was call. Given me a chance to freshen up a bit."

"You look fresh as a daisy to me, Vel. Anyway, I wanna show you something. But how 'bout we do it in the kitchen so I can taste some of that good stuff of yours."

***

Sherman was seated at the kitchen table. "Honey," he said, "a cup of coffee with whatever it is you're baking would sure hit the spot, particularly since I've been driving for about five hours nonstop. By the way, Billy is fine. I just dropped him off at the hospital."

"He's finer than you think, Sherman. Fact is, I've got some wonderful news." Velma hesitated for just a moment. "Oh yes, Captain Schtung called around 5:30. He wanted you to call him just as soon as you got home, no matter what time it was. Said it was important and that he'd be waiting for your call."

"I guess I'd better give him a call."

"Hold on, Sherman." Velma said, raising her voice slightly. "My news comes first! Dr. Stone gave this to me today. It's one of only three copies he has, and I promised to return it to him on penalty of death." Velma handed Sherman a shiny tan piece of paper. It was a copy of Doc Gunderson's Interoffice Memo to Colonel Harkavy sent on the day Billy was inducted. Sergeant Sack took a moment to read it. Below the typewritten portion there was a handwritten note in the part of the form entitled "Reply":

4/28/50 Doc: Per your request, I met with Rosen and told him all about his foot and the problems it could cause him during basic and afterwards. I offered him 4F. Surprisingly, he turned it down. He insisted on induction into the Army despite the foot. He also refused to consider OCS and wanted in as an EM. I hope his foot doesn't bother him, but it's his call. Nice kid.

Ken Harkavy

"Jesus," Sergeant Sack said after reading the Memo and Harkavy's handwritten reply note. "This completely clears Billy!"

"You got it, big guy." Velma paused. "Why don't we head on over to the hospital right now and tell him? I think after everything he's gone through he's entitled to know."

"Lemme make that call to the Captain first. I'll do it as fast as I can: from the den." Sergeant Sack started up the stairs.

***

"Evening, sir. I just got in. What's up?"

"Thanks for calling, First Sergeant. That Rosen thing has finally come to a head. Remember, you and I were going to decide on a plan of action? Well, now we don't have to. Harkavy fixed that." Sergeant Sack noticed that as he spoke Captain Schtung's voice trembled slightly.

"What do you mean, sir?"

"He confirmed to me what we both suspected: that Fuller was right all along." Now it seemed to Sergeant Sack that Captain Schtung was having difficulty breathing.

"Late zis zafternoon (Captain Schtung was beginning to mispronounce more and more of his words, further indication to Sergeant Sack of the Captain's agitation) I received a phone call from zat fucker, Harkavy. He starts off with his typical bullshit: 'Emil,' he says, 'how are you and your family?' Cockzucker never met my family, First Sergeant!"

Sergeant Sack now thought he was hearing gasping.

"But I played along with him," Captain Schtung continued. "I wanted to hear what he had to say, and whether he was gonna try to con me again. Then he bowls me over; does a complete one-eighty: 'Emil,' he says, 'I'm really very very sorry about this, but everything I told you about Rosen is all a terrible mistake. I've found out he never tried to lie his way out of the Army. For the Army's sake, Emil, I've got to ask you to put things right.'" There was a pause. Again, Sergeant Sack heard gasping.

"Just like fuckin' zat. The cockzucker just says 'put things right.' How in Christ's name do I do zat, First Sergeant? Zat's why I'm calling."

"Sir," Sergeant Sack said. "This is what we've been trying to do all along. Don't you see?"

"I suppose I do, First Sergeant. It's just zat Harkavy has made a mess of things and left me holding the goddamn shit bag. Fritzi came home last night. When I told her what happened in Chicago she called me an idiot. She wants me to resign my commission." Captain Schtung halted momentarily.

"But it's zat boy, First Sergeant. I keep thinking about him and what I've done to him." Now Captain Schtung began to wail. "For God's sake, help me! Please! I want to put things right! But what can I do? What can anyone do? It's too goddamn late!"

"Sir, sir!" Sergeant Sack said. "Please! You're no idiot. Didn't I say I would have done the same thing?"

"Ya, but…"

"And, sir, it's absolutely not too late. You have no problems at all! None." He waited, letting what he said sink in.

"Trust me. When all the dust settles, Rosen will be fine, and you'll still be the most respected company commander in the regiment. I promise. On my sacred goddamn oath!"

"But…"

"Please, Captain, listen to me," Sergeant Sack said. "How long we been friends?"

"I dunno. Maybe seven, eight years, I guess. Why?"

"Well, in all that time have I ever bullshitted you?"

"Never once," Captain Schtung replied.

"Okay, then, when I tell you everything's gonna work out will you please believe me, sir?"

"Ya," Captain Schtung said, "I'll try. But…"

Sergeant Sack cut him off. "Well then, sir, please let me handle this. Okay?"

"All right, but what should I do, First Sergeant?"

"You just stay put, sir. I'll get back to you in about half an hour, maybe sooner. But what I'm thinking right now is that maybe you and Mrs. Schtung should be joining me and Velma tonight at the hospital. I think that an apology from you to Private Rosen might be a help for starters. But, like I said, cool it. And one more thing, sir: you gotta let me orchestrate this whole thing. Okay?"

"I agree, First Sergeant. I'm putting my complete trust in you."

"Good. And please, sir, just wait for my call back."

"I will, First Sergeant," Captain Schtung said, relieved but nevertheless confused.

***

It took Sergeant Sack approximately ten minutes to fill his wife in on his conversations with Captain Schtung.

"So now, Vel, you know everything I know. I mean everything!" Sergeant Sack said.

"But why didn't you tell me about Billy volunteering for the draft and all that stuff between Schtung and Harkavy at that ridiculous luncheon in Chicago? That would have helped explain a lot of things."

"I couldn't, Vel. I gave Captain Schtung my word that I wouldn't tell anyone. And, frankly, I was afraid of what he might do if word got out. I knew he felt like a first-class imbecile the way he allowed himself to be seduced at that fancy restaurant by Harkavy and all his medals."

Velma nodded. She had more or less come to the same conclusion: that Captain Schtung had, on that particular occasion, made a complete fool of himself. "But then again," she thought, "there were many times in my life when I allowed myself to be seduced." She smiled.

"Okay, Sherman, so now that I know everything, what's to discuss? I'd say we better turn this whole matter over to the IG because I think this Harkavy's a no good liar. He's the one who should be drummed out of the Army. And he's the last person I can think of who deserves to be promoted to brigadier general."

"As I've said many times before, Vel, great minds think alike. But turning this thing over to the IG—well, strange as it may seem, that might be exactly the wrong thing to do."

"Why's that?" Velma asked, taken completely by surprise.

"Okay, here's the way I see it," Sergeant Sack said. "First, there's that Interoffice Memo. It's dated April 28th. When Harkavy met with Schtung at that restaurant, it was on Sunday, June 4th. That was only five weeks later. Very unlikely that Harkavy forgot about his interview with Billy and his notation on that Memo that Billy refused a 4F classification, don't you think?"

"I agree," Velma said. "Its pretty obvious to me that Harkavy intentionally lied to Captain Schtung at that luncheon. But I can't figure out why."

"I can't either," Sergeant Sack said. "But he didn't go to all the trouble of arranging that fancy lunch with Schtung just to get his jollies off, unless he's one sick bastard. And I don't believe that for one minute because they don't promote lunatics to general. No, I think he had a reason. But there's also something else."

"Which is?" Velma asked.

"Well, when Billy first got to the company I told Schtung that I had a problem with him. Schtung asked me if he was a 'bad apple,' and I said no, he wasn't; he was just the opposite. I said I thought there was something wrong with our orders. So Schtung and I called Colonel Paulson. We had a series of telephone calls. Paulson made us wait, and I got the impression he was making calls on his own. But after all the phone calling ended, we received our marching orders and they were, and I quote Colonel Paulson *verbatim*, 'to put the fuckin' blocks to Rosen, and that's a direct order.' So I think that what Harkavy told Schtung in Chicago, which of course was designed to put the maximum amount of pressure on Billy, was just an extension of what had been going on before. Maybe Harkavy was simply ratcheting things up. I dunno. But what I do sense is that all the shit thrown at Billy was intentional and sanctioned by some fairly heavy duty people in the Army." Sergeant Sack paused. "Am I making any sense, Vel?"

"You're making perfect sense, honey," Vel said. "You know, sometimes when that brain of yours surfaces, you scare me with your brilliance. Good thing it doesn't happen often." Velma laughed. "But Sherman, there's one thing that gets in the way of your analysis."

"What's that?"

"Why, suddenly, today, has all this harassment of Billy come to a screeching halt? What prompted Colonel Harkavy to make that phone call to Captain Schtung?"

"I guess if I knew the answer to that one, Vel, I'd have a solution to all this. But I don't and I probably never will. Given what I strongly suspect, that what was going on with Billy probably was done with the blessing of the powers that be of the

United States Army, I have a feeling we should tell Schtung not to mention to anyone his luncheon with Harkavy or today's phone call. After all, with that Interoffice Memo we have more than enough solid evidence to disprove all those allegations about Billy trying to lie his way out of the Army. If we mention the luncheon or the phone call, then, in effect, we're accusing Harkavy of outright lying—which may not be the wisest thing to do. Whaddya think, Vel?"

"I think you may be right, honey. And anyway, why don't we just let someone else point a finger at Harkavy. I'd hate to have you or Schtung thrown out of the Army because one of you stuck your nose in a place where it didn't belong. But, damn, Sherman, I'd sure like to know what prompted Harkavy to call Schtung today. Or putting it differently, honey, I wonder if someone got to him?"

"My take, Vel, is that someone wanted all this nonsense with Billy stopped; someone with an awful lot of juice. Sounds like a pretty heavy hitter to me. Fact is, we'll probably never know who that person was. But, Vel, who cares? It looks to me like it's all over. And thank God for that!"

***

"Sorry it took so long to get back to you, sir," Sergeant Sack said to Captain Schtung, "but I had to resolve a few things...which I've finally done." Sergeant Sack cleared his throat before continuing.

"So the ground rules still are that you're gonna let me orchestrate this thing, right, sir?"

"That's what I agreed to, First Sergeant."

"Okay, sir, then for starters I'm going to ask you never ever to mention anything to anyone about your luncheon with Colonel Harkavy in Chicago or his phone call to you today. This is important."

"But First Sergeant, how am I going to justify letting up on Rosen? Why would I suddenly consider all those allegations I charged him with to be bullshit if I hadn't gotten that phone call?"

"Because, sir, we've received written proof today that Rosen was offered 4F status and that he turned it down."

"Really, First Sergeant?" Captain Schtung said, obviously surprised. "Can you tell me about that?"

"I can, sir, but it's gonna piss you off good. It's a note Harkavy wrote when Rosen was inducted. In it he says he offered Rosen 4F status because of his foot, and that Rosen turned it down and insisted on coming into the Army despite his bad foot."

Sergeant Sack could picture Captain Schtung turning red with rage.

"Look, sir, Harkavy obviously lied to you. And I truly believe he did it for some reason we'll never know. My guess is that he wanted to get you to increase the pressure on Rosen. But to repeat, sir, he had to be doing it with a purpose in mind."

"But he fuckin' lied to me, First Sergeant!" Sergeant Sack knew Captain Schtung was seething.

"That's what I just said, sir. But we've known that he lied to you since that time in Fuller's office when we figured out that Rosen volunteered for the draft. The real question, Captain, is why did he lie to you? And my take is that Harkavy was acting on orders." Sergeant Sack stopped for a moment.

"Captain, you and I know we were ordered by Colonel Paulson to stick it to Rosen at the beginning of his basic training. Right, sir?"

"True, First Sergeant."

"Well I think what Harkavy got you to do when you met him at that restaurant in Chicago was all a part of that. What puzzles me is why today he suddenly called it off. But whatever, sir, please let's not be telling anyone about your Chicago luncheon or today's telephone call; or, for that matter, that Harkavy's a liar. I think there's a lot more to this than we'll ever know. It's very likely this whole thing with Rosen extends further up the chain of command than just Harkavy. What I'm saying, Captain, is who knows where all this bullshit with Rosen began or where it was intended to end. Why should you or I be the one to blow the whistle on something that's probably been okayed by the powers that be of the United States Army?" Sergeant Sack paused again.

"So I say leave it alone, sir. We've got more important things to do. We've got youngsters to train. Let's let the generals deal with army politics. Consider what happened to Rosen an oddball case of 'friendly fire' and let's get back to doing what we've always done, running the best damn basic training company in the regiment. Whaddya say, sir?"

"All right, First Sergeant. What time do you want me at the hospital?"

"Why don't we meet in the third floor visitors lounge around 2030 and we'll all go to Rosen's room from there. And, Captain, be sure to bring Mrs. Schtung. Tell her not to be discussing your Chicago lunch or Harkavy's phone call with anyone. Okay?"

"We'll be there, First Sergeant. And I'll tell Fritzi. Anything else?"

"I'm going to be wearing my Class A uniform. Could you do the same?"

"Certainly, First Sergeant."

Chapter 42

Third Floor Visitors Lounge,
Base Hospital, Fort Leonard Wood, Missouri,
Friday, 16 June 1950, 2010 Hours.

After hurriedly showering and then dressing, the Sacks arrived at the visitors lounge on the third floor of the Base Hospital. They were twenty minutes early and Sergeant Sack was still carrying the same large cardboard tube he'd brought into his house two hours earlier.

"Sherman," Velma said, "what is that damn thing anyway?"

"You'll find out soon enough, Vel," Sergeant Sack replied, winking at his wife. "But listen, dear, I wanted to get here a few minutes early so we could prepare Billy for Captain Schtung's arrival. Don't wanna see that boy pass out when Schtung marches into his room in about twenty minutes."

"Good thinking, Sherman," Velma said. "You go in ahead of me. But I want to show him a copy of the Memo."

***

"So…feel good to be back in your own deluxe room with all the trimmings, Private Rosen?" Sergeant Sack asked his erstwhile traveling companion who was seated comfortably in a chair reading the *St. Louis Post-Dispatch*.

"Hi," Billy said. Then he noticed Velma peeking in through the doorway.

"Velma!" he exclaimed. "Come on in." He got up and hugged her.

"Billy," Sergeant Sack said, "we don't have much time, so I wanna let you know that Captain Schtung's gonna be visiting you in about fifteen minutes."

"Shit!" Billy said, horrified. "What do I do?"

"Nothing, kid. Fact is, he's coming to apologize."

"Apologize?" Billy was stunned. "But…"

"That's right, kid," Sergeant Sack continued. "Now he knows all that stuff about you trying to lie your way out of the Army is pure bullshit; he also knows you volunteered for the draft and then insisted on coming in the Army even after you were told that left foot of yours could have gotten you classified 4F. Really, kid, he's terribly sorry about this whole mess. Truth is, he feels like a damn fool."

Billy looked questioningly at Velma. "It's true," she said. "He's got an awful lot of egg on his face. And the important thing is he knows it." She reached into her purse and withdrew the copy of the Interoffice Memo. "Here, take a look at this."

"Thank God!" Billy said after reading the Memo. "But how'd you ever get hold of this, Velma?"

"The Army works in strange ways, honey. Seems Dr. Gunderson and Dr. Stone…"

"Vel," Sergeant Sack interrupted, "the Schtungs should be here in a few minutes. We'd better get on back to the visitors lounge."

***

"Evening, sir," Sergeant Sack said to Captain Schtung who, as instructed, was wearing Pinks and Greens, his uniform coat adorned with four rows of ribbons. Turning to Mrs. Schtung, Sergeant Sack smiled. "Nice to see you again, ma'am."

"Hi, Sergeant," Fritzi Schtung replied. "It's been a while, hasn't it?"

"I guess it has, ma'am." Sergeant Sack noticed that Mrs. Schtung was carrying a large white box.

Velma stepped forward. "Good to see you, Captain; and you too, Mrs. Schtung. And what a beautiful outfit you have on, ma'am."

In fact, Fritzi Schtung was a handsome woman. And on this particular occasion it was obvious she had chosen her wardrobe carefully. She wore penny loafers, a long dark brown woolen tweed skirt cinched in at the waist by a plain wide leather belt, and a white silk long sleeve blouse. Besides a wedding band, she had on only one other item of jewelry, a long strand of white pearls. Her blonde hair was neatly arranged in a bun.

"Thank you, Mrs. Sack," Fritzi said.

Fritzi Schtung and Velma Sack had known one another for a number of years. The two tacitly understood they could never be close friends because of army protocol which frowned upon fraternization between the families of officers and enlisted men.

Nevertheless, as in the case of their husbands, Fritzi and Velma liked one another, and there was a strong bond of respect between them.

"First Sergeant," Captain Schtung said, his nervousness now becoming apparent, "when I'm in Private Rosen's room, what do you think I should be doing?"

"I don't want to make this too complicated, Captain, because it really isn't. Just be yourself. Tell Rosen how you feel and then apologize to him. That's about it, sir."

"All right, First Sergeant, that's exactly what I'll do."

"And, sir," Sergeant Sack said, "before we go on down to Rosen's room, I thought you ought to take a look at something." He motioned to Velma who handed Captain Schtung the copy of the Interoffice Memo.

***

Billy heard a timid knocking at his door. He put down the newspaper he'd been trying unsuccessfully to read and got up. Unexpectedly, a feeling of nausea swept over him and he began to sway unsteadily. He sat back down on his bed and took several deep breaths. Finally, trying to sound as normal as he could under the circumstances, he said, "Come in." The door opened and an attractive woman in her mid-thirties entered. Quietly she closed the door behind her.

"Private Rosen?" she said. Billy thought her voice was kindly, maybe even friendly.

"Yes, ma'am."

"I'm Fritzi Schtung." She placed the box she'd been carrying on the table next to Billy's bed and extended her hand which Billy clasped. "I've been looking forward to meeting you." She smiled.

Still holding her hand, Billy asked, "You're Captain Schtung's wife?"

"Yes. The Captain's down the hallway with the Sacks. Is it all right if they come in?"

Billy nodded.

Fritzi Schtung went over to the table and lifted the cover of the box. Inside was an assortment of pastries and cookies. "I didn't bake them," she said apologetically. Then she walked to the door and opened it. Stepping out into the corridor, Billy heard her call out, "Come in."

"God, how strange this all is," Billy thought. "Here I am a basic training recruit and I'm hosting a damn soiree for my commanding officer who almost killed me trying to drum me out of the Army, and for my first sergeant who, up until recently, has been harassing the shit out of me."

***

"Private Rosen," Captain Schtung said. "There's no way I can tell you how badly I feel about what happened. Please believe me: I never intended to physically harm you. And the things I accused you of, well…I now know they were based on damnable lies. I apologize. I'm so very sorry about all this. Can you maybe consider forgiving me? It would mean so much to me and Mrs. Schtung. I'm so ashamed I…" Stopping in mid-sentence, he looked up at Billy pleadingly.

Billy looked over at the Sacks and Fritzi Schtung. The three were standing silently near the doorway to his room. Instinctively, Billy knew that this was the moment, that the words he was about to utter could destroy Captain Schtung's career. Or they could resurrect it.

Billy reached deep within himself. He needed his father's advice.

"Dad," he said, "help me!"

"Hey, son, no big deal. How many times have I told you we're all alike? Forget titles, uniforms, that kinda stuff. Remember what I've said so often: 'We all put our pants on the same way: one leg at a time.'"

"Meaning?" Billy asked.

"Meaning we're all fallible, kid. No one's perfect. He just went off the deep end. Didn't check out his facts, that's all. Maybe not the brightest of lights, but you'll survive. Just learn from his mistakes, Billy."

"So I don't cashier him?"

"'Course not. He didn't intend to harm you. Just went overboard. We've all done that."

"Thanks, Dad," Billy said.

Billy looked up. Captain Schtung was still standing there. And the Sacks and Mrs. Schtung were still by the doorway.

"Sir," Billy said, "I accept your apology and I forgive you."

***

"Captain," Sergeant Sack said, as he popped an éclair into his mouth, "I wanna show you something." Sergeant Sack opened one end of the large cardboard tube he'd been lugging around with him and emptied its contents.

"What's all this, First Sergeant?"

"Hold on a sec', sir."

Sergeant Sack placed seven large targets on Billy's bed, one on top of the other. He reached for a cookie, ate it, and continued. "Recognize this target on the top of the stack, sir?"

"I believe it's an 'A' target, isn't it, First Sergeant?"

"You got it, sir."

"What's an 'A' target, Sherman?" Velma interjected.

"These are all riflery targets, honey," Sergeant Sack said, pointing to the stack on Billy's bed. "The one on top is an 'A' target. It's the smallest. It's the one we use for slow fire at two hundred yards." Sergeant Sack paused for a moment. He wanted to make sure everyone was listening.

"These are all Billy's targets."

"What are you talking about, First Sergeant?" Captain Schtung asked, totally confused.

"Emil," Fritzi Schtung said, "what is the matter with you? Don't you understand? Sergeant Sack is telling us that Private Rosen has been firing his rifle."

"But how could that be, First Sergeant? Hasn't he been in the hospital under a doctor's care all this time?" Captain Schtung asked.

"Well, yes and no, Captain. He has been under his doctor's care all this time, but he's been out of the hospital a few days."

"Really, First Sergeant," Captain Schtung said. "Please tell me how that came about?"

"Well, sir, as you know, Rosen's my responsibility. I decided that he was getting behind in his training and I didn't want him recycled. At the same time his doctor, Colonel Stone, wanted him to get as much fresh air as possible. So I simply arranged to have him get away for a few days, and, while he was at it, take two of those days to get qualified on the M1."

"But you can't do that in two days, First Sergeant," Captain Schtung said, still perplexed.

"Begging the Captain's pardon, sir, you can with the help of Major Touhy."

"Touhy? So you took Rosen down to Touhy's place in Arkansas?"

"Correct, sir. And lemme show you what we've got."

Billy could see that Sergeant Sack was beginning to enjoy himself. He also saw that Velma was smiling. Mrs. Schtung stood quietly by, but she too was beginning to see something of interest in all of this—although she wasn't entirely sure what it meant.

"Sir," Sergeant Sack said, "here's that 'A' target. See," he pointed, "all four of his shots came together in the bull's-eye. You could cover them with a half dollar; maybe even a quarter. And, as you know, sir, this is from a standing position."

"I'm having difficulty believing what I'm seeing, First Sergeant," Captain Schtung exclaimed.

"I did too, sir, first time I looked at this target. Grouping's unbelievable, don't you think?"

"I repeat, First Sergeant, this is incredible!"

"Now, sir, let's try a 'sustained' target." He uncovered the next target in the stack. Then, turning to Velma and Mrs. Schtung, he said, "This target is used for what we call sustained fire. The shooter has to fire off nine shots in 51 seconds or less from 200 yards. He begins by standing and then goes into a kneeling or sitting position. Private Rosen here chose kneeling. Now let's take a look at the results." He pointed. "See," he said, "eight shots in a half dollar cluster in the bull's-eye. He unfortunately dumped one shot into the ring just outside the bull's-eye, but no big deal."

"Can we get to the bottom line, First Sergeant?" Captain Schtung asked anxiously.

"Meaning you wanna know his overall score, sir?"

"Exactly."

"He shot 204."

"Fritzi," Captain Schtung said, turning to his wife, "that's out of a possible 210. Remarkable!"

"And, sir, here's Major Touhy's certification. Shows the scoring." Sergeant Sack handed Captain Schtung a letter size document.

"Spectacular, Rosen!" Captain Schtung said, clapping Billy on the back. "You're to be congratulated, soldier. We can certainly use someone like you on the company's rifle team."

"I thought you'd be pleased, sir," Sergeant Sack said.

"Well, Private Rosen, I think a special company formation is in order," Captain Schtung said. "Could you possibly absent yourself from the hospital tomorrow morning for a few hours?"

"Mrs. Sack?" Billy asked, turning to Velma.

"Well, Captain, as his supervising nurse, I don't see why not so long as it's only for a few hours. You name the time, sir, and we'll make sure Billy's there."

"Do you think 0730 is acceptable, First Sergeant?" Captain Schtung asked.

"Okay by me, Captain. Tonight I think I'll run over to the company area and get hold of La Droop. Have him round up a clean uniform and spit shined shoes for Billy to change into tomorrow morning."

"Excellent, First Sergeant. And now that we've made a pretty good start at tidying up the mess I created, I think it's time for the Schtungs to get on home."

"And for the Sacks too, Captain," Velma said.

Captain Schtung smiled. "Well then, good night all."

Captain Schtung turned to Billy. "You're an extraordinary young man, Private Rosen. I respect you, *sir*." With that, Captain Schtung drew himself to attention and saluted Billy. Billy smiled, saluting in return.

***

Before leaving, Velma came over and hugged Billy. Then Sergeant Sack leaned over and said, "Nice going, kid. I'll pick you up 'round 0630 tomorrow morning. Now get some sleep."

Chapter 43

Drill Field, Company B, Fourth Battalion,
Second Training Regiment (Basic),
Fort Leonard Wood, Missouri,
Saturday, 17 June 1950, 0720 Hours.

Fat Jerry was pissed. The bus that was to take him on his prepaid USO tour of St. Louis was scheduled to leave the main gate promptly at 9:00 AM, and here he was cooling his heels on the drill field with the rest of the company on a Saturday morning.

"Goddammit," he cursed to himself. "Can't plan a fuckin' thing in this man's army."

Earlier that morning (at 5:15 AM to be exact) Sergeant Gomez had switched on the lights in the barracks and announced that a special company formation had been called and that the men were to be in Class A uniform and out on the drill field by no later than 0715 hours. "Any particular reason, Sarge?" Jerry had asked. "Just get your ass outta your bunk and get going, Krazinski. It's Saturday and the mess hall closes at 0700, so move it if you want breakfast."

As he stood there, Jerry looked around. The others appeared as irritated as he was, with the exception of Craig Billington. "Fucker's all army," Jerry thought, looking at Craig. "They could put his head in a grease trap and he'd be happier 'n a pig in shit."

Then Jerry saw First Sergeant Sack exit the OR. Behind him La Droop was dragging the loudspeaker out through the doorway. As he had done on at least six prior occasions, La Droop went back in the OR and came out a second time with the insulated mike cords and the stand with the microphone attached to it. When the microphone was hooked up and operating, Sergeant Sack stepped up to it and began speaking. "Okay, listen up." He waited, making sure he had the men's attention.

"We all know it's Saturday morning and that many of you have plans. And we're aware that some of you signed up for that St. Louis tour. We'll try to make this quick. We should be done, hopefully, by around eight o'clock. So please bear with me."

"What the fuck's going on?" Jerry asked, turning to Vin who was standing next to him on his right. "Never heard him speak so civil to us."

"Can't be good," Vin replied.

Just then Captain Schtung came out of the OR. Behind him they saw someone they hadn't seen in almost two weeks: Billy Rosen. He too was wearing a Class A uniform.

"Shit," Jerry thought. "Those no good cocksuckers are gonna drum him outta the Army right now…in front of all of us!"

"Gentlemen," Captain Schtung said, speaking into the microphone, "I wish to echo what your First Sergeant just said. I too regret having to interfere with your weekend plans. However, it's imperative that I deal quickly and decisively with the matter at hand, Private William Rosen." Captain Schtung cleared his throat.

Jerry felt a sinking feeling in the pit of his stomach. "They're really gonna do it, goddamn 'em!" he thought.

Captain Schtung began speaking again. "Some of you were in the barracks that evening almost two weeks ago when I accused Private Rosen of trying to lie his way out of the Army. My accusations, gentlemen, were based on what I thought was reliable information. Yesterday I learned that my information was totally false, and that my accusations were completely unfounded." He stopped for a moment, trying to collect his thoughts.

"What happened is that Private Rosen injured his foot when he was quite young. Because of this, the examining doctor at the time of his induction concluded that he probably should be classified 4F, but wanted to leave that decision up to Private Rosen. When Private Rosen was told of this, he chose to go into the Army despite his bad foot. And by the way, gentlemen, Private Rosen was not drafted; he volunteered for the draft.

"So you see, gentlemen, what I accused Private Rosen of was untrue, and, I might add, unjust. Last evening I met with him. I apologized. Private Rosen accepted my apology. I respect him, gentlemen, and I am very happy to tell you that once he is discharged from the Base Hospital where he is currently recovering from injuries to his windpipe, he will be restored…" Captain Schtung stopped momentarily, "*welcomed*…back to the company." Then Captain Schtung turned to Billy.

"Private Rosen," he said, "would you like to address the company?"

Billy thought for a moment. "Sure, sir," he said.

Billy walked to the microphone and took hold of its stand. He was about to begin, when he heard someone chanting, "Bil-ly, Bil-ly, Bil-ly." It was Jerry. Then others began to join in and the chanting grew louder: "Bil-ly! Bil-ly! Bil-ly!"

"Christ," Billy thought, "you guys are gonna get yourselves court-martialed!"

Suddenly, Jerry broke ranks. He was out of control. He ran up to Billy, knocking over the microphone stand. As he lurched forward, he grabbed Billy in a bear hug refusing to let go.

"God, man, I'm so glad you're coming back! Jesus, I'm so fuckin' glad! I thought they was gonna kick you out. Honest, man, I knew all that shit wasn't true. And, man, you fuckin' saved my life!"

Now others from Billy's platoon began to break ranks, to run up to Billy. Craig was there shaking his hand, while, at the same time, Vin grabbed him by the elbow and was trying to pull him away from the others.

In the midst of the melee Sergeant Gomez managed to bull his way in next to Billy. Putting his arm around him, he said, "Rosen, we're all happy for you. Most of us thought you got a raw deal, including me. Welcome back!"

Captain Schtung and Sergeant Sack stood by looking on helplessly. Finally, Sergeant Sack said, "Sir, I think we'd just better walk away from this. After all, it's a celebration of sorts."

"Well I for one am going home, First Sergeant. Too bad, though. I wanted to award him that Expert Rifleman's Badge."

"Some other time, sir," Sergeant Sack replied.

***

The crowd surrounding Billy had dispersed and only Craig remained. He and Billy were chatting as Sergeant Sack approached.

"Well, Private Rosen," he said, "whaddya say we head on back to the hospital?"

But before Billy could answer, they heard a woman's voice nearby say, "Hold on a sec', guys!"

Billy and Sergeant Sack turned in surprise. They hadn't seen the middle-aged woman come up to them. And when Sergeant Sack looked carefully at her he was even more surprised.

The woman, who was barely five feet tall, wore an ankle length black woolen suit badly in need of pressing. She carried a large overloaded briefcase which, because of her height, hung to within an inch of the ground. Her disheveled red hair was spotted with gray, and much of her face was covered with freckles.

"Excuse me, ma'am?" Sergeant Sack said.

"Hi, there, Sarge. I'm Rose Applebaum. Billy the Kid here and I are close friends and, with your permission, I'd like to drive him back to the hospital. He and I need to discuss a few things. Okay?" With that, she handed Sergeant Sack her business card:

Rose Applebaum
Secretary-Treasurer
The Boys, Inc.
995 Lariat Lane, Rolla, Missouri
RO4-7755

Sergeant Sack took the card, read it, and turned to Billy with a questioning look.

"First Sergeant," Billy said, "I'd like to introduce you to my friend, Rose Applebaum, CMW."

"Huh?" Sergeant Sack said.

"As in 'Certified Miracle Worker,'" Billy replied, smiling.

Hearing this, Rose blushed. "Flattery will get you everywhere," she said as she took Billy's hand and nuzzled up against him.

"So, whaddya say, Sarge? You gonna give me some private time with my boyfriend?"

"Is that your Packard over there, ma'am?" Sergeant Sack asked, pointing to the large blue coupe parked next to the OR.

"Nah. Belongs to my employer. But it'll get us to the hospital."

"Well, kid," Sergeant Sack said to Billy, "looks like you're ridin' in style."

***

Rose sat on a pillow behind the steering wheel. As they drove toward the hospital she began to speak.

"Well, babe, that was quite a shindig. I can't wait to tell The Boys about your 'welcome home' party."

"It was really great, Rose."

"So babe, in that briefcase behind your seat is a copy of an Interoffice Memo I think you outta see."

"Is that the one from Dr. Gunderson to Colonel Harkavy? Because if it is, I've already seen it."

"Cripes," Rose groaned. "How'd you see a copy? I wanted the fun of showing you that!"

"Never mind," Billy said. "You can show me your copy. I'll pretend like I never saw that Memo before."

"You're a sweetheart, babe. But I still got some more good news for you, I think." Rose reached for her sunglasses and put them on.

"So here's the scoop, Billy: from a read of that Memo you know that Captain Schtung was blowing smoke out of his you know what the night he was screaming at you in your barracks, right?"

Billy nodded.

"But what you don't know is whether all the harassment has come to an end, do you?"

"Not really, I guess," Billy replied. "I don't think Schtung's gonna be bothering me anymore. And I know Sergeant Sack has backed off. No, I don't think it's gonna continue."

"Oh yeah? You sure? Ever think that maybe they were ordered to stick it to you?"

"It never really occurred to me," Billy replied, shaken by the thought.

"Well they were. And the good news is that all that's been stopped." Rose was smiling.

"Wonderful," Billy said. "And I assume this was your doing?"

"Sorta, babe. The Boys and I more or less figured out who the bad guy was. But we weren't the ones who stopped it."

"Then who did?" Billy asked.

Rose paused. "Lemme say this, Billy. It was someone working with us. That's all I'd better say for now."

"Chris Haslett? It had to be her, Rose."

As the car pulled up to the Base Hospital's main entrance, Rose nodded. "Promise me you'll never say I told you, okay?"

"I promise," Billy replied. "And now I know who was behind all this nonsense: her father." Billy knew it had to be her father because he was the only person Billy could think of who Chris could have badgered into backing off. Furthermore, Billy remembered how puzzled he had been at the Haslett home when General Haslett had referred to him as "Private Rosen" without anyone ever mentioning his last name to the General. "Of course," Billy reflected, "he had to be the one."

Billy could see that Rose was becoming uncomfortable. "I guess I gotta release a little more information, because I don't want you thinking that General Haslett was behind all this. He wasn't. But, Billy, I don't think I should be saying anything more."

Billy could sense that it was time for him to back off, that Rose may have come close to betraying a confidence.

***

Late that evening in his darkened hospital room Billy lay in bed exhausted. His throat was slightly sore and sometimes when he took a deep breath or coughed his chest ached. Still, he wasn't nearly as bad as he'd been twelve days ago. And soon, he knew, he'd be well enough to be discharged from the hospital.

Billy closed his eyes. Time to sleep after an exciting day. But he couldn't. Questions again, dammit. Not the same ones that had plagued him about Sergeant Sack going through his medical records or General Haslett calling him "Private Rosen," but new ones, all concerning Chris Haslett.

What was she really all about? How had this seemingly unsophisticated college girl, away at school in the East and in the midst of final exams, put a stop to the dreaded treatment that someone somewhere in the Army had willed upon him? And why was he so strongly attracted to her?

Background Check: Sherman C. Sack

Sherman Cullum Sack was born on May 16, 1918, almost five months before a distant cousin, Corporal (later Sergeant) Alvin Cullum York, earned the Medal of Honor and the French *Croix de Guerre* on a battlefield in France and became the most famous hero of World War I, the great war to end all wars.[6] But following in the footsteps of his hero-cousin was not the reason Sherman enlisted in the Army; rather, it was a sad and hardly noteworthy incident which occurred seventeen years later.

Sherman's mother, Maria Cullum Sack, called her only child "Shermie," something which, after attaining the age of twelve, made Sherman cringe. But nicknames were used in the Sack household. For example, his father was referred to by everyone as "The Lieutenant" because he was a Lieutenant in the prison guard system at Clinton Correctional Facility, a maximum security prison in Dannemora, New York, some seventeen miles west of the Sacks' home in Plattsburgh, an historic city located on the westerly shore of Lake Champlain. And his mother was called "Cullie," a takeoff on her maiden name. So in the grand scheme of things Sherman could hardly object to a pet name, although he truly hated the one his parents had chosen for him. In fact, he didn't much like "Sherman" either.

Despite Plattsburgh's hot humid summers and icy winters often accompanied by temperatures well below zero, Sherman's life there was, for the most part, a pleasant one. In his senior year at Plattsburgh High he was getting fairly good grades, mostly A's and B's. He had also lettered in track running the 440 yard dash in a respectable 54.7 seconds. And, at the urging of his father, in his sophomore year he had joined the school's ROTC program and two years later had risen to the rank of Cadet Captain. He particularly liked close order drill; and he was in the Honor Guard which meant that he marched in parades just behind the Cadet Colonel. At community functions he and the other members of the Guard often performed the Manual of Arms using mock Springfield '03 rifles which had been issued to them when they joined the ROTC. To the Manual which they performed in unison they had added several flourishes including the Queen Anne Salute and a special rather perilous maneuver in which two members of the Guard (Sherman was one of them) spun their rifles high above their heads in mid-air. This seemed to thrill the crowd of onlookers which gave Sherman a particularly good feeling. Maybe this was why he took such pride in keeping his uniform clean and pressed, his brass brightly polished, and his Sam Brown belt and brown plain-toed shoes spit-shined.

In fact, when he thought about it, things in Plattsburgh were almost all good with only two exceptions: his girlfriend, Lydia Fermer, and his younger cousin, Tobias ("Toby") Mitchell.

Lydia, his primary irritation, was not only a source of physical frustration to Sherman, but the cause of some private embarrassment as well. Moreover, if the truth be known, because she was so shallow Sherman wasn't particularly fond of her. Nevertheless, he found her to be both sensual and physically attractive. Although she was only sixteen, Lydia looked more like a young woman in her mid-twenties. She was 5'6" with soft wavy shoulder-length brown hair, a pleasing olive complexion marred only by the fewest of acne blemishes, large seemingly innocent brown eyes, and a captivating smile which she often used to showcase her perfectly aligned bright white teeth. But most of all, it was her figure, unusually well-developed for her age, which captivated Sherman: her long slender legs, her narrow waist, and her large well-proportioned breasts. "God," he would muse, "if only I could see them, touch them!" And finally one night, after a year of dating, in the back seat of the Sacks' Chevy sedan Lydia had surprised him by removing her sweater and brassiere and welcoming him to her bosom. Yes, he could touch them, squeeze them, kiss them, whatever he wished. But then when he developed an erection and tried to reach up under her skirt, she had responded by pushing him away. "No!" she had said with surprising firmness. "Take me home now!" "But couldn't you even…?" Before he could finish, she had replied coldly, "No! I said take me home!" Which of course he did. After that evening Sherman knew that even though Lydia was both beautiful and much admired by many of his male friends at Plattsburgh High (some of whom had asked him how far he'd gone with her, a question he carefully avoided answering), their relationship would be short-lived; after all, they shared little physically and they hardly had a thing to say to one another. To him she was simply a pretty face, something to be draped from his arm when he attended a high school dance or a prom, but not someone he could truly befriend. And besides, Sherman was embarrassed when he thought of the many times he had returned home from a date with Lydia and had gone up to his room and masturbated.

The second irritation in Sherman's life was his cousin, Toby. In some ways he was the little brother Sherman always wanted. But in other ways he was a downright nuisance. "Damn him," Sherman would curse to himself. "Always appearing on the scene at exactly the wrong time, and Cullie insists that I watch over him while he's visiting us."

Thus it was that at dinner on Thursday, December 12, 1935, two days before the beginning of Christmas vacation in his senior year, his mother unexpectedly announced, "Shermie, your cousin, Toby, will be arriving from Albany Saturday night and he'll be your responsibility for the next week. And Sunday if the weather holds The Lieutenant has decided to take us all on a day trip to Montreal to tour cathedrals. He wants to drive over the new bridge that opened a few years back."

"Crap," Sherman thought. He had made plans with some friends and he hadn't seen Lydia in over a week, ever since a massive ice storm had immobilized the city. Babysitting an eight-year-old for seven days was hardly his idea of fun, particularly because Toby always brought a satchel of toy soldiers with him and insisted on playing "war" with Sherman at every free moment. Added to this was the even more upsetting thought of wasting a day of vacation in Montreal looking at churches. Although he had never been to Canada, Sherman could think of nothing more boring. But The Lieutenant had spoken. "Goddammit!" he swore under his breath.

***

They would never visit any cathedrals. When they reached the two-mile long Jacques Cartier Bridge which spanned the St. Lawrence River connecting the Canadian community of Longueuil with the City of Montreal, a thick sheet of ice on the surface of its three auto lanes and two sets of trolley tracks (one on each side of the auto lanes) unexpectedly caused the Sacks' Chevy to swerve back and fourth out of control losing almost all traction.

When he felt the skidding, The Lieutenant instinctively slammed on the brakes, perhaps the worst thing he could have done because they were so badly out of adjustment. This in turn caused the car, which was traveling at thirty miles an hour, to veer ninety degrees to the right and head straight for the metal guardrail which was encased in a mound of ice. Instead of acting as a barrier, it served as a ramp and launched the vehicle and its occupants into the air out away from the bridge.

As cars stopped and people ran to the bridge's edge they could just barely make out the top of the Sacks' Chevy as it settled into the river below. *"Mon Dieu!"* one man said. *"Pas person survive dat!"*

Thankfully, he was wrong. Although The Lieutenant, Cullie, and Toby all drowned in the freezing waters of the St. Lawrence, Sherman was pulled to safety from the sinking car by a startled Captain Auguste Aucoin, skipper of a tugboat that happened to be anchored only two hundred yards away. After his rescue, Sherman was transported to Montreal's Royal Victoria Hospital where he was pronounced fit to leave on the afternoon of the following day. His Uncle Mickey and Aunt Ruby were there to take him back to Plattsburgh where he moved in with them.

***

Uncle Mickey, whose full name was Meyer Newcomb, was a state court judge and The Lieutenant's closest friend. When he first ran for judicial office his campaign slogan had been "I admire Meyer." People laughed, and he was elected. But that was in 1915, and in the ensuing twenty years he had earned universal respect as an honest and decent no-nonsense jurist. Sherman both liked and trusted him.

Two weeks after the accident Sherman and the Judge were seated in the library of the Newcomb home.

"Well, Shermie, I've got some news for you. The family house will belong to you just a soon as I can get title cleared by the probate court. I'm told the house is free and clear and, according to several brokers I've checked with, its value is somewhere between $6,000 and $8,000. Besides that, your father carried a $20,000 life insurance policy. Those proceeds are also yours." The Judge sat back in his chair before continuing.

"Shermie," he said tenderly, "Ruby and I always wanted a son. We're glad you're living here with us."

"So am I, sir," Sherman said.

"Good, my boy," the Judge said. "You just stay here as long as you want. We'd like you to consider our home to be your home."

Sherman was touched. "Thank you, sir," he said. "You've both been wonderful to me."

***

Shortly after the accident Sherman called Lydia, mostly because he hadn't heard from her. She was strangely aloof. She didn't mention anything about the deaths of his parents and his cousin or offer a single word of condolence. Rather, she told him that their relationship was over, and that she was involved with someone else, a student at Plattsburgh State who was older and more mature. Sherman felt surprisingly indifferent and unmoved when the phone call ended.

Sherman never spoke to Lydia again, although occasionally he saw her at a distance. A month before graduation he heard that she was pregnant and had dropped out of school.

***

On Saturday, June 13, 1936, Sherman graduated. Mickey and Ruby were there to see him receive his diploma. Ruby had enjoyed the serendipitous experience of having Sherman become a part of her family, even if only for six short months. And now he would be off. He had talked about college, or perhaps enlisting. Wherever he went, she would miss him.

***

"So it's the Army, is it?" the Judge said to Sherman two days after graduation while the two were seated in the Newcomb library once again.

"Yes, sir. I've enlisted."

"Well, keep in touch with us, will you? You know your Aunt Ruby and I will miss you?"

"I will, sir. And I'll miss you both."

The Judge hesitated. There was something else he felt he had to say. "And what about the house and your insurance money?"

"I hadn't thought much about that, sir. Maybe I could use some of that money to repay you for all you've done."

"Nonsense," the Judge replied. "I suppose you know you've added a ray of brightness to our rather dull lives?"

Sherman looked down, slightly embarrassed.

"No, son, collecting room and board was not what was on my mind. I was wondering if I could help you with those assets. I think we should sell the house and then invest your money. You feel comfortable letting me do that?"

"Of course, sir," Sherman replied.

"Good," the Judge said. "And I'm thinking of buying some vacant land around here. I'll do the best I can. You'll hear from me." Then, withdrawing some papers from a large envelope, he continued, "Here, Shermie. Sign these. They create a trust for you. I'll be acting as trustee."

***

Although he never saw the Newcombs again after he left for the Army, he would regularly hear from the Judge—at least twice a year, on his birthday and at Christmas. The letters would be short and newsy. And he would always reply, even when writing was difficult, as it was when he was in the South Pacific during World War II.

But in all his letters the Judge never once mentioned anything to Sherman about his money or how it had been invested. Because of this, at some point in time, probably just before he and Velma were married in 1941, Sherman more or less concluded that Judge Newcomb, like most lawyers, was not much of a businessman and had lost everything. No matter, Sherman felt sure that the Judge, true to his word, had done the very best he could. But he vowed never to mention anything to Velma about the Newcombs, his correspondence with the Judge, or his money. He just couldn't have her asking questions. If she ever learned of the disappearance of his inheritance, she would hardly be forgiving. Instead, she would blame him for failing to look after his financial affairs.

Chapter 44

First Sergeant's Office, Orderly Room,
Company B, Fourth Battalion,
Second Training Regiment (Basic),
Fort Leonard Wood, Missouri,
Monday, 19 June 1950, 1230 Hours.

First Sergeant Sherman Sack was seated at his desk. The door to his office was closed, and at the moment his inbox was empty. Translated, this meant he didn't have a thing to do other than twiddle his thumbs. This was not because he'd previously disposed of the day's paperwork, but because there'd been none for him to deal with. "Sign of a successful administrator," he thought, smiling with some satisfaction. But nevertheless he was tired. He had just returned from a four-hour orientation in Building CR-C given by Major James Touhy to the members of the four company rifle teams who would be shooting in the battalion marksmanship competition. Each team consisted of six shooters, and most had qualified as Expert Riflemen. In the case of Company B's team, only five shooters had attended the orientation because one of the team members, specifically, Private William Rosen, still hadn't officially rejoined his company. The competition would take place the following day and, come hell or high water, Sergeant Sack vowed to make sure that Billy would be there. As Sergeant Sack began to drift into a pleasant relaxing reverie, he heard someone knocking at his door. "Come," he said. The door opened, and, with irritation, he saw Private La Droop standing in the doorway.

"What's your problem, La Droop?"

"Sorry to bother you, Top, but here's a letter for you sent in care of the company. Looks kinda official."

"Oh yeah? Well let's have it."

With some trepidation, Private La Droop took two steps into the First Sergeant's office, leaned forward, and carefully placed the letter on the desktop. Then, obsequiously, he shuffled back out of the office and quietly closed the door.

Sergeant Sack reached for the letter. He noticed that his name, rank, and the company address had been neatly typed on the envelope, obviously the work of a professional. But it was the return address which caught his attention:

New York State Court of Appeals
Court of Appeals Hall
20 Eagle Street
Albany 7, New York

Hurriedly, he opened the envelope and withdrew two pieces of paper: a handwritten letter and a typewritten schedule. He read the letter first.

Justice Meyer Newcomb
New York State Court of Appeals
Court of Appeals Hall
20 Eagle Street
Albany 7, New York

June 10, 1950

Dear Shermie:

I know that in my prior letters to you I never mentioned the status of the money I've been managing on your behalf. That was mostly intentional on my part because I always had it invested in vacant land. What I have been doing since you left was going into one land deal after another, each time taking a profit and then reinvesting everything after I've paid any taxes due. It seemed to be working, and then in 1946 I suffered a small loss...not a large one, mind you.

Finally, at the end of last year my efforts paid off. I sold all the land I bought and invested your funds in government securities which Manufacturers Trust Company in NYC is holding as custodian.

I'm fairly pleased with my efforts although, to be honest with you, I attribute much of my success to luck and good timing.

What I did when I took over your funds ($26,700) was match them with an equal amount of money from your Aunt Ruby. Then I formed a partnership, the Ruby Sherman Company. That was the company that has been buying and selling land these past 14 years. Last December I dissolved the partnership, and you and Aunt Ruby now have exactly the same investments. Each is in a separate custodial account at Manufacturers Trust Company.

I have enclosed a schedule of your assets. They are still in that trust we created just before you left for the Army, and we can terminate it if that's what you'd like to do. However, even with the trust intact you can withdraw as much of the income and principal as you wish. The officer at the bank who is familiar with your account is Chip Bosworth, TR 4-2000. Call him to get funds transferred, or for anything else.

Aunt Ruby joins me in sending warmest regards. We miss you a great deal and hope to see you one of these days. We would very much like to meet your wife.

By the way, I may not have mentioned that I was recently appointed to the Court of Appeals. From your high school civics class you may recall that this is New York State's highest appellate court. It's a real honor to serve on it. I plan to remain on the Court for a while, particularly since I have discovered that I'm able to take a fair amount of time off; and when court is in session and we are hearing appeals I have a number of excellent young clerks who help me with my legal research and opinion writing.

The Lord continues to be good to me and Aunt Ruby. We are both still in excellent health as I hope you and your wife are.

Fondly,

Uncle Mickey

After Sherman read the letter he looked at the Schedule. At its top the heading "**Assets of Sherman C. Sack Trust as of May 31, 1950**" appeared. There followed a list of government securities. At the end of the list there were four line items:

TOTAL FACE VALUE OF TRUST ASSETS:	$1,221,432.81
TOTAL FAIR MARKET VALUE OF TRUST ASSETS:	$1,242,387.04
ESTIMATED ANNUAL INCOME:	$29,314.89
CASH ON HAND:	$12,214.33

Sherman sat transfixed. He could hardly believe what he'd read. My God, how many other first sergeants were millionaires! Christ, what the hell should he do? Call Velma?

"Hold on, ol' buddy," he thought. "Let's think this through carefully."

And so Sergeant Sack sat at his desk trying as best he could to figure out what he should be doing. Finally, after five minutes had passed, he withdrew a sheet of letter size paper from the center drawer of his desk and began to make a handwritten list of people he needed to speak to right away:

Schtung (taking afternoon off)
Bosworth (funds transfer)
Don Shisler (Roubidoux Ford, Rolla)
Velma

Satisfied that he had covered all the bases that needed covering for the moment, he carefully replaced Mickey's letter and the Schedule in the envelope, folded it, and tucked it away in the back pocket of his pants. Then he got up and walked into the OR outer area. As usual, La Droop was seated at his desk reading a comic book.

"Hey genius," he said. "You seen the CO?"

La Droop looked up. "Stepped out a few minutes ago. Said he'd be right back. Probably went to the latrine."

"Okay, I'll be in my office. Lemme know when he gets back."

"You got it, Top," La Droop replied returning to his comic book.

Back in his office, Sergeant Sack placed a long distance call to Manufacturers Trust Company in New York City. When the bank operator answered, he asked to speak to Mr. Chip Bosworth.

"I'm very sorry, sir," the operator replied. "Mr. Bosworth is in conference. He won't be available for the rest of the day. May I please get your name and a number and I'll have him call you tomorrow?"

"I'd really like to speak to him right away."

"What's your name and number, sir?" the operator asked.

"Sherman C. Sack, ma'am..."

"Oh, Mr. Sack. Just one moment, sir," the operator interjected before Sherman could give her his number.

A few seconds later Sherman heard a different voice come on the line. "Chip Bosworth here, Mr. Sack. I'm sorry you had to wait. I did give specific instructions that if you called I was to be interrupted no matter what."

"That's okay, Mr. Bosworth. It's just that I want to surprise my wife with a little gift tonight and I'd like some funds transferred to me today here in Missouri if that's possible."

"Not a problem, sir. How much did you have in mind?"

"Oh, let's say $3,000."

"Fine, Mr. Sack. And where do I transfer the funds to?"

Sherman thought for a moment. "Is it possible to get them to Western Union in Rolla, Missouri?"

"I believe so, sir," Chip Bosworth replied. "If you give me your number I'll get back to you in, say, fifteen minutes. Is that okay?"

"Sure," Sherman said. "And here's my phone number."

***

Twelve minutes later Chip Bosworth called back. "Mr. Sack, you can pick up the money at the Western Union office in Rolla anytime after three forty-five this afternoon your time. Our bank will pay all wire charges."

"Thanks, Mr. Bosworth. And in the future please call me Sherman since it looks like we're going to be working together. One of these days I'll introduce you to my wife, Velma, who should also be authorized to withdraw funds."

"Thanks, Sherman; and you can call me Chip. And while we're at it, I think you should open a checking account with us, don't you? That way you can write a check for the amount you want without the need to call me or go through Western Union."

"Good idea," Sherman said. Then he gave Chip Bosworth his Waynesville address so that the checking account forms could be mailed to him.

***

Several minutes later the door to Sergeant Sack's office swung open and Captain Schtung entered.

"You needed to speak to me, First Sergeant?"

"Yes, sir. I know we're busy and all, what with the rifle competition tomorrow, the drill competition on Thursday, and the ceremony on Saturday, but something's come up and I need to take the rest of the afternoon off."

"Of course, First Sergeant. Is everything okay?"

"Just fine, sir," Sergeant Sack replied, although he knew that Captain Schtung would never know just how fine things really were.

When Captain Schtung left Sherman placed a call to Don Shisler at Roubidoux Ford in Rolla. After they had talked for a few minutes, he called Velma.

"Sweetheart," he said, "how 'bout taking the afternoon off and going into Rolla with me? And last time I drove your car I noticed the brakes were pulling slightly. Could you meet me at the house? Then we'll take your car so we can have the brakes checked."

"Okay with me, Sherman," Velma replied. "I could use some time off anyway. And I can do the shopping for tomorrow night. Don't forget, the Touhys are coming over for a barbecue."

"I won't, Vel. And while we're in Rolla I'd like to pick up some big juicy steaks for the four of us."

"Hold on, Sherman," Velma replied testily. "We're almost over budget for the month. Chicken will do just fine…which I'll be buying, not you."

"Sorry, Vel," he said. "You're right, honey, and I'll stay the hell out of your business. And, Vel, thanks for watching over our finances so carefully ’cuz we both know I’m no good at that.” He paused. “See you at the house in, say, half an hour?”

“See you then, baby,” Velma said.

But after they’d hung up Velma began to wonder. Had she detected just the slightest note of facetiousness in Sherman’s voice when he’d said to her “And, Vel, thanks for watching over our finances so carefully ’cuz we both know I’m no good at that.” Dammit, when it came to Sherman, she knew she was almost never wrong. Was he up to something? She’d soon find out. And come to think of it, the brakes on her car were working perfectly.

Chapter 45

939 East Seventh Street, Rolla, Missouri,
Monday, 19 June 1950, 1620 hours.

Sherman couldn't remember the precise wording of the age-old adage about the best laid plans, but the joyful afternoon he'd intended was turning to shit. First, Velma had not been shy in letting him know just how irritated she was when, after he'd asked her to wait in the car for a "minute or two" while he went into the Western Union office to pick up a telegram, he had kept her waiting almost forty-five minutes. And now they'd just parked in front of the Ford dealership and he'd gotten another shot. "Sherman, how come you parked on the street instead of driving into the service department? Just confirms what I thought. Not a damn thing wrong with my brakes. Why are we here, because I've got things to do today? You jerkin' me around or something?"

Then he'd handed her the envelope containing Uncle Mickey's letter and the asset schedule. At the moment he was sitting in the car awaiting her reaction. He had no idea what it would be.

When she finished reading, Velma looked up at Sherman. "Goddamn you," she said. There were tears in her eyes. "Why in all these years didn't you tell me you had family? What with both our parents gone and neither of us having any brothers or sisters, why?"

Sherman was dumbfounded. Not a word about the money. Nothing!

Velma opened her purse and withdrew a handkerchief. She wiped her eyes. "They could'a been with us Thanksgivings, on Christmas, Easters. Could'a stayed with us. I've always missed not having family. You know that."

Sherman could see that Velma's hands were shaking.

"Sherman, why did you keep this from me? I'm your wife, you know. Least I thought I was before I read this letter. Are you ashamed of me or something? These people are like your parents. And now they're old, and look what we've missed!"

"I'm sorry, Vel," Sherman stammered. "When my folks died the Newcombs took me in 'til I graduated high school. It was only for six months. I never thought you'd care..."

"You never thought I'd care!" Velma began to gasp for breath.

"Goddamn you, Sherman Cullum Sack, stop bullshitting me. These people obviously love you. And you never bothered to tell me about them."

Finally, after catching her breath, she continued. "Sherman, we can't undo the past. But they're coming here right now!" She paused for a moment.

"You got some of that money on you, Sherman? Is that why you went into the Western Union office?"

"Yes," he replied, looking down, unable to meet his wife's gaze.

"Okay, then, hand it over. We're going to a travel agency and send them tickets. Just in case you don't understand, Sherman, they're our only family!"

Sherman reached into his pocket and withdrew the $3,000 in cash he had just picked up at the Western Union office. He handed it to his wife. And as he did, he made a mental note to call Don Shisler at Roubidoux Ford and tell him that he'd decided not to go forward with the purchase of the red convertible he'd planned to give Velma, at least not for now. Velma was right. The Newcombs really were their only family, and he longed to see them.

***

"That will be $267.00, ma'am," Louisa Garrett, owner of All-Points Travel, said as she handed Velma two open first-class round trip tickets on TWA between Albany, New York, and St. Louis, Missouri.

Velma looked over the tickets. They were issued in the names of Meyer Newcomb and Ruby Newcomb, and everything else appeared to be in order. Velma reached into her purse and handed Miss Garrett six fifty dollar bills.

As Louisa Garrett was preparing a receipt for the Sacks, Velma said, "Come to think of it, Sherman, we've got one more item of business with Miss Garrett here."

"Whaddya mean, honey?"

"Well I seem to recall that you told me about a nice lady you met at some restaurant on your way down to Jim Touhy's place. Ring a bell?"

"'Lori' of 'Lori's Diner'?"

"That's the one, Sherman. And I also seem to recall you telling me it was her son who saved us a fortune in additional insurance premiums."

Sherman nodded.

"And didn't you also tell me Lori picked up the tab for you and Billy when you ate at her place and then told you she considered all army people to be 'family'?"

Sherman nodded a second time.

"Well," Velma said, "we are one big family. And now that we're here do you maybe know her full name and address?"

Sherman withdrew his wallet from his pants pocket and found Lori's business card in it. He handed it to Velma.

"Seems we're finally making a little progress, Sherman."

Velma read over the card carefully. It contained the name of the restaurant, Lori's Diner, its address, and the name of the owner, Lori Billingsley.

"Miss Garrett," Velma said, "we'll be needing another open first-class round trip ticket, this time between St. Louis and Frankfurt, Germany. We've got a friend who's gonna be visiting her son."

***

In the car on the way home Velma turned to Sherman. "Now you listen to me, big boy. And you listen carefully. We tell no one, I mean no one, about that money. And no more withdrawals without my okay!"

Sherman nodded a third time.

"And just so you know it, Sherman, I did buy us four big juicy sirloin strip steaks like you wanted. But that's the last of the luxuries for a long time." Velma looked over at Sherman to make sure he was listening. "And one of these days we'll talk about that money. But not right now when I feel like hitting you over the head with a frying pan. You understand?"

Sherman was getting weary of nodding so instead he saluted.

Chapter 46

Range #4, Fort Leonard Wood, Missouri, Tuesday, 20 June 1950, 0800 Hours.

There are six rifle ranges at Fort Leonard Wood, all located to its south beyond the terminus of Iowa Avenue and hopefully out of earshot (and gunshot) of nearby Forney Field, Fort Wood's airport. To the uninitiated the ranges all look alike and most people couldn't possibly tell one from another. Not so in the case of Major James Touhy, former captain of the championship U.S. Army Pistol Team and, since his retirement four years ago, a member of the Arkansas National Guard.

Three years earlier Major Touhy had been asked by Lieutenant Colonel Jonathan Q. Paulson, Commanding Officer of the Fourth Battalion, Second TRB, to take charge of the battalion's inter-company rifle competition held a few days before the end of each eight-week basic training cycle. At the time Major Touhy told Colonel Paulson he would only accept this assignment if the competitions were held at Range #4. When Colonel Paulson seemed to balk at this request, Major Touhy went on to make clear that because of its location and topography Range #4 was by far the best of the six shooting venues. He explained that shooters would be firing in a northerly direction which meant that sunlight was generally not a factor; moreover, there was a land rise to the west of Range #4 which served as a natural wind barrier. At the time Colonel Paulson told Major Touhy that he'd have to think about all this, but that he would get back to Major Touhy in a few days. And two days later he "reluctantly yielded" to Major Touhy's demand. In truth, Colonel Paulson didn't give a crap which range was used. What he wanted most of all was to have Jim Touhy honcho the competitions. He knew that Touhy was the best damn person in or out of the Army for the job.

Thus far in 1950 Jim Touhy had run two rifle competitions for Colonel Paulson. Neither had produced any noteworthy shooters, and the only saving grace had been the pleasant evenings that Jim and his wife, Nancy, had spent with their close friends, Sherman and Velma Sack. But Jim knew that today's competition would be different. Private William Rosen would be shooting, and in the many years he'd been around rifle and pistol competitions Jim had never seen anyone quite like Billy. The kid was a goddamn phenomenon.

And so, as he stood before the assemblage involved in the day's competition ready to give last minute instructions, Jim took careful note of the weather, the people who were present, and just about every other detail he could possibly absorb. He wanted very much to remember this particular day because he was certain some kind of shooting history was going to be made.

"All right, people, listen up," he said. "After that lengthy orientation we had yesterday you know you'll be firing the same routine you did when you qualified. But I've still got a few things for you." He cleared his throat. "First, earplugs. I strongly recommend you use 'em. I don't wanna be responsible for any hearing loss. They're on the table over there." He pointed to a portable table that had been set up nearby. "We'll have someone there who can show you how to use 'em if you don't know already." He looked around. They were listening.

"Okay, shooters, a word about the particular M1 you'll be firing. The one you shoot will be based on a draw. There are twenty-four M1's over there in four racks." He looked in the direction of the rifle racks. "Their stocks are numbered 1 to 24. Six came from each company after being thoroughly checked by the company's armorer. He's cleaned them, blackened their sights, and sighted them in as best he could." He waited a moment. "Sergeant Williamson, front and center!"

"Sir!" Sergeant Williamson replied snappily as he quickly went up to Major Touhy. He was carrying a shoe box.

Those present at the shoot who were permanent party knew and liked Master Sergeant Theodore ("Teddy") Williamson, the battalion sergeant major. He was highly popular with all of the officers and noncoms of the Fourth Battalion and, whenever he could, Teddy always tried to be helpful. When Jim had taken over the job of running the rifle competitions, Colonel Paulson had introduced him to Teddy and the two immediately hit it off, probably because, when it came to shooting, the sergeant major was not exactly a slouch. He was a damn good shot in his own right. And so it had become custom that when each rifle competition was to take place, Teddy would be there to help Jim out. Like Jim, Teddy was also looking forward to today's shoot, mostly because of what Jim had told him about Private William Rosen.

"Thank you, Sergeant Major," Jim said. Turning back to the others, he continued. "As you folks can see, the Sergeant Major here has a shoe box. In it are twenty-four folded slips of paper numbered 1 to 24. When I finish my little spiel I want each shooter to take a slip of paper. The number on it serves three purposes:

"First, and most important, it identifies you to us by your number after you've signed the log sheet. So right after you've gotten your number we want you to come on over and sign Sergeant Williamson's number log sheet so we know who got which number.

"Second, your number designates the M1 you'll be shooting. That M1 will have your number taped to its stock. So, as I said, your rifle is really assigned by lot. After you've gotten your number go draw the M1 with the same number from the rifle racks. Corporal Svendsen, Company B's Armorer, will be there to help you." Corporal Svendsen raised his hand and waved it.

"And last of all, your number indicates the location you'll be shooting from." Jim pointed to the firing line.

"We got twelve shooting spots. The first one is over there on the far left. It's for numbers 1 and 13. The second, next in line to the right, is for 2 and 14. And so on. The four company first sergeants will be working the firing line. They'll check your slip of paper against your rifle and where you're shooting from, so don't lose that slip of paper or remove the number from your rifle." He paused.

"Now a couple'a final things:

"Shooting groups. We'll be shooting in two groups of twelve. The first group will be numbers 1 through 12, and the second group will be numbers 13 through 24.

"Next, zeroing in. You'll have twenty minutes to zero in your rifle. Take as many shots as you want, but they'll all have to be from two hundred yards. Remember—and we went over this at the orientation—if you're sighted in at that distance, then you know how to correct for the other shooting distances, three hundred yards and five hundred yards, without firing off any more rounds." He looked up. No confused faces.

"Okay, we've finally come to the end: the scoring. You won't be told today what you shot." He heard a few groans which he ignored. "The first sergeants will have the scores by Friday. They'll be recorded using the numbers you've drawn, not by names, so, again, signing that log sheet is important. And on Saturday at the ceremony we'll announce the winning company and the best shots." Then he took a small piece of paper from his pocket. It had handwritten notes on it. He looked it over to make sure he hadn't forgotten anything.

"Questions?" he asked. No one had any.

"All right, then, come on up and draw a number outta the shoe box."

***

Billy was standing next to Vin and Jason "Jack" Russell. He felt good. His throat and windpipe seemed to be okay, and it had been great to be back in the barracks for the first time in weeks. In fact, last night he'd slept like a log in his bunk. He knew he was whole once again, and that, finally, things were close to being sorted out. In fact, the only thing he hadn't done in a long while was go for a run with Sergeant Sack. He hoped to do that shortly, and he would mention it to him later on in the day.

Billy, Vin, Jack, and three others Billy didn't know well, Charlie Courtney, Tony Mateo, and Jan Hildemuth, made up Company B's rifle team. Everyone had shot Expert, and Billy had heard that Vin was an absolute natural and had scored over 200. "We've come a long way," Billy thought as he remembered the time when he'd tried to help Vin at the end of that haircut line. Now Vin's hair was as short as it had been after that first haircut, he looked scrubbed and shaved, his fatigues were pressed and pleated, and his brass and boots shined. "Christ," Billy thought, "he looks like something fresh out of VMI. Who would'a predicted that armying would replace that gang member hairdo!"

As Billy walked over to Jim and Sergeant Major Williamson, Jim smiled. "Good luck, soldier," he said. Billy nodded in reply, not wanting to let on that he and Jim were on a first name basis. "Thank you, sir," he said as he reached into the shoe box. He drew number 15 which meant he'd be shooting with the second group. Vin drew number 9.

And then Billy remembered the conversation he'd had with Sergeant Sack down at Touhy's place in Arkansas at the end of his first day there:

"Lemme tell you something, kid," Sergeant Sack had said. "You're learning it all the right way. In basic the other recruits only get lectures and group instruction. You're getting it one-on-one from the best there is."

"If what Jim has shown me works," Billy remembered saying, "I think I'll do okay."

"Guaranteed it will," Sergeant Sack had said.

And so, as he had done so often at Harvard just before an exam, Billy closed his eyes and tried to remember the important things Jim had taught him during those two days at Elk Hill Dude Ranch. It took a few minutes, but then he knew he was ready, as ready as he would ever be.

Chapter 47

336 Pippen Road, Waynesville, Missouri, Tuesday, 20 June 1950, 1940 Hours.

Even though it was almost eight o'clock in the evening, it was still light. And because it was so warm, Velma had left the back door of the Sacks' rental home open. But she had closed the screen door to keep the bugs out. She was standing in the patio leaning back against the side of the house. Subconsciously she was listening for the sound of the front doorbell chimes; but, at the same time, she was watching her husband stoke their flimsy portable barbecue cooker with additional charcoal briquettes as he tried to get the fire as hot as possible. He liked his steaks charred on the outside and pink inside, and so did she. Velma's eyes weren't entirely concentrated on her husband. She was also gazing dreamily out over the backyard, the one part of their home she disliked. Its crabgrass lawn was interspersed with brown dead areas and its concrete walkway was haphazardly cracked, each a testimonial to Missouri's harsh climate. "Wouldn't it be nice to own our home," she thought, "with a beautifully landscaped backyard…maybe even a manicured dichondra lawn surrounded by flower beds and a used brick patio. Some day after Sherman retires, if we can afford it." And then she remembered: they could easily afford it, even now while he was still on active duty. She began to smile at the thought of spending Sherman's money, something she had discouraged, almost forbidden, only yesterday. Was she on her way to becoming a spendthrift? She would have to watch herself! It was at this moment that she heard the front doorbell chimes announce the arrival of the Touhys.

"Vel," Sherman called out. He too had heard the chimes. "Looks like our guests are here. Can you get the front door?" He was still working on the barbecue's fire which didn't seem to want to cooperate.

"On my way," Velma replied.

***

"Sorry, Tou," Sergeant Sack said. "Things are a little discombobulated 'round here. We thought we'd eat outside, but the table and chairs are still in the garage. My fault. I got home late from today's shoot."

"No problem, Sacko. I'll get them." Then Jim held up a chilled bottle of champagne.

"And, here, ol' buddy. Special for tonight's occasion. We got a little celebratin' to do."

"So tell me."

"In good time, First Sergeant, in good time. You just get to work on those steaks I see there. I'll take care of the table and chairs. I'll even set the damn table."

"Hardly something for a field grade officer to be doin', I'd say," Sergeant Sack replied, smiling.

"Screw you, Sacko! I'm no active duty officer. Just a plain old Arkansas National Guardsman, and a lot less lazy than some first sergeants I know."

***

Twenty-five minutes later the two couples were seated on the patio at an elegantly set table adorned with a white linen tablecloth, candles, and Velma's best china and silverware. In the center on a large platter were four charred New York strip sirloin steaks, steamed fresh string beans, and Velma's specialty, mashed potatoes made with butter, sour cream, salt and pepper, paprika, and bits of crisp bacon. Next to each place setting there was a salad plate with a Caesar's salad on it and also an empty champagne glass.

A moment later there was a popping sound as Jim began the celebration. "I'll do the honors," he said as he poured the champagne.

"First, I wanna make a toast to good health, happiness, friendship, and…" he looked at Nancy, "love. I think we've all got a lot to be thankful for, and that's what it's really all about, isn't it?"

"Hear, hear!" Velma said as she took her first sip of champagne.

"Tou," she said. "This is delicious. Thanks so much for bringing it. And thanks to you both for coming tonight and being with us…and for being our friends."

"Hold on. I'm not through," he said. "See, today, Sacko and I thought some history might be made at our shoot. We thought maybe a young man who showed a little promise might do fairly well." He was smiling.

"That young man is someone we've all put a little effort into one way or another, and…"

"And, what?" Sergeant Sack said.

"And I guess we've proved our efforts weren't in vain. Seems that Private Billy Rosen didn't let us down."

"For Christ's sake, Tou, what?"

"You ready for this, Sacko?"

"Jesus!" Sergeant Sack replied. "Tell us, will you!"

"Would you believe he shot a possible!"

Velma saw her husband's eyes widen in astonishment. He appeared stunned.

"What's 'a possible,' Jim?" she asked.

"That's the max, Vel. The most you can get. Billy scored 210 out of 210."

Turning to Sergeant Sack, he continued, "Yep, Sacko. He pulled a real tack-driver in that rifle draw. Then proceeded to drill the bulls by the numbers."

"Ho-lee shit!" Sergeant Sack finally whispered. "Holy fuckin' shit!" Suddenly aware of his choice of language, he looked over at Velma apologetically. "Sorry, honey. It's just…"

Velma was laughing. "It's okay, First Sergeant. Billy Rosen seems to be full of surprises, don't you think?"

Sergeant Sack nodded.

"So where does all this leave us?" Nancy asked.

"Wish I knew," Jim replied. "But I think it gives us a good excuse for my second toast, this one to me and you, Sacko, for turning Billy into one of the best damn shooters in the U.S. Army!"

"We'll all drink to that, Tou," Sergeant Sack said as he raised his glass and then, in one swig, emptied it.

***

"Nice evening," Jim said as they were finishing dessert and coffee. The table had been mostly cleared, the dirty dishes were in the sink, and the bottle of champagne, now a "dead soldier," was in the trash can.

"So Sacko, what about the drill team competition and the battalion awards for the outstanding recruit and the top company?"

"All gonna be announced at the ceremony Saturday. Drill competition'll take place Thursday. Sergeant Gomez is in charge for our company. He tells me he's got a drill squad leader for this cycle who's exceptional. Kid by the name of Craig Billington. I'll get to see all four company drill teams compete Thursday. You can attend if you want."

"No thanks," Jim said. "I'll just wait until Saturday and see the winner perform. But tell me about the Outstanding Recruit Award. Think Billy has a chance?"

"Not likely. Remember, he's missed a lot of training," Sergeant Sack replied. "He is well liked, though. But you know how it works. Each of my four platoon sergeants will be giving me two recommendations tomorrow. Then the Captain and I will make the cut down to two, and I'll send in our company's two names to Teddy Williamson along with a letter spelling out our reasons for selecting them. Same thing for the other three companies. Teddy and Colonel Paulson will make the final decision from the batch of eight…by Friday night at the latest. But no one finds out until Saturday. 'Course, when it comes to the top company it's pretty automatic. It's based on the best shooting team and best drill team. But where the winning shooting and drill teams are from different companies, Teddy and Colonel Paulson again make the call. But, like I said, everything will be announced Saturday." Then Sergeant Sack looked up at Jim.

"Tou, you got any idea which company shot best today?"

"Sorry, ol' buddy, I don't. As a favor, Teddy just gave me Billy's score. You'll get your answer when you get all the other scores on Friday. Guess we'll all have to wait until then."

Just then the doorbell chimes sounded.

A minute later Sergeant Sack walked in with an unexpected guest, Teddy Williamson, who was carrying his own bottle of champagne.

"Hi guys," Teddy said. "Got some news about another one of the shooters from your company, Sherm. Thought you might wanna hear about him."

"Really?" Sergeant Sack said. "And who's that?"

"Kid by the name of Vincent Foggerty."

"And?"

"He shot a 201!"

"Hot damn!" Sergeant Sack replied. "That means I got two over 200."

"Right," Teddy said. "Plus four more in the 190's."

"Jesus, wait 'til I tell the CO!"

"No hurry about that. I already called Captain Schtung. Man, was he excited. I'd say your company's rifle team for this cycle is about the best you've ever fielded. That's why I brought this." Teddy held up the bottle of champagne. "Thought our celebration deserved a little bubbly."

"Sure does!" Velma said, her eyes twinkling. "Why don't you take my chair, Teddy. Have some dessert. I'll go in the kitchen and get some glasses."

"Deal," Teddy replied. "But none of us should have more than a couple of glasses or tomorrow may turn into a horror story."

"We wouldn't want that, now would we?" Jim said smiling. "Hey, Vel," he called out. "Hurry up with the glasses or all the fizz'll escape."

"They're on the way, Major," Velma answered. "And it isn't often I get to drink champagne." Velma turned to Nancy and winked.

"Same for the rest of us," Nancy said. "Good way to end a perfect evening. Thanks for thinking to bring it, Teddy."

"My pleasure," Sergeant Major Williamson replied. He felt exceptionally pleased with himself. For once he'd done something right. He'd surprised them all with champagne, something they obviously hadn't had in a quite a while.

***

Their guests gone, Sergeant Sack was in the kitchen helping his wife clean up when she turned to him. "Honey, I've been wondering about something."

"What?"

"You have any idea what's gonna happen to Billy after Saturday?"

"Matter of fact I do, Vel. Although he hasn't gotten his orders yet, I know what they are. He's been assigned to the Public Information Office at Fifth Army Headquarters in Chicago."

"Meaning?"

"I don't understand," Sergeant Sack replied.

"Well, meaning, is he going to be getting any additional training?"

"Not exactly, Vel. He'll be going there for OJT."

"That's too bad, Sherman. What you're saying is that his army experience will just about end when he leaves here."

"Oh, I dunno, Vel."

"Sure it will, Sherman. With that assignment he's not gonna be exposed to anything new…just office work."

Sherman thought for a moment. "I guess you're right. But nothing much I can do about that. Fact is, he's probably better off."

"Whaddya mean?"

"Well, most of the people in the company have been assigned to advanced infantry training here at Wood for eight more weeks. But with the gaps in Billy's training which I've sorta overlooked he really shouldn't be doing that."

"Gaps? What sorta gaps?"

"Well, you know…things he missed while he was in the hospital."

"Like what?"

"Oh, like the infiltration course and bivouac, for instance. Also he never got bayonet training or instruction in hand-to-hand combat; and he's never tossed a grenade or fired a 45 automatic, a Carbine, or a BAR."

"Aw Christ, Sherman, the infiltration course…that's nothin' but keeping your head down and crawling around; and bivouac, shoot, that's just sleeping in a damn tent. And the rest of that stuff, why you could show him all that in half a day."

"And what difference would it make if I could, Vel? He'd only be needing that if he were staying here for advanced infantry training…which he isn't."

"I know," Vel said. She was quiet for a moment. "Sure would be nice, though, having him here a while longer. You two could take your runs and all."

"Vel," Sherman said, "we've been 'round the Army long enough to know how things work. Billy'll move on like all the rest. We'll try to stay in touch with him, but you know that doesn't generally last. He'll just be someone special we met along the way."

"I sure hope we run into him sometime in the future, Sherman."

"So do I, Vel. But it's not in the cards."

Chapter 48

Office of the Commanding Officer, U.S. Army Induction Center, Chicago, Illinois, Wednesday, 21 June 1950, 0800 Hours.

Colonel Kenneth Harkavy was seated at his desk in his office at Chicago's Induction Center. As usual, he was paying no attention to his Spartan surroundings. Instead, his thoughts were focused on his upcoming promotion to brigadier general in just over a week. It was something he'd always wanted. Once there, he knew the addition of more stars to his rank would be far easier. But the challenge of getting that first star had been the greatest of his military career, and he felt relieved that it was now behind him. His reverie was interrupted when Mildred poked her head in through the open doorway.

"Colonel, Wally's here."

"Thanks, Mildred. Send him in. And hold my calls, will you."

"Yes, sir," she replied.

***

"So, Sergeant Marks, take a seat, and tell me what you've got."

"What you asked for, sir: Rosen's assignment orders. Here." Sergeant Marks handed Colonel Harkavy a letter size sheet of paper which the latter took a moment to read.

"Christ, Wally, this assignment to the PIO at Fifth Army Headquarters in Chicago is no damn good. Doesn't come close to serving our purposes. Not even slightly."

"I know, sir. I honestly can't figure it out. When I called the AG's Office in D.C. six weeks ago I was assured that Rosen would be assigned to advanced infantry training down at Wood—which we both know is more or less customary."

"Yeah, well, he wasn't. I wanna know why—and I want you to get this thing fixed ASAP. We're running out of time!"

"I'll give it a try, Colonel."

"Goddammit, I don't want you to try. I want you to do it. This is absolutely critical, Wally!"

"Understood, sir," Sergeant Marks replied as he left Colonel Harkavy's office.

***

Forty-five minutes later Sergeant Marks was back in Colonel Harkavy's office. "Colonel," he said, "Rosen will be going into advanced infantry training at Wood. I'm heading over to Fifth Army Headquarters on the South Side in about thirty minutes to pick up copies of his orders. Mildred's gonna get them on today's 11:00 AM air courier to Wood. Plus I called the Assignments Section down there and told them to be on the lookout for Rosen's new orders.

"And, sir, I found out what happened. About four weeks ago the Honorable Ronald G. Lourdes, U.S. Senator from Illinois, went over to the Pentagon in person and arranged for Rosen's cushy Chicago assignment. So what I did was get in touch with one of my master sergeant buddies who owed me a favor. He knew exactly the right person to call in D.C. to get us what we wanted."

"Terrific, Wally," Colonel Harkavy said. "I knew you could do it. Thanks."

"You're welcome, sir. But the whole thing only confirms what I told you when we first talked about Rosen, Colonel."

"Which is?"

"That his father's powerful and influential."

"Yeah, well it only confirms to me that Rosen's father and that Senator don't have a clue." Colonel Harkavy was smiling.

"About what, sir?"

"Who they're up against."

Chapter 49

Orderly Room, Company B,
Fourth Battalion, Second Training Regiment (Basic),
Fort Leonard Wood, Missouri,
Thursday, 22 June 1950, 0730 Hours.

First Sergeant Sherman Sack's initial stop of the day was the OR. He had planned to spend no more than ten minutes there going over a few things before taking off for Gammon Field, Fort Wood's main parade field, to watch the Fourth Battalion drill team competition which was scheduled to begin at 0900. Sergeant Gomez, the NCOIC of Company B's team, had been unusually tight-lipped when Sergeant Sack had tried to find out how things were going. No matter. He would see for himself in a couple of hours. As he walked into his office, he noticed four large manila envelopes on his desk. He knew what they contained: the assignment orders for the recruits in each of the company's four platoons.

Sergeant Sack reached for one of the envelopes, the one with "First Platoon, Company B, Fourth Battalion, Second TRB" printed on it. He opened it and thumbed through the orders. They were arranged alphabetically. There it was: Rosen, William, NMI, Private (E-1), ER16548889. Sergeant Sack began to read it. "Son of a bitch!" he whispered. Then he picked up the phone and called his wife.

"It's me, and I know I shouldn't be calling right now 'cuz it's your private time, but something's come up."

"That's okay, Sherman. What's going on?"

"Well I won't be coming home until late. And there's an outside chance I might have to be out all night."

"Meaning?"

"I've finally seen Billy's orders."

"And?"

"And he's staying right here. Going to advanced infantry training."

"That's great isn't it?" Velma asked.

"Sure it is. But at the same time somebody's been messin' with him again, Vel. Remember, I told you he was gonna go to the Fifth Army Headquarters in Chicago for OJT."

"Hmm," Velma said. "At least whoever's been switching his orders around seems to have made sure he's not being treated differently from the rest."

"Yeah, I know. But I don't like it," Sergeant Sack said.

"Not much you can do about it, is there?"

"Guess not. But now I'll have to miss the drill competition and give Billy that additional training we talked about."

"I agree, Sherman. So go to it."

"See you when we're finished," Sergeant Sack said. He hung up and stepped into the OR outer area. He beckoned to Sergeant Whitney.

"Whit, I need your help ASAP. Get hold of Svendsen and then the two of you come on into my office."

Turning to La Droop who, surprisingly, had traded in his comic book for a girlie magazine, Sergeant Sack said, "Hey, whiz kid, I got something for you. Get your ass out the door; go find Rosen and get him over here on the goddamn double. Make sure he's wearin' fatigues. Now!"

***

Corporal Arvin Svendsen, the company armorer, and Sergeant Don Whitney, the company clerk, were seated in Sergeant Sack's office.

"Okay, listen up 'cuz we don't have much time. I'm givin' Rosen some special training today. I gotta have him catch up to the others in the company. And I need your help." He paused.

"Whit, go on over to the motor pool and wangle me a vehicle. Jeep or truck, I don't care. But bring it back here soon as you can. Okay, take off!" Sergeant Whitney left immediately.

Turning to his pan-faced company armorer, Sergeant Sack continued. "Arv, round up two M1s with bayonets, a Carbine, a 45, and a BAR. I'll need a dozen clips of ammo for each 'cept I don't need any M1 ammo. And get me a box of grenades. When Whit brings the vehicle back here, stick all that stuff in it. Got it?" Corporal Svendsen nodded, and got up. It was at this point that

Sergeant Sack heard Captain Schtung. He had just arrived and was in the OR outer area. Sergeant Sack went over to him.

"Captain, I need to speak to you."

"Of course, First Sergeant. What is it?"

"Well, sir, it's kinda personal. Could we talk in my office?"

"Certainly, First Sergeant."

***

Back in his office with Captain Schtung, Sergeant Sack closed the door.

"Sir, I need you to help me with Private Rosen."

"Help you with Rosen? What kind of help, First Sergeant? What's going on?"

"Well, sir, I think someone's been fucking with him again."

"What?" Captain Schtung said in a raised voice. "Goddammit, I thought that ended!"

"So did I, sir. But I don't think so. See, I checked with the Assignments Section some days ago and I know for sure Rosen's assignment was to the Public Information Office at Fifth Army Headquarters in Chicago for OJT. When I heard this, I decided to forget about bayonet training, hand-to-hand combat stuff, or firing the Carbine, the 45, and the BAR…or even tossing a grenade. But this morning the orders for everyone came in. Here're his." Sergeant Sack handed Captain Schtung the copy of Billy's orders.

After he'd read them over, Captain Schtung thought for a moment. "I see what you mean, First Sergeant. This isn't exactly harassment, but, still, from what you tell me, his orders have obviously been changed. Maybe that fucker, Harkavy, interfering again. And now you want me to help you bring him up to speed. Is that it?"

"That's it, sir. And we haven't much time."

"This, First Sergeant, is my cup of tea. Something like what we used to do at the 'U' a day or so before a big game. I'd say you and I can show Private Rosen a thing or two about the bayonet and hand-to-hand combat."

"A bit like old times, Captain," Sergeant Sack replied. He too was smiling. "So let's meet at the gym in, say, an hour?"

"I'll see you there, First Sergeant. I've gotta go home and change into fatigues. And I'll stick with you until we both feel Rosen's been fully prepped."

When Captain Schtung left his office, Sergeant Sack thought to himself, "Emil Schtung, you're a good man. I never even had to tell you that this was all part of your payback to Billy, did I?"

Chapter 50

Orderly Room, Company B, Fourth Battalion, Second Training Regiment (Basic), Fort Leonard Wood, Missouri, Friday, 23 June 1950, 1110 Hours.

Exhausted from having been up most of the night giving special instruction to Private William Rosen, Sergeant Sack entered the OR holding a cup of black coffee. He headed straight for his office. Strange. Its door was half-open and cigar smoke appeared to be coming from within. Quickening his pace, Sergeant Sack went over to the doorway and looked inside. A large obese man wearing civilian clothes and puffing on a cigar was seated behind the desk working a crossword puzzle. Putting the puzzle aside, the man looked up. "Come on in, Sherm. This hole in the wall belongs to you, not me."

The voice. Sergeant Sack recognized it immediately. "Bad News!" he exclaimed. "What in hell you doin' here?" From his tone, it was obvious that Sergeant Sack liked the man immensely.

"Thought you'd never ask. Guess you might call it working."

"'Working,' my ass. You don't even know what the word means, you lazy fuck. Christ, it's good to see you. You okay?"

But as he spoke, Sergeant Sack realized his friend was hardly okay. He was fatter and sicklier in appearance than he'd been eighteen months before when the two had last seen one another. Now Sergeant Sack looked at him closely. Sprouting from a more corpulent body than he remembered were the man's stubby arms and legs. His hands and feet were still unusually tiny, but his limbs were flabbier. Disturbingly, his large bald head resembled that of a corpse, and his complexion was a pasty off-white. Because he had put on so much weight, his eyes had turned to slits and his nose appeared broader and more pig-like. And now he noticed that his friend had three chins, not two. Only his mouth with those annoyingly thin lips hadn't changed.

The man, Anthony "Bad News" Edmunds, was no stranger. When he was younger and leaner, he had served with Sherman Sack and Emil Schtung in the South Pacific during the last war. When it ended he had elected to remain in the Army. His first assignment had been to the Army's Criminal Investigation Command at Fort Holabird, Maryland, where he had attended its renowned agent's course from which he graduated first in his class. Police work agreed with him and he soon made his mark as one the Army's top sleuths. Because he so often was the bearer of bad news for those he was investigating, he had gained his nickname. Like other members of the CID, Bad News never displayed his rank, and Sergeant Sack didn't know what it was. And if he wore a uniform, it was that of an officer but without insignias or other markings. More often than not, though, he simply wore civilian clothing.

Bad News reached down and hoisted a battered briefcase onto the desktop. He opened it and removed a half-inch thick manila file folder. He shoved it toward Sergeant Sack who was now seated in one of the two pull-up chairs in front of the desk. "Read this," he said as he took a puff of his cigar before returning to his crossword puzzle. Sergeant Sack noticed that the name *Furax* was typed on the label affixed to the file tab.

***

Fifteen minutes later Sergeant Sack put the file down. Bad News looked up. "So, whaddya think?"

"Nothin' surprises me anymore. Just another scheme to separate the Army from its property. But on a fairly grand scale. Violent too, with that guy being murdered."

"That's all?" Bad News chuckled. "And what if I told you it's been goin' on here right under your nose?"

"Horseshit!"

"Well it has been. But don't feel special. We think it's spread to the other companies 'round here; other places too. It's a damn cancer. 'Bout six weeks ago we were all set up to nab your mess sergeant, one of his helpers, and the guy who runs the Fort Wood Commissary. But for some reason the food pickup was aborted. I wanna know why." As he said this, Bad News suddenly began to gasp for breath. His face turned even whiter and he started to sweat profusely. Almost automatically he reached into his shirt pocket and withdrew a small bottle. Opening it, he shook out a tiny pill and placed it under his tongue. Then he leaned back and closed his eyes. A minute later he appeared completely normal.

"Sorry about that. Ticker's been acting up lately." He paused for a moment.

"Sherm," he said, "I need some help."

"Sure. You want me to get a doctor? Or call Velma?"

"No, no. I don't mean that kinda help. I gotta meet with some of the Wood Commissary people for a couple of hours; and after that I was hopin' to knock off early. Head on back to the BOQ and rest up…that is, if you'd cover for me."

"Glad to. Just tell me what I'm supposed to do."

"Okay. You got a KP Roster?"

"Sure. Hold on." Sergeant Sack got up and left his office. A few minutes later he returned with a three-hole notebook which he handed to Bad News. The latter began flipping through the pages until he came to one listing six names under the date "9 May 1950." "Huh," he said.

"What?"

"I know a little about one of these guys." Again he reached into his briefcase and withdrew a file—this one rather thin—which he gave to Sergeant Sack. It was labeled *"Rosen, William NMI (ER16548889)—Security Clearance."*

"Before I got here I was in Chicago working on this. From all indications, his father's a hoodlum…involved with some pretty unsavory underworld characters."

Sergeant Sack was puzzled. Immediately he opened the file. Among other items, it contained a series of interview reports including one with a Chicago Sun-Times crime reporter who talked about Louis Rosen's supposed Mafia connections and illicit business dealings. That surprised him. But he was also confused. Why in hell would Billy be getting checked out for a security clearance?

***

"So what I'd like you to do, Sherm, is interview these six guys and write up interview reports on them. Have 'em typed in triplicate and delivered to me in the BOQ by 2100 hours at the latest. I gotta know what went on while they were on KP that day. I'm lookin' for anything involving Furax. And I also gotta find out why that pickup didn't happen."

"I'll take care of it," Sergeant Sack replied.

***

By 1600 hours Sergeant Sack had finished compiling interview reports on every one of the six except Billy. His last interview with Vin Foggerty had been the only one which had shed any light on "Furax" and why the pickup hadn't occurred. It had also confirmed to him that Cookie and his helper, Ben Cross, were in this thing up to their eyeballs, and he had made a mental note of this. Even if they weren't prosecuted, he would deal with them in his own way at a time of his choosing. He got up and opened the door to his office. Billy was seated in a chair in the outer area reading. "Come on in, pal," he said.

As Billy entered, he asked, "Name 'Furax' mean anything to you, kid?" He thought he saw a look of shock cross Billy's face, but only for an instant.

***

The interview had proceeded as he'd expected it would. Billy had more or less repeated what Sergeant Sack had learned from Vin Foggerty. But there were still a few loose ends to clear up.

"So lemme recreate the scene, kid. You had this guy pinned to the dock with your foot on his throat, right?"

Billy nodded.

"And you were gonna call the MPs?"

Billy nodded again.

"But then Foggerty hands you this guy's business card and you decide not to call them. How come? What made you change your mind?"

"Good old Sack," Billy thought. "Never misses a beat. He's brought us right to the crux of the matter. I wouldn't have expected anything less from him."

"First Sergeant," he said, looking directly at Sergeant Sack, "I changed my mind and didn't call the MPs for precisely the same reason you've been helping me these past eight weeks."

"I'm not sure I understand what you're driving at, kid."

Billy stopped for a moment. He wanted to choose his words carefully. He knew that what he was about to say was important.

"First Sergeant," he began, "you and I...we've come a long way over the past eight weeks, haven't we? And I want you to know—although I already think you do—that I owe you everything. Without your help I wouldn't have made it. And that probably would have destroyed my life. I couldn't have survived being branded a liar and drummed out of the Army. That's the easy part." Billy saw that Sergeant Sack was listening intently.

"The hard part is explaining why you helped me, a stranger, a lowly trainee; why you went to such lengths to bend the rules. Whoever heard of someone in your position allowing a recruit to recuperate in his home? When in the history of the Army did the first sergeant of a basic training company ever take one of his charges out of state for M1 instruction? Or to put it in more military terms, where is it written that what you did is sanctioned by protocol or regulation or by the Uniform Code of Military Justice? The answer of course is 'nowhere.' So why did you help me, First Sergeant? Why?"

Sergeant Sack looked down, unable to answer.

"I'll tell you why. In fact, Shakespeare tells us both why. Ever read any of his stuff?"

Sergeant Sack shook his head.

"In *Hamlet*, First Sergeant, Polonius gives advice to his son. The last thing he tells him is *'This, above all: to thine own self be true.'* Sound familiar?"

"Maybe…yeah, I think so."

"So there's your answer, First Sergeant. When you helped me what you were doing was being true to yourself. *And that was more important to you than your army career.* In some deep sense you were answering to a higher authority."

Sergeant Sack thought back to the time he'd gone out to check on Billy in that furnace room at three-thirty in the morning, how he had rescued him from that blood-soaked cot, and how he had driven him to the hospital. He remembered feeling that his army career was over and that he really didn't give much of a shit if it was. He looked up at Billy and nodded.

"And when I decided not to call the MPs I was also answering to a higher authority. In a way I was being true to myself. At that moment not alerting the MPs was more important to me than anything else I could think of."

Sergeant Sack remained silent for a moment. "Okay, kid," he said, "I'll accept your answer. I'm not gonna press you further."

"His father," Sergeant Sack thought. "He was somehow protecting his father." Sergeant Sack would make sure this conversation never found its way into Billy's interview report.

"Billy, you go on back to the barracks and rest up for tomorrow's graduation. It's gonna be a big day for all of us."

As Billy was getting up to leave, Sergeant Sack said, "Hey, kid, you got any interest in joining me for a run later on…say around seven?"

"Wouldn't miss it for the world, First Sergeant," Billy replied.

***

In his small room back at the BOQ five hours later Bad News Edmunds was seated at a desk reading through the six interview reports. When he finished he reached for the phone. After the operator came on the line, he gave her a number. He heard a woman answer on the second ring. "Harkavy residence."

"Ma'am, this is Warrant Officer Edmunds. I'd like to speak to the Colonel."

"One moment, please," the lady said. There was a clicking noise and then he heard Colonel Harkavy's voice. "Harkavy."

"Sir, it's me, Edmunds. Sorry to bother you so late at home, but I think it's important."

"Edmunds!" Colonel Harkavy's heart skipped a beat. "There a problem with Rosen's security clearance?"

"Not exactly, sir."

"Not exactly?"

"We're gonna issue his clearance, Colonel. But there are some things I think you need to know."

"Like what?"

"Well, first there's Rosen's father. We can't prove it, but all indications are that he's Mafia…or damn close to it. He may be involved in some pretty nasty stuff. Not someone I'd wanna cross, that's for damn sure."

"Christ!" Colonel Harkavy replied, a note of unease in his voice. "Anything else?"

"Yes, sir. There's Rosen himself. He's not what you think he is, Colonel: a Harvard dilettante or a rich man's son. And that's really why I'm calling. I'm down at Fort Wood. I'll be in the Chicago area tomorrow and I'd like to deliver Rosen's security clearance to you along with some other interesting reading material."

"Other interesting reading material?"

"Yes, sir. The name 'Furax' mean anything to you?"

"'Course it does. It's been a goddamn embarrassment to the Army. I hope they catch those sons of bitches and hang 'em from the tallest tree."

"I've been working on doin' just that."

"You? I thought the MPs had the case."

"No, sir, CID's got it. For some reason the MPs weren't called in. And I've been busting my ass on Furax for over a month now and not making any progress."

"Huh. So how does this concern me?"

"Well, our investigation's generated some fairly interesting interview reports. Two involve Rosen. They give you a pretty good idea of what he's all about, Colonel. Tomorrow when I deliver his security clearance to you I'll drop off copies of those reports. By the way, tomorrow's Saturday. You gonna be in your office or should I go to your home?"

"I'll be in the office 'til three. Come on by anytime before then."

Colonel Harkavy was silent for a moment. "Good thing you and the CID are working on Furax, Mr. Edmunds. I doubt that I'd be seeing those interview reports if the MPs had the investigation."

"You're probably right, Colonel. The MPs don't run security checks so they wouldn't know about your interest in Rosen."

"I'll see you tomorrow, Mr. Edmunds. And thanks for the call."

"A pleasure, sir," Bad News said as he hung up the phone.

Chapter 51

Suite 12, Warnall House,
Smith College, Northampton, Massachusetts,
Friday, 23 June 1950, 1730 Hours.

Books, clothing, and other personal items were strewn about Suite 12 of Smith College's Warnall House which, for the past school year, had been occupied by Sarah Childs and Christine Haslett. Now both had finished final exams and were packing in preparation for their departure for the summer. Chris had an 11:30 PM flight to catch to St. Louis, and she had scheduled an REA pickup of her trunk, three suitcases and half a dozen boxes for 6:30 PM. She was in a rush, but knew she could make it easily. Then the phone rang.

"I'll get it," Chris called out, lifting the receiver.

"Princess," she heard Johnny Ludrakis say. "Frank and Rose are on the phone with me. We know you're coming back here tonight and that you're probably harassed at the moment, but we wanted to alert you to a problem."

"Honey," Rose said, "Uncle Ken's up to his old tricks again."

Chris was shocked. "Impossible!" she said. "He gave me his word!"

"Yeah, well his word's no damn good," Frank said. "See, Billy has had orders for almost two weeks to the PIO at Fifth Army Headquarters in Chicago. He was supposed to receive On the Job Training. Then first thing the day before yesterday we got a call telling us that his orders had been changed to advanced infantry training here at Wood. We were told to be on the lookout for copies of his new orders which would be arriving later that day. Wanna guess where that call originated and where the orders were sent from?"

Chris was almost unable to speak. In a whisper she replied, "Chicago Induction Center?"

"Exactamente," Rose said. "The caller was Master Sergeant Walter Marks, the Induction Center's Sergeant Major...which means that Harkavy has started messin' with Billy again. Not that the change in his orders is so terrible. Just not right. Billy's being singled out like before."

"Dammit," Chris said. "I'll have to think this through on the flight back tonight. Thanks for telling me."

"We thought you'd wanna know ASAP," Johnny said.

"You were absolutely right to call. I'll see you tomorrow." Chris hung up.

"Dammit," she swore as she continued packing.

Chapter 52

Forney Field Terminal Building,
Fort Leonard Wood, Missouri,
Saturday, 24 June 1950, 0820 Hours.

Dressed in chauffeur's attire, Aaron Lawrence was standing just outside the glass door of a flimsy wooden structure, Forney Field's excuse for a terminal building. He watched as a Douglas DC-3 with the Edenbrau logo painted on its fuselage taxied to a location roughly thirty feet away. The pilot cut both engines and the aircraft came to a full stop. The door immediately aft of the wing was pushed open, a small ladder-like stairway fell into place, and five passengers began to deplane.

Shortly afterwards Hatcher "Hatch" Peterson, President and Chairman of The Edenbrau Corporation, the second largest brewer in the country, approached Aaron. "How was the trip down?" he asked.

"Not bad, sir. Almost no traffic out of Chicago yesterday and an easy drive in from St. Louis this morning."

Hatch nodded. "Had a chance to look around?"

"Yes, sir. I went over to Gammon Field where today's event is taking place. Only five minutes from here. There aren't a whole lot of seats, and the best have been cordoned off. I was told they're expecting a large crowd."

"Really?" Hatch said, somewhat surprised. "I didn't think many people attended basic training graduations." He thought for a moment.

"Aaron, why don't you round up our bags. Be sure to get the one with Billy's clothes in it. Put them all in the limo. And arrange for a rental car for Billy. I want him to have transportation while we're here. I'll see what I can do about making sure the five of us have seats." With that, Hatch walked over to where his wife, Carolyn, his brother-in-law, Matt Irwin, and Billy's parents were gathered.

He beckoned to Billy's father. Speaking in a low voice so he couldn't be overheard, he said, "Louie, I'm told seats at this thing are in short supply and that a number of them have already been reserved. I know it's early Saturday morning, but could you call one of your army cronies and get us squared away?"

Louis Rosen smiled and went inside the terminal building. Looking through the building's glass door a short while later Hatch saw that he was speaking to someone from a pay phone.

***

The flight in from Chicago had annoyed Carolyn Peterson. Why hadn't they simply left yesterday with Aaron in the limousine? Hatch had said it was too small for five, and that it could barely accommodate four. Carolyn had disagreed. It was spacious enough for all of them, she had said, and it was certainly a lot safer than that damn plane. In addition, they could have spent a comfortable night in St. Louis at the company suite in the Stanbury Regent Hotel and then driven on to Fort Wood this morning after getting up at a reasonable hour…instead of 2:30 AM! But Hatch liked to fly, and that was that.

And besides, Hatch wanted the plane available first thing tomorrow for a flight to Washington, D.C. because Monday morning he was to meet with Secretary of Defense Paul Galt. He had insisted that Carolyn accompany him on the trip since he knew that the Galts enjoyed a night or two out on the town. But for Carolyn this was bad news. Unlike Hatch who held Galt in high regard, she disliked him almost as much as she detested flying. She considered his reputation sullied by the heavy-handed way he reputedly ran the Defense Department. And she also found particularly obnoxious his well-publicized scuttling of the program to complete the carrier *USS Old Glory* after its construction had already begun. Carolyn shuddered at the thought of having to socialize with someone she considered a boorish small town accountant turned political opportunist. How she wished she would be returning to Glencoe tomorrow in the Edenbrau limousine with Doreen, Louis, and her brother, Matt. For all she cared, Hatch could head off to Washington, D.C. on his own.

But most of all Carolyn Peterson feared that Galt had a hidden agenda in meeting with her husband. She felt certain he was plotting to get Hatch to take on some senior post at Defense. If Hatch got caught in that web, it would mean that he would have to end his rewarding twenty-eight year career at Edenbrau and that they would be forced to leave Glencoe. The thought of this sickened her. With effort, she would try to make today a joyful occasion for Billy and his parents. But deep down she was extremely troubled. She felt her life would soon be changing—decidedly for the worse.

Chapter 53

Gammon Field, Fort Leonard Wood, Missouri, Saturday, 24 June 1950, 0915 Hours.

Captain Jess Martin, General Haslett's aide, had to take a roaring piss. His bladder had just about reached the point of overflowing as a result of all the coffee and OJ he'd consumed earlier in the morning and he felt like his teeth were about to float away. And, son of a bitch, he couldn't just walk across Constitution Avenue to the Headquarters Building where he officed and where he knew there was a latrine because General Haslett had just called him and ordered him to be at Gammon Field by no later than nine-fifteen to meet and greet some VIP in the beer business who, God knows why, was intent on attending today's basic training graduation ceremony. This bigwig was supposed to be arriving at any moment in a limousine with an entourage of sycophants. "Goddammit to hell," he cursed under his breath, "if that limo doesn't show up soon I'm gonna have to go behind the stands and drain my lizard."

Captain Martin was standing next to a concrete helipad located at the end of a short paved driveway leading in from Constitution Avenue. Cars had begun to arrive, and when they reached the helipad they were being directed by several MPs to a section of Gammon Field which had been set aside for parking. Still other MPs in the parking area were helping the arrivals park in rows.

Behind Captain Martin a group of enlisted engineers from the Seventh CB were putting the finishing touches on the erection of the portable stands. Several were checking the structural joints which were connected by large nuts and bolts; and a couple of others were wiping down the seats including those near the podium which had been cordoned off. The stands could accommodate roughly two hundred guests and dignitaries. Those who were unable to get seats would be forced to view today's events from the edge of the field, not far from where the portable toilets were being set up. Because it was already sunny, with every indication that it was going to be very hot later on, some were already there reclining in lawn and beach chairs while others were simply standing idly by waiting for the ceremony to begin. A few had spread blankets or large towels out on the ground and had placed picnic baskets, thermos flasks, and other items on them.

After watching car after car arrive, Captain Martin saw a large black Cadillac limousine making its way toward the helipad. The Edenbrau logo was painted on its side. This most certainly was his quarry. The limo slowed, almost coming to a stop, directly in front of him and he rushed forward and tapped on a front window. The driver looked up and Captain Martin gestured to him to stop. Then Captain Martin turned and spoke to one of the MPs. Finally, he opened the rear door and beckoned to the passengers.

***

Hatch Peterson was the first to get out. "Son, I'm Hatch Peterson. Thanks for meeting us. Looks like I underestimated this thing. Didn't think there'd be this much interest."

"Captain Jess Martin, sir. Welcome to Fort Leonard Wood. General Haslett asked me to extend his compliments. We've reserved seats for your party, and after the ceremony, which should last a couple of hours, the General has invited all of you to the Officers Club for a buffet luncheon."

"Very nice of him, Captain," Hatch said. "Only problem is that my favorite nephew's a private, not an officer, and we came to spend time with him. We'll all be leaving tomorrow. My wife and I will be flying to D.C. and the others will be taking the limo back to Chicago. But let me introduce you."

Before Hatch could begin the introductions, Louis Rosen came forward. "I've got a personal request, Captain. I could use a visit to the restroom. Is there one close by?"

Captain Martin smiled. Closing his eyes, he began to pray inwardly: "Dear Lord, thank you for sending this man to me."

"That's an easy one, sir. See that large building over there across the road?" He pointed. "It's our Headquarters Building where I work."

Louis Rosen saw where Captain Martin was pointing. "Anybody care to join me and the Captain?" he asked. There were no takers.

"Let's be off," he said.

"A moment, sir. Let me show the others to their seats."

***

Captain Martin and Louis Rosen had entered the Headquarters Building through a side door, the only door to which Captain Martin had a key. And now after visiting the men's room they were headed down a hallway toward the front door which could be opened from the inside but was locked from the outside. As they approached the entrance, Captain Martin saw that the door to one of the offices was ajar.

"Just a moment, sir. This is General Haslett's office where I work. I think the General's in." He walked through the doorway. The ceiling light was on in the General's interior office, and someone was inside. "Hello," he called out. A feminine figure came out. Captain Martin smiled. "Well look who blew into town!" It was Chris Haslett.

"Jess, what are you doing here? I would have thought you'd be out there with the rest waiting for the party to begin."

"I guess I could ask the same question of you, Princess. It looks to me like you've turned your father's office upside down. You looking for something?"

"Oh, you know my father. He couldn't keep his papers straight if his life depended on it. He's been frantically searching the house for his notes for today's program. Last thing he did before he left for Gammon Field was send me over here to see if they were in his office."

"Not to worry, Chris. I've been carrying them around with me. I told him I was gonna give them to him, but I guess he forgot."

"Why don't you hustle on over to the field, Jess; and I'll escort this gentleman back."

"Thanks, Chris," Captain Martin said. He turned and hurriedly left the office.

Chris saw that the man who'd been with Captain Martin was smiling, and that he also appeared amused. She walked over to him.

"Please forgive us," she said. "My father's great at giving orders, but when it comes to details or keeping track of papers, well…" She laughed and rolled her eyes.

"I'm Chris Haslett," she said, extending her hand.

And as she drew closer she could see there was something about the man that intrigued her: those twinkling steely blue eyes.

"Louis Rosen," he said, taking her hand.

Chris' eyes widened and she stiffened. "My God!" she thought. "Billy's father! Those eyes!"

There could be no mistake, but, still, she had to make sure. "You're obviously here to attend the graduation?"

"My boy's just completed basic. His great uncle missed his college graduation last year and wanted to make up for it by coming here today. My wife and I tagged along."

"I believe I know your son, sir. Billy Rosen?"

Now it was Louis Rosen's turn to be surprised. "Yes," he said. "But how could you possibly know Billy?"

She hesitated for a moment. "Mr. Rosen, Billy needs help. Please, sir, it's important. If we could just talk…"

"Sit down," he said, motioning to the couch.

***

Twenty minutes later Louis Rosen and Christine Haslett emerged from the Headquarters Building. They were walking side by side, almost touching. It was as if, in that short span of time, a special bond had been forged between them, much like the one linking a father and daughter. Louis Rosen knew that never in his life had he met such a remarkable young woman. After Billy had almost died at the intentional hands of the military, she and others he soon hoped to meet had come to his aid. When Billy had been defenseless, they had put a stop to a cruel and unwarranted attack on his character, something which obviously had been designed to rob him of all self-respect and shame him forever.

The last thing Louis Rosen told Chris Haslett before leaving her father's office was that she and her friends had done enough. Now it was his turn. From now on he would take over as Billy's protector. All he wanted of them was to be kept informed.

And so, as they walked from the Headquarters Building to Gammon Field, Louis Rosen was not smiling; nor was he amused.

And his steely eyes no longer twinkled. Instead, they had turned hard and cold.

Chapter 54

Gammon Field, Fort Leonard Wood, Missouri, Saturday, 24 June 1950, 0950 Hours.

The men of Company B, Fourth Battalion, Second TRB, were gathered together in an informal group at the far side of Gammon Field. They were all wearing red armbands which, ten minutes earlier, Sergeant Whitney had passed out. These signified that once again the company had received the Best in Battalion Award, the result of its rifle and drill teams winning their respective competitions. The men had first learned of this from Sergeant Sack the prior evening. And from the way they were fussing with their armbands—continually looking at them, straightening them so they contained no wrinkles or creases, and making sure they were properly placed with the lower edge two inches above the elbow of the right arm—it was obvious they were filled with pride. There was also a certain electricity in the air because they all knew that at 8:00 AM the next day basic training would officially end. That meant the start of a fifteen-day leave, their first extended break from army life since they'd been inducted eight weeks ago. Many had family and friends attending today's ceremony which was expected to begin in about ten minutes.

Above the din of the chatting men one particularly loud voice could be heard, that of Fat Jerry Krazinski. Jerry was strutting around like a peacock trying hard to be noticed. He was wearing his red scarf and reddish silver helmet liner, his way of telling the world he was a member of the company's drill team. The other members of the team were dressed like all the rest, without scarves and wearing olive drab overseas caps. They would put on their scarves and helmet liners just before it was time for them to perform, near the end of the program. Until then, these items, and their polished rifles, would remain in a large wooden container resting at the field's edge and watched over by Private Dewey La Droop. But Jerry, without permission, had already grabbed his scarf and helmet liner from the container and had put them on. Now he was wandering among the men making as much noise as possible.

Craig Billington, selected as drill team captain by Sergeant Gomez, looked over at Jerry in disgust. How he wished he'd never asked that asshole to join the team. The son of a bitch was constantly disrupting practice. But some of his other antics were even more bothersome, particularly his insistence that the team's routine be performed with fixed bayonets. Sergeant Gomez, the NCOIC of the team, had absolutely forbidden this. But since he'd recovered from his surgery, which was just before he'd joined the team, Jerry had been out of control. And, trouble was, there were three other team members, Charlie Cook, Hank Wolf, and Ron Douglas, who were just as crazy as Jerry. Craig hoped the drill team would get through today's performance without a hitch. Then during advanced infantry training, which he and Jerry would be starting just after their upcoming leaves ended, he would give him as wide a berth as possible. It was at this moment that Craig saw Jerry approaching. He groaned.

"Hey, man," Jerry ranted. "We're gonna do it! We're fuckin' gonna do it! We're gonna give them people a fuckin' show they'll never fuckin' forget!"

As Jerry spoke he lurched and swayed, almost as if he were drunk, although Craig knew he hadn't been drinking. He was just high on the moment and more out of control than ever.

With pointed finger, Jerry extended his right arm in Craig's direction, attempting to poke him in the chest, trying to punctuate what he was about to say. Craig deftly stepped back out of the way. Undeterred, Jerry pressed on. "Fuckin' A, we're gonna do it! And I'm calling it, not you, mother fucker!"

Still ranting, and lurching and swaying, Jerry turned and headed in the direction of some of the others. And as he did, the first sergeant stepped out in front of the men.

***

"All right, listen up," Sergeant Sack said in a relatively low voice. The men quieted down immediately.

"Now we've been over this enough times to know what we're supposed to be doing. So for Christ's sake don't be worrying or getting nervous. You're the best damn group of recruits I've ever had. I know you'll all get it right. It's time, so let's do it!" Then, drawing himself up to attention, he called out, "Platoon Sergeants, have your men fall in!"

As an afterthought, Sergeant Sack looked over at Jerry. "Krazinski," he shouted. "Give La Droop your damn scarf and helmet liner. You'll have plenty of time to show off later on!"

***

Lieutenant Colonel Jonathan Q. Paulson, Fourth Battalion Commanding Officer, stood in the first row of the stands immediately behind the podium. Brigadier General Stanton M. Haslett, II, Regimental CO, sat in the chair next to him. The General's wife, Beth Haslett, was seated alongside her husband. Next to her there was a vacant chair that should have been occupied by the Hasletts' daughter, Chris, but wasn't. Instead, she was sitting in the uppermost row of the stands in the far corner. She was with four others, two uniformed sergeants, a middle-aged redheaded woman, and a middle-aged man. Captain Jess Martin, her father's aide, had tried to convince her that according to protocol her proper place was next to her mother in the first row, but Chris had told him to buzz off. She was much more comfortable with her friends, she had said. One of the two sergeants, Johnny Ludrakis, was sitting on one side of Chris, his hand resting lightly on her forearm, and the middle-aged man, Louis Rosen, was seated on her other side. The other two members of the group, Rose Applebaum and Sergeant Frank Kaye, were talking to one another.

From his location high up in the stands Louis Rosen looked down. He saw his wife, and her aunt and uncle, Carolyn and Hatch Peterson, and Carolyn's brother, Matt Irwin, in the center of the second row directly behind Colonel Paulson and General Haslett. Although he was in a somber mood because of what he had learned from Chris earlier that morning, he could hardly keep from smiling at the sight of Matt who had donned a bright red University of Wisconsin sweater with large white "Ws" sewn on its front and back. "He just never leaves the campus," Louis Rosen thought as he waved to his wife. When he finally got her attention he pointed, motioning to her to move down one row and take the unoccupied chair in front of her that had been reserved for Chris Haslett. Doreen Rosen possessed a number of qualities.

Shyness was not one of them, and so, intrigued at the thought of sitting next to the commanding general's wife, she got up and changed seats. As she sat down, Beth Haslett glanced over at her: "Tastefully dressed, slightly understated," Beth thought. "She appears friendly enough, and there's something about her that reminds me of someone I know. Obviously one of Stan's invited guests. I've got to find out who she is." She was about to ask the general when Colonel Paulson leaned toward the microphone which was resting on the podium. Clearing his throat, he began to speak.

***

"General and Mrs. Haslett, honored guests, ladies and gentlemen, officers and men of the Second Training Regiment and the other units present, good morning. I'm Colonel Paulson, CO of the Regiment's Fourth Battalion, and I'd like to welcome you all to the basic training graduation ceremony for our current group of recruits. As you will soon learn, this is going to be a bit of an unusual graduation today with what I hope will be some nice surprises for you all." He looked down at some notes he'd placed on the podium. "Would you please rise for our national anthem to be performed by the Fort Leonard Wood Army Band under the direction of Major Mack Perry."

While people were getting to their feet, Colonel Paulson looked out over Gammon Field. He could see the four companies of his battalion lined up facing him. The band and a four-man Color guard stood in front of the companies. An officer stepped to the front of the band. He raised his baton, nodded, and then lowered it; and as he did, the band began playing *The Star-Spangled Banner*. Those in uniform saluted; most of the others placed their right hands over their hearts; some began to sing.

When the national anthem ended, Colonel Paulson returned to the microphone. "Lined up in formation in front of you are the four companies of the Fourth Battalion. Members of the company on your far right, Baker Company, are wearing red armbands. They signify that this company, commanded by Captain Emil Schtung, a highly decorated veteran of the last war and a former All-American football player from the University of Wisconsin, has won the Best in Battalion Award because its rifle and drill teams placed first in our competitions. This, by the way, is the ninth consecutive basic training cycle in which Captain Schtung's company has been 'Best in Battalion.' In a few minutes the four companies will pass in review. Please give them a hand as they pass by. And, incidentally, the tune the band will be playing honors Baker Company." Colonel Paulson nodded, and the band began playing the University of Wisconsin Fight Song as the four companies marched past the stands. When Company B, the last company in line, approached, Sergeant Sack shouted, "Let's hear it for Captain Schtung!" and immediately the men began singing:

We are Schtungmen, we are Schtungmen,
we are trained to fight
to protect our nation's honor
through each day and night!

Because…
We are Schtungmen, we are Schtungmen,
we love liberty;
and we pledge
to keep our country free!

Billy's Uncle, Matt Irwin, long-serving president of the University of Wisconsin's National Alumni Association (who hadn't missed a U football game in years), was both surprised and delighted, first at seeing his old acquaintance, Emil Schtung, even if only from a distance, and then, unexpectedly, hearing the band play his *alma mater's* Fight Song. It was almost too good to be true, and he was overcome with joy. When he finally saw Billy march past him in the midst of the others singing along with them, he could no longer contain himself. He too began to sing while jumping up and down and pumping both fists into the air.

From his seat Louis Rosen looked down at Matt and chuckled. He leaned over and whispered something to Chris, at the same time pointing to Matt. She nodded and also began to laugh. Matt's enthusiasm was obviously infectious. Like Matt, Louis Rosen was beginning to enjoy himself despite what he had learned earlier about Billy.

***

After the four companies of his battalion had passed in review, Colonel Paulson once again began to speak. "It's my honor and pleasure to introduce to you General Stanton Haslett, Regimental Commanding Officer." Turning, he said, "Sir," as the general made his way to the podium, notes in hand.

"Good morning to you all, and welcome," General Haslett began. "As Colonel Paulson indicated earlier, this morning's graduation ceremony is somewhat exceptional. It's exceptional for two reasons. First, the performance of one of the recruits is, well…" General Haslett hesitated. "Off the chart. None of us has ever seen anything like it. And second, the Outstanding Recruit Award has caused a great deal of consternation among those deciding who should receive it. But I guess I'm getting a little ahead of myself." He paused for a moment.

"So for starters, we've got some trophies to present. The first I'm going to be handing out to the recruit captain of Company B's championship drill team. Private Craig Billington please come up here."

Even though Craig knew that he would be called up to the podium to receive the drill team's trophy, he began to feel butterflies in his stomach. Trying hard to ignore them, he quickly approached General Haslett. "Sir," he said, saluting, "Private Billington reporting as ordered."

"Nice to meet you, son," General Haslett said quietly so he wouldn't be heard over the amplifier. Then he spoke into the microphone. "Folks, Private Billington here is the recruit captain of Company B's championship drill team. We're going to see them perform a little later on, but I personally want to congratulate him and the other team members on an absolutely outstanding performance in the competition. These young men had only a few weeks to learn their drill routine. I'm told that Private Billington, and Sergeant Manuel Gomez, the NCO in charge of the team, spent an awful lot of off-duty time perfecting the team's program. It's the kind of dedication, folks, that goes way beyond the call of duty and these young men deserve a lot of credit for what they've accomplished. I applaud them and I hope you will too."

When the applause subsided, General Haslett handed the drill team trophy to Craig. "Congratulations, again, Private Billington, on a job well done by you and your teammates." Holding the trophy, Craig thanked the general and returned to the company formation, but not before placing the trophy on a portable table that Dewey La Droop had set up nearby.

"Folks," General Haslett said, "I think now would be a good time for a twenty-minute break. As you'll see, we've got a number of portable rest rooms set up for you. We're also serving refreshments over there next to the stands." He pointed. "Compliments of the United States Army."

***

When Doreen Rosen heard General Haslett call for a break, she was overcome by feelings of abandonment and disappointment. Her husband had left her to sit elsewhere. She didn't have the foggiest idea what he was doing with that group of people high up in the stands: two soldiers, a woman her age, and a younger woman. And now she was surrounded by strangers, people with whom she would have to make conversation, something she despised. Coupled with this was her extreme disappointment that a fuss hadn't been made over Billy. She thought back to his days as a Cub Scout and, later, a Boy Scout and Eagle Scout. He was always being praised and rewarded. Then she remembered his graduation from New Trier. He was class president, valedictorian, had lettered three years as a member of the track team, and was one of only twelve inducted into Triship, an organization of outstanding students. She also recalled the time he'd applied to colleges. He'd been the only one in his class to be accepted by Harvard. There had always been something for her to brag about. But today…absolutely nothing. Billy had just marched by in his olive drab uniform. Just another recruit in a sea of drabness. Probably most of the youngsters in his company hadn't even graduated from high school. Doreen Rosen felt embarrassed and depressed—and mediocre. *And more than anything else, Doreen Rosen hated mediocrity.* As she brooded, General Haslett's wife unexpectedly began speaking to her.

"I'm Beth Haslett. I couldn't help noticing you're not my daughter, Chris."

"Oh, I'm sorry. I thought my husband motioned to me to sit here. I'll move back."

"No, stay," Beth said, extending her hand. "If Chris surfaces she'll have to find a seat somewhere else."

Doreen Rosen clasped Beth's hand while forcing a smile. But she hardly felt sociable.

"And what brings you here?" Beth asked.

"My son is one of the recruits."

"Really? You must be very proud."

"Well, not exactly. I'd be much happier if he were in graduate school. But he insisted on joining the Army…and as an enlisted man, no less. And what about your daughter?"

"Chris? She just finished her third year at Smith. That's her in the top row with the dark hair," she pointed.

"If you mean the attractive young woman in the yellow sun dress, she's sitting next to my husband." Doreen Rosen said.

"They certainly look like they're having quite a time up there," Beth Haslett replied.

"I can't imagine how they'd know one another. We just arrived."

"I think it's time we find out," Beth Haslett said as she and Doreen Rosen got up from their seats and headed toward the aisle.

***

"Mother," Chris Haslett said, "sorry I didn't sit next to you, but, as you can see, I'm with The Boys and Rose; and I've also gotten involved with a married man along the way." She began to laugh. "Mr. Rosen," she said, "I'd like you to meet my mother, Beth Haslett."

"Nice to meet you, Mrs. Haslett." Then turning to his wife, Louis Rosen said, "Doreen, this is Chris Haslett, a friend of our son's. And this kind lady, Rose Applebaum, and these two sergeants are also friends of his. When I get a chance I'll explain to you how much time and effort they've put into helping him get through basic training, particularly Chris."

As Chris listened, she began to smile. "Mother," she said, "don't you see the resemblance?"

Beth shook her head. She had no idea what Chris was talking about.

"Mother, this is Billy Rosen's father. You remember Billy, Gram's boyfriend?"

"Why, yes, of course," Beth Haslett said, suddenly realizing that the lady who had been sitting next to her, "Doreen," and the gentleman she had just met, "Mr. Rosen," were the parents of the young recruit her mother had befriended at the Base Library and brought to their home. Turning to them, she said, "My family and I had the pleasure of your son's company at Sunday dinner a few weeks ago."

"Seven weeks ago, to be exact," Chris interjected.

Listening to this exchange, Doreen Rosen realized an opportune moment had arrived: the perfect time to let this woman and her daughter know a little something about Billy. "Chris," she said, "it's finally dawned on me who you are. I should have put two and two together when your mother told me you went to Smith. At last I get to meet Billy's special lady from Smith. I was so looking forward to meeting you last June at the dinner party Harvard's President, Dr. Lindsay, gave for the summas. I can't tell you how disappointed we were when you called and said you couldn't make it."

"Doreen, for Christ's sake!" Louis Rosen said, irritated at his wife's enormous *faux pas*. "This is not the same girl! That other one has been out of Billy's life for almost a year."

"Oh, Lord, I'm so sorry," Doreen Rosen said to Chris. But inwardly she was smiling. She had accomplished what she'd set out to do. She had wanted Beth Haslett and her daughter to know that although Billy was completing basic training as a lowly recruit, he was much more than that: he was a *summa cum laude* graduate from Harvard College. And now that they knew, she felt decidedly better; not nearly as mediocre as she'd felt when she watched him march by in that dreadful sea of olive drabness.

Louis Rosen knew his wife. And he knew precisely why she'd said what she'd just said. He looked over at Chris hoping her feelings hadn't been hurt. Could she handle something like this? He wasn't sure.

Chris Haslett's expression was intentionally enigmatic. But although she tried not to show it, she was about as pleased with herself as she'd ever been. First, what she'd just learned about Billy confirmed what she'd always suspected, that he was exceptional. A *summa cum laude* from Harvard. Not bad! Not bad at all. She'd chosen her man well. Secondly, what Billy's mother had told her—and obviously it had been told to her intentionally—cleared up something that had puzzled Chris on and off for weeks, that strange notation in Billy's 201 File, "*HUSCL*" Now she knew what it meant: "Harvard University *summa cum laude*." That obviously had impressed the person who made the notation, more than likely Ken Harkavy. Now it was time for her to respond.

"I will say that had I been invited to that dinner for the *summas* I certainly would have attended. After all, who wouldn't want to meet President Lindsay? Quite a man. We probably would have lost the war without his help in increasing our production of synthetic rubber. Don't you agree?" Chris knew that she was right. Without the genius of Jonas Everett Lindsay the war really might have been lost. She stopped for a moment before continuing.

"And when I first met your son, Mrs. Rosen, it was obvious that women were attracted to him. I certainly can't fault him for that. Why even my mother and grandmother found him charming. So I'm not bothered by what you've told me about Billy's other women, including the one from Smith. But just between us, they're all history."

"*Touché!* That's my girl!" Louis Rosen thought. "I think I now understand how you must have gotten that Colonel Harkavy to back off!"

"Mr. Rosen," Beth Haslett said, "the General is probably looking for me. I'd better be getting back to my seat. Boys, Rose, good seeing you. I may be needing your services shortly. I'll give you a call."

"Anytime, Mrs. Haslett," Rose said.

Annoyed on hearing all this, Doreen Rosen turned to her husband and gave him one of those looks he knew so well. "Lou, will you be coming down to your seat with me?"

"I think I'll stay up here, dear. You go on back with Mrs. Haslett."

Louis Rosen knew why he wanted to remain where he was. He just liked the company, most of all the young woman seated next to him. But there was another far more important reason. He knew that his wife had been caught totally off guard when Chris Haslett had told her that she alone had replaced the other women in Billy's life, and he was certain that this had threatened Doreen. Sad, but she always had difficulty sharing Billy. The mere thought of it sent her into a funk. From years of marriage Louis Rosen knew that whenever this happened she was best left alone.

***

Returning to the microphone ten minutes later, General Haslett said, "I believe it's time for us to resume. I'd now like to introduce to you Major James Touhy, U.S. Army, Retired. Major Touhy was in the Army for many years and had a distinguished career. Currently he's a member of the Arkansas National Guard. I knew him when he was on active duty, when he captained the Army's championship pistol team. He's recognized nationally and internationally as an expert marksman both with pistols and rifles; and folks, he's competed in literally hundreds of shoots. A few years back Colonel Paulson talked him into running the Fourth Battalion's riflery competitions. We feel very fortunate to have Jim helping us out. So I'm going to turn the microphone over to him and ask him to present the marksmanship trophy to the captain of Baker Company's rifle team. Jim."

Jim Touhy, who had been seated at the end of the first row next to the aisle, got up and walked to the microphone. "Thanks, General," he said. "Ladies and gentlemen, I'd like to introduce you to a rather unusual young man. Some weeks ago he was seriously injured in a gas mask training accident and was recuperating in the hospital. Because he'd spent so much time away from his company, he'd missed almost all of his M1 training." Jim looked up. People were listening. "He and I met when his first sergeant asked me to teach him to shoot the M1 in two days. I'd like to ask Private William Rosen to come forward."

On hearing this, Doreen Rosen's jaw dropped in astonishment. "Billy seriously injured! My God!" she thought.

Billy, who was standing next to Craig Billington in the company formation, marched smartly up to the podium. "Private Rosen reporting as ordered, sir."

Major Touhy continued. "Now teaching someone to qualify in the M1 in only two days is a pretty tough assignment. But producing a world-class shooter in that length of time is, well…next to impossible, unless the shooter just happens to be a natural. After spending only a few hours with Private Rosen I discovered that that's what he is, a natural. Billy is probably one of the most promising marksmen living today—and, with a little more training, there's no doubt in my mind that he'd be a top shooter on the All-Army Rifle Team. In the battalion competition he shot what we refer to as a 'possible'—a perfect score, 210 out of a possible 210! We checked, and no other recruit in the history of Fort Wood has ever done that. This may not mean much to you folks, but to people in the shooting world it's, to use General Haslett's words, 'off the chart.' With Billy's superb performance and the help of one other shooter, Private Vincent Foggerty, Company B's team easily won the riflery competition. So, Private Rosen, as captain of Company B's rifle team, I'd like to present this trophy to you and your teammates. Congratulations!" Jim handed Billy the trophy.

"Thank you, sir," Billy said. As he spoke he was surprised to see his mother seated close by, next to Mrs. Haslett. He had no idea that any of his family would be attending the day's ceremony. And then to his further surprise he saw Aunt Carolyn and Uncle Hatch, and, finally, Uncle Matt. Hatch winked at him and he saw his mother nod approvingly. And then he caught a glimpse of his father high up in the stands seated next to someone resembling Chris Haslett. Somewhat puzzled, he turned and walked to Dewey La Droop's portable table. He placed the trophy on it and returned to the company formation.

"Well that is a little better," Doreen Rosen thought. Her son appeared well, even though what she'd heard about him being injured had greatly disturbed her. It was about time someone gave Billy a little recognition, even for something as uninteresting as shooting his rifle. But that Major—whatever his name was—had said some complimentary things about him. Something or other about being one of the most promising marksmen living today. That sounded nice.

She looked up at her husband, but couldn't make out his expression. She wondered how he and that girl from Smith were reacting to the Major's little speech about Billy.

***

"Folks," General Haslett said, returning to the podium, "we're almost finished. First, we'll be presenting the Outstanding Recruit Award. Master Sergeant Theodore Williamson, Fourth Battalion's sergeant major, will do the honors. And then we're in for a real treat. We'll get to see Company B's drill team perform." He looked down at his notes.

"So without further adieu, I'd like to call upon Sergeant Williamson. Teddy."

"Sir," Sergeant Williamson said, stepping to the podium.

"Ladies and Gentlemen, I'm glad you're here for this part of the ceremony. It's the part I like best. I get to introduce the outstanding recruit to you. And then I get to tell you something about him.

"First, though, you should know that in each of the four companies we have roughly one hundred seventy-five recruits going through basic. That means the current batch of basic training graduates from the Fourth Battalion totals about seven hundred. Our outstanding recruit is the best out of a group of seven hundred.

"So how do we choose him? The answer is by a process of continually refined selection. First, in every company each of the four platoon sergeants picks two outstanding recruits from his platoon. He turns in the names to the company first sergeant. Then it's up to the first sergeant and company commander to pick two of the eight as the company's best recruits. Their names, along with a letter explaining the reasons why they were chosen, are sent to me. Colonel Paulson and I go over the eight candidates and make the final selection. If the Colonel and I can't agree, which almost never happens, I get to make the call.

"Okay, that sounds easy, doesn't it? Well the selection of the outstanding recruit from today's group was anything but that. To quote General Haslett, it 'caused a great deal of consternation among those deciding who should receive it.' The general was referring to Colonel Paulson and me. We were the ones deciding who should receive the award, and I can assure you it caused us a lot of concern. But we finally made the selection, at least up to a point. And then we were stymied. There were two young men who we felt deserved to be the outstanding recruit, and both Colonel Paulson and I were unwilling to eliminate either one of them. So..." Teddy smiled, "for this graduating group only—because Colonel Paulson and I don't want to be setting a precedent—we've decided to have co-outstanding recruits. In other words, both of these young men will receive the award." Teddy continued to smile.

"So let me tell you a little about these two. And let me also tell you that Colonel Paulson and I have done our homework. We know all about them. We think each represents what being a member of the United States Army is all about: honor, courage, duty, perseverance, excellence, concern for your fellow soldiers, resourcefulness...all those qualities, and more."

***

While Sergeant Williamson was speaking Doreen Rosen was becoming increasingly bored. It was all so dull, so banal, so run-of-the-mill. Nothing at all like the commencement speeches last year at Billy's Harvard graduation. Why had Billy done this to her? Why had he chosen to throw away two precious years of his life? It was all so sad.

***

Sergeant Williamson continued. "The two came into the Army at the Induction Center in Chicago and almost immediately struck up a friendship. One was concerned about his performance on our Achievement Test, but the other told him not to be concerned because that wasn't what soldiering was all about. I won't go into detail, but it was interesting how we learned this.

"The two wound up in the same platoon, and when one of them was subjected to special field exercises, the other made sure his personal things were put back in place.

"These are little things, folks, but the two were becoming buddies as well as leaders in their platoon.

"Then came the day they took gas mask training together. Both of their gas masks leaked."

***

When Billy heard this, he turned to Craig. "I'll be damned. He's talking about us."

Craig shook his head. "No way."

"Listen," Billy said.

***

"They were in a tear gas shack with leaking masks, and they couldn't get out. One started banging his canteen against the glass door of a case which had a fire ax in it, but the glass wouldn't give way; so the other rammed his fist through the glass. Then the first one pulled the ax out of the case and made his way to the door. Unfortunately, he passed out. But the other grabbed the ax, chopped open the door, and dragged his friend and a third soldier out into the fresh air. All three survived. One of the two receiving our award needed stitches in his arm; the other had to be hospitalized."

***

Louis Rosen had been listening carefully. "Chris, are they talking about Billy?" he asked as he looked over at her. Unable to speak, she nodded.

"Jesus!" Louis Rosen said.

***

"But that's not all," Sergeant Williamson continued. "In their platoon there was a soldier with a medical problem that needed surgical attention. One of these men discovered this, told his first sergeant about it, and the boy was operated on. I'm glad to report he's doing fine.

"Want more? A recruit was having a personal problem complying with some of our appearance requirements. Mostly about the short haircut we insist on. The way things were going, we would've had to discharge him. And it would have been less than an honorable discharge. But one of the men receiving today's award recognized this and talked him through the problem; and it went away. And the man who had it is now one the finest soldiers in the battalion. Not much, you say? I disagree. A few well chosen words changed a man's life.

"Folks, Colonel Paulson and I spent a lot of time on this. We think these two young men are highly deserving co-recipients of the Outstanding Recruit Award. You've already met them, but let me introduce them to you again. Will Privates Craig Billington and William Rosen please come up here."

***

At this moment Doreen Rosen's eyes widened. She had almost fallen asleep, but now she was fully awake. How nicely things were working out after all. Maybe Billy really didn't have to be an officer. What was happening this morning was beginning to please her. Unable to catch her husband's attention, she turned and smiled at her aunt and uncle.

"Dori," Hatch said, "that nephew of mine is a born winner. Why do you think that is?"

"Takes after you, Unc," she said. "Plus Lou's brilliance. Between the two of you, he didn't have much of a choice, did he?" But in truth Doreen Rosen didn't understand why her son excelled. He just did. Which of course was precisely what she had always insisted he do. It was what she expected of him. It never crossed her mind that she might just be the moving force behind Billy's accomplishments.

***

Billy looked over at Craig. "He called your name first, ol' buddy. I'll follow you."

"Horseshit," Craig said.

"Stop the Alphonse-Gaston business and get going, Craig," Billy said.

"After you, Billy."

Finally, the two walked up to the podium side by side.

***

The Outstanding Recruit Award to those two young men, particularly Billy Rosen, had both moved and impressed General Haslett; but now, as he watched Baker Company's drill team go through its routine, he found he was even more impressed. It wasn't the routine itself which caught his attention—for they were all about the same—but rather the precision, the teamwork, the attitude. He had a sense that there was something special about this group of twelve recruits. He wondered if this were also true of Baker Company as a whole. How would they conduct themselves in combat? He suspected they would do well. That young drill team captain who was also one of the outstanding recruits—Billington he believed was his name—seemed to be the leader. The others were obviously working off of him, following him. Leadership was a subtle quality which defied definition. He had seen it so often over the years, starting at West Point and then continuing on during his time on active duty. It wasn't a function of rank, although leaders rose quickly on up through the ranks; rather, it was a personal quality. Like Rosen, young Billington seemed to have whatever it took to be a leader. And his drill team was providing the crowd with some damn good entertainment. An excellent way to end today's ceremony. He'd have to remember to mention something to Schtung about the team's performance; maybe even talk to him about sending Billington to OCS.

***

Out on the field Craig was beginning to feel better about things. He had been worried that Jerry would do something crazy. But so far everything had gone as planned and the team's performance had been flawless. Now they were getting ready to go into the Queen Anne Salute which marked the end of their routine, as it typically did for most drill teams. Following this Craig supposed that there would be some closing remarks, either by General Haslett or by Colonel Paulson, and then the graduation ceremony would officially be over. And all of Jerry's boasting about "*giving them people a fuckin' show they'll never fuckin' forget!*' and '*I'm calling it, not you, mother fucker!*" would prove to be nothing more than meaningless palaver.

Craig looked over at Sergeant Gomez who was standing in front of the team. "By the numbers, the Salute," he heard him shout. "Hup, toop, threep, four!"

As he and the others had practiced, on four Craig began to spin his rifle in his left hand while at the same time bowing his head and dropping to a kneeling position with his left knee resting on the ground, his rifle coming to an upright stop in front of it. Flattening the palm of his right hand, he swung it smartly to the left so that his forefinger rested on the upper edge of the rifle's front hand guard. Sergeant Gomez let the team members remain in this position for several seconds before finally calling out, "Reform!" On hearing this, they shouldered their rifles and marched back to the company where they rejoined its formation. "Thank God!" Craig thought, relieved that all this was now over. He looked toward the stands and saw Colonel Paulson stepping up to the podium.

And then, as if out of nowhere, he heard Jerry yell, "Special Unit…front and center!" To his total astonishment, he saw Jerry, Charlie Cook, Hank Wolf, and Ron Douglas line up in front of the company.

"Left face!" Jerry hollered. "Forward march!" The four marched some thirty feet beyond the company formation before Jerry yelled, "Unit halt! Form up!"

Immediately the four formed a square with Jerry and Charlie Cook in front and Hank Wolf and Ron Douglas behind them.

"Fix bay-o-nets!" Jerry cried, as Craig watched in horror.

"By the numbers, hup, toop, threep, four!" On four Jerry and Charlie Cook began to spin their rifles. Then they tossed them high in the air directly to the rear. Just as they were about to come crashing down, bayonets first, Hank Wolf and Ron Douglas each took a step to the side. The two rifles plunged into the ground quivering as they remained upright. Then it was the turn of the two in the rear. Each executed an about face. Then they spun and tossed their rifles high up behind them to the two men in front who, like their counterparts, side-stepped the bayonets which buried themselves in the ground.

"By the numbers," Jerry shouted again as each man withdrew and shouldered the nearest rifle. "Hup, toop, threep, four!" On four each man spun and tossed his rifle high up and over to the man diagonally opposite him with all four rifles appearing to collide in midair in the center of the square. Remarkably, they didn't. This time each man caught the rifle thrown to him by its front hand guard just below the gleaming bayonet.

"Remove bayonets and reform!" Jerry yelled. The men sheathed their bayonets, shouldered their rifles, and formed in a line.

"Right face!" And then he cried, "Forward march!"

When the men were in front of the company, Jerry shouted. "Unit halt!" Finally, he again ordered them to reform, and the four rejoined the company formation.[7]

***

General Haslett turned to Colonel Paulson. "Jon, what the hell was that?"

"I dunno, sir. I'll have to ask Schtung."

"Do that, will you. Looked damn dangerous to me."

"I agree, sir. I don't ever recall seeing anything like that. I certainly never authorized it."

Colonel Paulson walked up to the podium. "Ladies and gentlemen, the Baker Company drill team!" Everyone applauded. When the applause subsided, Colonel Paulson said, "Well, folks, that does it for our graduation ceremony. We hope you've enjoyed it, and we thank you for coming. General Haslett joins me in congratulating our graduates." He waited a moment. "Have a nice day, folks. We've put out more refreshments for you to enjoy." He stepped from the podium.

***

"Screw it," Craig thought, faintly amused. Jerry and his cohorts had probably made a two-month reservation for themselves in the stockade, but he couldn't care less. Whatever sanctions would be meted out to Fat Jerry Krazinski and the other three no longer concerned him. Shortly he'd be heading back to the barracks where he'd pack so that he'd be ready to take off for his home in Decatur in the morning. He looked forward to telling his folks all about basic, his friend, Billy, and how the two had won the Outstanding Recruit Award. He'd come a long way since that first day at the Chicago Induction Center.

***

As people were leaving the stands, Louis Rosen approached his wife's uncle. "Hatch," he said, "we've gotta talk. I'm damned upset over what happened to Billy during his training, and I think it's something you should know about."

"I'm listening, Louie," Hatch replied.

Chapter 55

Lenny's Octane-Plus Station, Doolittle, Missouri, Saturday, 24 June 1950, 1420 Hours.

A 1950 light green Chevy Business Coupe with Rolla Rent-A-Car stickers on its front and rear bumpers was parked near a phone booth located alongside Lenny's Octane-Plus Station. Lenny's was one of only two gas stations in Doolittle, Missouri, a small town on US 44 eight miles west of Rolla. A tall black man in his early forties was standing inside the booth; and even though it was humid and the temperature was in the 80s, he'd completely shut its partitioned door to keep from being overheard. He was facing the wall of the station's building as he spoke quietly into the phone.

"No, Colonel, I don't believe anyone recognized me, not even General Haslett. I was out of uniform, and I had on a raincoat, a hat, and sunglasses. I sat in a crowd in the middle row of the stands off to one side."

"Excellent, Wally. So tell me what happened."

"Certainly, sir. The bottom line is that we were right about him. He captained the winning rifle team. He shot a possible, sir—an unbelievable 210 out of 210. That's world class. And he was one of two who received the battalion's Outstanding Recruit Award."

"One of two? I don't get it?"

"Well, Colonel, apparently this go-around they couldn't decide between him and another recruit, so they gave them both the award. Co-winners."

"Interesting. Who was the other?"

"Kid named Billington. He came in with Rosen. But when you consider all the problems Rosen had in basic, I think he did a remarkable job."

"Anything else?"

"Yes, sir. During the ceremony that Haslett girl sat next to Louis Rosen, his father. I recognized him from photos in the newspapers. I could see them fairly well and it looked to me like they were getting pretty chummy."

"What's so important about that?"

"I have no idea, Colonel. I just thought I'd mention it, that's all."

"It's something to think about, I guess." Colonel Harkavy paused for a moment. "And when will I see you?"

"I'm taking the week off, Colonel. I've got family in St Louis I'm gonna be visiting. I'll be back in the office a week from Monday, just in time to be one of the first to call you 'General.'"

"Have a nice vacation, Wally."

"Thanks, Colonel. You have a good trip to D.C. And congratulations again on your promotion, sir."

***

After he hung up with Sergeant Marks, Colonel Harkavy began to think about Chris Haslett and Louis Rosen sitting next to one another during the ceremony. They had obviously talked. But about what? Definitely not a good sign. Not a good sign at all.

Chapter 56

Town Center, Kaesong, South Korea, Sunday, 25 June 1950, 0525 Hours (Korean Time).

While Colonel Harkavy was mulling over what Louis Rosen and Chris Haslett might have been discussing, halfway across the globe in Kaesong, South Korea, the ancient Korean capital close to the 38th parallel, it was five twenty-five in the morning on the following day. First Lieutenant Jared Berringer, a KMAG advisor to the ROK Army, was in the process of parking his jeep in Kaesong's center, next to the railroad station. Earlier that morning his house on Kaesong's outskirts had come under artillery and small arms fire and he'd hurriedly dressed and driven into the town to investigate. Now, as he was about to turn off the ignition, he looked over in the direction of the station and, to his amazement, saw a large group of North Korean soldiers, probably more than a thousand, brazenly disembarking from a long train. Without waiting to see where they were going or what they were doing, he turned his Jeep around and floored it. One hour later he was at KMAG Headquarters in Seoul, some forty miles to the south. He banged his fist repeatedly against the main entry door, but no one answered. He had forgotten that it was early Sunday morning. He had to wait for over an hour before a car drove up. It was Captain Bart Curren, the OD.

"What the hell are you doing here, Berringer?" he asked.

"Nothing much, sir. I just thought I'd drop by and let you know we're at war, that's all."

"Huh?"

"You heard me, Captain. My house got shot up pretty badly this morning, so I hightailed it into Kaesong to find out what was going on. At the station I saw what I'd estimate to be a full regiment of NKPA detraining. They didn't get an invitation to cross the 38th parallel and join us for breakfast, did they?"

"You better come on in," Captain Curren said, "because we got some calls to make."[8]

Chapter 57

Suite 106, Lebanon Country Club, Lebanon, Missouri, Saturday, 24 June 1950, 1715 Hours.

It had been a long day, but, surprisingly, Hatch Peterson felt good. He'd been able to nap for an hour and then shower, shave, and put on some fresh clothes. Now he was standing outside on the patio of his suite at the Lebanon Country Club with a scotch on the rocks in one hand and a lighted cigarette in the other. As he gazed out at the Club's perfectly manicured seventh fairway he began to feel nostalgic. How he wished he'd stuck with golf when he was younger. But he hadn't; instead, he'd opted for tennis which gave him a more vigorous workout in much less time. In those days he'd been focused on building Edenbrau's sales, not on lowering his handicap.

He felt a hand on his arm. It was Carolyn. "Isn't this a lovely place?" she said. "And to think that we almost spent the night in that broken down hotel in Rolla."

Hatch smiled. "How're we coming with the dinner?"

"Everything's under control right down to the last detail, and I haven't had to lift a finger."

"Really. Mind telling me how you managed that?"

"Rose Applebaum, dear."

Hatch looked puzzled.

"You remember. We met her and those two sergeants they call 'The Boys' after the ceremony."

"Right," Hatch said, also recalling that Louie had told him how they had helped Billy.

"I just happened to mention to her where we were staying in Rolla and she had a fit. And when I told her you'd decided to give a dinner party for Billy and his friends tonight, she insisted on taking over. Since then all I've had to do is sign a few checks. For starters, she canceled our original hotel reservations and got us all in here, even Billy. She told me she'd spoken to his first sergeant and he didn't have to go back to his barracks tonight. Then she made the dinner arrangements, everything from inviting the people, to the hors d'oeuvres, the food and drinks, and the music, and...she's bringing half a dozen chilled bottles of champagne compliments of her company."

"My kind of woman," Hatch said. "Not surprising, though, when you consider everything they've done for Billy."

"I'm sorry, dear?"

"I'll tell you all about that on the plane to Washington tomorrow."

Hatch looked at his watch. "I'd better get going. I'm due in the cocktail lounge in a few minutes. I'll see you at our dinner in half an hour."

***

"Lou's upstairs in the room with a headache," Doreen Rosen said as she joined her Uncle Hatch who had been waiting for her in one of the booths in the country club's cocktail lounge.

"Doesn't surprise me one bit," Hatch thought to himself.

"What's your pleasure, Dori?"

"I'll have my usual, a Manhattan."

Hatch nodded and motioned to a waiter who hurried over. "A Manhattan for the lady, son. And I'll have a refill."

Hatch turned to his niece. "How much has Lou told you about Billy?"

"About Billy? Nothing, really. What I know is pretty much what I heard at today's ceremony, although Lou did mention that Billy had some problems during his training. But he hasn't bothered to tell me what they were. Why do you ask, Unc?"

"Well, honey, seeing as you're his mother you need to know everything Lou and I know about the hell he's gone through. And more important, I want you to know who his real friends are and how they went out of their way to help him. It's quite a story. One of the reasons I wanted to have this little dinner. They're special, Dori. Seems these good people took a liking to your son. And thank God for that!"

Doreen Rosen was puzzled. "I know Billy was injured. Is that what this is about?"

"Unfortunately, there's a lot more. But I want you to know that Lou has assured me that nothing like this will ever happen again to Billy."

"Nothing like *what* will ever happen again to Billy? I don't understand, Unc? What in the world happened to him?" Doreen Rosen could feel her heart beginning to pound.

***

Fifteen minutes later when the waiter looked over at the booth he saw that the gentlemen's scotch on the rocks and the lady's Manhattan were untouched, and that the lady was quietly crying. He thought it best not to be asking them if everything was all right. Obviously, it wasn't.

***

"You gonna be okay, Dori?"

"I'll try, Unc. But I feel sick. My poor boy. I don't think I'll be able to make it through the dinner party."

"You will, dear."

"What about that girl, Unc? What do I say to her? I feel like such a fool."

"Just speak to her from your heart. You're a good person, and so is she. You love Billy and, from what I hear, I think she does too. She'll understand."

"I hope so. I truly do." She thought for a moment. "And the others, Unc. How do I thank them?"

"Why not let me do the thanking, Dori. I'm pretty good at that."

Chapter 58

The Wyota Room, Lebanon Country Club, Lebanon, Missouri, Saturday, 24 June 1950, 1755 Hours.

When Carolyn Peterson walked into the Country Club's Wyota Room, the private dining room where the dinner was to be held, she saw Rose standing near the doorway attired in an elegant floor-length light blue dress and high heels. Her hair was tastefully coiffed. Next to her stood two young men, both in dark business suits. She had to look closely before she recognized that they were the two sergeants everyone called "The Boys."

Standing next to them was the striking young woman Doreen had mentioned earlier to Carolyn, someone Carolyn felt certain Hatch would have been attracted to in his younger days. She was tall, perhaps 5'7", with long shapely legs and a light tan healthful complexion. Her short dark brown hair, almost black, was brushed in an upward accent in the style of college girls of the day, and she wore pale lipstick, but no other makeup. Around her neck there was a sterling silver loop. Her silk dress was soft beige in color with a large open neck. This caused it to hang from just above her shoulders. The remainder of the dress seemed to follow the contour of her slender figure: wide shoulders, full bosom, flat stomach, narrow waist, and hips slightly narrower than her shoulders. The dress ended an inch below her knees. Her high heel shoes were also beige and added almost an inch and a half to her overall height. Her posture was confident and erect, and she carried a small silk purse. Her voice was friendly and she was laughing as she chatted with The Boys and Rose.

"Hello," Carolyn said. "I'm Carolyn Peterson, Hatch's wife, Billy's aunt. I'm so glad you're all here. And Rose, I can't thank you enough for your help. I certainly couldn't have done it without you. This place is perfect."

"You're most welcome, Mrs. Peterson. Here's a list of the people who'll be coming." She handed Carolyn a letter size paper. Then she asked, "You do know The Boys, don't you?"

Carolyn nodded, still smiling.

"And Chris Haslett?"

"I don't believe we've met."

Chris smiled, extending her hand. "I did get a chance to meet the others: your husband, Billy's parents, and his Uncle Matt. And please forgive me if I'm not too good with names this evening. I was traveling all last night and I haven't slept in almost thirty-six hours."

"You could have fooled me, Chris," Carolyn said. "You look lovely. And I understand you've just completed your third year at Smith?"

Chris nodded. "My last exam was yesterday morning." As she was speaking, Hatch Peterson and Doreen Rosen arrived. Doreen was particularly ill at ease. She had to set things right with this young woman who had done so much for her son. She came over. "Chris," she said, "when you have a moment I'd like to talk to you...please."

Chris Haslett sensed that this was not going to be a continuation of their earlier confrontation but, rather, something else. "Of course, Mrs. Rosen," she replied.

***

The two women were standing in a far corner. "Chris," Doreen said. "I apologize for acting so childish this morning. Can you ever forgive me?"

"Mrs. Rosen, please. There's absolutely nothing to forgive."

Doreen Rosen took hold of both of Chris' hands. "You must call me 'Doreen.' And I hope we'll always be friends. From now on if you ever need anything from me, or from Billy's father, we will see that you get it."

"Even if it involves turning your son's head ever so slightly in my direction?"

"That and more, Chris."

"Strange. I haven't spent a lot of time with your son, but from the moment we met, well..."

"When you met, what, Chris?"

"I can't explain it. I just wanted to be with him, to have him in my life..."

"I don't think that's strange. I remember meeting Billy's father. The moment I laid eyes on him I knew he was the one. I wanted him desperately. And I didn't care what anyone else thought. If I had, we wouldn't be together today. He and I were so different. I was wealthy in my own right, Presbyterian, and from what in those days was considered a socially prominent family; he was poor, his mother was Italian and his father was Jewish, and he hadn't even graduated from high school. My parents hated him. They flatly refused to accept him. But not Uncle Hatch. He saw in Lou what I suppose I saw in him...a brilliant and caring man who would be a wonderful husband and father."

"How unusual," Doreen Rosen thought. "I don't ever remember telling anyone that."

"So to answer your question, Chris, I will do everything I can to turn Billy's head in your direction if that's what's required. But why don't we wait and see if it is."

***

As they walked back to rejoin Hatch, Rose and The Boys, Chris noticed that the other guests had begun to arrive. "I only know one of them," she thought. She began making mental notes:

Two couples together. One in their thirties. The man is wearing a Master Sergeant's uniform and the woman has on a tailored white dress. The other couple: both much older. The man has a full head of gray hair. Looks very distinguished.

Another couple. The man is a major and has unusually broad shoulders. He's much taller than the woman he's with.

Some Colonel in the Medical Corps. That's the one I think I know. Must be Dr. Stone, Billy's doctor. He's the one who got hold of that Interoffice Memo with Harkavy's handwritten notation on it.

Another couple, obviously married. The man seems to know Billy's Uncle Matt. What a weird physique: solid muscle, 5'7" tall and about as wide. His wife is surprisingly attractive.

"Forgive me," Doreen said to The Boys and Rose, "for dragging Chris away. We had a little matter we needed to discuss." Just then Billy walked into the room. He was wearing a blue blazer, dark gray slacks, a light blue oxford button-down shirt, a blue rep tie with yellow diagonal stripes, and penny cordovan loafers. He came directly over. And, as he did, Chris stiffened. Suddenly she was afraid.

"Well, Mother," he said. "What do you think?"

"About what, dear?"

"About this wonderful woman standing next to you?" He put his arm around Chris.

Doreen Rosen smiled. She knew that her head-turning skills would not be needed this particular evening.

***

"Where's Dad?" Billy asked his mother.

"He's got a headache, dear. But I expect he'll be here shortly."

"Well I want you and Chris to meet some of my friends." He approached the Sacks.

"Mom and Chris, this is Sherman and Velma Sack. Sergeant Sack is my first sergeant, and I've never had a better friend; Velma was my nurse when I was in the hospital."

"Hi," Velma said. "Nice to meet you both. And Chris, we've all heard so much about you. Are your parents coming?"

"'Fraid not, Mrs. Sack; military protocol," Chris replied. "Truth is, I think they both wanted to be here; I know for sure my mother did."

"Come," Velma said. "I'd like you two to meet Sherman's stepparents, Mickey and Ruby Newcomb. They're visiting us from Upstate New York."

Mrs. Rosen smiled. But Chris was staring intently at Mickey Newcomb—just as she had stared at Billy when she first saw him in the dining room of her parents' home. Then she took her glasses from her purse. Putting them on, she said, "Pardon me, sir. 'Mickey': is that short for something?"

Mickey looked up, surprised. "Meyer," he said.

"As in 'I admire Meyer'?" Chris asked.

Mickey began to smile.

"As in *McClanahan v. Optima-Whitebock Construction*?" she continued.

Now Doreen Rosen, Billy, and the Sacks were listening intently. Ruby had a resigned expression on her face, and her husband was beaming. "And how would you know anything about my old campaign slogan or the *McClanahan* case, young woman?"

"Because, in my pre-law class at Smith we all learned to 'admire Meyer.' My professor thinks you're one of the country's outstanding jurists. And we spent over a week on *McClanahan*." Then turning to the others, Chris said, "This gentleman happens to be the Honorable Justice Meyer Newcomb of the New York Court of Appeals, the highest appellate court of that state. He wrote the opinion in *McClanahan v. Optima-Whitebock Construction*, the landmark decision which solved a problem that had plagued the construction industry for years. Other states are now beginning to follow *McClanahan* and Justice Newcomb has been written up in all sorts of legal publications for his judicial excellence."

"My Lord, you'll make his head swell," Ruby Newcomb said.

"Would you believe it if I told you two of my clerks prepared the first draft of that opinion?" Justice Newcomb said.

"Maybe, Your Honor," Chris said. "But I'm sure they had a good deal of input from you."

"And what brings you to this event?" Justice Newcomb asked.

"I'm a friend of the guest of honor," Chris replied as she leaned back pressing herself against Billy.

***

They were all seated at a long table in the room's center. The Boys found themselves on either side of Hatch Peterson and the three were speaking quietly together. Emil Schtung and Matt Irwin were enjoying their reunion, and Fritzi Schtung seemed to have made new friends in Rose Applebaum, Ruby Newcomb, and Nancy Touhy. Carolyn Peterson was sitting next to Dr. Stone and across from Justice Newcomb and Velma Sack, and found them all to be excellent company; moreover, she couldn't have been more pleased with the food Rose had selected, particularly the strip sirloin steaks. Louis Rosen had finally come down from his room and was seated between Sherman Sack and Jim Touhy. The three were discussing Billy's two days of M1 instruction at Elk Hill Dude Ranch which seemed to fascinate Louis Rosen. And, despite his reputed underworld connections, Sergeant Sack found Billy's father to be not only extraordinarily likable, but a decent and caring parent as well—which went a long way in explaining why Billy had gone to such lengths to protect him.

Doreen Rosen was sitting next to Billy, with Chris flanking him on his other side. It was the first time he'd had a chance to be with Chris, to talk to her at length. But, at the same time, he wanted to touch her. He placed his hand behind her, on the inside of the chair back. When it slipped down below her waist, she pressed back against it, all the while continuing her conversation with him and his mother. Billy knew, though, that she too wanted to feel his touch. Finally, she leaned in his direction. "Sport," she whispered, "Rose got me a room upstairs." Billy could feel her slip a piece of paper into his pocket.

***

While coffee was being poured, Hatch began striking his water glass with a knife. Billy felt a sinking feeling in the pit of his stomach. He hated being the center of attention and hoped that whatever his uncle was about to say would be kept to a minimum.

"Ladies and gentlemen," Hatch said. "You have been invited here this evening because each one of you in some way helped or protected Billy. On behalf of my grandnephew and his family I would like to express our gratitude."

Billy was the first to raise his glass. "To all of you," he said.

"And thank God all's well that ends well," Hatch added.

Billy drained his glass and the others did the same. And as they did, Rose nodded to the brass quartet that had been providing the evening's music. Immediately they began playing the Wisconsin Fight Song followed by a song whose Irish melody was familiar to everyone present but whose lyrics held a special meaning for Billy, *Fair Harvard.*[9]

***

Billy was in his room. He had just gotten out of the shower and a towel was wrapped around his waist. He looked at the slip of paper Chris had put in his pocket. She had written "Room 267" on it. It was just down the hall. He felt nervous and excited, just as he'd felt so many years ago when, in that makeshift sitting room on the fourth floor of the Louella, he'd pointed to the red-headed woman sitting opposite him and the two had gone down the hall and into that dingy room. But of course tonight would be different. Chris Haslett was someone who had been in his dreams since the moment he'd met her. Putting on a bathrobe, he opened the door to his room and stepped out into the hallway.

Chapter 59

Room 267, Lebanon Country Club, Lebanon, Missouri, Saturday, 24 June 1950, 2210 Hours.

Billy knocked quietly on the door to Chris' room. When she opened it he gasped. She was clad in a short white almost see-through satin robe and, as far as he could tell, nothing else. He found her breathtakingly beautiful.

"My goodness, Sport, you do take your time," Chris said, reaching for his hand. Grasping it, she gently pulled him into her room, closed the door, and then moved close to him, looking at him directly and unflinchingly, as she had done when they first met. "And just to set the record straight, Billy Rosen, I've never loved anyone as much as I love you. And I never will." She released his hand and put her arms around his waist drawing him to her.

"Chris," Billy whispered in her ear, "I love and adore you."

"Glad we've cleared all that up, Sport. I don't know about you, but it's way past my bedtime."

***

Their lovemaking had been slow and tender, a gentle intimacy fashioned of distant dreams. And now in a sense they were one. There was nothing they would not share.

"Billy," Chris said, a note of discomfort in her voice. "We have to talk."

"About what?"

"About the way you were treated. About your terrible ordeal."

Billy tensed. "I've thought and thought about that. What in hell did I do?"

"You didn't do anything. You were just singled out."

"But why?"

"I wish I knew, Sport. I don't. But I know who was behind it." She took a deep breath before beginning.

***

As Billy listened his head began to throb, as if his blood pressure were skyrocketing. When Chris finished he was silent for several minutes trying as best he could to calm himself. Finally he whispered to her, "You must believe me, Chris. I love you. But there's something I've gotta do. It can't wait."

"Not now, Sport. You need sleep. Then tomorrow we'll…"

"No!" Billy said, with a firmness which surprised her. "I'll be back in a day or two."

He got up and put on his robe. Then he was out the door.

"He's gone," Chris reflected sadly. "And all because of what I told him!" With effort she closed her eyes and fell back into a lonely sleep, only to be awakened forty minutes later by the sound of ringing.

***

Groggily she reached for the phone. "Hello."

"Miss Haslett?"

"Yes?"

"Sorry to bother you ma'am, but I need to speak to Billy right away. He there?"

"Who is this?"

"His first sergeant, ma'am. Sherman Sack."

"No, he's not here."

"Well it's important. If you hear from him please tell him his leave's been canceled and that he's gotta report back to the company on the double."

"Leave's been canceled? Why?"

"North Korea just invaded South Korea. Our battalion's on orders. We'll be shipping out sometime next week. We're at war."

"Oh, God! I'll tell him if I hear from him."

"Thank you, ma'am." Sergeant Sack hung up.

As Chris replaced the receiver, a feeling of bitterness came over her. Having been raised in the military, she knew that women weren't permitted to weep when their men went off to war. But that didn't rule out anger, and she was infuriated: at the North Koreans, at the Army, and at Billy's fate. "Dammit!" she seethed. In frustration, she grabbed a pillow and punched it ferociously—

over and over again. Like her life, she watched as it began to come apart at the seams.

Chapter 60

Chief Detective's Office, River Forest Police Department, 832 Central Avenue, River Forest, Illinois, Monday, 26 June 1950, 1640 Hours.

Chief Detective Jack Greenwald was seated behind his small desk hole-punching various papers which he was about to insert in a new manila file labeled "Bartolo Trucking Company Theft, 6/26/50."

"If my granddaughter could only see me now," he thought, smiling. What he was doing reminded him of a child playing with cutouts. But he wasn't playing games. In fact, he was finishing up an investigation of a rather bizarre occurrence. Even though they hadn't caught the perp—a job he would pass on to one of the two more junior detectives—he knew he'd soon be accumulating a fair number of brownie points with the lieutenant.

Greenwald got up, walked to the door and, grabbing hold of the doorknob, pushed it open. "Hey 'M-J,'" he said. "Do me a favor and tell Lieutenant Quinn to come on over to my office. I got some good news for him."

Mary-Jane Stamos, the typist for the three detectives on the River Forest PD, popped a stick gum into her mouth, began noisily chewing it, and then started walking in the direction of the front office.

***

"So tell me, Jack, what's all this good news?" Lieutenant Francis Xavier Quinn asked after seating himself in the Chief Detective's office.

"I want you to listen carefully, Frank, while I make a call to your dear friend from Chicago, the Honorable Giovanni Bartolo, Alderman of the Third Ward. In exactly two minutes that asshole will be off your back."

As Greenwald picked up the phone he could see that the Lieutenant had leaned forward and was listening intently.

When he heard someone answer, Detective Greenwald said, "Ah, yeah. This is Chief Detective Jack Greenwald of the River Forest PD. Is the Alderman available?"

There was a pause and then Greenwald began. "Afternoon, Giovanni. I've got somethin' for you. I hope it'll mean you'll stop bothering us about your family's stolen truck." There was another pause.

"Yeah, 'bout two hours ago we found the truck at Midway Airport in the same parking lot where it was originally parked. Its front end was pretty badly damaged; I'd say to the tune of about $300. And guess what? In the glove compartment there was an envelope with $500 cash in it; and 'To Cover Damages' was typed on the envelope. So I guess that ends it as far as you're concerned, right?"

There was a further pause. "That's it, Giovanni. I'd say your family business just made a fast $200."

Detective Greenwald listened for a moment. "You're welcome, Alderman." Then he hung up. He looked over at Lieutenant Quinn who was smiling.

"Thank God for small miracles," Lieutenant Quinn said, sighing with relief. "But what in thunder's going on?"

"Someone stole one of the Bartolo trucks early this morning, used it as a battering ram, and returned it along with the cash. Here, take a look." Detective Greenwald handed Lieutenant Quinn an official looking multi-page document which the latter immediately recognized as a River Forest PD Witness Statement Form.

Statement of Witness

My name is Oliver Honab. I live at 195 Clinton Avenue, River Forest, Illinois. Our house is located on the Southwest corner of the intersection of Clinton Avenue and Pleasant Street. Detective James Davis of the River Forest Police Department interviewed me for this Statement at my house at approximately 11:10 AM on June 26, 1950. When the interview ended, we both drove to Detective Davis' office at the River Forest Police Station. I listened while he dictated this Statement to a typist. I made some corrections while he was dictating. After this Statement was typed, I read it over, dated it, inserted the time, and signed it. It accurately and correctly sets forth what I told Detective Davis in my interview:

At about 5:30 AM this morning my wife and I were awakened by a loud noise. It sounded like two cars colliding. I ran downstairs and went to the living room window which looks out onto the intersection of Clinton Avenue and Pleasant Street. In the intersection I saw two vehicles which had been in an accident. They were about thirty feet apart. As best I could piece together what happened, it appeared that a 1942 black Chrysler Station Wagon with wood paneling (Illinois License JVX214) had been struck on the driver's side by a 1949 red Chevrolet Pickup Truck (Illinois License LLR101). The pickup truck had the name "Bartolo Trucking Company" painted on its sides. There were only two people involved in this accident, a male driver in each vehicle.

When I first observed the scene it appeared that the driver of the station wagon was unconscious and the driver of the pickup truck was unharmed. Then something happened which totally surprised and confused me. The driver of the pickup truck got out of his truck and walked over to the station wagon. He was wearing gloves, sunglasses, a black knit navy watch cap, a red woolen shirt, khaki pants, and military boots. In one hand he was carrying a tire iron, and in the other a military canteen. When he reached the station wagon he pried open the driver's door with the tire iron. Then he reached in and pulled the unconscious driver of the station wagon out of his vehicle and threw him to the ground. Next, he unscrewed the cap of the canteen and poured water over him. The driver of the station wagon appeared to regain consciousness, and then the driver of the pickup truck raised the tire iron. I thought he was going to hit him with it, but he didn't; instead he dropped the tire iron to the ground and almost immediately began pummeling the driver of the station wagon with his fists. I don't think he said anything; he just kept beating him until it looked like the face of the driver of the station wagon had turned into a bloody pulp. From time to time the driver of the pickup truck would pour more water onto the driver of the station wagon. It looked to me like he was trying to prevent him from going unconscious. After this had gone on for a minute or two, the driver of the pickup truck dropped down on both knees directly in front of the driver of the station wagon. Again he poured water onto the driver of the station wagon. But this time instead of continuing to beat him, the driver of the pickup truck tore off his sunglasses and cap, and then grabbed the driver of the station wagon by his throat pulling him up so their faces were inches apart. It seemed like the driver of the pickup truck was trying to identify himself to the driver of the station wagon, but I can't be sure of that. When this happened I think the driver of the station wagon passed out again. Then the driver of the pickup truck started walking back to his truck. Halfway there he stopped, turned around, and walked back to the station wagon. When he reached the unconscious driver of the station wagon he started going through his pockets. I saw him take out a small dark colored box. He opened it, removed its contents (I don't know what they were), dropped them on the ground, and began to crush them with his right boot. Finally, he went back to the pickup truck and drove off.

This all happened in the span of about three or four minutes. I was really too shocked to do anything until I saw that the driver of the station wagon was alone. I ran over to him and tried to revive him, but I couldn't. His face was badly battered, but he appeared to be breathing. I looked in his pockets and found a wallet and a plane ticket. His name was Kenneth Harkavy. He was some kind of a military officer and he was on an early flight this morning out of Midway to Washington, D.C. On the ground I saw two small silver stars. I think these were the items from the small box which the driver of the pickup truck had been stepping on and trying to crush.

I ran back to the house and called the River Forest Police. I reported the accident and told them to send an ambulance as soon as possible. About ten minutes later the ambulance and two squad cars arrived. The driver of the station wagon was put into the ambulance and driven off. Shortly after that I was interviewed for this Statement by Detective James Davis.

Dated: June 26, 1950, 2:15 PM

Oliver Honab

Chapter 61

***Room 1801, Jason Memorial Hospital,
1900 South Ellis Avenue, Chicago, Illinois,
Tuesday, 27 June 1950, 1330 Hours.***

Colonel Kenneth Harkavy was resting quietly in his hospital bed. The pain killers had finally taken hold and now his head and mouth no longer ached, although his face and neck were sore and severely bruised. "Billy's payback," he reflected.

The door to his room opened and Colonel George Gunderson, MD, quietly entered.

"Ken," Doc Gunderson said. "You've got a couple of visitors. One kinda distinguished. You up to seeing them?"

It was difficult for Colonel Harkavy to speak, but, in a raspy voice, he asked, "Who are they?"

"A Detective James Davis from the River Forest Police Department. And the Chief of Staff, General Thaddeus Watson."

Colonel Gunderson saw Colonel Harkavy mouth the word "Jesus" and Doc smiled. It wasn't often that someone of General Watson's rank and stature paid a visit to a lowly bird colonel.

"I thought that under the circumstances you might want to postpone talking to Detective Davis, and I told him so. But he was pretty insistent. I finally got him to agree to leave if you answered one question: You got any idea who the driver of the pickup was?"

Colonel Harkavy knew he'd be asked to identify Billy Rosen, and he also knew what his answer would be: "No idea whatsoever."

"Right. I'll tell Davis. And I'll tell General Watson to come in. Okay?"

Colonel Harkavy nodded.

***

"Sir," Colonel Harkavy said in his raspy voice, as General Watson entered.

"Stay put, Colonel. Too bad about your accident. How you feeling?"

"Much better, sir. I should be discharged in a few days."

"Glad to hear it. I'm sorry to bust in on you like this, but I was in Chicago for the day. And I felt we really needed to speak face to face." He paused. "By the way, we met some years ago. Shortly after D-Day."

"Yes, sir. I remember."

"Look, I'm on a tight schedule. I gotta be back in D.C. tonight. And you've got a fair amount of healing to do. So lemme get to the point. I received that report you sent in a week ago, and I've got some serious reservations about your man. He just doesn't seem to cut it. Smart as hell, Harvard grad and all that, cross-country runner, survivor of an enormous amount of harassment. But that's it. How do we know he's like you, me, or, say, General Conroy? Mean, cunning, and…" General Watson paused for effect, "tough. The five others we've selected are all junior officers and we've been able to keep close tabs on them. We've got efficiency reports, interview reports. We know a lot about each of them, and they all make it. But we don't know jack shit about Rosen, mostly because he's a draftee and all he's done is survive basic …rather successfully, I might add. I gotta know that given some very unpleasant circumstances he could rise to the occasion, become one no good uncaring nasty smart son of a bitch. You with me, Colonel?"

Colonel Harkavy thought for a moment. "Will you give me your word, General, that what I'm about to tell you will never be repeated?"

"You got it."

***

Some minutes later when Colonel Harkavy had finished, General Watson sat silently. Then he shook his head. "I'm afraid what you've told me only confirms what I suspected. Rosen may be tough, but he's spoiled. We don't tolerate temper tantrums; and we're not in the market for loose cannons." He looked at Colonel Harkavy. "I guess you didn't hear me, Colonel. I said we were looking for *smart* sons of bitches, not *dumb* ones. Assaulting you the way he did was pretty goddamn dumb."

"Please, sir, before you close the books on Rosen let me show you something."

"I really gotta go, Harkavy."

"One moment, sir. Please!" Colonel Harkavy pulled himself out of his hospital bed and, ignoring the pain he was in, made his way to a closet at the far side of the room from which he removed a briefcase. Opening it, he withdrew two sheets of paper and handed them to General Watson.

"Rosen and another trainee were interviewed at the request of the CID, General. All part of an investigation into a food theft scheme."

"The Furax thing?"

"Yes, sir."

General Watson began to read. Several minutes later he looked up at Colonel Harkavy. "Interesting," he said. "Your young man did a damn fine job that night on KP. Stood up for his buddy too. I'd say he's exactly what we're looking for. Glad you had me read these reports, Colonel."

"Thank God!" Colonel Harkavy thought. "Three years of effort won't be going down the drain."

"Thank you, sir."

"Let's just hope he learns to keep that temper of his under control."

"I don't see a problem, General. I think most of us would have lost it long before he did…considering everything I put him through."

"Maybe, maybe not. Only time will tell." General Watson was silent for a moment. "Now that we've resolved Rosen's status, I think it's time for me to take off."

"Thanks for stopping by, General."

As he got up to leave, General Watson turned to Colonel Harkavy. "Drop in on me anytime when you're in D.C., Colonel. And by the way, your promotion is on track. Not a thing to worry about there."

Chapter 62

Motor Pool, 100 Artillery Circle, Fort Leonard Wood, Missouri, Wednesday, 28 June 1950, 0600 Hours.

As dawn was breaking, three women stood in the pouring rain at the entryway to Fort Wood's motor pool. Although they knew what they were doing was probably a futile act, they were nevertheless searching intently for one last glimpse of those they loved, this despite the fact that almost all of the men of Company B were now in the canvas-enclosed backs of the trucks whose engines had just started up.

Earlier these women had said their goodbyes. They realized then, as they did now, that it could be months, maybe years, before they saw their loved ones again—that is, if they were fortunate. And if they were unfortunate? This was something they never discussed.

Two of the women had been through this before, long ago when World War II was raging. For the third, young Christine Haslett, this was a new experience. Perhaps this was why Velma Sack had her arm protectively around Chris' waist.

All three were women of the military which meant they were not permitted tears. Yet two of the women had wept years ago when their men had gone off to war. And now, beset by the reality that their men were actually leaving, they and Chris Haslett had wept twice: earlier when they had said their goodbyes and only minutes ago. However, at the moment there was one saving grace: the rain. Thank God for the rain! It cooled them as it soaked into their outerwear and clothing, their shoes and stockings, their skin, their hair; it soothed them; it calmed them; it quieted them; and, as it ran down their cheeks, it washed away their tears.

"C'mon, honey," Velma said to Chris. "Best we be leaving. They'll be gone in a few minutes." Slowly she turned and began walking in the direction of the parking lot, her arm still around Chris. Fritzi Schtung followed.

"Let's go on back to my house," Velma continued. "I'll put on a pot of coffee. Then we can talk. Talk is good. And I have a feeling we'll be needing an awful lot of it in the months ahead."

Chapter 63

Office of the Chairman of the Joint Chiefs of Staff, The Pentagon, 2E872, Washington, D.C., Wednesday, 28 June 1950, 1600 Hours.

Seated at his large desk, General Glen Conroy felt decidedly uncomfortable, like a merganser out of water. He had been serving as Chairman of the Joint Chiefs for over ten months—since his appointment last August 9th—but, still, he knew that to the core he was a field commander, not a damn politician. He looked outside. Another one of those summer showers. He reached for the switch on his intercom. "Miss Carlson," he said, "I'll be going home shortly."

"A few minutes ago Captain Riley, General Watson's aide, dropped off an envelope for you, sir. Shall I bring it in?"

"Oh, all right," he replied, resigned to his paper-pushing fate. How he envied Thad Watson, his replacement as the Army's Chief of Staff, a job he had thoroughly enjoyed.

The door to his office opened and a shapely young brunette in her early thirties entered carrying a letter size envelope. She handed it to General Conroy.

"Captain Riley said to tell you your meeting tomorrow with General Watson has been canceled. General Watson will be out of town."

Before he opened the envelope, General Conroy nodded to Miss Carlson, his way of telling her he needed to be alone. He had recognized Thad Watson's handwriting on the envelope which had been addressed simply to "General Conroy—Personal."

With his office door closed, he withdrew a single sheet of letter size paper from the envelope on which General Watson had penned a note to him in longhand:

28 June 1950

Glen,

I'm off to Tokyo to meet with senior staff on the Korea mess — which means our meeting tomorrow will have to be scrubbed. In any case, there's not all that much to report.

First, per our last meeting in March I've arranged to protect our little investments. Each of the five now has a "mentor" (read "bodyguard"). And by the way they're all doing just fine. They're all First Johns. Three are going to Korea and the other two have been assigned to combat-ready outfits in Germany.

Secondly, Water Walker #15 was finally selected. I'm glad we gave Harkavy all that time because I really think he hit the jackpot. He got himself a topnotch youngster (talk about coincidences — I understand this kid's uncle, a beer baron, is under serious consideration as Galt's number two man at DOD).

Lastly, this morning I was on the phone moving heaven and earth trying to find someone to guard Water Walker #15's backside because he's also on orders to Korea. I'm pretty concerned because he's refused a commission and will be going over there as an EM in a rifle company — which will undoubtedly place him in *harm's way (not exactly what we had in mind for someone slated to be a three or four-star general twenty-five years from now!).*

I finally tracked down the guy I was looking for, a retired army officer who captained our Pistol Team when it won all those trophies some years back. I had to play mortgage banker to get him to commit to thirty more months of active duty. I agreed to pay off the mortgage on a guest ranch he owns and operates down in Arkansas. Our special fund will take an $85,000 hit, but I think it's worth it.

That's about it for now. I'll be in touch when I get back — which I expect will be in two weeks. Meanwhile, you know how to get hold of me.

Thad

General Conroy replaced the note in its envelope, and, reaching down, unlocked the lower left hand drawer of his desk. He put the envelope in the drawer and relocked it. But all the while he was thinking: life was so damn full of coincidences. Tomorrow he and Secretary Galt would be lunching with Hatcher Peterson, the man Galt had chosen to be his second in command at the Department of Defense—who, *by coincidence*, just happened to be Water Walker #15's uncle. "Not only full of coincidences," he thought, "but goddamn incestuous!" Smiling, he got up from his desk and walked over to a nearby coat rack from which he removed his trench coat and brimmed general officer's hat. Then he headed for the doorway.

Epilogue

It was Thursday, June 29, 1950, four days after Louis Rosen had returned to the Chicago area from Fort Wood. At his behest, Joseph "Joey Store" Storzoni had joined him for lunch in one of the rooms set aside for private parties in the back of Abramovitz' Deli, a kosher delicatessen located on Chicago's North Side.

Joey was a small muscular nondescript man in his late forties who, for most of his adult life, had lived inconspicuously, trying as best he could to maintain a low profile. To a great extent he had succeeded. In addition, by intent he almost never displayed anger or any other emotion, even to those he knew well. In many ways he and Louis Rosen were very different. Yet despite this, the two had been friends for years.

During their lunch Louis Rosen had told Joey about Billy being en route to Korea, as an army private, no less. Joey, who knew Billy well, had been surprised. But now that he had finished his corned beef sandwich and was sipping his coffee Joey felt it was time to discuss business, for he knew that this was what Louis Rosen had intended in setting up their luncheon.

"So what else is going on, Lou?" he asked.

"Unfortunately, Joey, I think I've got a problem which requires your expertise. It may be under control, but I have my doubts. So I'd like to go over it with you just in case I need to have you solve it for me."

"You referring to a 'permanent solution,' Lou?"

Louis Rosen nodded. He withdrew an envelope from an inside pocket of his sport coat and handed it to Joey.

"This should cover today's expenses, Joey. And I've also included a name and address."

Joey took a piece of paper from the envelope and examined it. "Army guy," he said, somewhat surprised. "He gonna be around the area for a while?"

"I'm not sure. Tomorrow he's being promoted to brigadier general. That may mean a transfer."

"No big deal. When you want us to do him just let me know where he's at. If he's out of town I may have to bring in an associate." Joey took another sip of coffee. "Can you tell me what this is about?"

"Sure. While Billy was going through basic training his throat, windpipe, and nasal passages were badly damaged because of this guy's shenanigans—which, by the way, involved only my son and no one else. Fact is, Billy damn near died. I was told that he'll be fine, but I don't believe it. He's gonna suffer from this for the rest of his life."

Louis Rosen saw Joey Store sadly shake his head. "Unbelievable!" he said. "Not a lot for me to say, Lou, except that I know your kid and he deserves better." Joey took a last sip of his coffee.

"So you'll let me know when I'm supposed to move on this, Lou. And since it's your son, it's on the house provided this guy hasn't been transferred out of the Chicago area. Remember, I've known Billy since he was a boy."

"You'll hear from me if and when it's a 'go,' Joey. And I really want to pay you."

"Not a chance," Joey replied.

And then, in what Louis Rosen would come to view several years later as an unusually prescient remark, Joey Store placed his hand on his friend's shoulder and said, "Lou, I'm real sorry about Billy, what with his injuries and all. But I guess what's bothering me most is where he's headed. See, I got this feeling he and his buddies are not exactly on their way to some summer camp in the Catskills."

Author's Note

When our troops first arrived in Korea they found it was decidedly not a summer camp. It was a war zone. And the war they were about to fight would turn out to be hardly the cakewalk they expected. Close to 36,500 Americans would lose their lives while almost triple that number would be wounded, many to suffer permanent disabling injuries.[10] Those who were fortunate would make it back to the States physically intact. But even they, like all the others who fought as combatants in the Korean War and survived, would forever be traumatized by its horrors.

The Korean War, sometimes dubbed America's "Forgotten War," would end where it began, at the 38th parallel, roughly three years later—and at a terrible cost to so many.

Billy's journey continues in the sequel, *The Furax Deception.*

Endnotes

---

[1] For more on the amazing career of Archibald MacLeish, see: www.wikipedia.org/wiki/Archibald_MacLeish

[2] Its official title is *On Wisconsin*. Its melody was composed in 1909 by W.T. Purdy, and its lyrics were written by Carl Beck. Currently, it is also the official song of the State of Wisconsin (with some changes made to its lyrics).

[3] Mumbly Peg is a somewhat hazardous game played with a jack knife and involves throwing the knife in twenty-four different ways so that its point sticks into the ground. The first player to complete successfully all twenty-four throws wins.

[4] While the name "Elmer Posley" is fictitious, the names of the players mentioned in this chapter are not. The actual Cardinals' manager was Eddie Dyer, truly a baseball great—perhaps one of baseball's finest managers of all time. During his five years at the Cardinals' helm his team won 446 games and lost 325 for a stellar .578 winning percentage. For more on his achievements and noteworthy career, go to: www.wikipedia.org/wiki/Eddie_Dyer

[5] This is an actual Burma-Shave® commercial. Burma-Shave® signs were common in the 1950s. The trademark Burma-Shave is a registered trademark of AMERICAN SAFETY RAZOR COMPANY which has generously consented to use in this novel of this Burma-Shave® commercial.

[6] For more information on Sergeant York go to: http://www.worldwar1.com/heritage/sgtayork.htm

[7] Routines with fixed bayonets similar to those described in this chapter are actually performed by some military drill teams. See, for example: http://www.army.mil/OLDGUARD/specplt/usadt.htm

[8] Approximately one thousand NKPA troops disembarked from a long train at Kaesong's railroad station in the early hours of June 25, 1950, as witnessed by Captain Joseph R. Darrigo, a KMAG officer. See *Korea, The Untold Story of the War* by Joseph C. Goulden, McGraw Hill, 1982, p, 43; and *In Mortal Combat Korea, 1950-1953* by John Toland, William Morrow and Company, Inc., 1991, p. 26.

[9] *Fair Harvard*, the commencement hymn of Harvard University, was composed by the Reverend Samuel Gilman, Class of 1811. The song is set to the tune of *Believe Me If All Those Endearing Young Charms*, lyrics by Irish poet Thomas Moore and music from a song entitled *My Lodging Is In The Cold, Cold Ground.*

[10] The statistics vary. One source puts the actual U.S. losses as follows: 54,229 KIA; 103,248 Wounded; 8,142 Missing In Action; 3,746 Captured; 169,365 Total (Note: KIA includes 20,600 Accidental Fatalities). See *Korean War Casualty Statistics,* copyright Dongxiao Yue, 1999, http://www.centurychina.com/history/krwarcost.html

The following is found on the Korean War Memorial in Washington, D.C. for US participants in the war: Dead—54,246; Wounded—103,284; Captured—7,140; and Missing—8,177. The foregoing death figure includes not only deaths of those who died as a direct result of the war but also military deaths which occurred during the period of the war. The more commonly accepted number of US deaths from the war itself is 36,516.